CENTRAL PARK WEST

'A great read. Brimming with been-there-done-that authority, it's clear James Comey knows this world like the back of his hand. And he delivers it with the addictive style of an expert storyteller.'
MICHAEL CONNELLY

'It reeks of authenticity and the plot goes like a train. The courtroom scenes are tense and the cast of characters vivid and compelling.'
IAN RANKIN

'A winning legal thriller... Memorable characters, a gripping plot, and breathless pacing combine for a truly outstanding debut – one that announces a bold new talent in the mystery genre.'
HARLAN COBEN

'A masterful blend of legal thriller, police procedural and psychological drama.'
JEFFERY DEAVER

'Truly outstanding... Grabs the reader from the opening scene and doesn't let go.'
DOUGLAS PRESTON

'James Comey combines his insider knowledge of every level of the justice system with a natural storytelling voice to create a winning debut. More books, please.'
ALAFAIR BURKE

'Comey's experience as a New York City mob prosecutor brings plenty of credibility to this fast-paced legal drama.'
READER'S DIGEST

'I loved this novel... It's a modern 'good guys vs the bad guys' story in which nearly all of the good 'guys' are actually strong, smart, steely women. It's a smart and satisfying read that I could not recommend more highly.'
NICOLLE WALLACE

ABOUT THE AUTHOR

JAMES COMEY was born in New York City and attended the College of William and Mary and Chicago Law School. He worked in federal law enforcement, first as an assistant US attorney in New York, where he prosecuted organised crime figures, then on terrorism cases in Virginia, before becoming the chief federal prosecutor for the Southern District of New York. He served as the seventh Director of the FBI from 2013 until May 9, 2017, when he was fired by President Donald Trump. *Central Park West* is his first novel.

Follow James on @Comey

JAMES COMEY

CENTRAL PARK WEST

HEAD
of ZEUS

An Aries Book

Published in the US in 2023 by Mysterious Press,
an imprint of Penzler Publishers

First published in the UK in 2023 by Head of Zeus,
part of Bloomsbury Publishing Plc

9 7 5 3 2 4 6 8

A catalogue record for this book is available from
the British Library.

ISBN (HB): 9781837932672
ISBN (XTPB): 9781837932689
ISBN (E): 9781837932658

Interior design by Maria Fernandez

Printed and bound in Great Britain by
CPI Group (UK) Ltd, Croydon CR0 4YY

Head of Zeus
First Floor East
5–8 Hardwick Street
London EC1R 4RG

WWW.HEADOFZEUS.COM

To all who have dedicated their lives to justice.

PROLOGUE

The doorman barely glanced up as she breezed past, bright blonde hair spilling from under her navy blue Hermès scarf, fancy Jackie O sunglasses on even at night, black Prada gabardine raincoat. *She was never very friendly anyway.* But he didn't want to upset her because she was a good holiday tipper—better than most of the tight-asses in this fancy place. Besides, tonight he had these two poodles from 12D in quilted dog vests yipping and nipping at him. Why people thought it was okay to hand him the leashes to their little mutts while they went to the package room was beyond him. No, he knew why. Tips. They had money and he needed money. *But one of these little things better not crap in my lobby.* The place to do that, apparently, was out on the sidewalk, on Central Park West or the Eighty-First Street side, where he would have to hose it off in the morning.

When he looked up from the dogs, Mrs. Burke was gone, into the tasteful maroon-carpeted elevator with the little fold-down seat on the wall where the operator would sit back in the day, because old-timey rich people apparently couldn't press their own floor button. *So we've made some progress; course some poor elevator operator lost a job while the residents pushed their own buttons and just kept getting richer.* He watched the bronze arrow above the door slowly turn to the penthouse. *Must be nice*, he thought.

After receiving the security code, the elevator doors opened softly, directly into the apartment, onto an entryway identical to the black-and-white marble tile of the building's lobby. She walked quietly in the enormous space, through the living room, down the hallway lined with dozens of pictures of the former governor flanked by politicians and celebrities—none of whom wanted anything to do with him now that he had been exposed as a creepy perv of a boss—past the music room with its grand piano, and into the office, with its view of Central Park and the American Museum of Natural History just down the street. There wasn't much of a view after the sun went down; mostly what Antonio "Tony" Burke could see, if he bothered to look up from the book he was reading, was his own reflection in the twelve-foot-high wall of windows. Of course, that wasn't a view that bothered him, if the rows of pictures on his "me wall" were any indication. And even after all those women violated their nondisclosure agreements to bad-mouth him to reporters, his love of self hadn't been shaken.

By the time he heard her steps and looked up into the window's reflection, she was pressing the cold barrel of a gun against the back of his neck.

"Don't move," she whispered. He recognized her voice and his heart started pounding. *Breathe*, he thought, *keep breathing and think*.

He went with his usual move—bravado. "What the hell are you doing here?" he said, his voice not as strong as he wanted it to sound.

"You're gonna do exactly what I tell you to do."

Now he found his executive cadence. "No, I'm not, and you better get the fuck out of my apartment before the cops get here."

She laughed quietly. "For once, you're not in charge, Mr. Governor. And the beauty of being on the top floor in a prewar building is—what's that expression?—nobody can hear you scream. You'd be much better off just doing what I say."

Gesturing to the pen and pad on the desk in front of him, she ordered him to write, *I'm sorry for hurting so many people.*

When he hesitated, she pushed the gun barrel into his neck and said, "Do it or I'll shoot you right now. Think I'm kidding?"

He hated that his hand shook slightly as he wrote the words. Finished, he sat back, his mind racing, trying to stall, to keep her engaged, so he returned to the bluster that had served him well for decades in politics. "I know you're in bed with my guy Conor. I know everything. Just tell me what you really want. Money? It can't just be that stupid note."

She ignored him. "Don't move," she said, staying directly behind him. He could hear her coat rustle. In the window, he saw her removing something from her pocket with her left hand and working her gloved fingers, while still pressing the small handgun into his neck with her right hand.

"Sit back, arms on the chair with your palms up, where I can see them. Good. Now close your eyes," she said.

He did what she asked, but squinted enough to see her suddenly stab his forearm through his shirt with a large syringe, depressing the plunger in the same move. It took less than a second.

"Ow! What the hell was that?" he gasped.

"The world becoming a better place," she answered as she set an empty bottle of insulin and the used syringe on the end table next to him.

He wanted to yell, to struggle, but it was too late. He slumped in the chair, deep in a hypoglycemic coma, headed for death. She pressed the syringe into his limp right hand, placing his thumb on the plunger before dropping it to the floor and leaning over to roll up the sleeve on his left arm.

In the lobby, she was past the doorman before he even saw her. "Evening, Mrs. Burke," he called. She acknowledged him with the back of a gloved hand and was gone.

These fucking rich people, he thought.

Ten minutes later, a black electric-motor bicycle skidded to a stop on the sidewalk out front and a short man wearing a large insulated backpack walked into the lobby. He had a delivery for Mr. Burke in the penthouse, dinner from a fancy steakhouse. The doorman knew Mr. Burke loved the coffee-rubbed Wagyu strip. He rang upstairs several times, with no answer. He couldn't allow the delivery guy into the elevator, so he signed for the dinner box and called the janitor to the lobby, telling him he was running food up to the penthouse. He punched the penthouse code into the elevator and moments later quietly stepped into Mr. Burke's home, using his most subservient tone to call the great man's name. Calling and stepping, calling and stepping, he slowly made his way through the apartment to the office, finding the body, open-mouthed and staring with empty eyes. *Dead fucking rich people.*

CHAPTER ONE

Hoboken smelled like coffee. Nora Carleton stepped up to the sidewalk from her basement apartment and took a deep breath of morning air. For decades, this once-shabby little New Jersey city on the west bank of the Hudson River had been home to coffee-roasting factories. There was coffee in the air when Hoboken was an Italian enclave and Frank Sinatra was a local hero. There was coffee in the air when the Italians moved out in the 1970s and Puerto Ricans moved in to raise their families. And it was still in your nose now that Hoboken was a gentrified city where Manhattan commuters paid six bucks in upscale cafés for what they could almost get with a deep breath.

Nora's rental in her hometown—the Mile Square City—was a basement with little natural light—nothing like the grand brownstone apartments in the floors above—but at least she could afford it on a federal prosecutor's salary. And Eleventh and Bloomfield was a fancy spot—for Hoboken. It meant a short commute; she could stroll one block to Washington Street and then to the PATH train station into Manhattan. It also meant that every morning she passed within sight of what her father long believed was America's holiest ground. Nora didn't see it that way because she didn't love baseball—and no matter how much you loved the game, there was nothing left to see—but, yes, she passed the location of Elysian Fields, where the first-ever baseball game was played in 1846. Underneath all those apartment buildings and townhouses was earth on which the game was invented, despite the fairy tales they tell tourists in Cooperstown.

It was a warm September morning, so she carried her Brooks Brothers navy blue suit jacket over her arm as she walked, a black canvas computer bag slung on her shoulder, her rubber-soled Clarks shoes making no sound on the sidewalk. Thanks to an awesome two-for-the-price-of-one Labor Day sale, she now owned four pantsuits—two blue, one black, and one gray. The salesman said the off-the-rack fit her six-foot frame perfectly, saving her on alterations. Her only splurge was the not-on-sale Brooks Brothers 100 percent cotton white shirts. She had to spend extra money getting them cleaned and pressed every week, but she decided it was worth it because she represented the United States of America. The first time she rose in court and said that—"*Nora Carleton for the United States, Your Honor*"—she got chills, and they had never fully gone away.

Being an Assistant US Attorney for the Southern District of New York was her dream job and she was determined to look the part. Her former boss liked to say they did good for a living. That was inspiring, but "good" didn't pay much, so she shopped at sales and clearance racks to represent her country. She would also splurge for a trial haircut to clean up her chin-length auburn bob, and buy a little makeup—just blush and mascara—to play up what her dad had called her BBB eyes—Big, Brown, and Beautiful. Remembering his words made her feel more confident. It also made her lift her shoulders. She had heard it a hundred times. *Stand up straight, my beautiful girl. Show 'em exactly how tall you are. Show 'em those BBB eyes. No one's gonna mess with you then.* God how she missed him.

She didn't think much about Hoboken history, ever really, but especially not today. She would be late to work because she had to pick Sophie up from her mom's house to take her to school. Not that she *had* to; her mother could easily walk five-year-old Sophie around the corner to Joseph F. Brandt Elementary. No, she wanted to, because with a big mob trial coming up, she wasn't going to be a great parent this fall. The chance to hold her ladybug's hand on the way to school—full-day kindergarten!—was too precious.

So today Nora walked in the opposite direction from the hallowed baseball ground, going two blocks west on Eleventh and then left on Park. In the middle of the block between Ninth and Tenth, she bounded up the four stone stairs to her childhood home, a three-story brick townhouse, two windows wide, built in 1885. The heavy wood door was unlocked—she needed to remind her mother to keep it locked; there really were bad people in the world—and she stepped into the front hall. Nick was coming down the stairs and still looked like a high school kid, backpack over his shoulder, messy black hair, running shoes, jeans, and a hoodie. "Wall Street back-office casual," he called it. He worked in a technical support role for a big bank in their Jersey City complex, moving money or analyzing something; she was never quite sure.

"Hey, prosecutor-lady," he said, "you look fancy."

"Hey Nick," she answered, ignoring the awkward sorta compliment. "How's ladybug today?"

"She's great. Kid talks more in the morning than most people do all day." He brushed past her. "Have a good one."

"Yeah, you too."

He wasn't a bad guy. In fact, he had been a good partner in figuring out what was best for Sophie. Nora thought he was pretty cool in high school and liked having a boyfriend to do things with, but she never felt the spark people wrote songs about. She didn't meet any other guys at college in Connecticut, and apparently, he didn't meet anybody at Seton Hall, so they just kept rolling along, Nora and Nick, the couple from Hoboken. The only time they ever fought was when he said they should fool around more often. When she was in law school, they almost broke up after he said she was "frigid." She got drunk that night on Thanksgiving break—too drunk to think clearly—and they had sex. Nora got pregnant, which was both the worst and the best thing that ever happened to her. Sophie was born the summer following graduation, just after Nora passed the New York bar exam.

She and Nick agreed to share custody of Sophie in a "nesting" arrangement, made possible by Teresa Carleton, Nora's mom. Teresa had mightily offended her own family by marrying a non-Italian, but she and Rick Carleton had had the good sense to repair the damage by buying an old townhouse near her family—before prices got crazy—to raise their daughter. Now Rick was gone, Teresa was a widow, and Nora needed help, so Sophie lived in Nana's house, in her own room, and her parents alternated weeks staying there. Nick had been part of the Carleton family since high school, so it felt natural to everyone, and Sophie thrived. Nick looked for love on the apps, but didn't bring dates around Sophie, at least not until it got serious. Nora didn't date; she had enough on her plate and was married to her job anyway. She liked to tell friends she had only four things she cared about outside work: Sophie, food, exercise, and sleep.

Teresa came out of the kitchen. "Hey, beautiful, how are you this fine morning?"

"I'm good, Ma," Nora answered, welcoming her mother's hug. "How's our big girl?"

"She is very excited. Has the lead for show-and-tell at circle-time today. Big stuff, big stuff. Gonna go with the Junior FBI Special Agent badge you got her."

"Awesome. And I'm gonna take her to Lisa's for a bite on the way, if that's okay. Sorry if you made breakfast."

"No problem. She's in a toaster-waffle phase, so they'll keep."

Nora squeezed her mother again. "You rock." Breaking away, she leaned over the stair railing and called up to the second floor. "Ladybug! Your favorite mom is here! Let's roll!"

She could hear Sophie's feet pounding above before she appeared at the top of the stairs looking like Nora's personal mini-me. "Mommy!" she shouted and galloped down, one hand on the railing, her Skip Hop Zoo butterfly backpack already on. Three stairs from the bottom, Sophie launched herself into Nora's arms.

"Nana says it's okay if we stop at Lisa's for breakfast," Nora said. "You up for it?"

"Yes!"

"Okay, let's do it. Hug for Nana, then we stroll."

Since Nora was a little girl, Lisa's Italian Deli had occupied the corner of Ninth and Park, just down the street from their house and across from the school. Nora leaned in the front door of the small store and waved, calling out her familiar order. "Hey Freddy. Two OJs and two bacon-and-egg on whole-wheat toast, please." She and Sophie found chairs in the fenced sidewalk eating area under a black-and-red umbrella.

While they waited, Nora did what her mother had always done for her. They "pre-gamed" the big circle-time presentation, even if Sophie didn't yet realize that's what was going on.

"Tell me how the show-and-tell will go," Nora said.

"I'm gonna show them the cool badge you got me."

"I can't be there, so can you do it for me like you will for them?"

"Sure, Mommy." Sophie switched to her louder school voice. "'My mom is a federal prosecutor in New York, which means she works with the FBI to put bad people in jail. She got me this badge from the FBI. I want to be like my mom someday.' Then I'm gonna hold it up."

Nora was surprised by the wave of emotion—affection, guilt, worry—washing over her. She took a breath. "Wow, I wish I could be there. It's gonna be great. And you are gonna be a great prosecutor someday—or whatever you decide to be. Work hard in school and always be kind, okay?"

Then she reached across the table, extending her little finger. "And no secrets between us, ever. Pinky swear?"

"Pinky swear," Sophie answered, linking fingers before dropping her hand as Freddy put the sandwiches on the table.

Nora sat watching her chomping her breakfast. *This is so fucking hard*, she thought. *School loans, no life, no sleep. Yup, all worth it. For this.*

"Why you smiling, Mommy?" Sophie mumbled, her mouth full.

"You make me so happy," Nora answered. "Now don't talk and eat, baby girl."

An hour later, Nora walked onto the bricks of the pedestrian plaza in front of the Church of St. Andrew and stopped to buy a coffee from a vendor's stand. At the far end of the red bricks—past the enormous *5 in 1* statue that was supposed to represent the city's five boroughs, but instead seemed to represent five huge red poker chips—she could see NYPD headquarters, which was why the area was known to most New Yorkers as Police Plaza. Since opening in 1973, the fourteen-story red stone, brutalist-style police building had claimed the address of One Police Plaza, or "1PP" to insiders.

When the US Government opened a new office the next year for Manhattan's federal prosecutors, squeezing a building between the Catholic church and 1PP, the feds couldn't bear the thought of being on the NYPD's turf—with the added indignity of being called "2PP" and enduring decades of urination jokes—so they made up an address that had bedeviled delivery services ever since. "One St. Andrew's Plaza" didn't seem to exist to Grubhub or Uber Eats, but it was a real ten-story living indictment of 1970s federal procurement. Its eyesore of a gray prefabricated facade was horizontally striped with tall, wide windows on each floor, ensuring that bad people could always see into the building, at least until the window seals failed and the double-pane glass clouded with mold.

Nora thought her boss, Frederick Simpson, the current chief federal prosecutor—the presidentially appointed United States Attorney—was an insufferable ass, which is why she so loved the story of Simpson ignoring the office manager's advice to not put anything near the wall of windows that ran down one side of his huge triangular eighth-floor office. *Yes, the thirty-foot-long black HVAC housing, sitting just a couple feet off the royal blue wall-to-wall carpet, is a tempting place to put photos and knickknacks but, Mr. Simpson, sir, it would be a mistake because the wall of windows has been a weather-sealing challenge since 1974.* He did it anyway. It didn't rain hard for the first two weeks of his tenure, but then it did and a whole lot of his me-wall photos got soaked, and he screamed at everybody for being idiots. *So great.*

Nora's office, which was neither triangular nor grand—nor carpeted really, except in the sense of mismatched glued-down gray padded squares—was four floors below the US Attorney's, but Nora didn't look out on St. Andrew's Plaza. From her fourth-floor spot in the Violent and Organized Crime unit—known by its initials and pronounced *vock*—she looked out across an alley to the federal prison, the Metropolitan Correctional Center. The MCC was built at the same time as the US Attorney's building and connected by a loading dock and a small power station, making them appear as conjoined twins of bad architecture.

Like most Assistant US Attorneys for the Southern District of New York—the federal district that covered not just Manhattan, but also the Bronx and six counties to the north and northwest of the city—Nora was fiercely proud of how dumpy the offices were. Dented file cabinets as old as the building jammed everywhere; sensitive papers stacked on top; the private offices along the exterior walls crowded with government-issue desks, beat-up chairs, and the occasional—and coveted—faux-leather couch. Non-lawyers usually sat in the hall, their workspaces separated by wobbly gray "privacy walls" that only provided privacy from really short people. The office had long ago outgrown the space, forcing the attorneys who represented the government in noncriminal cases—the Civil Division AUSAs—to move to another building blocks away.

One St. Andrew's was awful and it shocked visitors, especially those from other US Attorney's offices—This *is the famous Southern District of New York?*—but alumni of the office grew misty-eyed telling stories of the awfulness, like surgeons regaling colleagues who were never fortunate enough to serve in a MASH unit.

Nora bounded up the stairs toward the entrance, waving to the guards as she passed through the two visitor-screening posts and into the elevator lobby. On four, she used her access card to open the bulletproof entry door and strode down the hall to her office. A deep voice stopped her at her doorway.

"Ms. Smooth, we should talk about the Frenchman."

It was Benny Dugan, a mountain of a man and legendary Mafia investigator whose office was next to Nora's. His crew-cut hair still blond in middle age, he was six foot five, 250 pounds of Brooklyn, and he'd been doing the work for thirty years, starting as the youngest detective in NYPD history. The US Attorney's office hired him years ago as a federal investigator because he knew more about the mob than anyone in the FBI, which was technically the lead agency on federal Mafia cases. Benny connected with criminals in extraordinary ways, somehow both frightening them and communicating respect. Although Benny and Nora were twenty years apart, they'd become close and established a familial banter, which might have had something to do with Dugan's own family story. His beloved wife was dead and his two sons were estranged from their father, who had been absent—on surveillance, likely—during their childhoods.

Benny was fond of calling Nora "Ms. Smooth" because she was good on her feet in court. In return, Nora called Benny "Mr. Rough"—a nod to his complete lack of diplomatic skills—frequently adding in a tone of mock apology, "Just messing with you. Don't mean anything bad about you."

Benny would invariably give her a sideways look, adding, "I'm not as good a person as you think I am."

Nora's practiced reply was the final piece of this shtick: "Did I say you were a good person?"

She turned and looked into Dugan's large office, which he shared with FBI Special Agent Jessica Watson, detailed to the United States Attorney's office to show the Bureau's "support" for the prosecution of Dominic "The Nose" D'Amico. In truth, the supervisor of the FBI squad dedicated to the Gambino Mafia Family didn't care much about the D'Amico case. Mostly, Nora thought, because the FBI hadn't made it themselves; Dugan had, with his uncanny ability to develop witnesses.

So the FBI's "support" took the form of Watson, a twenty-nine-year-old fresh-out-of-Quantico agent and former Northern California high school chemistry teacher, with smooth dark skin and a soft Afro kept very short. She was a happy teacher—and weekend triathlete—until a friend dragged her to an FBI Bay Area recruiting event. She found herself riveted as the Bureau rep—a ramrod-straight Black woman in her forties—explained the need for diversity in law enforcement and dared the audience to try a job with moral content—one where fitness was part of the mission description. She felt the call, became a Special Agent, and got sent to New York, her forty-seventh choice in the Quantico field office ranking exercise.

Dugan had long ago come to understand the FBI's approach to "supporting" cases the agency didn't believe in. It was, he explained, like the expansion draft in a professional sports league, where teams jealously guard stars and make only lowly rookies available to other teams. His comparison invariably launched one of his favorite routines with "the new kid," whom he had come to like.

"But a lot of the so-called stars are turds, and sometimes the low pick is the GOAT," Dugan would say. "We got us the next Tom Brady. So fuck them."

Watson corrected him every time. "Dude, seriously? I look like Tom Brady to you? Can't I be Kobe in your little metaphor? He wasn't a top-ten pick."

"I'll consider it," Benny always answered, with a grin.

This morning, Benny wanted to talk about one of the witnesses he had developed; nicknamed Frenchie, he was to be the key witness in Nora's case against D'Amico—a bad man out on the streets pending trial after the judge denied Nora's motion to detain him as a danger to the community. She dropped into one of the chairs scattered around Dugan's office.

"What's wrong with him now?" she sighed.

Dugan shook his head. "Nope, nope. First I get a full report on our angel. You took her out to breakfast today on the way to school drop-off?"

Nora laughed and looked at Jessica, who held the backs of her hands up, flexing her fingers toward her chest—the classic "gimme, gimme" signal. So Nora beamed and told the story of breakfast alfresco and the planned show-and-tell, her head ping-ponging between the beaming Benny and Jessica. The mob could wait.

CHAPTER TWO

Pomander Walk was a hard street to find, and even harder to get into, which is why Kyra Burke's lawyer, Matthew Parker, wanted to meet her there. The paparazzi who were stalking Kyra's every move were stuck at the gates that blocked the entrance to the secret little block between Ninety-Fourth and Ninety-Fifth Streets on Manhattan's Upper West Side. The press could stand at either end, but could see nothing through the tight metal mesh. Since separating from her now-deceased husband, former governor Tony Burke, Kyra had lived quietly in one of the attached two-story Tudor-style homes in the tiny make-believe-looking development, which had somehow survived the onslaught of high-rise apartment buildings for a hundred years.

Now settled into a quiet academic life as a law professor, Kyra cherished the walk uphill along West End Avenue and then Broadway to her office at Columbia Law School. She even loved the faculty lunches, although it took focus not to roll her eyes at colleagues asking endlessly long questions that were always about themselves and not about the paper under discussion. Good times. But no more. She was the accused murderer known as Killer Kyra, at least according to the screaming tabloids. Quiet walks and academic reflection were gone. People with cameras stalked her every move.

"These people really need to get a life," Kyra vented, looking across her butcher-block kitchen table at her lawyer. She was a strikingly beautiful thirty-nine-year-old woman, her high cheekbones framed by a long honey-blonde Jennifer Anniston bob cut. Not old enough yet to be tempted by the plastic surgery and Botox that were epidemic in her circles.

At the other end of the rectangular table, Matthew Parker looked pained, rubbing his face from top to bottom with an open palm. He also looked tired, but only his combed-back silver hair betrayed his sixty years; the rest of his six-foot-two frame was toned by hours on a Peloton bike and in the pool, and somehow his skin was smooth and his blue eyes unclouded. Now he blinked those eyes slowly, silently recalling a prayer—*grant me the serenity to accept the things I cannot change*—as he stared at Kyra. He had spent a career in federal law enforcement and then the past fifteen years as a defense attorney. Despite all the bullshit about Martha Stewart flourishing in jail, women like Kyra Burke didn't do well in prison. And Martha had done five months in a minimum-security Club Fed; Kyra was staring at life in a New York state prison. It was to be avoided at all costs; well, at least at the cost of his $3 million retainer.

He had never met Kyra Burke until two weeks earlier, inside the 24th Precinct. At dawn that day, the NYPD had executed an arrest warrant at her Pomander Walk home and also searched the place. Parker had been sound asleep in Brooklyn Heights when he got a call from Conor McCarthy, longtime aide to former governor Burke, recently deceased. It seemed the Manhattan DA had decided Kyra was responsible for that death and had charged her with murder. She was walked in handcuffs from a squad car into the police precinct in front of dozens of photographers, who all somehow knew to gather on One Hundredth Street in Manhattan as the sun came up. *The mysteries of New York law enforcement*, Parker thought. Once inside the 24th Precinct—known in the NYPD as the "Two-Four"—Kyra had used her one phone call to reach her dead husband's closest aide, Conor McCarthy, who in turn had called Parker, woke him up, and assured him that the funds would be available for a robust defense and to secure her release on bail before trial.

He had found her lying on a bench in the Two-Four precinct's holding cell. Parker had helped Kyra sit up and introduced himself. It had been a media circus ever since, a fact that didn't thrill Parker's partners at his Wall Street law firm, who were more accustomed to representing corporations accused of financial crimes than estranged spouses accused of murder.

There had been no time at the beginning to really review the case with his client but, with the arraignment behind them and discovery received from the prosecution, they now had the chance to come to know each other and what she faced.

Like any good investigator, Parker began with open-ended questions, letting the witness—in this case, his client—decide where to go.

"Okay," he began, "tell me your story."

"My story?"

"Yeah, your story. Tell it to me, as if you were introducing yourself to a class, or a jury." He looked down at his notepad, a technique he knew made it easier for the witness to speak freely.

She stared at his bowed head for a moment. "Okay, weird, but okay. My name is Kyra Burke, and I'm thirty-nine years old. My maiden name is Podolski. I was born and raised in Easton, Pennsylvania, by my grandparents—my father was never in the picture and my mother was dead from an overdose before I was five."

Kyra took a deep breath and seemed to reset. "Anyhow, my grandparents raised me and I went to public high school in Easton and then to Yale for college, which I paid for through some financial aid but mostly loans and campus jobs. I'm a lawyer. I went to Columbia Law School, where I now teach gender and employment law classes. I started mentoring programs for at-risk girls in Easton, in New Haven, and in the South Bronx. We have to do more than just get them through high school. They need role models and mentors who empower them to build careers and be leaders. I've always been interested in public policy and politics. When I was thirty, I met the then-governor, Tony Burke—he was in his first term—at a charity event and we hit it off; we seemed to care about the same things and started dating—he was recently divorced—and we fell in love.

"Maybe I was naive—no, I *was* naive—but he seemed the kind of leader we need in this country. He was a leader who believed in the power of the free market, but he also cared deeply—or said he did—about things I cared about: a strong social safety net, constitutional policing, women's rights, progressive taxation, and protection of the environment. It seems silly now, but he gave off a *Camelot* vibe and said he wanted me to be his partner in it. Guinevere to his Arthur, I guess. I told my friends he was JFK but without the zipper problem. Jesus, was I wrong.

"He told me he was a feminist and advocated for women, but I discovered he was a lying, vicious predator, who tried to screw everything he could get his hands on, whether they consented or not. A total fraud. Honestly, I was relieved to get away from him, to have my own life back, here"—she gestured around the kitchen—"in this little place. And then he goes and dies and, poof, my new life is gone. It's almost enough to make me sorry he's dead. Almost. Not quite."

Kyra paused before adding, "So how's that, story-wise?"

Parker stopped writing and looked up. "Perfect, exactly what I was looking for. More to come, but now let's talk about the case."

He briefed her on the research their jury consultant had already done. It was an ugly picture. Everybody seemed to have a view—that she was guilty. Kyra exhaled through pursed lips. "So I'm still waiting for a potential juror who has formed a view that I actually *didn't* kill Tony. Everybody just believes all the tabloid crap?"

"Look, we're gonna get a jury," he answered. "There are lots of people in Manhattan who don't read and have no idea what's going on in the world. Which, as a citizen, I'm not sure is a blessing, by the way. But we will get twelve people who say they can be fair and impartial. I'm not worried about that. I'm more worried about the evidence the jury is gonna hear and how we deal with it."

Kyra leaned forward in her ladder-back farmhouse chair, putting both forearms on the kitchen table. "Tell me."

"Well, they got the doorman, for starters. He's known you for years and says you walked in and out of the building at the time Tony was killed. Video backs him up. The stuff you were wearing is stuff they found during the search here at your house: scarf, glasses, fancy raincoat . . ."

"That's silly. Anybody could have an Hermès scarf."

"Right, course. Then there's the fact that the fake you, which looks on tape just like the real you, used the family code in the elevator to get up to the penthouse."

"Lots of people have that code. Tony's entire staff and all the women he screwed probably know it."

"Look, I'm not saying we don't have arguments here. I'm just tryin' to lay out what they have. No struggle at the scene, so it was somebody your husband knew. Oh, and your phone was turned off during the time window around his death. Came back on an hour later."

"That is some . . ." Kyra began.

"So they have some decent opportunity proof, with the doorman and video and all, and we're gonna have a hard time undercutting it, what with you being here alone and reading during that time. But I digress."

"Yeah, but no video of me leaving here, right?"

"True, in a sense," Parker answered. "Only shitty, blurred video of lots of figures coming and going through the gates from this weird little block in the dark. So our alibi kinda sucks."

He exhaled before continuing. "And they got motive proof comin' out the ass. Seems you really did bad-mouth the deceased to your Columbia colleagues before his untimely demise. Bunch of them are on the witness list to lay out what a womanizing, abusive, lying, evil piece of shit you said he was."

"All true," Kyra answered, "both in the sense that I said it and in the sense that he was a womanizing, abusive, lying, evil piece of garbage. But I didn't kill him and if I'd wanted to, I sure as hell wouldn't get caught."

Parker grimaced and leaned back in his chair, looping his thumbs behind his suspenders and stretching them forward, hands sliding up and down, up and down. "No doubt, no doubt, but, uh, not great evidence for us, right?"

"Not great," she agreed.

"Then they're gonna call his lawyers to tell the jury about the divorce proceedings, and that, with the prenup kicking in, you were gonna get next to nothing. Oh, unless he died first. In that case, you'd get it all."

Releasing the suspenders, he added, "So there's that."

Parker's sarcasm was wearing on Kyra. "You enjoying this?" she asked sharply, leaning back in her own chair.

He looked pained. "I most definitely am not." Pointing to her, he added, "I believe my client is actually innocent, which doesn't happen to me a lot, and that's good because it scares the shit out of me. Much rather represent guilty people. Less pressure on me. So, no, I'm not enjoying this."

He leaned forward, putting both forearms on the table. "But I just want you to see clearly what we're up against. You hated this guy, you were gonna lose a ton of dough if you two got divorced, and the doorman and a video say you came and left when the killer did."

Kyra didn't hesitate. "I still think we argue it was a real suicide."

Parker offered a tight smile. "Yeah, we've been through that and, look, it's your life and I'm your lawyer, so I will do what you want, within reason. But the visitor and the dinner make it a really steep hill to climb. If it was a real suicide, what were you doing there? And if it wasn't you, what was a look-alike doing there? And the steak. Nobody orders their favorite dinner in the world and then kills himself before the food gets there. Oh, and the forensics are bad for the real-suicide theory. They found a small hole in his shirt and cotton fibers from the shirt on the needle."

"And so?" Kyra asked, confused.

"Well, that means he injected himself through his shirt and then rolled up his sleeve after he was dead. Seems unlikely, although I'm no doctor."

Kyra studied the stripes of the wood table. "And the note. No way that jerk felt bad about anything."

She exhaled audibly. "Yup, somebody killed him. Which was a public service, but I didn't do it."

"Yup," Parker echoed. "It's gonna come down to your testimony creating a reasonable doubt. We don't have many handholds to pull down the DA's proof. You just gotta convince the jury—or at least one of them, anyway—that you didn't do it. And that's gotta start with you not celebrating his death. This 'public service' stuff is out, 'kay? You gotta be more disciplined than that."

Kyra flinched, but then slowly nodded. "So, Mr. Defense Lawyer, let's write a statement for the press about how sad I am that my husband was murdered and that one of his many enemies is trying to get away with it by framing sweet innocent me. Anything to get a new narrative out there."

"Okay," Parker answered wearily, flipping his legal pad to a clean page. "So who are the suspects?"

"His first wife, Marian, hates him—sorry, hated him. She gave up her life for his career, had a kid with the bastard, and he still screwed her over, worse than with me. The gaslighting, the humiliation. Thirty years of it, and she put up with it because—well, I don't know why, probably for her son, who she thinks is the anointed one. And after putting up with all that, he still dumps her, and has his people stab her to the press: unstable, mentally ill, a burden he could no longer carry and still serve the voters. Really sick stuff."

"And so why would she kill him now, after so long?"

"For the golden child, would be my guess. She thinks Edward should be president. He's the picture of a modern major conservative: married to his high school sweetheart, bunch of kids, born-again, pro-life, tough on borders, blah, blah, blah. Always wearing the new team uniform—red vest that says, 'I may be a hedge-fund millionaire but I will fight for you and the other deplorables.' She lies awake at night imagining her room at the White House, wherever it was the Obamas let Michelle's mother sleep. Course, Tony was not gonna let that happen; he was too sick a guy to let his son get what he couldn't. Hard to blame her for killing him."

"Okay, maybe Marian. Who else?"

"Edward would have the same motive, I suppose. And I should have started with this one, but the mob. I don't know who or how, but Tony Burke was covered in the stink of that world. I never knew details but I heard enough echoes to know he'd been doing favors for some bad people for a long time. Contracts, bids, union issues, zoning problems. He would say it was 'constituent service,' but these weren't the ordinary constituents. They had some hold over the guy that I never understood. Who knows how he screwed them over, but with

him out of office—and unlikely to get back in now that the world knew
he was a sexual predator—they'd have very little patience for getting
screwed over."

"Got it. Who else?"

"Well, any of the girls he laid hands on, or people close to them. I
mean, this guy was the Harvey Weinstein of politics. Think of how
many girls—well, women, but he liked them young—he hurt and
threw away. Not a shocker that they would want him to pay for that."

"Got it. So what is it you think we should tell the press about all
this?"

Kyra paused for a few seconds, then began dictating. "Okay, here's
the theme I think you start putting out, all on background . . ."

Parker sighed and flipped to another clean page. *Why can't my
clients ever just shut up and do what I say? Why am I even still taking
this tabloid shit?*

". . . Kyra Burke is innocent, and a victim of our obsessive media
culture and politically ambitious prosecutors. She was raised by her
deeply religious grandparents, put herself through school, and committed her life to service through the law. But that life was derailed by
an abusive, manipulative older man, a predator who tried to destroy her,
as he had so many others. Fortunately, she escaped from him to focus
on teaching the law to talented young people, only to be accused—in
a cruel twist—of murdering the man she had already successfully
escaped. Now, falsely charged in a tabloid rush to judgment, she is
being victimized all over again. This prosecution is a travesty."

Parker was scribbling furiously. "You just came up with this off the
top of your head?"

Kyra laughed. "I have a lotta free time."

CHAPTER THREE

I t was one of those fall mornings that remind you winter is coming. But Nora didn't feel it as she walked through chilly Hoboken. Her mom would walk Sophie to school today. Nora was in trial mode, her head already in the courtroom. When she grabbed a bagel with cream cheese at Seventh Street, she was planning the day in court. When she shuffled with the crowd down the stairs to the PATH train for the short ride to Manhattan, she was thinking about her key witness.

She didn't even notice the tabloid headlines shouting from newsstands. The *Daily News* went with its nickname for the murdered former governor whose record of sexual harassment was exposed shortly before his death: LUV GUV SLAY TRIAL. The *Post* focused on the accused: KILLER KYRA IN THE DOCK. Sure, Nora knew the murder trial of Kyra Burke, the dead governor's estranged wife, was starting soon, but that was a local case handled by the Manhattan District Attorney. She was a fed—an Assistant US Attorney for the Southern District of New York—prosecuting a mobster, and she didn't much care about the "Luv Guv" or "Killer Kyra". The feeling was mutual, in a way; the media didn't care much about mob cases anymore, didn't seem to care that there were still sophisticated and dangerous criminals out there, didn't seem to care that the elusive Dominic "The Nose" D'Amico was finally going to jail.

But Nora wasn't worrying about the press this morning. When the commuters flowed out through the Oculus, the gigantic ribbed white bird of a transportation hub emerging from the wreckage of the original World Trade Center site, she was worrying about Frenchie. Would Frenchie hold up? Would he freak out? Would the jury believe him? When Frenchie pointed at The Nose in that cavernous courtroom today, would that finally get D'Amico off the streets and into prison?

She marched along Park Row past City Hall and instinctively lowered her head as she prepared to pass the forty-story white granite David N. Dinkins Municipal Building. For some reason, it was always into the wind here, which was why, on trial days, she broke a personal rule and used some hairspray to hold her bob together. Juries didn't trust prosecutors with crazy hair.

But she wasn't thinking about the wind or her hair right now. Nora's mind was across "the bridge" which connected her building to a more dignified piece of stone, the Thurgood Marshall United States Courthouse, named for the legendary civil rights attorney.

United States v. Dominic D'Amico, aka "The Nose," was being tried in courtroom 318 of the Marshall Courthouse. That was unusual, because most federal criminal hearings these days were held in the Daniel Patrick Moynihan Courthouse—the so-called "new courthouse"—finished in 1996 and wedged into a tiny piece of land behind the state courthouse, over which it towered, and across narrow Pearl Street from the MCC jail. Most federal trial judges now sat in the new courthouse, leaving the Marshall building, with its feeling of an old Ivy League eating club—all rich carpet, dark paneling, and whispering—to the federal appeals court. But there were no bridges to the new courthouse, so it was inconvenient and nerve-racking to move dangerous defendants and incarcerated witnesses on the street for court proceedings.

Room 318 was a grand old courtroom with ample space for spectators and press, but its best feature was that, behind the judge's bench, it was secretly connected to the bridges to the MCC and the US

Attorney's office. Witnesses could be brought in and moved without being seen. And Nora needed her key witness not to be seen until the moment he stepped up to take the oath.

There was no banter with Benny Dugan this morning. He had already been to the US Marshals Witness Security holding facility to see their star witness, the one who was going to bury Dominic D'Amico, *if* he didn't melt down first.

"You should check in with Frenchie before he hits the stand," Dugan said.

"Hanging on?" Nora asked.

"Barely. Feels like he could come apart any minute."

Daniel Albert Joseph, aka "Frenchie," was a career thief who looked like the actor Denis Leary. A handsome man with thick wheat-colored hair, he had the same gravel in his voice as the actor, but with a hint of *la langue française* of his childhood. He was normally charming and confident, traits that had been essential to his living to the age of forty-eight.

Frenchie first met The Nose when he needed to unload a highly recognizable bronze sculpture he'd stolen from the Bolton Gallery in Manhattan. The Bolton had been around since 1857 and occupied a grand townhouse at Seventy-Ninth Street and Madison Avenue; it specialized in American and Western paintings and sculpture. Frenchie wanted their Remington bronze. So late one night, he stole it, working alone and climbing the elevator shaft as his way in and around alarms. With the heavy sculpture in a canvas bag on his shoulder, he pushed a door open and vanished. He couldn't unload something like that on an ordinary fence, so, through fellow criminals, he managed to meet The Nose, who was a recently made member of the Gambino Crime Family, the most powerful of New York's five Mafia Families.

Their first meeting was in the parking lot of a diner near Kennedy Airport, where they made a deal for the Remington. D'Amico took to

Frenchie immediately, explaining that he sold high-end stuff like that to people who would never display the art. "They just wanna touch themselves while they look at it," he explained. But that was none of Frenchie's business; what mattered was that D'Amico said he liked Frenchie's style and asked him to bring him more stolen valuables.

Frenchie and The Nose rose together, each becoming more sophisticated and successful in their criminal worlds. Frenchie would scout art and check with D'Amico to see if he had a buyer. From time to time, D'Amico suggested a focus for Frenchie. The Valnaghi was their best work. D'Amico asked Frenchie to case it, and the thief came back wide-eyed, for two contradictory reasons. The Madison Avenue gallery's walls were covered with amazing paintings. That was the good news. The bad news, he told The Nose, was there was no way to get to those walls because the large gallery floor was honeycombed with sensors and the entire open space, which extended upward for three floors, was equipped with a heat sensor that would detect even small changes in air temperature. Frenchie didn't say it couldn't be done, only that it would be really hard. D'Amico responded by offering him 40 percent of whatever he made reselling the pieces.

Several weeks later, Frenchie used a diamond blade to cut the glass in a roof skylight at the gallery. Wearing a head-to-toe wetsuit to contain his body heat, he lowered himself on a cable into the main display space, swinging from wall to wall—above the motion sensors. He skipped stuff he knew was overpriced junk and cut twenty-seven Old Master paintings and drawings from their frames, including two panels from the early 1400s by Italian Renaissance master Fra Angelico, gently rolling and storing each piece in a large portfolio tube slung over his back, before retreating up through the skylight. It was an impressive job clearly done by somebody who knew a lot about both burglary and art. D'Amico paid him $800,000 for his end. Frenchie knew that was well below 40 percent of the sales price, but he said nothing. D'Amico by this point had become a capo in the Gambino Family, supervising his own crew of made members and answering directly to the Family boss. He was not one to entertain complaints about accounting.

To Frenchie's dismay though, D'Amico wasn't interested in Persian rugs, despite Frenchie's insistence that they were an underappreciated SWAG—a term purportedly derived from the police report category of "Stolen Wares and Goods." D'Amico responded that rugs were stupid because more than one person was needed on every job, given the weight of the things. "Helpers," he explained, "bring risk. Stay the fuck away from that kind of risk. You are the best there is, alone. Keep it that way."

But Frenchie couldn't stop thinking about rugs, especially after he burned through the money from the Valnaghi job. Before he'd met The Nose, Frenchie had orchestrated an audacious rug heist at the Regency Manhattan art storage warehouse and was itching to do it again. With coconspirators, he built a custom crate for himself and shipped it—and himself—to the warehouse. A corrupt employee ensured the huge, heavy wooden box was placed inside a special vault that held Persian rugs, each worth tens of thousands of dollars. That evening, Frenchie emerged from the box. He removed the heavy material that gave the box its shipping weight and replaced the weights with dozens of carefully selected carpets. It was a long process, but he had all night and he had snacks and water he brought with him. Before dawn, he climbed back into the box with his pile of rugs, sealed the box from the inside, and waited. First thing in the morning, the corrupt employee "discovered" the misaddressed crate and immediately shipped it—and Frenchie and the Persians—out of the warehouse.

The Regency Manhattan rug job had been so lucrative—and so goddam fun—he had to do it again. He had promised to avoid rugs and to work only for D'Amico, but what The Nose didn't know wouldn't hurt him.

So he returned to the Regency and, with the help of four others, used a jackhammer to open a burglar-sized hole in the wall from an adjoining roof. The hole easily accommodated the twenty Persian carpets he stole that night. That was the good part. The bad part was that D'Amico was right: helpers were risky. One of the other four got jammed up on something unrelated and fingered Frenchie and his helpers.

Frenchie was sent to Rikers Island—New York City's main jail complex, on an island in the East River—for five months before trial. He had never cooperated with law enforcement but, as he sat in the bleak jail, now forty-five and looking at a seriously long stretch in New York state prison, he was receptive when two detectives from the NYPD robbery squad came to see him. Their pitch was simple: wear a wire for us against other thieves and fences, and we'll spare you many years upstate. He signed up and spent the next eighteen months working for law enforcement, making cases against his former colleagues. Everyone except The Nose. He didn't tell the cops about D'Amico. And what? Wear a wire against a capo? That was too dangerous. Instead he gave up rug guys, guys he had sold small stuff to, little people. The cops ate it up.

Frenchie was so good at dealing with people that his undercover tapes usually produced guilty pleas. But not always. Two corrupt rug merchants went to trial in state court, and Frenchie dreaded revealing himself at a public trial. Under stress, Frenchie secretly returned to the two things that relaxed him—heroin and stealing. He began visiting Saks and Bergdorf Goodman, two high-end department stores on Manhattan's Fifth Avenue, to steal crystal, silver, and anything else he could resell for drugs. But he cleaned himself up before testifying through an in-patient treatment program and the rug dealers were convicted. Frenchie was going to get a reduced sentence, which, at his request, he was going to serve in a state prison away from New York City, where he was less likely to be recognized.

Except he had been recognized and he was no longer safe in prison, which is how Nora and Benny met him.

Frenchie was in solitary confinement near Buffalo, about as far from New York City as one could get without leaving the state. His lawyer called Carmen Garcia, the chief of the Violent and Organized Crime unit at One St. Andrew's. He told Carmen his client wanted to get into the federal witness protection program—known as WITSEC—and had information about "a significant organized crime figure." Carmen explained that she didn't do deals over the phone, how getting into WITSEC would be complicated for a state prisoner, and she would never buy without a test drive anyway. She sent Nora and Benny to Buffalo, where Frenchie told them everything he knew about The Nose.

Now Frenchie was in "the program" and about to hit the stand. He was still in custody and would be until he finished his state jail term, but he was doing that time in a special witness protection prison run by the federal Bureau of Prisons and the United States Marshals Service.

Nora and Benny stood as the WITSEC marshals brought Frenchie into the small room just behind courtroom 318. He was in a prison jumpsuit, the way Nora wanted it. The defendant D'Amico was out on bail and appeared every day in a tailored suit; she wanted the jury to see that Frenchie was being held accountable and now it was D'Amico's turn.

Frenchie seemed jumpy, nervous. "Hey, you ready to do this?" Nora asked.

"Yeah, yeah, ready as I'll ever be," Frenchie answered in a low voice.

Benny hit it directly, his own voice a rumble. "What, you scared of this piece of shit?"

Frenchie exhaled a short laugh. "Nah. Not for me. But I still worry about my kid."

His adult son, Albert, had declined the offer of relocation with a new identity, something the marshals routinely provided to willing family members of a witness. But Frenchie's son was not willing. They weren't close enough for him to abandon his whole life because a father who had been distant most of his childhood was now doing something really dangerous.

"You heard from him?" Benny asked. "There a problem?"

"No, no, I never hear from Albert. Still, everybody in my old world knows I have a son, and they might hurt him just to hurt me. Only good thing I ever did was have that kid and then stay away so he grew up normal. I didn't fuck him up. But now I may have fucked him."

"They know he's a civilian, Frenchie," Benny said. "They ain't gonna mess with him. They know if they ever did, we would fuck with them 'til the end of time."

"I appreciate that, Benny, I really do." Looking at Nora, he added, "I appreciate both of you, but this has me feeling like I'm making a mistake."

Nora paused, a feeling of panic rising in her throat. Before she could speak, Benny jumped on it. "Don't be a putz. We made you promises, we kept our promises. Now you gotta keep yours and testify. You told us in motherfucking freezing Buffalo that you were an honorable man. I believed it then, I believe it now. So fucking act like it."

The room went silent. Frenchie studied the table, while Nora and Benny stared at him. After several long beats, Frenchie looked up, jutted his chin out, and broke the silence. "You're right. Fuck it, let's do this."

"Good man," Nora said, standing. "Marshals will bring you out in just a couple minutes. Be yourself out there. Tell the truth and get on with your life."

CHAPTER FOUR

Nora could tell something was wrong the moment direct examination began. Granted, courtroom 318 was an intimidating place for anyone. It was like an architecture class final exam—thirty-foot-high dark-stained oak walls with round arches and fluted Ionic pilasters supporting what seemed to be an acre of cream-colored ceiling, which was blazingly lit by recessed can-lights and divided by elaborate molding into dozens of rectangular coffers. Four enormous brass and cast-ivory bowl-pendant lights hung menacingly down from the ceiling, ready to drop on anyone who disrespected the gods of justice. And if looking up didn't freak you out, a glance at the bottom of the walls might. There, the architect had chosen to wrap the entire room in ten-foot-high gray-on-black marble wainscoting, as if to prevent people from escaping by digging through the wood walls. It was cavernous and over the top with institutional symbolism—like testifying from the Speaker's Chair to a joint session of Congress. But it was more than the architecture that was freezing Frenchie.

"Sir, could you please state your full name?" Nora began.

Frenchie answered in an irritated voice. "Daniel Albert Joseph." Unlike their prep sessions, he seemed tense and didn't add his trademark humorous quip, "Yeah, I know it seems like three first names, but my mom liked them all."

"Do you go by a nickname?"

"Yes" was his only answer.

Nora squinted, her face begging Frenchie to snap out of it. "And what is that nickname?"

"Frenchie."

"Why are you known by that nickname?"

"Kids just do stuff, you know?"

Something was wrong. Although Frenchie didn't like testifying, he was normally highly verbal and demonstrative. Suddenly, he was withdrawn, his words coming out in pieces, not sentences. The next hour was agony, Nora constantly forced to the edge of improper leading questions as she tried to get Frenchie to tell the story of his life of crime, his introduction to The Nose, his stealing for the mob leader. When it came time for the usual midmorning break, Judge Edgar Whitney smiled pleasantly at the career criminal witness and the jury. "Mr. Joseph, the marshals will escort you to the back. Ladies and gentlemen, we will take our ten-minute recess."

Nora and Benny walked casually toward the door next to the witness box. When it closed safely behind them, Nora exhaled loudly. She was careful not to speak as they headed down the hall past the jury room and into the witness prep room but, once the heavy wood door was closed, she let loose at her witness. "What. The. Actual. Fuck, Frenchie? You're killing me out there."

Frenchie didn't look up. "Funny you say it that way. Because I'm the one they wanna kill."

"What happened?" Benny asked.

Frenchie explained that, as he walked into the courtroom, D'Amico looked at him and mouthed, "You're dead."

Nora's face went red. "Son-of-a-bitch. I gotta tell the judge."

Frenchie's energy returned in a flash. "No, no, don't do that. It's gonna happen. We really—I just want to get it over with."

"Look," Nora replied, "I know you're not happy with this, I know you don't want to do this, but we have to protect the system. It's something that can't just go away. Defendants can't be threatening witnesses during a trial, and not in a fucking federal courtroom. We have to bring it to the attention of the judge." Frenchie didn't answer.

Shaking with anger, Nora returned to the courtroom, leaving Benny in the witness room with Frenchie. She told the courtroom clerk she had an issue to raise with the judge before the jury and witness returned. Judge Whitney took the bench, mildly irritated by the delay. "What is it, Ms. Carleton?"

Still having trouble controlling the anger in her voice, Nora disclosed the threat. She hadn't seen it, but her witness told her about it and she'd seen a dramatic change in Frenchie from the moment he took the stand. Something had turned Frenchie into a different, very frightened person. She asked the judge to immediately revoke D'Amico's bail.

Judge Whitney looked confused. He was squeezing the muscles on his handsome, lightly tanned face, the muscle bumps rhythmically stretching the skin at the corners of his jaw. His was a world of Big Law firm partnerships, Connecticut country homes, and golf partners who conceded three-foot putts. His three years as a federal judge hadn't made him any more comfortable with the awfulness of these criminal types. Without speaking, he looked to the defense table, and flexed both eyebrows toward his hairline.

The Nose's lawyer, Salvatore Butler, was even more associated in the public mind with the Mafia than D'Amico was. He now rose in practiced indignation, his bald head reddening. "Your Honor, I saw no such thing, and I'm sure the court didn't either. My client is accused of being a major organized crime figure, and now he's supposed to be dumb enough to threaten a federal witness while looking directly at a federal judge? And in front of a jury? So which is it? Is he an idiot or a criminal mastermind? And this whole thing comes from the mouth of a career criminal. I suggest, respectfully, that we continue with the trial. There is no basis to detain my client." He dropped himself back down into his chair.

"Very well," the judge began, "let us proceed. Ms. Carleton, I saw no misbehavior and I have no basis for assessing a change in your witness's demeanor." Ever the gentleman, he paused before adding, "Of course, I accept your representation that the witness told you what you have proffered to the court and counsel. Bring in the jury and return the witness to the box."

Waiting back in the witness room, Frenchie's mood had been swinging ominously, a prominent blood vessel bulging on his reddened forehead. "Look," he told Benny, "they know about my kid. If anything happens, if they go after Albert, I'm going to be out of here in a couple years myself and I'm going to have to do something. They *will* fucking answer for that."

Benny urged him not to worry about that now. "Just take care of your business in that courtroom. Be a pro. We'll handle the rest."

Back on the stand, Frenchie found his sweet spot, a blend of anger and charm. The forehead vein was gone, as he smoothly answered the rest of Nora's questions on direct, painting detailed pictures of the Valnaghi job, the Old Masters in a tube, and the delivery of millions of dollars of stolen art to D'Amico. He was back on his game.

On cross, he walked right up to the line between feisty and inappropriate, but never went over. Even Judge Whitney seemed to enjoy watching the show, his jaw muscles invisible.

D'Amico's lawyer tried to rattle Frenchie with the story of his failure to surrender to start a jail term in an earlier case. His voice dripping with sarcasm, Butler asked, "Despite all we've heard today about your respect for the judicial process, there came a time not very long ago when you were supposed to obey a judge's order and report to jail and you didn't go, did you?"

"Sure, but there are reasons why I didn't go," Frenchie answered.

"No doubt. But it took an arrest to get you there? They had to drag you there?"

"Right. That's the way I like to go."

"Kicking and screaming?"

"I'm not much of a kicker or screamer, but—"

"You weren't happy?"

"Would you be happy if you had to go to jail?" Frenchie asked.

"I'm not happy now," Butler answered in a role reversal.

"All right," Frenchie answered. "That makes two of us."

Benny had been watching the jury. He had watched dozens of cooperating witnesses in court. He leaned toward Nora's ear. "Frenchie's killing it. They love him, they believe him."

Dominic D'Amico had also been to his share of jury trials. He had penetrating green eyes and might have been dubbed "The Eyes" if those striking features didn't frame a simply enormous nose, one with the classic "Roman" sloping curve and exaggerated bridge. Those eyes saw the same thing Dugan did. So, The Nose decided to write a note. With his mob-appointed counsel standing far away at the lectern across the enormous well of the courtroom, he scribbled on a small piece of paper before folding it repeatedly until it was the size of a postage stamp. At the next break, following the completion of Frenchie's testimony, he stood with his hands in the pockets of his chalk-striped navy blue suit pants, occasionally removing his right hand to greet someone, always the gregarious, confident hoodlum. He slowly drifted toward the government table. In a loud voice, he addressed Benny. "Dugan, a worthy adversary," he said, extending his hand. Never rattled by a mobster, especially one he'd been surveilling for twenty years, Dugan wrapped his enormous paw around D'Amico's. "Just a job, Dom, just a job. Nothin' personal."

Benny never called him "The Nose." He knew D'Amico accepted the nickname; it was predictable, given the most prominent feature of his face, but Benny also knew it chafed D'Amico, knew he wished he were "The Butcher" or something more mob-like. So, just as he would never serve a subpoena at a mobster's home and embarrass him in front of loved ones, Benny didn't use nicknames that offended their dignity. As they broke the handshake, Benny felt the postage stamp note move to his own palm, which he smoothly slid into his pocket. He read it when he was alone in the conference room off the courtroom.

> *Dear Mr. Dugan,*
>
> *I would like to meet with the government without my lawyer to discuss my future and information I have about the murder of Governor Burke.*
>
> *With respect, Dominic D'Amico*

CHAPTER FIVE

That evening, Nora and Benny stood on the Persian carpet in Judge Whitney's courthouse waiting room. Nora stared at the floor, wondering what Frenchie would think of the rug. Benny stared at the two long walls, one of which was covered with paintings of sailboats. Actually, they all appeared to feature the same boat, just in different sailing conditions in different places. The other large wall featured paintings of dogs, again appearing to be the same hunting dog in each picture, standing, pointing, or running in different settings. *Are you fricking kidding me? What planet is this guy from?* Unable to keep it all inside, he turned to whisper to Nora. "Can't speak to the boat thing, but we share a love of dog art, me and the judge."

She was too nervous to laugh, so she shook her head with the slightest of grins. Before Dugan could make another attempt to crack her up, the judge's assistant ushered them into his office, which was enormous. An acre of deep blue wall-to-wall carpet seemed to separate his desk from the entryway. He was seated behind the desk, wearing a tie and suit vest but without his jacket. As they crossed the lawn of carpet, Benny noticed that the vest had lapels on it and a gold pocket-watch chain strung across the middle. *Seriously?*

The judge looked up. "Ms. Carleton, I understand you wished to speak to the court privately about a sensitive matter. And without opposing counsel or a court reporter present? This is highly unusual."

"Yes, Your Honor, that's right, it is unusual, but we're in an unusual situation. If the court will permit me to explain?"

"Very well," Judge Whitney replied, not inviting them to sit.

Nora told him about the note to Benny in court that day, which she held up in a heat-sealed clear evidence envelope. She moved to hand it to the judge but he pulled back as if it were a used tissue. Still holding the envelope, she explained that this had happened before, years ago, when another Mafia boss—Salvatore "Sammy the Bull" Gravano—wished to cooperate. The trial judge met with the defendant to be sure of his wishes and then appointed a trusted "shadow" lawyer to secretly represent him in his effort to cooperate with the government. She explained that the government wished to handle this in the same manner, separating D'Amico from his lawyer so he could meet privately with the judge and then with his new appointed lawyer.

"Am I to understand you wish me to trick Mr. D'Amico's lawyer?"

"Not at all, Judge," Nora answered. "We'll take care of getting Mr. D'Amico to your robing room at lunch tomorrow without anyone knowing. Once there, and with a court reporter, he'll describe his wishes for the court. And we'll arrange for appointed counsel to be present."

"It all seems a little theatrical."

Benny hadn't planned to speak but couldn't contain himself. "I'm not sure I know what that means, Judge, but if his current lawyer finds out, Mr. D'Amico will be murdered. No doubt about it."

The judge sniffed, looking up at Benny. "Now *that* seems theatrical, Mr. Dugan. His attorney, Mr. Butler, is a member of the bar of this court with clear ethical requirements to safeguard client confidences."

Nora moved an inch closer to Benny, hoping to drain some of the heat she felt radiating next to her.

"Judge," Benny said, "Mr. Butler is house counsel to the Gambino Crime Family. I'm sure he has important obligations as a member of the bar, but they would kill *him* if he helped D'Amico cooperate. D'Amico is Cosa Nostra in all but name and, to Butler, his obligations to the Family supersede any obligation he feels to this court or to the fricking New York bar. This isn't a TV show, Your Honor."

Actually, it all felt very *Sopranos* to Judge Whitney, but he decided not to say it. Instead, he waved one hand side to side. "Very well, as you wish. Make the arrangements and I will see Mr. D'Amico, without Mr. Butler, but with a court reporter. Now, what is your plan for the so-called 'shadow' counsel?"

Nora gently pushed her elbow against Benny's arm. She would take this. "We intended to ask the court to offer Mr. D'Amico the choice among several trusted defense lawyers, all former Assistant United States Attorneys. I can give you their resumes."

The judge was already shaking his head from side to side. "No, no. The court is responsible for appointing counsel. I will appoint a suitable lawyer for Mr. D'Amico. You have impressed upon me the sensitivity of the matter and I will be guided accordingly. I require nothing further from you."

"Judge," Nora began, but he cut her off.

"Very well, that completes this matter. Good day."

Nora didn't move. Now it was Benny's turn to nudge her, but she ignored him. "Judge, I would ask you to reconsider," she said, barely concealing her frustration. "It has to be someone with both the discretion and the experience to handle a matter like this. That's a very small group of people."

"I said 'good day' to you, Ms. Carleton. If you wish me to cooperate in this little play of yours, you would do well to leave my chambers—immediately."

"Yes, Your Honor," Nora mumbled. They turned and left.

At the lunch break the next day, The Nose told his entourage he had forgotten something in the courtroom and would meet them at their usual table at Giambone's, a restaurant just behind the federal and state court buildings. He made his way back to the third floor, taking the stairs as instructed. He turned right out of the stairwell down the hallway behind courtroom 318 and then turned left through a heavy wood door into the judge's robing room.

Judge Whitney was sitting behind the desk, still in his black robe. A court stenographer was in a chair next to the judge's desk, fingers already on her keys. Nora and Benny stood to the judge's left. To the right was a well-dressed man, about the judge's age, his hair combed back like the judge's and wearing a dark three-piece suit. *Bet he's got fucking lapels on his vest*, Benny thought.

At least the judge was fast. He quickly confirmed D'Amico's desire not to have his lawyer present and his wish to have shadow counsel appointed to help him deal with the government. "Very well, then," the judge said, gesturing to his right. "I have appointed Charles M. Blatchford as your counsel. Mr. Blatchford is well known to this court, an experienced counsel and advisor to individuals and institutions, and is someone the court has known and trusted since we were at Amherst together. You will be in good hands, Mr. D'Amico. I wish you both fair seas. In the meantime, the court will continue to conduct this trial as if nothing has happened, until informed otherwise. Good day. Mr. Blatchford, you and your client may use this room for the next few minutes."

With that, the judge and court reporter left. Nora turned to Blatchford and extended her hand. "Nice to meet you. We will be right outside and would like to spend five or ten minutes with your guy, under the standard queen-for-a-day agreement."

Blatchford looked confused, but said only, "Very well."

In the hallway, Nora was on her phone, Googling Blatchford. Benny was venting. "'Very well'? Another fucking 'very well'-er? That some kinda preppy disease? More goddam sailboats and dogs? This isn't some fucking game."

Nora heard none of it. She looked up from her phone. "He's a mergers and acquisitions lawyer with a big firm. Amherst, NYU, twenty years of deal lawyering. He doesn't know shit about this stuff. He's just buddies with Whitney. Unbelievable."

"Maybe that makes him more trustworthy," Benny said. "Couldn't find a mob guy if his life depended on it."

"Listen to you," Nora said. "All 'bright side'. Well, *D'Amico's* life may depend on that."

The robing-room door opened and Blatchford motioned them in. "My client says we have very little time. His, uh, colleagues, are expecting him at a restaurant. He has explained to me what the queen-for-a-day agreement is—as I understand it, a use-immunity agreement that prevents you from using what he says here directly against him—and he is willing to sign it. He would like to give you—his words—"a taste" and then meet again for a fuller conversation. Satisfactory?"

Nora nodded and found herself suppressing a grin. *The mobster just explained the proffer agreement to his lawyer. That's definitely not normal.*

They all signed the one-page agreement. Then Benny took over. Looking at D'Amico, he said, "Okay, Dom, gimme the taste and then get to Giambone's."

D'Amico actually sounded nervous, which surprised Nora and Benny. He took two long breaths and then began. "Governor Burke was whacked. Wasn't no suicide and it wasn't no murder by his fucking estranged wife, Kayla, or whatever her name is. All bullshit. Lotta guys in the Family sayin' it was a Gambino hit, by a specialist. Somebody who came up through Joey Cufaro's crew, who the Family keeps away from the usual shit and uses only for the most important wet stuff. I've never met the hitter but I hear rumors it's a she. Anyhow, that's what I got, and I can get more if you make it worth my while."

Dugan was cool. "Okay, get to your bucatini. We'll work with your lawyer here to get together again. In the meantime, think about what more you know and how you're gonna find out what you don't. Capisce? Go back the way you came. We'll stay here. Go."

D'Amico shook Benny's hand and left the room. They sat in silence for a full minute before Nora turned to Blatchford. "We expect you to keep this entirely confidential for the safety of your client. We'll be in touch," she said as she and Benny hurried from the room and back across the bridge to the US Attorney's office.

CHAPTER SIX

Nora, Benny, and Nora's supervisor, Violent and Organized Crime unit chief Carmen Garcia, stood staring at the big framed black-and-white photo over the couch. Hundreds of people, mostly white men, and all in formal attire, were seated at round tables and smiling up at the camera, which must have been near the ceiling of the huge banquet space. Georgene Jackson, the US Attorney's secretary, was sitting at her desk watching them look at the picture, like a museum docent. She was a heavyset woman in her early sixties, with a round face, thick braids kept tied back for work, and warm eyes. Her voice combined the dropped *er* of a longtime "New Yorkah" with the lilt of her childhood in Trinidad. "That's from the office's two hundredth anniversary dinner, at The Plaza," she said. "Years ago. Been on that wall forever"—it came out *fa-ev-ah*—"Nothing changes here."

She lowered her voice and added, "Except for the rug." Nora, Benny, and Carmen turned to face her just as she gestured with her head toward the closed door to the US Attorney's private office, and added in a whisper, "He stole my rug."

They had heard stories about the rug. Georgene had served as secretary to many presidentially appointed US Attorneys, who came and went about every four years. On leaving office, one of them thanked her by giving her a burgundy and blue six-by-ten Persian rug. For years, it occupied the space in front of her desk and she beamed whenever a visitor glanced down at the striking carpet. "You know, Nathaniel Seymour gave me that rug," she always said. The legendary New York lawyer was long retired, but his rug remained, a reminder of Georgene's value to the office.

Until Freddy Simpson stole it. The newly appointed Simpson, still smarting from the water damage to his photos along the HVAC cover, brought his wife in one weekend to help him decorate. Together, they decided the beautiful rug in the reception area would look spectacular under the coffee table in his office, perfectly tying the oxblood couch and armchairs to the royal blue carpet. So they dragged it into his office. Georgene never said a word to him. Of course, it was possible the Simpsons simply assumed it was all government property, but no matter.

She hated him over the rug. Also over "the girl"—a full-grown woman really, but quite a bit younger than the boss. They had also all heard the stories about her as well.

Assistant US Attorney Jill Untermeyer was a junior prosecutor in the office, in the introductory unit, handling cases involving counterfeit currency and illegal gun possession. She had no cases that warranted the attention of the United States Attorney, and no obvious business on the eighth floor, where the leadership offices were, yet she frequently found herself up there, in private conference with the US Attorney himself, usually in the evenings. Georgene resented it for a bunch of reasons, maybe the lack of discretion most of all. Two or three evenings a week, the tall, attractive Jill would walk briskly into the reception area after seven P.M., her long brown hair held back by a gold band and swaying behind her as she walked. She would stand where the rug should be, and ask with a broad smile, "Hi Georgene. Is he available?" Georgene would pick up the phone and press the intercom, informing her boss, "Ms. Untermeyer is here."

Simpson invariably answered, "Send her in. And thank you, Georgene, that'll be all for tonight. I'll see you in the morning."

Jill Untermeyer then disappeared into his office, closing the door. It infuriated Georgene, sometimes more than the rug theft, which was why she told so many people.

The three of them now stood in awkward silence. "You sure you don't want to sit?" Georgene asked. "He knows it's urgent, but you never know. He gets delayed sometimes, although I don't know of any appointments this evening." They began shuffling their feet, trying to decide whether to sit and who should sit where, when they were startled by the sound of a valve toilet loudly flushing. The noise roared through the wall just to the right of the closed office door. "Oh, he'll be with you shortly now," Georgene said, her voice taking on an odd sing-song quality. "He's finished whatever he was doing."

The intercom rang, Georgene answered, and then hung up. "Mr. Simpson will see you. Go right in. I'm sure he appreciates your patience while he handled his business." Nora smiled at her as they walked toward the office door. She liked Georgene. *But this is some dysfunctional shit.*

Simpson was behind his desk at the far end of the triangular office. He was middle-aged, with a slight olive tint to his skin and a prominent chin and long nose, between which were two rows of capped white teeth, seemingly too large for his mouth. His most prominent feature was his forehead, which would have extended uninterrupted to the back of his head but for an aggressive comb-over of his straight, dyed black hair, which was plastered in an arc from his left temple up and across to his right.

Nora hadn't been in the eighth-floor office since Simpson became the United States Attorney, but it felt the same. To her right, forming the office's hypotenuse, was the wall of windows looking out over the lights of the plaza to the Manhattan landing of the Brooklyn Bridge. Nora and Carmen took the two chairs closest to the enormous wood desk; Benny pulled a side chair from the wall and sat behind the two of them.

Simpson lifted his chin toward Carmen. "So, what can I do for you?"

"Thanks for seeing us on short notice, sir. You may know Nora Carleton from my unit and"—turning to look over her shoulder—"Benny Dugan, the office's lead organized crime investigator."

Simpson nodded and didn't make it clear whether he knew them or not, answering, "Nice to see you both."

She then launched into a briefing on the developments with D'Amico: the secret note about having information on Tony Burke's murder, the judge's appointment of shadow counsel, the secret meeting.

Simpson seemed riveted. "Very cool," he said. "So what'd he give you on Kyra Burke?"

"That's just the thing, sir," Carmen said. "He says she didn't kill the former governor; the mob did."

Simpson made a face. "Oh, that's some bullshit, for sure. DA says he has her dead-to-rights. Trying to save his own ass, I'm guessing."

"Well, sir," Carmen continued, "we don't have details yet, because this was just a preliminary meeting, but Benny—and Nora—both assess D'Amico as credible. He is taking an enormous risk to cooperate here. We'd like to continue the debriefing and explore whether there are opportunities to use him proactively to get more information on the killer, or killers. Since he's on the street—out on bail—maybe wire him up to get some conversation about it."

Simpson was shaking his head. "Whoa, whoa, whoa. You're getting way ahead of yourself. Isn't this D'Amico a seriously bad guy, somebody we've been trying to nail for years?"

Nora answered. "He is."

"And won't he be looking for some kind of deal with us in exchange for his cooperation?"

"He will," she said. "What that might look like, I can't say at this point."

Simpson raised his voice. "Well, I sure can. We aren't gonna do it. That's what I say. We aren't gonna get in bed with some piece-a-shit mobster over some bullshit about a case that's already being prosecuted by the DA down the street. Nope. Not gonna happen."

Carmen stepped in. "Sir, he is offering us information that the Mafia murdered a significant public figure and that an innocent woman may go to jail for it. It's our obligation to pursue this."

Simpson's face reddened and he began almost shouting. "No, it's not. That case is the DA's responsibility. I've had to work hard enough to repair our relationship with that office after my predecessor crapped all over them. And, as I recall, your unit was part of that—stealing their cases. Our job—" he said, before pointing to Nora, "*your* job—is to convict Dominic D'Amico, and not get manipulated by this nonsense. We are not—"

Carmen interrupted, her tone on the edge of insubordination. "Sir, with all due respect, that makes no sense. We've always made mob cases through cooperators. D'Amico could give us all kinds of things. We haven't even debriefed the guy, so to cut it off now isn't right."

Somehow Simpson's face grew redder. "Don't talk to me like I'm a child. The President of the United States appointed me to run this office and make decisions, and I've made one. We are not getting in bed with a mafioso over some fairy tale. Nope. No negotiations with this maniac. Hasn't he murdered thirty people himself? I only wish you had come to me sooner; we wouldn't have dragged Judge Whitney into this sideshow. But it ends here. Am I clear?"

Carmen answered. "Yes. Very."

Simpson broke the awkward silence that followed. "Good. I wish you luck with the rest of the trial." He looked down at his desk and began reading something.

Without speaking, the three of them filed out, the windows now on their left, the sitting area just to the right of the doorway. Nora glanced at the Persian rug. *Looks kinda nice there.*

CHAPTER SEVEN

"I s the judge always gonna take Friday afternoons off?" Kyra asked. They were back in the kitchen of her Pomander Walk home.

"No," Matthew Parker answered. "She just didn't want to do openings and then send the jury home for the weekend. Better to open Monday morning, she figures, and then go right into the evidence. Hard to disagree with her. So, how you feelin' about our jury?"

After four and a half days in the state courtroom, they had finished picking a jury of twelve, with six alternates. They were diverse in all sorts of ways, except one: Parker had used his strikes to ensure there was nobody in the top twelve who had heard anything about the case.

Kyra laughed and shook her head. "I'm surprised and pleased—and maybe a little hurt, although I'm kidding—that so many people have never heard of Killer Kyra. You were right; there *are* a lot of people in Manhattan who don't read or follow the news."

"Yep." Parker said with a laugh. "Now, let's talk about Monday. They're gonna open with the medical examiner—guy was dead, insulin overdose, blah, blah, blah. No shocker there. Then they'll go with the doorman and the lobby video, trying to put you in the shit right away. And—"

The street-gate buzzer rang.

"That's probably Conor," Kyra said.

"Conor?"

"You know, Conor McCarthy, the guy who called you to represent me? I asked him to come by and talk strategy with us."

"What? Why?"

"He's smart and I trust him. He knew Tony really well. Also got screwed by him—figuratively in his case—and I think he can help us."

Parker started rubbing his face.

"Look," she said, "lemme at least let the guy in. I told him to come."

She got up from the table and went to the front door, returning a minute later with a slim, well-dressed man of average height, about her age, with unblemished, tanned skin. He wore his brown hair slicked back, with a yellow V-neck sweater over a pink button-down dress shirt, tan corduroy pants, and tasseled loafers with no socks. *Just back from a J. Crew fashion shoot*, Parker thought. *Maybe some spray-tan action as well.*

Kyra introduced them and they shook hands. *Gives new meaning to "buttery smooth,"* Parker thought. As they took their seats around the butcher-block table, Kyra spoke first. "Tell Matthew your story, Conor. He likes to start that way."

"Okay," Conor began, his accentless voice as smooth as his hands. "I grew up in the city. My dad was a doorman. Mom was a hotel maid. Went to Yale on a scholarship. First in my family to go to college. Met *this* amazing woman there. We hit it off immediately and became close friends. After school, the law was not my thing, so Kyra and I went in different directions—at least for a while. I went into political consulting, lots of different jobs, then ended up working for Tony Burke—a gofer at first, then I did comms, leg affairs, fundraising, ending up as chief of staff in his second term. He was a difficult boss, but I learned a lot. Then Kyra came back into my life more regularly when she started dating the bastard—and I should add I didn't know yet that he was as bad as he was. I thought at that point he was a politician and they're all bad in a certain way, but not in the way that he turned out to be. I was just as fooled by Burke as Kyra. And when he died, and these morons decided Kyra killed him, I had to help her. So I called you that morning, I tapped a lot of our friends to raise the money for your fee and bail, and I'm willing to help in any way I can."

Parker looked up from his notepad, although he hadn't taken any notes. "Look, I appreciate all that, Conor, I really do, but you aren't my client, or a member of this legal team, so we don't enjoy the protections of attorney-client privilege or the work-product doctrine. Everything you say or hear could be discoverable."

"But I want him here," Kyra said. "And he can help, as I said."

"I get that, I really do," Parker answered, "and he can stay for now, but you have to be very careful about what you say."

"That's a little silly, Matthew. I've already told him everything. He's one of my closest friends. If I've told him too much, then it's too late, but all I've told him is that I didn't do it. That I'm completely innocent, which is the truth."

Conor nodded and turned to Parker. "That's right, and I believe her. And so do lots of other people. I've spoken to both Marian and Edward Burke. They are convinced Kyra didn't kill Tony, which is one of the reasons they contributed money for your fee. It's a big deal that the man's own son—and his first wife—believe in Kyra's innocence. I don't want to be part of your legal strategy, but I know communications and I'd like to get that out there."

Parker sat up straight. "Look, I can't ask you, or counsel you, to engage in any communication that might reach the jury now that the trial is underway. I have to abide by the court's publicity rules."

Conor was instantly apologetic. "Oh, no, I'm not asking you to do anything or approve anything. That has nothing to do with you. I just wanted you to know that a lot of people think Kyra is innocent, including me and members of Tony Burke's family. That's all. What I do with that is my business. But good people will not sit silently by and watch an innocent person go to jail for life. And I'm sorry for the speech."

"No, no, that's okay, Conor," Parker said. "If you're okay in Kyra's book, that's good enough for me. And she *is* innocent. No doubt about that."

Turning to Kyra, he added, "Have we covered everything on how you thought he could help?"

"Actually, no," she answered. "The other day he reminded me of something I think is good for us."

Now Parker swiveled to Conor, raising both eyebrows. "And that is . . ."

"Yeah, yeah," Conor said, "thanks Kyra. That was actually the reason she wanted us to chat. I remember Burke telling me he wasn't going to enforce the prenup against Kyra. Said he didn't want to be a complete prick. He said he would give her a big chunk of cash, so long as he got an NDA on anything related to him, going back to when they first met. So it really wasn't about being a good guy; it was about keeping her quiet. But either way, Kyra was gonna get paid, big, although he didn't say exactly how much."

"Okay," Parker said dismissively, "so that's hearsay."

Kyra jumped in. "But that's the thing, Matthew. Conor *told* me that before Tony died, which goes to my state of mind, making it non-hearsay. We can get that in. It totally undercuts their motive proof. I was gonna get good money with him alive, so what reason would I have to kill him?"

Parker sat without speaking for a long time, before mumbling, "Well, somebody paid attention in law-school evidence class."

In a louder voice, he added, "And you were gonna tell me this when?"

"Conor reminded me of it just this week," Kyra said. "And even then it didn't seem a big deal until I had a minute to think about it. Then I asked him to come see us."

Parker paused again. "Okay, listen, I'm gonna need to think about this one and interview each of you separately, which I can do this weekend. But I think you're right, it could be useful, as long as we think through how the idea of you being willing to take cash for a nondisclosure agreement squares with you not wanting Tony to victimize others and all. But let's take some time to think about it."

He dropped his hands on the table and exhaled loudly. "Okay, Conor, thanks for helping the team." Nodding to a bottle of Redbreast 27-Year on the table, he added, "We were about to end the week with a well-earned Irish whiskey. You in?"

"Conor McCarthy's the name," he answered. "I was born 'in', especially for a taste of 27-Year."

"Another glass please, Kyra."

They spent the next hour sitting at the kitchen table, enjoying whiskey and Conor's extraordinary storytelling ability. His tales of navigating the snobbery of Yale and the snakery of politics were hilarious. Parker found himself charmed by this working-class kid made good.

"Thanks for a good end to a tough week," he said, gathering his papers.

"My pleasure," Conor answered. "I can't imagine the burden of representing an innocent person, but we're grateful for your shouldering it and confident that you'll save Kyra."

"I'll do my best," Parker answered. He paused a moment before continuing.

"And it may be easier than it seems. I have lots of friends in the legal world, for obvious reasons. And it's early yet, but somebody on the inside let me know today that the feds have good reason to believe the Mafia ordered a hit on Tony Burke, which would prove Kyra is innocent."

Both Kyra and Conor took audible breaths.

Parker continued. "Some mobster decided to do the right thing and be an informant to save his own skin. Good for him. Maybe better for Kyra. But I see reason for hope. I mention it because we may need help dragging Kyra's case out a bit longer while this develops. If you can work with me to line up people like the Burkes to testify, that'll both help and buy us time."

Turning to Kyra, he said, "And maybe after Conor leaves, I can give you the details, just to be sure we protect the confidentiality of it all."

She nodded.

"Got it," Conor added, rising from the table. Looking back and forth between Kyra and Parker, he added, "Of course I'll help get anyone to testify—the Burkes, anyone. And I won't say a word about this."

As Kyra stood to walk him out, Conor wrapped both arms around her, holding the hug for several seconds, his tightly closed eyes facing Parker over her shoulder.

Kyra was irritated when she returned to the table from the front door. "So when were you gonna tell me about this?"

"I wasn't sure I was going to at all, yet. It's too early and I'm sure I'll know more in a day or so. But my friend said the feds are prosecuting a mobster named D'Amico. Apparently he decided the trial is not going well for him, so he reached out to try to cooperate. As an appetizer or something, he told them you didn't kill Tony, the mob did. Some specialist killer from the Gambino Crime Family did it. This D'Amico is out on bail and is gonna try to get more details. That's all I got so far.

It's important that this stays close-hold. Not a word to anyone, and I hope your friend can keep his mouth shut too."

"Of course, of course," she said.

"And speaking of shit that wasn't shared," Parker went on, "this bit about Burke not enforcing the prenup seems a little too good. So you really forgot about that, and also forgot to tell me once you no longer forgot?"

Kyra locked eyes with him, hers filling with tears. "It's the God's honest truth, Matthew. I've been under a mountain of stress; this whole thing has messed with my head in ways I never imagined. But I'm telling the truth, and Conor's telling the truth."

Parker looked away first. "Okay, okay, I believe you."

The kitchen was quiet for several beats before Kyra spoke. "Is it too soon to have another whiskey?"

Parker laughed. "*You* can. I gotta get home to Brooklyn. I'll call you tomorrow. And, again, not a word about this to anyone. We don't want to do anything to jeopardize our ability to use this to get all charges against you dropped."

"Got it," Kyra said, her eyes welling up. "Then this nightmare will finally be over. I can't thank you enough."

"Don't thank me yet. Tomorrow we'll talk about what I'm gonna ask the doorman on cross."

CHAPTER EIGHT

There were Chinese characters on many of the storefronts on Eighteenth Avenue in the Bensonhurst section of Brooklyn now. Some Spanish signs as well. That was hard to get used to, but The Nose was one of the few mob guys with a progressive view of immigration. "How do you think youse ended up in this great country and not stuck in some Sicilian shithole?" he routinely asked his colleagues. "People come to Brooklyn, they do well, they move to the suburbs, other people take their place. America never stops, amiright?" He was right, but they didn't get it. And, as open-minded as he was, even he was consoled by the constant of the Caffè Giardino, which had been on Eighteenth Avenue since, well, back in the day. Way back.

It even smelled like the old country, the streets of Palermo rushing at him as he pushed the glass front door open, the little brass bell rattling on the frame to announce his arrival. He grunted a greeting to geezers at the bar sipping their Sunday morning espresso. The bartender jerked his chin up, silently asking whether he wanted one. The Nose held up a single finger as he walked through to the back stairs. *Later.* He would grab one after his meeting.

The basement of the Giardino held two small bathrooms and an office, which was once the man cave of John Gambino, deceased after getting out of prison—of natural causes, which was the way to go. Now the office was the mob version of WeWork, available to any made member who needed a quiet place, one regularly swept for electronic surveillance devices.

The linoleum-covered wood stairs groaned as The Nose headed down. At the bottom, he ducked under the low ceiling pipe and walked toward the closed office door. *Must be here already,* he thought. *Wish I knew what the fuck this was.*

The Nose walked in to find himself looking at a silenced black semiautomatic pistol. He had seen many, but wasn't sure if it was a Glock 17 or a 19. Hard to tell if it's the short or long pistol grip when it's in someone's hand. No matter; guns didn't freak him out, even when pointed at him in the basement of a mob hangout.

But the bird rattled him. There was a dead yellow canary on the small round table between the two chairs. Somebody had crushed the poor little thing. *Sick fucks.* Determined not to show anything, he sat, facing the gun.

"Been a long time," he said. "I thought you were supposed to be the one who got out, went straight. Wasn't that your old man's dream?"

"Hardly, Dominic. My father believed what *we* are supposed to: You only leave Cosa Nostra when you die. And you don't rat. Ever. Omertà means something. It means you don't make friends with Benny fucking Dugan."

The Nose could feel it all slowing down. He had been there for this moment so many times, the excruciating seconds as time dilated before the flicker of someone's consciousness was blown out. *Goddammit.* He wasn't gonna beg, wasn't gonna fight, but he had to ask.

"Who the fuck told ya that?"

He got his answer, cold as ice. "The old man's gone, but he still has lotsa friends in high places, people who appreciate loyalty, who believe oaths matter."

That was all the explanation he was going to get.

"Fuck it," he said. "Been a good run. Just do it." He slid to the end of his chair and stiffened his back, hanging his clasped hands between his thighs, eyes closed, chin lifted.

The silencer was so good that the only sound in the office was the metallic rub of the slide moving as the Glock spit two nine-millimeter bullets through the center of Dominic D'Amico's forehead, just above his famous nose.

Monday morning, Salvatore Butler, Esquire, was on his feet, nervously wiping the top of his shaved head with a monogrammed white handkerchief as he waited for Judge Whitney to take the bench.

The judge swept through the back door, robe flowing behind, and up to his high-back leather chair. "Mr. Butler, any sign of your client? You know how important promptness is to this court, and how reluctant the court was to release Mr. D'Amico on bail, especially without an ankle monitor. And over the government's strong objection, as you will recall. His tardiness is deeply concerning and erodes the trust this court placed in him."

"Judge, I don't know what to tell you," Butler answered. "I tried all his numbers. His family has not heard from him since Saturday. I'm very concerned. We've been feeling good about our defense and he's not a man to run, especially after this court placed confidence in his ability to abide by the terms and conditions of release."

The judge looked at the government's table. "Ms. Carleton, I assume your office is doing all in its power to locate Mr. D'Amico?"

"We are, Judge. We have the US Marshals fugitive task force, which includes the FBI and NYPD, out looking for him."

"Very well. Most unfortunate. The court will stand in recess until further word." With that, he was off the bench and out the back door.

Six hours later, Nora, Jessica, and Benny walked together across the bridge to courtroom 318.

"This is seriously fucked up," Benny whispered. "We met with the guy *three days ago*, and just for 'a taste,' as he said. Then we get that shit from the boss. Now this? Somethin' is seriously sideways."

Nora whispered back intensely. "Agreed. Seriously. Let's just do this and then go back to my office to talk to Carmen."

Judge Whitney was already on the bench as they walked into the courtroom, and he addressed Nora before she reached her seat. "Counsel, I understand you have an update on Mr. D'Amico?"

Nora remained standing. "I do, Your Honor. Unfortunately. Responding to an anonymous tip, the NYPD found Mr. D'Amico in the trunk of a car abandoned off the Belt Parkway in Canarsie— southeastern part of Brooklyn. He'd been shot twice in the head. And a dead bird was forced into his mouth. A canary, I believe."

The judge looked genuinely confused. "What?"

Because Nora wasn't sure what confused him, she explained it all. "He appears to have been executed by someone who wished him to be found, to deliver a message. Two shots in the forehead. Best guess at this point is that he was killed yesterday. The canary in the mouth is an old mob warning to those who might cooperate with law enforcement."

The judge still looked confused, so she added, "You know, those who sing will die?" *And he never should have been out on bail in the first place, you pretentious fool.* She didn't say that last bit, but still enjoyed the thought. "I have photographs of the body, should the court wish to examine them." She lifted an iPad in two hands, almost daring Judge Whitney to look at the pictures of D'Amico curled in an open trunk, yellow feathers in his mouth, maroon-colored bullet holes in his forehead, eyes frozen open. *Sorry, no dogs or boats, Judge. Just a dead guy in Canarsie, a place you've never been in your life.*

The judge seemed to get it now, raising his palm to decline her offer, slumping back in his chair. After an awkward silence, Nora added, "Your Honor, we would respectfully suggest you dismiss the jury. My office will be filing a death nolle prosequi to end this case."

After another two beats of silence, the judge stirred. "Very well, Ms. Carleton. I will go back and speak to the jurors. And await that filing. Is there anything further?"

"No, Your Honor."

"Very well," the judge said, rising. "This court will stand in recess." He turned to leave, then paused and said. "I assume this will be investigated."

Nora wasn't sure that was a question and, if it was, one directed to her, but she answered anyway. "I sure hope so, Judge."

Jessica left directly for the FBI field office and Benny was silent during their walk back across the bridge. Nora looked up at him. "You okay?"

"Yeah, yeah," he said. "Just thinkin'. Hey, meet you in your office, okay? Gotta run an errand."

"Sure," Nora said, pressing the up button for the elevator as Benny pressed the down. He grinned as her elevator doors closed. As soon as Nora disappeared, he turned and walked to the fire stairs, where he climbed to the eighth floor and headed toward the executive suite.

"Hey, Benny," Georgene said as he entered the waiting area. "What's up?"

He jabbed his left thumb toward the closed door to the US Attorney's private office. "Need to see him. Now."

"Sure," Georgene answered, "he's free." She reached for the phone. "What should I tell him it's about?"

"Personal," he replied, taking two long strides and opening and closing the office door behind him.

Simpson was nowhere to be seen, but the door to the private bathroom was closed. He'd wait. Benny took a seat on the oxblood couch, feet on the Persian rug. A minute later, the blast of the valve toilet flush announced Simpson's imminent return.

As the US Attorney stepped into the room zipping his fly, he was startled to see the enormous investigator on his couch, legs crossed, with one penny loafer resting atop the opposite knee, exposing on his bare leg—he never wore socks—the ankle holster with the Smith & Wesson revolver he always wore.

"Can I help you?" Simpson asked.

"Geez, I sure hope so," Benny said, adding, "have a seat, boss." He pointed to a chair and Simpson moved as directed. He seemed either curious or intimidated. Benny couldn't tell but, regardless, his boss took a seat in the wing chair.

Benny waited. He knew the unsettling power of silence. Finally, Simpson broke it, lifting both hands off his lap, palms facing up. "So?"

Benny's voice came out an octave lower than even his normal baritone. "So," he echoed, "this will be brief. I don't know what the fuck is going on with you and this D'Amico/Burke thing, but that shit stops now. You and I never spoke, but you are gonna call Carmen Garcia and tell her to go balls to the wall to figure it out."

It was intimidating, although Simpson worked hard to conceal it. "Now why would I do that?" he sneered.

"Cause I know you're bangin' that General Crimes chick and I will burn you to the fuckin' ground otherwise. Don't doubt for a second I could do it or that I will do it. Look, I could give a shit where you put your dick, but I'm guessing your wife cares. And EOUSA cares maybe even more than your wife does, given that you're puttin' it in a kid who works for you."

The reference to the Executive Office for United States Attorneys—the Department of Justice office responsible for overseeing the nation's US Attorneys—seemed to rattle Simpson even more than the reference to his wife. He was now studying his unwashed hands, which were back in his lap.

Benny waited a bit for him to digest, then added, his voice slightly higher, "Just give Carmen the green light, step back, and we never speak of it again."

Simpson didn't look up.

"We good?" Benny asked.

Still looking down, Simpson nodded his head several times and whispered, "We're good."

Benny stood and moved toward the door, then stopped and turned back toward Simpson, pointing toward the US Attorney's feet. "And give Georgene her fucking rug back. Today." With that he was through the door, past Georgene, and into the fire stairs down to four.

CHAPTER NINE

Carmen Garcia was standing in the hall so she could see Nora and Benny in their adjoining offices at the same time. She was a five-foot-three ball of energy and humor, with the dark eyes and tan skin of her native Puerto Rico. Her parents had moved to New York when she was a toddler, and both worked long hours at low-paying jobs while dreaming big for their little girl. And she didn't disappoint, first going to law school, and now becoming the chief federal organized crime prosecutor, a job she liked because it gave her more predictable hours and the opportunity to mentor younger lawyers. Carmen always wore her black hair short—"Saves me time having to tell people I'm a lesbian," she liked to joke—and she lived with her wife and their three-year-old son in suburban New Jersey. "And, yes," she was quick to add, "there *are* gay Puerto Ricans. Took my parents a while to realize it, but they got there."

Now she seemed confused, which didn't happen often. "Unfuckingbelievable. I feel like I'm being punked."

"What?" Nora asked, looking up from her desk. "What happened?"

"Can we confer?" Carmen asked, assuming a scarecrow stance to point at each of them. "My office, now?"

Benny was on his feet. "Cool if Jessica joins us?" he asked, pointing into the corner of his office, where Special Agent Watson was obscured from Carmen's view.

"Of course," she answered. "We need the whole A-team."

Carmen closed the door to her fourth-floor corner office. The VOC unit chief job came with a lot of stress, but it also brought a nice office overlooking the plaza. "Okay," she said, turning to face them, "I just got a bizarro-world call from Simpson. He ordered me to aggressively investigate not only D'Amico's death, but his information about Burke's killing. 'Do whatever it takes to get to the bottom of it,' he said. And he added that I didn't need to keep him posted. He knows he can count on us to do the right thing. What the hell?"

"Did you ask him why the change of heart?" Nora asked.

"You kidding? Hell no. I pocketed it. 'Thank you, Mr. US Attorney. We're on it.' And I hung up to come tell you."

"You sure it was him?" Jessica asked, adding a small smile so they knew the new kid was being funny.

Carmen laughed. "Yup, caller ID and voice all matched."

"Holy shit," Nora exhaled. Then, looking at Benny, she added, "You're mighty quiet."

Benny laughed. "Just shocked at the way the wheels of justice turn sometimes. Okay, let's get to it." Turning to Jessica, he said, "Let's you and me start looking at where D'Amico coulda got his information. Need you to shake the Bureau tree. They gotta pulse every CHS, and do it now while it's still fresh. Including all TEs."

The FBI's Confidential Human Sources—called CHSs in Buspeak—were its lifeblood, and the FBI had developed dozens in Cosa Nostra over the years, including high-ranking mobsters out on the street who secretly supplied information—the Top Echelon, or TE, sources.

"Got it," Jessica answered.

Benny turned to Nora. "We're gonna need 2703(d) orders on all D'Amico's devices, including location data. Need to see who he's touched and where he's gone in the last week. And then we'll need them on everyone he contacted. Gotta put together a full link analysis on him."

Nora nodded as Benny continued, "I'll get with the PD to find out what Brooklyn South Homicide has on this. And I'll start going through my stuff to see if there's something we missed on ol' Dom."

They all knew what he meant by "my stuff." For decades, Dugan had conducted surveillance of mob gatherings and taken photographs. He sat outside social clubs endlessly, but he maintained he was most productive with a zoom lens at weddings and funerals. "That's when these assholes cross family lines and really show us who's who." He insisted on printing out the photos and storing them in black three-ring binders, each with the name and date of the event written on the spine, always in his hand and always using liquid white-out. Dozens of colleagues had urged him to consider digital files or at least printed labels on the binders. "Nope," he invariably replied, "stuck in my ways. And I like to be able to spread 'em out and study the pictures. Hard to do that on a screen."

He had consented to having the photos digitized, but he never looked at them that way. Instead, he would stand before the rows of black binders on steel shelves from floor to ceiling all around his office and decide what wedding to check, what wake or funeral might be interesting.

"I'm off to my books," he said, unfolding from the couch. Jessica followed him out the door, on her way back to the FBI office across the street.

Carmen and Nora sat a moment in silence before Carmen broke it. "You good?"

"Yeah, I'm good," Nora said. "I just wish I felt better about our boss. This is some whiplash shit. And I assume he knows we're gonna have to talk to the DA on this, maybe mess up their big Killer Kyra case in the middle of trial. If he's so proud of rebuilding that relationship, shouldn't he be on that with us? Our frigging leader should at least make the first touch over there to block for us a bit. I'm just not sure his weird call to you gives us the authority to make those contacts on our own."

The relationship between the Manhattan DA and the United States Attorney's office—sitting two blocks apart in lower Manhattan—had been fraught for decades, a tension born of shared jurisdiction, but also the talent—and crossbreeding—in both places. Assistant district attorneys sometimes became AUSAs, who often returned to the DA's office as senior supervisors. A longtime US Attorney, Robert Morgenthau, became the longest-serving Manhattan district attorney in history. And he did everything in his power to steal high-profile cases from his former office and stop them from stealing his. It was made even more complicated by the ability of the NYPD to play the two prosecutors' offices against each other. Congress had seen to it that nearly every state crime could also be prosecuted federally, so the cops could decide where to take the fruits of their investigations. The constant warring between the FBI and NYPD only added to the tension. And New Yorkers were naturally a pain in the ass. It was all a recipe for chronic tension

It was true that Freddy Simpson had tried to patch things up with the current DA. The prior US Attorney had several times gone nuclear in turf battles with the DA, indicting cases that the two offices were competing for. Under New York law, a federal indictment prevented a later state prosecution of the same matter. And to the DA's frustration, they had no such weapon because the reverse was not true; the feds could still pursue a case even after the locals prosecuted it. After that particularly ugly stretch, Simpson took the DA to lunch several times and promised a new era of transparency and trust.

As a senior supervisor, Carmen Garcia knew all this. Still, she paused before answering. "You know, you're right. He should at least be with us on the initial approach, maybe call over there to prep the ground for us. Let's pop upstairs and see him."

They saw it the moment they stepped into Simpson's reception area: the beautiful six-by-ten burgundy and blue Persian rug sat directly in front of Georgene's desk. Nora and Carmen stopped short of the rug and each looked at Georgene with the same wide-eyed expression. She chuckled. "Look at you two. Like you've never seen a rug before."

They drew close to her desk, Carmen whispering, "What the hell?"

"Don't know," Georgene whispered back. "About an hour ago he dragged it out here, mumbled something about not knowing it was mine, and went back in there. Haven't seen him since."

"He still here?" Carmen asked.

"Think so," Georgene answered, "unless he jumped out the window, but I woulda heard the sirens."

"Would you mind telling him we need to speak with him briefly on the D'Amico case? Just a quick follow-up."

"Sure." Georgene lifted the phone and pressed the intercom, repeating Carmen's request to the US Attorney. They couldn't make out his words, but could hear him speaking sharply to Georgene, who said, "Yes, sir, I understand," and replaced the receiver. She stared at the phone for a moment and then looked up, speaking like she was in a hostage video.

"He's not interested in speaking with you and believes you have all the direction you need. He said his conversation with Mr. Dugan is the last he intends to have on this matter."

Nora jumped in. "What conversation with Mr. Dugan?"

"Benny was up here this afternoon," Georgene explained. "Went in without asking. Don't know what it was about. Few minutes later, he was gone. Little while after that, the rug got dragged." Georgene shrugged beneath a broad smile.

Nora and Carmen turned and walked quickly to the fire stairs. On four, they both started to turn toward Dugan's office, but Nora extended her arm in front of Carmen. "Wait. Let me do this. I'll let you know."

Carmen didn't answer but she stopped and changed direction, heading toward her own office.

In Dugan's office, Nora was hot. "You talked to Simpson about *our* case? Without us? What the hell, Benny? What did you say?"

He was standing by a shelf of photo books and turned to face her. "I did. I'm sorry, but it had to be done, and only I could do it. And it's best if you don't know more than that."

"What, did you threaten him? And why the hell did he return Georgene's rug?"

"Again, Nora, I love you like you were my own, but there are some things better left unsaid. I keep telling you I'm not as good a person as you think I am."

She paused, trying to decide whether she was too angry to say her line.

She was not. "Did I say you were a good person?" she said, adding, "Whatever it was, thank you. But I don't like this Lone Ranger shit." She turned and went into her own office.

Two minutes later, she was back, as if it had never happened. "Hey," she said, "I think we should go down and see Frenchie. He's been with the marshals since he got off the stand. Gonna freak when he hears the case ended like it did. We should tell him he's done and we'll hold up our end of the deal—he stays in WITSEC as long as he wants."

"Agreed."

Frenchie had heard it hours earlier from one of his US Marshal babysitters, but he was still hyped, talking rapid-fire. "Ha ha, they whacked The Nose. Son of a bitch. Wish that were on pay-per-view. Oh well, couldn't happen to a nicer guy. *Morceau de merde*, as my mom would say."

"Frenchie," Nora interrupted, "we wanted to be sure you knew, and also that you know your deal is still good."

Frenchie was so excited by D'Amico's demise that he had forgotten to ask. "Yeah, yeah, my deal. That's good, good. So I stay WITSEC until I finish my state time, then I can go into the full program as a civilian if I want. That right?"

"Yes," Nora said. "New identity, the whole thing. And the offer is still there for your son to come with you."

"We'll see how that goes," Frenchie answered. "But I appreciate you people holding up your end."

"Never in doubt," Nora said. "You did good."

Benny nodded his head in agreement. "But here's the thing, Frenchie. When you get out and you're in Omaha, or wherever, as Fred Flintstone, or whatever, don't steal shit. That's part of holding up your end. Clear?"

Frenchie nodded solemnly.

"And if you steal shit," Benny continued, "I will personally hunt your worthless ass down and lock you up. Clear?"

Frenchie looked pleadingly at Nora. "Why's he gotta be like this? Always the dark cloud in a blue sky."

Turning back to Benny, he said, "This is a happy day; the wicked witch got splattered by a big old house. Lighten up, big man. Don't you worry. I get it, I get it. New man, new life. Omaha has nothing to worry about. You won't see me again."

Before moving to the door, Benny extended his hand. "We're countin' on it," he said in his deepest voice, before adding, "but thanks. You were a stand-up guy."

Nora smiled at her witness. "Be well and be safe, Daniel."

As they walked down the street from the safe house, Nora turned to Benny. "What's wrong with me that I feel good after speaking to a career criminal about the murder of our defendant?"

He turned his head to smile warmly down at her as they walked. "Yup, this work is pretty fucked up, ain't it, kid?" before adding, "But pretty great, huh?"

Nora answered with a grin. "Mostly great. Mostly."

CHAPTER TEN

S tate criminal trials in Manhattan didn't happen where the movie-going public thought they did. The one-hundred-foot wide sweeping staircase up to the Greek-temple-looking courthouse at 60 Centre Street actually led to courtrooms filled with civil cases—fights over contracts or asbestos or property. The criminal action was a few doors down in a drab, vaguely greenish building that the criminal court judges shared with the District Attorney's office. There, at 100 Centre Street, visitors climbed five little stairs—or six if you were going to the north entrance. But that Soviet-looking building made a poor movie set, so the filming was done on the grand staircase up the street at 60 Centre, overlooking Foley Square.

At 100 Centre this morning, they were getting a late start. As in many New York courtrooms, the judge only planned for the jury to hear evidence from ten A.M. to four P.M., with an hour for lunch. And, still, jurors were late, blaming the subway system. After initial court legal instructions, they were finally underway in a third-floor courtroom, and Assistant District Attorney Andy Kwon was on his feet, introducing himself to the jury in *People of the State of New York v. Kyra P. Burke.* He wore a dark blue off-the-rack suit, looking tall, skinny, and very young. From the defense table, across the dimly lit courtroom, Matthew Parker noticed that Kwon put no notes on the little brown podium centered along the jury rail. In fact, he had nothing at all: no notebook, no charts, no exhibits. He was just going to stand there and talk.

We're fucked, Parker thought. He knew from his many years as an Assistant US Attorney up the street that the best prosecutors avoided the disease of nervous lawyers—"gilding the lily." In truth, Parker never fully understood the term—something about putting gold paint on already-perfect flowers to try to improve them, which, of course, killed them—but he got the gist: focus your case on your best facts so the jury can do the same. He liked that these days prosecutors called it going "thin to win." Of course, he liked it less now that he was a defense lawyer, watching an ADA without notes tell the jury it was all quite straightforward.

Yes, it was simple, ADA Kwon said to the jury. Tony Burke was murdered, Kyra Burke had a powerful motive, the doorman and lobby camera saw her arrive and depart in a tight bracket around his death, and the rest is distraction. He added that there would probably be smoke about the "real killer" being a look-alike with the elevator code and somehow known to Tony Burke. But it was just that, smoke, and . . .

Gotta break up this little prick's show. Parker was on his feet, deftly buttoning his suit before calling out, "Objection to the arguing, Your Honor. This is supposed to be an opening statement."

"Sustained," said New York State Supreme Court Justice Irene Zannis, a large and imposing jurist with a head of curly black hair, who long ago gave up trying to explain to proud Greek relatives that she was not "on the Supreme Court" and that, for reasons lost in the mists of time, New York had chosen to give that title to its *lowest* level trial court, calling its highest court the Court of Appeals. It was just as well they couldn't see the linoleum floor and hanging fluorescent lights here on the third floor of a building that towered five—or six—steps above Centre Street in lower Manhattan.

ADA Kwon wasn't rattled by the objection. He just kept rolling along in an engaging, conversational tone. Give both sides your attention, listen to the judge, apply your common sense. And, if you do that, you will see there is only one just verdict in this case—guilty. Thank you. Then he collected nothing from the podium and sat down.

Kid is good. Fuck.

"Mr. Parker," the judge called.

"Yes, thank you, Your Honor." Matthew Parker also brought nothing with him to the podium, nothing except twenty years as an organized crime prosecutor, including ten as chief of the US Attorney's VOC unit, and fifteen years as a criminal defense lawyer. *Thirty-five years of this shit. And now my last at-bat is in fucking New York Supreme.*

He pulled himself back into the moment, not because this was his last time, but because he had warmed to this case and to Kyra Burke. He actually believed what he was about to say. And he had to lean into it because, other than the jurors believing Kyra, he didn't have much to work with.

Without speaking, he looked at the jury, drew a deep breath, and then twisted his upper body away from them to face the defense table on the other side of the courtroom. Raising his arm, finger pointed, he nearly shouted, each word a verbal punch. "That. Is. An. Innocent. Woman. Not just 'not guilty.' Completely and totally innocent."

Turning back to the jurors, he continued in a more normal voice. "It's not often that a lawyer gets to say that about a client, that a lawyer is *permitted* by the rules of ethics to say that about a client. But I say it because it's true. I have the indescribable honor, and the terrifying burden, of representing a woman wrongly accused of murder. And, when we are done, you'll see it the same way."

The jurors were wide-eyed and pressed back in their seats, like front-car patrons at Space Mountain. Parker then lowered his voice further, adopting an almost grandfatherly tone. "Now Mr. Kwon over there seems like a real nice fellow, so there's nothing personal in what I say. This is about the state of New York. They have it wrong. They faced enormous pressure to solve the killing of a former governor, fell in love with a theory, and have been trapped in it, unable to see that they're walking us all into a miscarriage of justice. They have blinders on and—"

Now it was Andy Kwon's turn to object. He stood and started to speak, but Justice Zannis didn't wait for him.

"Yes, sustained. What's good for the goose is good for the gander." The moment she said it she realized she had no idea what that really meant or whether it might be inappropriate in some gendered way. Looking at the jury, she quickly added, "Openings are simply an opportunity for each side to lay out what they believe the evidence will show. Argument comes at the end. Please proceed, Mr. Parker."

"Thank you, Your Honor," Parker said, before turning back to the jury. "The *evidence* will show that Kyra Burke was home at the time of the former governor's death. The *evidence* will show that Kyra also had no reason to harm her estranged husband; in fact, she had every reason to want him healthy and able to sign the generous divorce settlement she expected. The *evidence* will show that Kyra Burke had no reason to do it, and didn't do it. And the *evidence* will also show that other people, including the Mafia, had reason to want to do it."

He paused, then added, "Mr. Kwon didn't mention that the state must prove its case to you beyond a reasonable doubt. They can't take

Kyra's liberty without doing that. Well"—he twisted again, pointing at Kyra and nearly shouting again—"there sits the world's biggest reason to doubt."

He turned back to the jurors, almost whispering now. "Thank you for your service to justice."

The courtroom buzzed as Parker returned to his seat. Justice Zannis rapped her gavel and called for quiet, before adding, "Mr. Kwon, call your first witness."

The prosecution's case went in as expected. It opened with a crime-scene technician who displayed pictures of the dead former governor, the insulin bottle on the table, the "suicide note," the syringe bearing the dead man's fingerprints on the floor by his chair. The technician showed close-up photos of the syringe, with tiny cotton fibers adhered to its slender steel stem, and pictures of the dead man's left sleeve, with a small circular hole in the fabric that lined up with the injection site in his skin only when the sleeve was extended.

Next, the medical examiner confirmed that a massive dose of insulin killed Tony Burke and the circumstances of injection were consistent with homicide. That is, he testified, it was highly unlikely that a person intent on suicide would or could inject himself through his shirt and then roll the sleeve up before dying. Based on the police response, he was able to fix the time of death within a small window bracketing eight P.M.

Not a terrible start for Team Kyra, Parker thought as he packed his briefcase. *Tomorrow we get slaughtered.*

CHAPTER ELEVEN

E arly the next morning, Nora and Benny sat on small metal chairs in a narrow tiled hallway at the Manhattan DA's office waiting to be summoned to meet Paul DePietro, chief of Homicide. One of his senior ADAs, Andy Kwon, was the one actually trying the Kyra Burke case.

They waited fifteen minutes before being ushered into a cramped conference room. DePietro introduced Jack Ackerman, who looked to be about sixty, explaining he was a longtime investigator with the DA's office. Nora shook hands with both men. Dugan reached across and shook hands with DePietro, but Ackerman abruptly sat and picked up a pen with his right hand when Dugan turned toward him. Not one to let a slight go, Benny said, "What the fuck, Jack?"

"You know I don't go for this fake diplomacy shit, Benny," Ackerman said. "Let's just get to it."

Dugan sat heavily in his chair, silently shaking his head.

Nora laid it all out for them. The Nose, the note to Benny, the "taste" about Burke's murder being a hit done by someone from the Gambino Family, the dead Nose, the canary, the end of the case.

When she was done, DePietro looked up with a strange smile and locked his eyes on her. "That's it? That's the big emergency that we needed to see you about this morning? So noted mob scumbag Dominic D'Amico, now deceased, came crying to you to get his neck out of the noose and said somebody else did it? And we're supposed to do what? Thank our Ivy League friends and drop the case against the woman who actually murdered the former governor? You must be kidding me. We have a slam dunk here. What fucking planet are you from, and just how stupid do you think we are?"

Nora felt ill. Benny almost came out of his chair, face red, voice loud and full Brooklyn. "You motherless fuck," he began. Ackerman started to move but Dugan extended an enormous palm in his direction, momentarily freezing him while Benny continued. "You talk to her again like that and I'll knock your fuckin' teeth down your throat. We aren't here to tell you shit about what you should do. We're here because we have information—that we didn't fucking ask for—that somebody else killed your vic. We assess it to be credible information. We thought you might care. Seems you don't. Well, that's on you and your office. You wanna keep your heads up your ass? Your business. We don't give a fuck. Meeting over."

With that, Dugan rose so forcefully that the draft almost pulled Nora out of her chair. In a flash, they were in the elevator. The doors closed and he was calm and apologizing. "Sorry I did that. Don't like anyone coming at one of my own like that. I have a temper."

"Huh," Nora said, intending the sarcasm, "I'm getting that."

She waited a beat and then turned serious. "Look, I appreciate that, Benny, but (a) I don't need it and (b) you kinda blew up that meeting."

"Like those pricks were gonna do something with our information. They just think we're trying to fuck with them. Ackerman and me, we got some history."

"You don't say?" Nora replied, smiling. "It was hard to tell, given that you didn't actually stab each other. What the hell, Benny?"

"He's been beefing with me and SDNY for twenty years. Thinks we stole some cases back in the day. We probably did, but we do better work and he's always been a dick."

Nora let out a breath. "Okay, let's go tell Carmen how well we did."

"Hey," Benny said as the elevator doors opened. "Since we're over in this shithole, why don't we pop into the trial and sit in the back for a bit? Not to make a scene, but just to see what a trial of an innocent person looks like. You up for it?"

"Sure," Nora said.

Next up in *People v. Burke* was the doorman, Ivan Ramirez, with his account of Kyra Burke's quick visit shortly before eight that night, the arrival of the delivered steak dinner, and his discovery of the body, which was just as depicted in the police photographs.

Andy Kwon had him narrate the lobby camera footage—in color but without sound—showing the blonde woman in glasses, scarf, and Prada raincoat coming and going. It was Mrs. Burke, all right, and he had greeted her by name, although she didn't speak to him. With the doorman still on the stand, ADA Kwon read a stipulation that several prosecution exhibits had been recovered from Kyra's home on Pomander Walk and would be admitted into evidence. Parker had decided to agree to that to avoid a detective testifying about the search, which would only highlight the importance of the items. But now Kwon could show them to the jury at the same time he played the lobby video. *Mighta been a mistake*, Parker thought. *Maybe shoulda broken up his rhythm*. Kwon handed the witness the scarf and sunglasses, stepping back to hold up the coat, as if offering it for sale.

"Mr. Ramirez, do these appear to be the things you saw Kyra Burke wearing that night?"

How the hell can he know that? But Parker decided not to object. *Better to save it for cross.*

"Yes," the doorman answered.

"No further questions, Your Honor. May I publish the exhibits to the jury?"

Why can't lawyers just say "show"*?*

"You may," Justice Zannis answered, gesturing to her clerk to take the sunglasses, scarf, and raincoat to the jury box. Silence followed as the jurors passed the items around. When the last juror handed them back to the clerk, the judge looked at the defense table just as Nora and Benny slipped into the crowded courtroom, quietly taking seats in the back row.

"Mr. Parker?"

"Thank you, Your Honor," he said. He took his notepad to the podium, which was now at the far end of the jury box, so as not to block the jury's view of the witness.

Parker's tone was gentle, and intentionally so. He didn't love being sixty or having gray hair, but there was value in contrasting the wisdom of age with his opponent's youthful energy. He was not going after the doorman. Ramirez was a good guy, a working man. He was just another victim of the state's blind rush to judgment.

"Mr. Ramirez, you can't say for sure that those things—the scarf, glasses, coat—were the same ones you saw in the lobby that night, right?"

"I don't know what you mean."

"All I mean is that the most you can say is that they *look like* the ones you saw, that's all I mean."

"Oh, that's right," he answered. "They look the same."

"And they look like the kind of stuff Kyra Burke often wore, right?"

"Yes, that's right. She was a stylish person."

"And if somebody wanted to *appear* to be Kyra Burke, that somebody would want to wear that kind of stuff, right?"

Kwon was on his feet. "Objection, argumentative, Your Honor."

Justice Zannis paused for only a moment. "No, overruled. This is cross-examination."

Ramirez seemed confused until Justice Zannis added, "You can answer, Mr. Ramirez."

"Oh, thanks. Yes, I suppose so. If you want to look like her, you should look like her."

That brought light laughter from the gallery, and Parker smiled to reflect it.

"That's right, that's exactly right, Mr. Ramirez. It might have been somebody trying to convince you it was Kyra Burke, right?"

"I don't know. Sure did look like Mrs. Burke to me."

"And that's right too," Parker said. "Sure did look like Mrs. Burke."

Justice Zannis cut in. "Mr. Parker, I will ask you not to repeat the witness's testimony. Please just ask questions."

"Certainly, Your Honor." Now Parker made his move. "But she didn't *act* like Mrs. Burke, now did she?"

"I don't know what you mean."

"Well, lots of rich people live in your building, right?"

"Yep. Compared to me, they're all rich."

More laughter came from the gallery. Parker smiled again. Ramirez was likable and funny, which was perfect. But Parker dropped the grin for his next question.

"Lotta rude, snobby rich people, am I right?"

Now the doorman looked tight. This could be really dangerous for him; people in the building were following this case—closely—and were very unhappy about it. He even had to take a vacation day to comply with the subpoena.

"Well," he began, searching for words, "people are complicated, all people."

"Mr. Ramirez, I'm not trying to get you in trouble, but let me just put it to you this way: There are a lot of people in that building who aren't friendly to working people like you. Is that fair? For whatever reason."

Ramirez now looked to be in physical pain. "Yes, I suppose that's fair, but I don't want to judge people. Sometimes money is a strange kinda burden for people."

"Okay, Mr. Ramirez, this isn't about those people, so I don't wanna spend a lot of time on this." He turned to point at Kyra. "But this is about *her*, so let me ask you this: Was she a rude, snobby rich person?"

"No," he answered quickly, relieved to be off the broader topic of his many pain-in-the-ass employers and dying to say something nice about one of them. And it was the clue Parker needed that Kyra was right, so he raised his voice.

"In fact, Kyra Burke was always friendly to you, wasn't she?"

"Yes, pretty much."

"Treated you like an actual human being."

"I think so."

"Knew your name and used it, with a smile, didn't she?"

"Yes, lotta the time."

Now Parker shifted his tone to deadly serious. "Was that woman in the scarf and glasses in the lobby that night friendly to you?"

"Not particularly."

"Did she smile at you, use your name, treat you like a human being?"

"Well, she just came in and out, but she did wave."

Parker was ready for that, the video remote control already in his hand. "Mr. Ramirez, let me ask you to take another look at that lobby video, if you would."

He played the entry portion on the courtroom monitors. "Did that woman wave to you, or even look at you?"

"No, but you can see I was busy with those dogs."

Now he played the departure clip. "Did that woman wave to you?"

"Well, she raised her hand after I said, 'Good night, Mrs. Burke.'"

Parker replayed the clip. "So that's where you say good night and that woman gave you the back of her gloved hand. She acknowledged your existence. Is that really a 'wave' where you come from, Mr. Ramirez?"

"I guess not."

"That's not the kind of person Kyra Burke is and you know it, Mr. Ramirez, don't you?"

"She was nice."

"Is that woman in the video 'nice'?"

"Not particularly."

"That wasn't Kyra Burke that night, was it?"

Ramirez wouldn't go all the way there. "It sure looked like her."

But it didn't matter to Parker, who had what he wanted. "Yup, it sure *looked* like her, didn't it? Nothing further, Your Honor."

In the back pew, Nora nudged Benny and whispered, "Her lawyer is pretty good."

"One of the best," Benny whispered back. "He was at our office a long time. Had Carmen's job."

"So that's Matthew Parker? Never met him. Heard great things."

Benny just nodded as the trial continued.

"Mr. Kwon, any redirect?" Justice Zannis asked.

"Yes, Judge, briefly." Andy Kwon actually seemed a little nervous. *How's your thin to win goin' now, fuck-face?*

"People have moods, don't they, Mr. Ramirez?"

"I'm not sure I understand."

"Well, you have no idea how Kyra Burke was feeling that night, do you?"

"That's right."

"Might not have been feeling herself, is that possible?"

"Sure."

"Maybe she just killed somebody, maybe not feeling real friendly?"

Parker was on his feet, but Kwon spoke first. "I'll withdraw that last question, Your Honor. Nothing further."

You clever little bastard. Okay, okay. Didn't know you had it in ya.

Justice Zannis announced that they would be taking the lunch recess early before calling another witness. Nora stood with the rest of the courtroom and turned to leave but Benny lifted his hand, silently asking her to hold on a minute.

As they waited, Kyra Burke stood at the defense table and turned toward the gallery, chatting with her lawyer. A strange feeling washed over Nora. She had seen pictures of the accused on tabloid front pages but had never seen her in person. Something about the way she moved—maybe in the shoulders or neck or something—seemed oddly familiar. It gave her a weird feeling, which she quickly shook off as Benny rapped her leg with his knuckles and stood.

Nora stood with him and waited to exit into the center aisle. Benny's enormous body blocked her for a moment before he stepped from the row and greeted Matthew Parker in the aisle with a bear hug.

Kyra kept walking toward the exit, glancing to her left at Nora as she passed. There was no hint of recognition. *Must have been mistaken,* Nora thought.

Benny and Parker held each other for a few moments, whispering. When they separated, Parker quickly followed after his client and Benny turned to Nora. "You ready? Sorry for the holdup."

"Wait," she said, "you and Matthew Parker dating or something? Because I have not seen a hug from you before."

Benny laughed. "We go way back. Been through it together, him and me."

As they began walking, Nora asked, "Does this mean we may hug someday?"

Benny chuckled. "Could be, could be. But don't want no sexual harassment situation," he said, holding up both hands, fingers balled. "Always keep my hands in fists huggin' girls. Women." He started to blush, eager to stop talking about this. "But no doubt we are going through it this time, aren't we?"

"Indeed we are," Nora answered.

From the elevator lobby, they walked down the five steps onto Centre Street and began walking left, toward St. Andrew's Plaza. As they crossed in front of the Marshall courthouse, Nora broke the silence.

"You know what, with our defendant dead and all, I'm gonna go home, get lunch, and pick Sophie up from school. I'll call Carmen on the way and tell her of our wildly successful diplomacy."

"Perfect," Benny replied. "Sophie is exactly what you should do. Me, I have no life, as you know, so I'm gonna go work the phones a bit, see what I can stir up on The Nose and this Burke murder. But please do come back tomorrow. Lost without you."

"Oh, I'm coming back," Nora said. "You're stuck with me." Then she paused, before searching his face and asking, "You doing okay, Mr. Rough? Haven't checked in for a while."

He nodded, looking down at her with a gentle smile as they stood on the edge of the plaza. "Yeah, I'm doin' good. I appreciate you askin'. Been keepin' the demons at bay. And I remember my promise: Will call you if I get stuck like before."

She knew what he meant. Six months earlier, as they'd prepared the D'Amico case for trial, Benny had hit bottom. Drunk and alone, he'd left his Brooklyn apartment at two A.M. to walk the streets, ready for a fight, hoping someone would attempt to rob him. Luckily for him, and any would-be robbers, officers in an NYPD patrol car had seen him staggering along the sidewalk and approached him. He'd slurred his words as he'd held up his credentials, but they'd found Nora's business card tucked behind his badge and called her rather than arrest him for public drunkenness. He and Nora had sat together in his little living room as the sun came up that morning, Benny leaning over the coffee table, holding his face in his huge hands. He had done it before, he explained, whenever he tried to drown the darkness with too much whiskey—wandering the streets looking for violence, to hit someone who deserved it, maybe kill someone who deserved it. He'd rejected her advice to speak to a counselor but promised he would call her if the darkness began to descend again.

Now Nora smiled back up at him. "Good," she said. "And I know you always keep your promises."

"Always," he answered. "Now go get your girl."

Benny turned left into the plaza, hoping he really could keep that promise, as Nora continued up Centre and into the wind.

CHAPTER TWELVE

After lunch, the prosecution offered a parade of Kyra Burke's colleagues from Columbia. Most of them seemed reluctant witnesses. Most. Two were young superstars in the modern elite legal academy who failed to entirely hide their schadenfreude. Of course, they had always been on pleasant terms with Kyra but, deep down, found her an ambitious, cold person and suspected she suffered from internalized white patriarchal self-loathing. And she seemed bored at the faculty lunches.

But supporter or not, they all testified to the same theme: Kyra hated Tony Burke—his lying, his hypocrisy, his mental torture of her. But most of all she hated what a courageous group of women revealed him to be: a serial sexual predator. He had mistreated dozens of women, of all ages and backgrounds, simply because they happened to walk across his consciousness in a room, or elevator, or hallway—and with no witnesses.

Of course, the prosecution witnesses said, learning about the flirting, touching, groping, kissing, and assaulting bothered Kyra, tremendously. But what bothered her more was that he terrified those women, before and after victimizing them, and he proceeded to savage them when they dared speak the truth, using all his power and all his contacts in the media. He said these women were not victims, they were the predators, and were continuing to victimize him now by seeking fame and money. "You drag a fifty-dollar bill through the streets of Albany, this is what you end up with." On and on. "He's the devil," she'd told a civil procedure professor.

The two who were not fans also told the jury that Kyra had confided in them that what really burned her was the humiliation of being a professor of employment and gender law and married to the predator whose behavior would be studied in those disciplines for decades. And if she hadn't used those exact words, that was the sentiment she communicated.

So, not good, Parker thought, watching the onslaught with his practiced resting-lawyer face. He offered no cross-examination. *Don't want the jury to think this bullshit faculty-lounge gossip hurts us.* Kyra would explain those statements during her testimony: Yes, the murder victim was a horrible person, but she didn't kill him.

Next up were the lawyers for the deceased to lay out more motive proof. Before the then-sixty-one-year-old Tony married the then-thirty-one-year-old Kyra, he required her to sign a prenuptial agreement governing their financial affairs in the unlikely event they should divorce. They would share joint custody of any children of their union, who would be supported generously—as she would—until they attained the age of majority. In the event the marriage dissolved without offspring, Kyra would receive a lump sum of $500,000. And that was all.

Parker didn't want to underscore the importance of this testimony, but he decided to briefly cross-examine to preview the defense testimony. That way, the jurors would think they had figured something out down the road.

"A prenup could be modified at any time by the parties in a divorce settlement, right?" Parker asked the attorney.

"Of course."

"And somebody like Tony Burke could even decide he wanted to give Kyra more than the prenup provided, right?"

"I suppose so."

"And he might want to do that, say, in exchange for her promising not to say bad stuff about him after the divorce?"

"I can't answer that."

And I don't really care if you do. "Okay, thanks. Nothing further, Your Honor."

The testimony about the prenup didn't seem like much until the second lawyer testified, about Tony Burke's will.

Shockingly, Tony Burke had failed to update his will, which by its terms provided that his estate should go to his wife and, if she should predecease him, to any children of their union. But at the time he signed the will, Tony was married to Marian Burke, with whom he shortly had his son, Edward. Of course, he was no longer married to Marian. And there laid the wrinkle that made his death of great financial benefit to Kyra.

Because she was his lawful wife, Kyra would inherit his $25,000,000 estate under one of two theories: Either a court would strike Marian's name and enforce the bequest to "my wife"—Kyra, at the time of his death—or the court would declare the entire will void, in which case the laws of New York provided the assets of a spouse dying without a will go entirely to the surviving spouse. So, either way, if Tony Burke died before he and Kyra divorced, she got $25,000,000.

So better than $500,000 under the prenup. Is that what you're saying? This was really testing Parker's bored look, because his mind was racing, trying to decide whether to cross on this at all. Kyra had said she had no idea what the terms of Tony's will were. But if he suggested that to the witness—"You have no reason to believe Mrs. Burke had any knowledge of the will"—the guy could make shit up and explode it in his face—"Well, actually, my client told me they had discussed the will." And what was he going to do with that?

Nope, better to let it go. Argue it later. Prosecution has the burden of proof, and they haven't shown she knew anything about the will. And when she hits the stand, she's gonna say she didn't know, so we're good. And worst case, they have strong motive proof. So what? People don't kill everyone they'd like to kill, or this courthouse'd be a hell of a lot busier.

"Mr. Parker, are you with us?" It was Justice Zannis, interrupting his reverie.

"Oh, yes, Judge. Sorry."

"I was asking, do you have any questions for this witness?"

Parker started to say no, but paused as a bolt hit him. He pulled on his suspenders. *Why the fuck not.* "Uh, just a few, Judge."

At the podium, he tried to look genuinely interested in a novel legal problem. "Mr. Appel," he began. "It is Mr. Appel, is that right?"

"Yes," the witness answered.

"Mr. Appel, isn't there a third possible legal outcome with respect to Tony Burke's will?"

"I don't know what you mean."

"Well, as you said, it's possible a court would interpret the will to give Burke's money to his wife and, crossing out Marian's name, the money would go to Kyra, because she was the legal wife at the time of his death, right?"

"That's correct."

"Or a court might just decide the whole thing is so screwed up that the will is invalidated and the estate governed by New York law, under which Kyra inherits anyway, right?"

"Well, I can't imagine a court using words like 'screwed up,' but I take your meaning. Yes, that is the other possibility."

"But there's a third, right?"

"Not to my mind, there isn't."

"The key words are 'my wife, Marian Burke,' right?"

"Yes."

"But rather than cross out Marian's name, a court might cross out the words 'my wife,' concluding that Tony Burke's intention—because he never changed the will, even after divorcing Marian—was that his estate actually go to Marian, whether they were married or not. Am I onto something here?"

The witness seemed rattled by this. "That seems highly unlikely to me."

"But it's possible, isn't it, Mr. Appel?"

"Maybe. Lots of possibilities in the law."

Parker paused and then went for it. *What the hell.*

"So the original Mrs. Burke may have been the one with the reason to want Tony dead, am I right? Before he could change that will?"

The audible reaction from the gallery almost obscured Andy Kwon's objection, but Justice Zannis heard it.

"Sustained. That's argument, Mr. Parker. The jury will disregard the question. Anything further, Mr. Parker?"

"No, Your Honor," he said, turning back to his seat. *Okay, that was a swing worth taking.*

CHAPTER THIRTEEN

Benny Dugan loped into his office, a paper-wrapped chicken-parm sandwich in his hand, to find Special Agent Jessica Watson standing before his wall of photo books. He was feeling motivated and hungry after the cathartic battle with the DA's office. "There she is," he boomed, "the future of the Federal Bureau of Investigation. Thought you were out finding us source info."

Jessica turned with a smile. "Was. Squad supervisor was breaking my chops so I talked to the ASAC who supervises all the organized crime squads, which I suspect is not a career-enhancing move, but I always loved teaching chemistry."

"And what did the exalted Assistant Special Agent in Charge have to say?"

"He ordered intel to push an urgent collection requirement to all New York personnel, the entire NYO. Everybody has twenty-four hours to pulse their sources on the D'Amico hit or anything on a hitter from Joey Cufaro world. We threw in anything on the Tony Burke homicide too. And both negative and positive responses must be reported, so nobody can just ignore it."

"Very impressive," Dugan said, smiling. "Okay, now that you've turned that ocean liner on a dime, I have a new project for us." Pointing at the enormous whiteboard behind his desk, he dropped the butcher-paper-wrapped sandwich, grabbed an eraser, and began cleaning the board. "I want a picture up here of everybody who might be connected to Tony Burke and his killing. I know it's low-tech, but I'm a visual guy. Need to stand in front of the thing and stare at it. Laptop doesn't do it for me."

"Same," Jessica answered. "How can I help?"

Pointing to a computer, he said, "You jump on the system, print DMV pictures of everybody I call out. We put 'em on the board, use different color Expo markers to connect them. Not that crazy yarn shit you see on TV."

An hour later, they had the board covered with pictures: Gambino mobsters, especially those connected to Joey Cufaro; Tony Burke's family—Kyra, Marian, and Edward all made appearances; Burke's staff and close supporters; women publicly identified as victims of Burke's predation; political rivals. It was a strange mix.

Benny and Jessica stood back to admire their work. "Lotta pictures and lines," he said.

"Yup," she answered. "Any closer to knowing who whacked him?"

"Nope. But we ain't done with our photo projects." Sweeping his arm toward the shelves lining the rest of the large room, he said, "I wantcha to go through photo books now, while I finally get a bite of my chicken parm. The Nose said the Burke hitter came from Joey Cufaro's world. So start there. Check the date labels and look for any coverage of Joey Cufaro and his crew, then branch out to all Gambinos."

"What am I looking for?" Jessica asked.

He reached back and tapped the whiteboard. "Start with any of the people on here. I don't know of any connections between Cosa Nostra guys and the Burkes or any of that group up there, but there has to be one, and maybe we'll get lucky.

"Anything that gives you a feeling," he continued. "Mostly, people with people that don't make sense—especially any of these people. Your colleagues at the Bureau never got it or wanted to put in the time, but these mob weddings and wakes and funerals are really important because the net is so wide. It ain't just guys from a crew showin' up. Guys from other Families and 'friends of the Family' are supposed to show their respect at these things, so you can pick up all kinds of weird connections."

He rapped on a binder with his fingers. "Anyhow, in the front, you got an index of all the players in the binder, and I wrote on all the hardcopy photos when I couldn't ID somebody. Mark the potential universe, give it a once-over, then flag stuff for me. My memory is good, but even I can't remember every event clearly. I do know all these mopes, though—hell, I took the damn pictures—so if you find anything, I should be able to tell quick whether it's somethin'."

"Copy that," Jessica said.

Benny started to tease her for the FBI Quantico training-academy talk, but stopped. Instead he reached to a top shelf and touched on a thick binder with "Cufaro Wake" written in white-out on the spine. "Start here, at the end of Handsome Joey's time on this earth. Wakes were always my most productive time; mopes come out of the woodwork to look and be sure a guy's dead. And they didn't have to be invited or bring a gift, so even better than weddings, attendance-wise. And for reasons I've never figured out, these guys seem to think these things are private. Stupid fucks."

As he settled behind his desk, unwrapping his sandwich, Benny saw Jessica stand on a chair to retrieve the "Cufaro Wake" book. He grinned. *I like a kid who doesn't ask for help.*

Jessica studied page after page while Benny sat facing her as he both chewed and worked the phones, touching his own sources, both in law enforcement and in the criminal underworld.

They worked for almost two hours. Then Jessica stood up. "Holy shit."

"What? What?" Benny asked.

"Remember the feeling you told me to watch for? I just got it! Look at this from Joey's wake."

She hurried around his desk and dropped the open binder on the butcher paper, her finger pointing at a picture. "That's Conor McCarthy at Joey Cufaro's wake." She turned to look up at the whiteboard photos. "He's younger, but it was nine years ago. And he has his arm around a woman who looks like a brunette Kyra Burke."

CHAPTER FOURTEEN

Sophie shrieked when she saw her mother waiting outside the school. "Mommy! Mommy!" She began running, backpack bouncing as she held some kind of glued and taped collection of colored paper in her hands. Nora swept her into her arms, careful not to crush the art project and hoping Sophie wouldn't ask her to guess what it was. "You like my turkey?" Sophie asked, the construction paper flopping as she tried to hold it aloft.

"Oh my goodness! It's the best turkey ever. Wait until we show Nana. She'll want to put it on the refrigerator for Thanksgiving!" Nora gave her an extra-long squeeze, closing her eyes and hugging away images of mobsters and murders and exculpatory evidence. Sophie finally broke the hug, squirming to be put down. Nora took her hand. "Ice cream, my ladybug?"

"Yay! Can we bring some for Nana? I know what she likes."

"Course we can," Nora said, steering them toward Washington Street, Hoboken's main drag, carefully following Sophie's example to never step on a crack between sidewalk slabs.

"Why are you home?" Sophie asked, carefully watching for cracks. "Is it because your big case is finished?"

"Yup, like I told you, my big trial got canceled, so now I can hang out with you more."

"Yay."

After they ordered and found a table inside the ice-cream shop, Nora asked, "You seem kinda serious today, Soph. Anything you want to talk about? School okay?"

"Yeah, school is awesome, but I know something. Kinda secret."

Nora's stomach flipped as she fought to hold her mommy-face. "What is it, ladybug?"

"I think Daddy is gonna marry Vicki."

"Wow. That's some scoop, Soph. How do you know that?"

"Well, she's been wearing a diamond ring on the marriage finger, but she takes it off when Nana is around, and last weekend she asked me if I knew what a flower girl was and wouldn't it be fun to be one someday."

Sophie paused, then added, with evident pride, "So kinda obvious, Mom."

Really, Vicki? Sneaking around, my daughter, your wedding? Who the hell do you think you are?

"Well, I guess Vicki will be part of our family then," Nora said. "Do you like her?"

"Sure, but what if she has babies? Or what if Daddy moves away with her and doesn't care about me anymore? At lunch, that's what Julia in my class said would happen."

"Oh Sophie, your daddy will always love you. And may be a little early to worry about babies, don't you think?"

Sophie nodded and leaned over her ice cream, whispering. "And I have one more secret."

"What?"

"I always hoped Daddy would marry *you* someday, not Vicki."

Nora had to gather herself, then said, "Oh sweetie, I probably should have talked to you about this before now. I love your daddy and care about him and always want him in our family, but I don't love him the way Vicki does—the way someone does when they wanna get married. Does that make sense?"

"Yeah, Nana says that kissy-face love is different from family love. That what you mean?"

"That is exactly right, Soph. You are one smart kiddo!"

Sophie smiled and went back to work eating her ice cream.

Nora's cell rang with *The Godfather* theme song she had assigned to Benny Dugan as a joke. Every head in the shop turned as she snatched it off the little stone table and whispered, "Hello?"

It was Benny, loud and seeming overcaffeinated. "Nora! Big news, big news. You got a sec? Jessica found something huge."

"Okay, Benny. I'm with Sophie having ice cream in a place," she said, watching her daughter paint bubblegum-flavored ice cream on her lips. Normally, that would be enough to end the call. *I'm with Sophie. And we are in a public setting.* Benny would instantly get it and say to call later. But this was different.

"Can you just listen?" he asked.

"Sure."

Dugan then poured out what Jessica found, his words coming fast and loud—Nora toggled the side of her phone to lower the earpiece volume.

"It looks a bit like Kyra Burke, but it's not. It's Gina Cufaro, Joey's only child. I watched her grow up. Went off the grid when he died. And Jessica's right about the guy with his consoling arm around her, looking like there's more between them than the average mourners, like they've been horizontal in the all-together. It's Conor fucking McCarthy, Tony Burke's right-hand man. Now what's he doin' years ago at a mob funeral, gettin' all PDA with the dead capo's daughter? Huh?"

Benny didn't wait for an answer, but lowered his voice to continue rapid-fire. "I been hearing echoes, whispers really, for years, that the

Gambinos got a hitter who's a woman. Their best. A shadow. Which is why I wasn't surprised by what The Nose said when he gave us his 'taste.' Remember? He said it was somebody who came up through Joey Cufaro's crew, only does the most important stuff, and is rumored to be a girl.

"I remember her. Joey's little girl. Always around her old man. Thick as thieves. Course, she couldn't join his crew 'cause she's a she—the Mafia not being what you would call a 'progressive' organization. So maybe Joey gave his little girl some special jobs to be part of the mob without the 'getting made' part. Then after he died—when I took the pictures—she disappeared. Poof. But who cared, right? Didn't have anything on her. What difference does it make? But maybe now she's back."

Benny paused and took a loud breath. "And maybe the biggest score is that slick dude with his arm around her. That's our connection to Burke."

When he finished, "Whoa" was all Nora felt comfortable saying—in a whisper—before adding in her public-restaurant-with-child voice, "I'll give you a ring when we get home, 'kay?"

She hung up and fought the urge to hurry Sophie. *Be in the moment. Be in the moment,* she told herself. "Sorry I had to take that call, ladybug. I'm so glad you told me about Vicki, and I promise everything will be fine."

As Nora watched her little girl savor the ice cream, she replayed Benny's report in her head: about Joey Cufaro's daughter maybe being a contract killer for the mob, and maybe having some connection to the dead governor through this Conor character. *Not sure what to make of all this.* Then a strange wave washed over her and she suddenly had the urge to again tell Sophie that she should never keep secrets from her mother. So she did, asking the angelic little girl to let go of the ice-cream cup and give her another pinky swear. Nora knew it was weird, but it made her feel better. *There are really bad people in the world and they usually operate in secret, and if anyone like that comes near you, I gotta know.* She couldn't say any of that, of course. Just the pinky swear.

When Sophie was good and ready, they got the to-go cup for Nana—chocolate with Heath Bar, always—and walked home, not stepping on a single crack.

After dropping Sophie at her mom's place on Park, Nora walked to her cramped basement home on Bloomfield. It was still light outside, but her apartment was in its usual state of perpetual twilight. Flipping on the kitchen light, she dropped her shoulder bag on the counter and opened the fridge. A White Claw called to her but was shouted down by Benny's words about the toxic mix of loneliness and alcohol. She grabbed a Diet Pepsi instead and sat on a stool, reaching for her work laptop before pulling her hand back. She got up and went into her tiny bedroom, returning with her personal laptop. She opened the device and stared at her draft dating profile. "Nora from Hoboken" looked friendly and outgoing. She liked museums, hiking, children, and Italian foods of all kinds. She was a never-married attorney with a young daughter. She was interested in finding a serious relationship.

Nora's fingers brushed the laptop's mouse pad as she gently moved the cursor across the incomplete profile, lingering over the drop-down menu where the app wanted to know whether Nora from Hoboken was looking for men, women, or both. The little black arrow just sat there. As she had dozens of times already, Nora watched it without blinking until her eyes watered and tears ran down her face. She slammed the laptop shut. *What is wrong with me? I don't even know who I am. I am so fucking lonely, and I don't have any idea who I want to be with.* She got up, exchanged the soda for the White Claw, and opened her work laptop. There was always work to do. So what if she had no love life. She had Sophie and her mom and her job. She would get back to the app another day.

CHAPTER FIFTEEN

T he prosecution finished with a blown-up aerial map showing the location of Kyra's Pomander Walk home in relation to the murder scene on
Central Park West—a twenty-minute walk or nine minutes in a cab.

Standing in front of the map, Andy Kwon read another stipulation,
laying out the parties' agreement that, if called as a witness, an NYPD
computer forensics expert would testify that Kyra's iPhone was turned
off between seven P.M. and nine P.M. that day, so no location data was
available for the phone. They were ending by essentially shouting to
the jury, "She has no alibi!"

With that, he announced, "The People rest, Your Honor."

Justice Zannis invited the lawyers to sidebar so she could hear, and
quickly deny, Parker's obligatory motion to dismiss. "Drawing all
inferences in favor of the prosecution, a reasonable jury could find
all elements of the crime beyond a reasonable doubt. Now please
step back. We will start the defense case without delay."

"Judge," Parker interjected, "I'd really like to get a fresh start with
our case, in the morning."

"I can understand that, Mr. Parker, but we have ninety minutes left
in the trial day and I will not waste the jury's time. Proceed."

Once the lawyers were back in position she added, "Mr. Parker,
please call your first witness."

"Yes, Your Honor. The defense calls Conor McCarthy." The witness stepped through the side door. *Jesus, pal,* Parker thought as he watched him walk to the stand, *that's the go-to-court outfit?*

Conor didn't actually hunch when he walked, but he appeared embarrassed, as if he hoped not to be noticed. That would be hard, given that he looked like he'd just walked off the runway at a Milan fashion show. He was wearing a slim-cut steel-gray suit, with a lavender checked dress shirt and solid lavender skinny tie. The suit pants were intentionally cut short, to show off lavender-and-black argyle socks and brown Gucci horsebit loafers.

As he identified himself, Conor's voice, as usual, was quiet and without an evident accent. He sounded like he had been born in that mystical place along the American mid-Atlantic coast where the voices of network TV news anchors came from. Justice Zannis had to ask him twice to speak up when spelling his name for the court reporter.

Parker began by speaking loudly, hoping to pull his witness up with him. "Mr. McCarthy, how are you employed, sir?"

"I'm unemployed at the moment, since the death of my last employer, Tony Burke."

"And what was the nature of your employment with Mr. Burke?"

"I served as his chief of staff. I had the same role when he was governor and, when he left, I went to work for his 'family office,' as they called it."

"Can you tell the jury what the 'family office' is?"

"Sure, it's basically the fancy term rich people use for the management of their lives and their money. For billionaires, the family office employs lots of people to invest, spend, or give away the family's money. Bill Gates has one, and Governor Burke liked the way it sounded."

"And could you briefly describe your responsibilities?"

"In the family office, or before?"

"How about both?"

"When we were in the state government, I was a New York state employee. I was responsible for ensuring his staff was functioning well, that he got the information he needed to do his job, that the schedule worked, that sort of thing. At the family office, it was different because he had a very small staff, so my job was to do everything the former governor wanted that his staff might do—scheduling, travel arrangements, speech writing, bill paying, you name it. And special projects."

"Like what?"

"Like working quietly on his behalf to see if he could save the Teddy Roosevelt statue in front of the Museum of Natural History next door to his apartment. He loved Roosevelt—another New York governor—and especially that statue of him on a horse. He could see it from his apartment. Folks said it was problematic because the artist put an American Indian and a Black man standing down below him. Governor Burke wanted to see if he could privately give some money or something to save it. Didn't work. The statue was moved to some place in North Dakota."

"Do you know the defendant, Kyra Burke?"

"Yes."

"Would you explain to the jury the nature of your association?"

"Sure. We met in college, became good friends, and stayed in touch over the years, like good college friends do. Or should, I suppose."

"And where did you go to college, and how did you come to be friends?"

"We went to Yale, in New Haven, Connecticut. She lived in my dorm—Yale called it a 'residential college'—and we were both from pretty humble backgrounds. There were a lot of rich kids at Yale, from all over the country, so I think that kinda pushed us together. And she was really smart and fun. I should have started with that."

"Were you two ever romantically involved?"

He answered quickly. "Oh, no, never. Not that she isn't a gorgeous woman. That just wasn't how it was between us."

"You mentioned your background: where did you grow up?"

"Off Mosholu Parkway in the northern part of the Bronx. An Irish and Jewish area. The kinda place you only find in New York."

"And what did your parents do?"

"My dad was a doorman at an apartment building on the Upper East Side of Manhattan. My mom worked in big hotels as a maid."

"You mentioned that your friendship with Kyra continued. Did you have any role in her marriage to Tony Burke?"

"Yes. I suppose it's my fault, in a way. We were in his first term as governor. He was single—divorced. I knew he was interested in dating, because he'd said so. They were a ways apart in age, but I also knew Kyra would be a huge asset to him—so smart, so committed to doing good, so pretty. I introduced them. And they got married like a year later. Honestly, I should have given more thought to how it would be for her."

"We've heard quite a bit in this trial about Governor Burke's, uh, shortcomings. Were you aware of those when you made the match?"

"No, although I should have been much more aware. Looking back, it seems obvious to me now, but I just didn't believe—or want to believe—bad things about him. I thought being married again would be good for him both publicly and privately, but I was wrong and Kyra suffered because of my bad judgment."

"Why did you stay after so much about him became public these last two years?"

"I ask myself the same question. I think it was just a sense of loyalty, misplaced loyalty, but I felt like I had been with him so long I just couldn't run away."

Andy Kwon didn't object, but Justice Zannis cut in. "Mr. Parker, is this going some place? The case isn't about former Governor Burke, in that sense."

"Yes, Your Honor. Just background. I'll move on."

Turning to the witness, he asked, "Mr. McCarthy, did there come a time shortly before Governor Burke's death that you discussed with him the prenuptial agreement between him and Kyra?"

"Yes. We were in his office at his apartment. The same room where he died. He said he wanted me to take a message to Kyra. They were starting the divorce proceedings. He said he—"

"Objection, Your Honor, hearsay." Andy Kwon was up now.

Justice Zannis looked confused. "Yes, Mr. Parker, I don't see how . . . Come up to sidebar please."

The lawyers and court reporter walked to the side of the judge's bench away from the jury.

"Mr. Parker," Justice Zannis began, "you are asking this witness to recount the out-of-court statement of an unavailable declarant, the victim in this case. Are you relying on some hearsay exception?"

"No, Judge. It's not hearsay, because I'm not offering Tony Burke's statements for the truth of the matter asserted. They are being offered only to show their effect on my client's state of mind, when Mr. McCarthy repeated them to Kyra. The prosecution is arguing Kyra had a financial motive to kill Tony Burke. Mr. McCarthy will testify Burke asked him to assure her that he intended to modify the prenup to give her much more money in a divorce settlement. For that reason, it is relevant non-hearsay."

He turned to look at ADA Kwon. *Yeah, bub, I'm a real fuckin' lawyer. How you like them apples?*

Justice Zannis also turned to Kwon. "So he says it's not hearsay. Goes to her state of mind. You still object?"

Do the stupid thing, kid. Object and get her to keep it out, so I have something to argue on appeal.

Kwon paused and looked up, like the answer was on the ceiling. Then he said, "The People withdraw the objection, so long as the court gives an instruction to the jury limiting the purposes for which this evidence comes in."

Smarter than you look.

Back in open court, Justice Zannis said, "The prosecution has withdrawn the objection. The witness may answer the question. Would the court reporter please read back the last answer?"

The stenographer grabbed the stack of folded paper spit out by her inexplicable machine and began pawing through it, somehow reading aloud from the strange markings on the paper. "He said he wanted me to take a message to Kyra. They were starting divorce proceedings. He said he . . ."

Conor looked confused, until Justice Zannis gently added, "You can continue, Mr. McCarthy."

"Oh, thanks. He said he wanted me to tell Kyra she would be okay. He wasn't gonna hold her to the prenup; he would make sure she was financially comfortable after they divorced, so long as she signed a nondisclosure agreement."

"Did you tell her what he said?"

"Oh yes, right away; either the same day or the next. I can't remember."

"And what did she say?"

Andy Kwon started to stand, but Justice Zannis didn't wait. "Mr. Parker, I assume you are offering this on the same basis?"

"Yes, Judge."

"Okay. Ladies and gentlemen of the jury, this is a good time for me to give you some legal instruction. Under New York state law, what someone says outside of court is normally not admissible as evidence. You may have heard the term 'hearsay,' which means any out-of-court statements offered as true. Normally, we don't allow that unless it falls within one of the recognized exceptions to the hearsay rule.

"But sometimes a statement is admissible evidence whether it is true or not, because it is relevant to something other than the truth of the statement. In this instance, the defense is not intending to prove whether or not Mr. Burke's statements about the prenuptial agreement were true; only that Kyra Burke heard them and they had an effect on her. That is the basis on which Mr. McCarthy was permitted to testify about Mr. Burke's statements, and it is the basis on which he is being allowed to testify as to what the defendant's reaction was. I hope this is helpful. Mr. Parker, you may proceed."

"And so what did Kyra say when you delivered Burke's message?"

"Something like: That's good to hear, but I'm not sure how I feel about an NDA."

"NDA?"

"Nondisclosure agreement. Governor Burke wanted her to agree not to say anything bad about him. He liked NDAs and had a lot of us sign them."

"Why would someone have a problem with an NDA?"

Andy Kwon leaped up. "Objection, Judge."

"Yes," the judge answered, "this witness has not been offered as an expert of any kind."

"Fine, Judge. I'll withdraw the question."

"Mr. McCarthy, did you ever hesitate to sign an NDA from Tony Burke?"

"Yes."

"Why?"

"Because it could limit my ability to speak about something I really should say something about. And it did."

"What do you mean?"

"I kept my mouth shut about stuff about the governor and women that I think now I should have talked about, but I was afraid of violating my agreement and getting sued."

"To your knowledge, did Kyra refuse to accept Tony's offer to modify the prenup?"

"I never heard any more about it before he died."

"Thank you. I have no further questions."

Andy Kwon was on his feet and, for the first time, sounding sarcastic.

"Mr. McCarthy, so is it that you didn't know Tony Burke was a sexual predator or that you were afraid of violating your NDA?"

Parker decided not to object. *Conor can handle himself.*

"Both and neither."

That forced Kwon to ask an open-ended question: "What do you mean?"

"I learned more and more about Tony Burke over time, which forced me to worry more about the NDA."

"Did you know he was abusing women?"

"I didn't, but I should have. It seems obvious now."

Kwon was getting nowhere with this, so he shifted. "Where did this conversation you say you had with Kyra take place?"

"I think on the phone."

"You think or you know?"

"I'm reasonably certain, because we didn't see each other in person much."

"And she understood that Tony Burke wasn't offering money without strings, right?"

"Yes, he wanted an NDA."

"And you knew by then that she hated him, and for good reason."

"I knew she hated him."

"And that she cared deeply about the sexual misconduct of powerful men?"

"Yes."

"And that she would never agree to remain silent about misconduct."

"I don't know that. I don't know one way or the other how she weighed it. Besides, lots of women were telling the truth about the governor by then and still are now."

"But she never told you her decision?"

"That's right."

"Tony Burke was murdered first."

"Well, I don't believe there is a connection between those two things, but you are literally correct that he was murdered before I heard her answer, because I've never heard her answer."

"Nothing further, Your Honor."

Parker paused for a moment. *That hurt a little, but Kyra can hit all of this.* "Nothing further, Your Honor."

CHAPTER SIXTEEN

They were in a conference room at Parker's downtown law-firm office, high in a glass-and-steel tower with an amazing view of New York Harbor and the Statue of Liberty.

"So, what do you think?" Kyra asked.

I think we are totally, completely fucked. "Well, we've got our work cut out for us," he said instead. "Their case went in pretty well, better than expected even. They got motive 'til the sun goes down, and opportunity . . ."

"But you . . ." she started to say.

"But I got Ramirez to say you were nice. But also that you coulda been a tad distracted after, you know, murdering your husband for money."

He looked down at the table, then back up at Kyra, who now looked deflated. "Look, I'm sorry for being a downer. I'm just tired. We knew their case would be powerful, but, hey, we got *you*. It's gonna be hard for those jurors to hear you say you didn't do it and then turn around and convict you.

"Conor helped today about the prenup modification, but you're gonna need to hit that NDA issue. And I'm gonna try putting Marian and Edward up there to say nice things about you and bad things about Tony."

Kyra cut in. "You really think Marian's gonna testify after you just publicly suggested she had a motive to kill Tony? That was great, by the way, but it feels like we should have chatted about that first."

"Yeah," he answered. "Sorry 'bout that. I was seized by the Holy Spirit, like I was when I threw the Mafia thing into my opening. But you're the one who put her on the suspect list, remember?"

"Yeah, but she's gonna be so pissed."

"Maybe," Parker answered. "Anyhow, she has no choice. She's under subpoena. And she may hate me, but she really hated Tony, so I think she'll still say nice stuff about you. It'll be a big deal for the first wife and the son to say that. And I'm gonna try to get one or both of them to slip in that Tony had powerful enemies in the mob. And maybe I'll get seized by the Spirit again and ask her if she killed Tony. Ya never know."

He turned serious. "But I really, really would like to offer some kind of alternative theory, something for those twelve people to grab on to as they do what they're gonna want to do, which is let you go."

"How're we gonna do that?"

"Not sure."

They sat in silence before Parker broke it. "My guy says the feds are running it down like crazy, but it's gonna take time and we don't have much time left. Also, I just found out the DA blew them off, so we aren't gonna get any help there. Maybe I'll just have a stroke and go to intensive care."

She didn't smile.

"I'm just kidding. Hey, hey, you with me?"

Kyra blinked her eyes to focus on him. "Yeah, I'm here. Just thinking. Can I ask you a question?"

"Sure," he answered.

"If they convict me, the judge'll revoke my bail, won't she?"

"Look, let's not—"

Kyra cut him off. She was glassy-eyed, sweat gathering on her nose and upper lip. "Please," she said, almost begging, "just answer the question. In a murder case like this, they'll lock me up right after a verdict, right?"

He shook his head at the question but answered. "Yes, most likely. Very hard to avoid being led away in handcuffs—'stepping back,' as they say—after a murder conviction."

Her breathing was now labored, her eyes filled with tears. "I can't do it, Matthew. I can't be locked up like that. Your friend convincing the DA down the road does me no good. You saw me that morning. It's the thing that scares me most in the world. I just can't be locked up. It'll kill me."

Parker laid one hand on top of hers. "Hey. Hey. Not gonna happen. We're gonna find a way out of this. Remember, we just need one juror to believe you. You can do this. Go home and get a good night's sleep. I'll see you in court first thing."

CHAPTER SEVENTEEN

I t was early, so everyone brought their cups of coffee to the meeting in Carmen Garcia's office. The VOC unit chief's office was four floors directly below the US Attorney's personal office—with a nice view of the plaza and the red poker chip sculpture of the five boroughs. Although much smaller than the boss's office above, it was big enough for a couch, a major perk in the fed world. Nora took the chair by Carmen Garcia's desk while Benny and Jessica dropped onto the blue faux-leather couch by the window.

Carmen listened without interruption to Nora's briefing about the discovery of a connection between Gina Cufaro and Conor McCarthy. "Okay, so what's the investigative plan?" Looking at Benny, she added, "Nora told me about your lovely little meeting with the DA's office yesterday."

Benny noticed Nora was staring out the window, so he jumped in. "Nora can check me on this, but the plan we worked out is to go balls to the wall seeing what we can put together on links between Gina and Conor. Full work-up on play, work, devices, travel, the whole nine yards."

He nodded toward Jessica. "FBI is finally fired up. Jessica spoke to her ASAC and they're gonna put full FISUR"—he pronounced it *fye-zure*—"on both of them, SSG and SOG here and out of Miami Field Office, where Gina lives now."

"Wow," Carmen answered. "They *are* fired up. Better late than never."

FISUR was FBI-speak for physical surveillance, which was the work of squads in major city offices devoted entirely to following people. A Special Surveillance Group, or SSG, was composed of unarmed FBI employees who were not agents and looked nothing like a spy or gangster might imagine FBI people look. The Special Operations Group, or SOG, similarly specialized in surveillance, but its members were all armed agents and so had less flexibility to role-play and blend in, a trade-off that made sense when they were dealing with potentially violent targets.

In practice, nobody saw the tail. The teams were like ghosts, which was their informal name in the Bureau. The ghosts used all manner of vehicles, body types, and disguises to perform a complicated ballet, blanketing a subject who never felt the blanket. Sometimes, when a bad guy went out for an important dinner meeting, the ghosts were literally every other patron in the restaurant—old, young, skinny, fat, white, Black, Latino, Asian, hip, uncool, clean-shaven, bearded—and sometimes they were every car on the block—ice-cream truck, sports car, motor bike, minivan, taxi.

Like real people, they moved, argued, turned, stopped, and visited the restroom, moving on and off "the set," as they called the area being blanketed. But these people were all listening to the ballet's director through tiny earpieces. It was one of the FBI's least-known and most-hallowed capabilities—critical to following foreign spies and sophisticated criminals—and so important that the ghosts avoided FBI offices, staging instead at remote "off-sites" where they parked their vehicles and got dressed for the day's ballet.

"We wanna see if we can put Conor and Gina together," Benny continued, "both historically and, if we're lucky, in real time. And I wanna map her movements against open mob hits. If she's the killer we heard whispers about, maybe there's a pattern that would be useful."

Nora stopped looking out the window. "And we'll pump out the sub-poenas and court orders we're gonna need to put together that picture. Jessica and her colleagues have already reached out to the providers to get things rolling on an emergency basis, paper to follow."

"Good," Carmen answered. "And the DA?"

"Right," Nora said. "They're pushing on with their Killer Kyra trial. Basically told us to fuck off without anything harder than 'a taste' from our dead cooperator. Soon as we get something, we'll get it to them."

Nora paused before continuing. "Weird thing is, from the press about the trial, it almost seems like the defense has some idea about the possible mob angle. Matthew Parker said something about it in his opening. Not sure what that's about, but we're keeping this close-hold until we have more to go on. We'll work it hard and keep you posted."

"Good," Carmen said. Pointing to the ceiling, she added, "And given we got a blank check from up there, I don't see any need to brief the boss at this point. So go get 'em."

"Hey, you okay?" Benny asked as they walked back toward Nora's office.

"Sure, why?" Nora replied.

"You seem a little outta sorts this morning. Everything okay with your ladybug?"

"Yeah, yeah. She's great. It's not that. Turns out Nick's getting married, which has me weirded out for some reason. I'll get through it. But thanks for asking."

They continued walking down the hallway, but Nora touched Benny's arm and stopped as Jessica went ahead. She was whispering now. "Hey, any chance it was you who gave your buddy Parker a heads-up on the mob angle?"

Benny stared at her. "You want the answer to that question?"

"Yeah," Nora said, "that's why I asked."

"I did."

"Before The Nose got whacked?"

"Yes."

"Shit, Benny. I get why you might want to, but you really trust him like that? I don't like the idea that his client might be innocent either, but somethin' got The Nose dead and, for all we know, Killer Kyra might actually be guilty."

"I trust him with my life. And I literally have in the past. I trust him like I trust you."

"Okay." They started walking but she touched his arm again and he stopped. "And you know I trust you like family, but you can't be sneaking around on me like that. I know you and Parker go way back, but I gotta know."

He nodded. "You're right. My bad. Never happen again."

They continued walking in silence.

Jessica was waiting for them in front of the whiteboard, now covered in photos with colored lines drawn between them. Nora stood beside her for a few moments, then asked, "We got other photos of Kyra Burke?"

"Bunch," Jessica answered, pointing toward her desk. "Media photos from all over the place. And the arrest file has her mugshot."

Nora walked over and lifted the file, opening it to look at the arrest photo stapled to the inside left flap. In a loud voice, she said, "I knew it. I knew something felt familiar in court, Benny. I know her, or at least I did. In Connecticut. When I was at Fairfield in college. She went by another name. I think she was 'Lizzy' then."

She continued reading in the file. "Yup, here it is. Her full given name is Elizabeth Kyra." Flicking the photo with her finger, she shook her head in disbelief. "That's Lizzy from Yale. Small world. Weird, too."

CHAPTER EIGHTEEN

"Good morning, members of the jury. Mr. Parker, are you prepared to continue?" Justice Zannis asked.

"Yes, Your Honor. The defendant calls Marian Burke."

The jurors all turned to watch an elegantly dressed woman enter the courtroom and walk toward the witness stand. She walked easily—glided, really—on black patent Christian Louboutin stilettos, below a black Chanel wool skirt and matching half-sleeved black button-front jacket with a turndown-style collar. She wore her hair as Kyra did—with the same professional dye job of blonde highlights and lowlights. She walked with a straight back and carried herself much as Kyra did. In fact, she looked and moved eerily like Kyra, except she was thirty years older, an age difference obscured by Marian Burke's extensive investment in skin products and related procedures.

"Ma'am, thank you for being here today," Parker began. "Would you please tell the jury about your background?"

Marian Burke glared at Parker. "I appreciate your gratitude, but you subpoenaed me to be here," she said, speaking with a faint and obscure patrician accent, like Grace Kelly in a black-and-white movie.

Then she turned her head to the jury and smiled. "As for my background, I grew up on the Upper East Side, in what they used to call a 'socially prominent family,' went away to boarding school, then to Sarah Lawrence College up in Bronxville, where I think my parents wanted me to be 'finished.'"

She turned back to Parker, who didn't want to ask what that meant, but had no choice.

"Finished?"

"Yes," she answered. "It's an old expression, conveying the idea that young women should become polished by their education to make them better spouses and hostesses."

"Did it work?" Parker asked, now starting to enjoy this.

"Hard for me to say, but I suppose not, because they were horrified by my career choice after college."

She was really going to make him work for it.

"Which was?"

"I became a fashion model, which was my life until I met and married Tony Burke."

"And how old were you at that point?"

"Midtwenties, so the modeling career was short, which I, of course, came to regret."

"How long were you married to Tony Burke?"

"The honest answer is 'too long.' Just over thirty-five years."

"Children?"

"Yes, one, which was the only good thing about that union. Our son, Edward, was born about a year after we were married."

"Why did you marry Tony Burke?"

"He was handsome, charming, and intelligent. To my foolish young self, he seemed perfect. Of course, he was also broke, but given where I came from, that was not an issue."

"What do you mean?" Parker asked.

Marian looked at him like he was an idiot. "My parents had lots of money, which meant I did as well, so Tony didn't need to."

"When and why did you and Tony Burke divorce?"

"I waited until after Edward was established on his own, with his own family. And as to the 'why,' I don't wish to speak ill of the dead. Let's just say Mr. Burke was not a faithful and reliable spouse, something that was true throughout the marriage."

"Then why did you stay together for so long?"

"Oh, for Edward of course, who was a remarkable child and has grown into a remarkable adult, something I hope the whole country will come to appreciate. I think we also stayed together to help Tony get elected governor. A divorce would have been 'bad optics,' as he liked to say. After he won, it turned out that in Albany, of all places, there seemed to be even more women for him, and that was it for me. I moved back here, had the lawyers negotiate a generous divorce agreement, and I was free."

"Can you just broadly describe the financial settlement?"

"Well, Tony came from nothing and he was a politician, so he never did any real work. But I didn't want him to struggle financially after the divorce—that would embarrass Edward—and I was well off, so I gave him the Central Park West penthouse and a significant collection of other assets."

Parker made a mental note not to suggest she killed Tony to get money through his will.

When another question didn't come quickly, Marian went on. "Of course, he still found a way to embarrass all of us."

She paused before looking around the courtroom and adding with a sigh, "And somehow he's managed to keep embarrassing us, even from the grave. Quite a trick."

Parker brought it back on track. Gesturing toward Kyra, he asked, "Do you know the defendant, Kyra Burke?"

Marian smiled warmly at Kyra. "Of course, I know her and like her. There's a certain camaraderie in this club of Tony Burke spouses."

"What do you think of her?"

"She's bright, funny, and committed to helping other people. I knew that from the moment I met her, which was before they actually got married, and why I ached from the first for her inevitable future as an emotionally abused spouse. Frankly, she reminded me of a younger me."

"Do you know her friends and associates?"

"Yes, many."

"And what is her reputation in that community as to honesty?"

"She is regarded as a fundamentally good and honest person, a view I share."

"Do you have an opinion as to whether Kyra is capable of murdering your former husband?"

Andy Kwon was on his feet, objecting.

Geez, that's dumb, Parker thought. *Only gonna highlight this.*

"No, Mr. Kwon," Justice Zannis said. "I'm willing to give some latitude in a defense case. Overruled."

"You may answer, Ms. Burke," Parker said.

"Oh, my dear, no. Never. Not in a million years. Not that he didn't give her and all of us plenty of cause, but no."

"So you hated Tony?"

"With the heat of a thousand suns," she answered, showing a slight smile that might have been a grimace.

"Are you aware that you and Kyra bear a striking resemblance to each other?" Parker asked.

Marian now actually smiled, the skin on her face tight, her forehead frozen. "First, thank you for that extraordinary compliment, Mr. Parker. My husband had a type, although I suspect I am more easily taken for Kyra's mother at this point. But, thank you. Yes, we look alike."

"Do you think you could pass for her?"

"I doubt it, but, again, I'm flattered by the thrust of your question."

"Do you own a navy blue Hermès scarf?"

"Of course."

"Jackie O–style sunglasses?"

"Again, of course. This is New York, Mr. Parker."

"What about a Prada gabardine raincoat?"

"What color?"

"Black."

"Probably. I'd need to check."

"Do you know the elevator code to Tony Burke's penthouse?"

"Unless they've changed it since it was *my* penthouse."

"Was that you in the lobby the night he was killed?"

Miriam didn't react at all. "It was not, Mr. Parker."

"Did you kill Tony?"

"I did not."

"Do you know who did?"

"I have my suspicions," she answered.

Andy Kwon was up, but Justice Zannis spoke first. "Mr. Parker, I've given you quite a bit of latitude, but you've reached the limits of it now. The witness is not here to offer alternative theories."

"Fine, Judge. How about this," he said, turning to the witness. "Do any of your suspicions include Kyra?"

Marian answered quickly. "They do not. I suspect the Mafia had him killed."

Justice Zannis was hot. "No, no, no. That answer is stricken, and the jury will disregard it. Ms. Burke, you are a sophisticated person. You do that again and there will be severe consequences. Am I clear?"

Marian was again unruffled. "Yes, Your Honor. Quite."

"Sit down, Mr. Parker. Your examination is completed. Is there cross-examination?"

Andy Kwon stood and made a move toward the podium, then appeared to think better of it. "No, Your Honor, nothing from the People."

"Ms. Burke, you are excused. Call your next witness, Mr. Parker."

"The defense calls Edward Burke."

Justice Zannis looked pained by the Burke parade. "Short leash, Mr. Parker, short leash."

"Got it, Judge." He paused at the defense table to lean toward Kyra. Whispering intensely, he asked, "How the fuck does Marian know about the mob-hit angle?"

Kyra shrugged. "No idea," she whispered. "She's a pistol though, huh?"

"Glad you're enjoying it," he whispered. "She almost got me held in contempt."

Edward Burke was tall, with his mother's posture, but somehow— maybe with his shoulders and the angle of neck, or the swing of his arms—he communicated the earthiness of his father. He smiled as he entered the courtroom—a smile that went all the way to his eyes—his head swiveling to point his warmth at people on all sides. His thick, straight hair, worn just long enough to produce a wave that bounced above his forehead, was the brown midpoint between his mother's blonde and his father's black. He was wearing a dark blue suit, white shirt, and red tie, apparently having decided that the trial of his father's accused murderer was the one place where he should not wear the red zippered waterproof vest he otherwise sported at public events in New York and far beyond. At forty-five, he was already time-to-stop-working rich and had begun preparing a run for national office.

Parker knew from his brief prep session with Edward that the man-who-would-be-president saw no upside to testifying at this trial. He was stuck with the same last name as his old man, which, of course, had value with low-information voters—and that's darn near all of them, he said—but he had no interest in generating information that would remind those voters of what an evil prick his father was.

Not that he would use language like that.

"Mr. Burke," Parker began, "please tell the jury something of your background."

"Sure," Edward replied, looking directly at Parker. "I'm the son of Marian and Antonio Burke. I grew up in Manhattan and went to Syracuse University, where I found the two most important things in my life: my amazing wife, Angela, and my lord and savior, Jesus Christ. In fact, I met Angela freshman year at an InterVarsity Christian Fellowship meeting. She and my faith have been at the center of my life since."

"Children?"

"Yes, four incredible kids."

"You mentioned the central role Angela and your Christian faith have played in your life. Did they have an impact on your relationship with your parents?"

"Not with my mom, who is still my closest advisor and friend. Except Angela, of course. But it strained my relationship with my father, who was not a person of faith, or a person who particularly respected the religious beliefs of others."

"What did you do after college?"

"I spent two years getting my MBA at Harvard Business School, then went to work for a money-management firm, where I stayed until just last year when I retired to spend more time with my family and to explore ways to serve this great country of ours."

Parker knew he had to be careful with what came next because Edward was much more guarded in his support of Kyra. As he told Parker privately, "I don't believe your client killed my father, but it's always possible she did, so I don't want to plant my feet too firmly, if you take my meaning."

Parker took it. Edward would not be volunteering suspicions that the mob killed his father, which was just as well, given Justice Zannis's pique.

"Do you know Kyra Burke?"

"Yes, of course."

"Do you know her friends and associates?"

"Many of them, from charity events, things like that."

"What is her reputation in that community as to honesty?"

Edward turned to the jury and, in a warm voice, said, "She's known as an honest, caring, and talented individual. And I share that view of her."

Not bad, Parker thought, *considering she's supposed to have killed your dad. Guy's gonna be one hell of a candidate.*

"No further questions, Your Honor."

Andy Kwon seemed less afraid of Edward but asked only one question: "Mr. Burke, you have no personal knowledge of the facts of this case or the evidence this jury has heard, is that correct?"

It was a stupid and compound question, but Parker let it go with Edward's simple "no."

Okay, not bad. The Burke show was actually okay. Now if Kyra can just stay on script too.

◆

After lunch it was time for Kyra Burke's last, best shot—her own testimony.

"Good afternoon, ladies and gentlemen. Mr. Parker, are you ready to proceed?"

"Yes, Your Honor. The defense calls Kyra Burke."

Kyra rose slowly from the defense table and began walking toward the witness stand. She really did eerily resemble the first Mrs. Burke, but her style today was much softer than stiletto-wearing Marian's had been. For her big moment, Kyra wore a modest knee-length navy blue dress with matching suit jacket and navy blue two-inch heel pumps. Her hair was clipped back in a ponytail, showing her plain silver hoop earrings. She looked anxious, with long visible lines bunched above her eyebrows.

With Parker's prompting, she told the jury her story, much as she had for him in her Pomander Walk kitchen. Messed-up and absent parents, including a dead mother. Raised by grandparents in gritty Easton, Pennsylvania. Yale, Columbia, mentoring programs for at-risk girls, work on feminist legal policy, academic job at Columbia, marriage to Tony, separation from Tony, arrest for killing him.

"Did you kill Tony Burke?" Parker asked, his tone solemn and his pace slow.

Kyra turned toward the jury and matched his tone and pace. "No, I did not."

"Where were you at the time he was killed?"

"In my home on the Upper West Side."

"What were you doing?"

"Catching up on recent scholarship, as best I remember, because that's what my job requires."

"You've heard the evidence about your phone being off during that time. Is that true?"

"Yes. I know it seems old-school, but I always turn my phone off when I want to get an uninterrupted block of time to concentrate."

"Why not just put it on silent?"

"Because if I do that, I still know it's on, and I think about it: What texts are coming in, what news alerts am I missing? The damn things light up and steal our attention by just sitting there, alive. So I power it down. And I read printed documents, as prehistoric as that sounds."

Parker picked up a piece of paper. "Your Honor, I'd like to read a stipulation between the prosecution and the defense, if I may."

"You may," Justice Zannis answered.

"It is stipulated and agreed that, if called as a witness, a representative of Verizon Wireless would testify that Defense Exhibit 1 is an accurate record of information pertaining to Kyra Burke's iPhone, in particular those times over the last six months during which the device was powered down. It is further agreed that Defense Exhibit 1 may be admitted into evidence without further testimony.

"On that basis," he continued, "we offer Defense Exhibit 1."

"Received in evidence," Justice Zannis replied.

Parker then used courtroom monitors to walk Kyra through a highlighted copy of the exhibit, showing dozens of times, usually in the evening, when her phone was powered off for two-hour intervals.

"So what's going on with your phone, Kyra?"

"Exactly what I said. That's me turning the darn thing off so it gets out of my head and lets me work."

Parker looked down at his notes and switched topics. "You heard all this stuff about your alleged financial motive, is that right?"

"I did."

"Let's take the will first. Did you have any knowledge of the contents of Tony Burke's will?"

"Not before this case I didn't. I had no idea."

"And what about this prenup agreement? Where did that stand?"

"As the jury heard, I signed an agreement where I would get a lump sum of $500,000 if we divorced."

"Why did you sign that?"

"I wanted to marry him and I didn't care about his money. I still don't."

"Was Conor McCarthy's testimony about that accurate?"

"Yes. He called me one day not long before Tony died to tell me that Tony intended to modify the agreement as part of a divorce settlement to give me a lot more money. But only if I was willing to sign a nondisclosure agreement to not speak about anything I might have learned during the course of our relationship."

"How did it make you feel about Tony?"

"It didn't surprise me. Everything in life was, for him, a transaction, a deal. I think he wanted me quiet and was willing to pay for it. That was Tony. Just another deal to be done."

"Were you willing to sign the NDA?"

"No, never."

"Why?"

"Because I saw what he did to those other women and how he used those agreements as a weapon. I wasn't going to be part of that. And I know it sounds strange, but I didn't care about the money. I was going to get $500,000 under the prenup, which is a lot of money, at least in my eyes. And I have a good job with health insurance at Columbia Law School. I wanted to be free to tell the truth about him."

Parker paused for effect. "Did you kill him?"

She turned toward the jury as she spoke. "No, I did not."

"I have no further questions, Your Honor."

CHAPTER NINETEEN

A ndy Kwon went to the podium and just stood there. The courtroom was silent for so long that jurors started turning their heads
to check on him.

Strong move by the kid, Parker thought. *Icing the kicker.*

At long last, Kwon spoke.

"Ma'am, what is your actual name?"

The question seemed to surprise Kyra. Parker thought he saw her
chest move—as if jolted—before she quickly recovered.

"I'm Kyra Burke."

"Yes, we've heard that quite a few times, but what was your full
name as a child?"

Again, Parker noticed the almost imperceptible recoil. "I was born
Elizabeth Kyra Podolski."

"You were actually known for most of your life as 'Lizzy,' is that
correct?"

"I was," Kyra answered, "at least through college."

"And after college, you told people to call you Kyra, right?"

"I did." Kyra was now staring hard at Andy Kwon, her jaw noticeably
tightened, the worry lines gone. Parker was holding both suspenders,
screaming in his mind. *I have no idea what the fuck this is, but I told you
to keep the same pleasant manner the whole damn time!*

"And you did that to reinvent yourself, is that fair?"

"No."

"It's not? Well, after being called Lizzy for twenty-two years, why did you decide to be Kyra?"

"Lizzy just seemed like a child's name to me," Kyra said, before adding, "Sort of like 'Andy.'"

Oh no, what the fuck are you doing?

ADA Kwon ignored the jab, keeping his level but persistent tone. "But *Elizabeth* was an adult-sounding name readily at hand. In fact, it was your actual first name. Did that also seem like a child's name to you?"

"It did not, but I didn't like it."

"Why?"

"I can't remember."

Now Kwon knew he was getting to her. "You were a recent Yale college graduate deciding not to use your actual first name and you can't remember why you didn't like your own name. Is that your testimony?"

"That's right. I just liked Kyra better."

Kwon inhaled audibly through his nose. "It wasn't about the names, was it, Mrs. Burke? It was about your need to reinvent yourself, right?"

"I suppose so."

Parker was now moving his thumbs on the suspenders. *Wait, so the stuff you told the jury like thirty seconds ago about not liking the name was bullshit? Did we just admit to lying to the jury? Oh my fucking God.*

"Reinvention has been a theme of your life, hasn't it?"

"I don't know what you mean."

"Well, Lizzy Podolski became Kyra Podolski, the law student at Columbia, which was a long way from Easton. Then after graduating from law school, you legally changed your name to Kyra Elizabeth Paulson, isn't that correct, Mrs. Burke?"

"Yes, I did. Lots of people change their names. It made sense because everyone called me Kyra and people had trouble pronouncing Podolski. So I legally changed my name to Kyra Elizabeth Paulson."

What the actual fuck is she doing up there and why didn't she tell me about this name-change bullshit during trial prep? She is going totally off the rails and now the jurors are all wide awake and leanin' in. Fucked.

"So then you became Kyra Paulson, law professor, and with that name you met the Governor of New York, courted and married him, and became First Lady of New York, Mrs. Kyra Burke. Another new name for you, correct?"

Kyra's answer was dripping with sarcasm. "Correct."

"So, Mrs. *Burke*, would it be fair to say that all these name changes were part of your plan to become a rich and powerful person in your own right?"

Parker was on his feet, "Objection, Your Honor!"

"Sustained," Justice Zannis said, sharply. "Next question, move along."

"Yes, Your Honor," Kwon answered. "Mrs. Burke, Tony Burke becoming a pariah, that wasn't part of your plan was it?"

Parker let go of the suspenders and jumped up. "Objection to the arguing, Your Honor."

"Sustained," Zannis said again. "Move along, Mr. Kwon."

Kwon now changed his approach, but he left his mark on Kyra, who looked coiled, cornered, and angry. For his part, Kwon switched to a mildly empathetic tone.

"Tony Burke was a vicious, lying sexual predator, is that what you told your colleagues?"

"Yes."

"And you believed that, right?"

"Yes, and I still do."

"And he took your thirties, didn't he?"

"Again, I don't know what you mean."

"You met him when you were thirty, separated last year when you were thirty-nine, and now that you are forty, he is dead."

"Your math is correct."

"You devoted a decade of your life, your physically prime years, to a vicious, lying sexual predator."

"I did, although I didn't know it going in."

"Because he lied, right?"

"Yes."

"So you were tricked into spending ten years with him, with his name becoming part of yours?"

"You could say that."

"And the things he lied about, the things he did to women, were things you devoted your professional life to studying and trying to prevent, right?"

"Yes. Empowering women and fighting the power imbalances that allow men to victimize women has been an important focus of my work."

"And now you have to reinvent yourself again, don't you?"

"I don't know what you mean."

"Kyra Burke the widow, a victim of predator Burke along with so many other women."

"Is that a question?"

"Here's my question, Mrs. Burke. Isn't it true that you gave a decade of your life to a man who turned out to be the very thing you said you stood against?"

"I think that's fair." Kyra was a long way from rattled now. She seemed cold, clinical, almost ruthless. Parker was very concerned, gripping his suspenders and working hard to look bored, perhaps even daydreaming.

"How did that make you feel?" Kwon asked.

"Angry."

"Angry? Didn't you *hate* Tony Burke? We heard his first wife say she hated him with something like 'the heat of a thousand suns.' Does that accurately describe how you felt?"

"Yes, I think so. Not my expression, but it captures some of my feelings."

"Are you sorry he's dead?"

Kyra paused, lifting her chin before calmly answering. "No, actually it's a relief."

An audible *oooooohhhh* came from the packed public gallery. The few jurors who were taking notes jerked their heads up. Justice Zannis rapped her gavel.

Parker was now frantically thumbing the suspenders. *We practiced this very fucking question ten times. The answer is, "I didn't like him, but I don't want to see anyone lose their life." Have you lost your mind?*

Kwon took a swing, his voice rising. "You would have killed Tony if you could get away with it."

"No, I wouldn't," Kyra answered.

You're a millisecond too slow with that answer! That's one you start saying no to before he finishes asking. I felt it. Jury felt it. They had to. What the hell are you doing?

As he wound up, Kwon lowered his voice, trying to sum up a bit through Kyra. "You knew he took insulin."

"Of course."

"You knew where the insulin was kept in the apartment."

"I did."

"You also knew the elevator code."

"Yes."

"And Tony Burke liked you, right? It was *you* who left him, am I right?"

"That's right."

"So he wouldn't have been unhappy to have you stop by?"

"I suppose not."

"He wouldn't struggle to stop you from coming in, right?"

"No, he wouldn't."

"And your alibi is that you were home alone, less than a mile away, with your phone conveniently turned off at the time the victim was murdered?"

"Yes."

"And you're asking the jury to believe that the woman we saw in the lobby video, who looks just like you, who the doorman identified as you, is not actually you?"

"Yes, I am." The courtroom was silent, the jurors mesmerized.

"I have no further questions, Your Honor." He looked into the jury box and shook his head almost imperceptibly before walking back to the prosecution table.

Justice Zannis cleared her throat, as if to get everyone's attention. "Mr. Parker, do you have any questions on redirect for this witness?"

Parker was up fast. "Just one, Your Honor."

His voice was rich with emotion, telegraphing the passion he needed from his client. "Mrs. Burke, Mr. Kwon asked you all these questions about your name, your life, your work, and Tony Burke and how he made you feel. Did you kill the man?"

Kyra didn't turn to the jury as they had practiced. Instead, she seemed irritated to have to deny it again and stared at Parker, before giving him a short, sharp, middle-volume answer. "No."

That's it? Are you fucking bored or something? We are screwed.

"Nothing further, Your Honor."

"Thank you, Mr. Parker. "Mrs. Burke, you may return to the defense table. Anything further from the defense, Mr. Parker?"

"Yes, Judge, but I'd like to be heard at sidebar first."

Justice Zannis glanced up at the clock on the wall above the jury box. "Okay, given the time, ladies and gentlemen, I'm going to release you for today. I will see you back here tomorrow morning, and please remember my instruction not to read or listen to anything about the case or discuss the case with anyone. See you tomorrow. Counsel, I will see you in the robing room with the court reporter in five minutes."

CHAPTER TWENTY

Kyra sat at the defense table, not speaking, staring off into the distance. Next to her, Matthew Parker was distracted, trying to frame the argument he needed to make in five minutes. He also wanted to yell at Kyra, but he couldn't yell in the courtroom, and it was her life anyway so what was the yelling going to be about? *If she goes to jail, it's her fault and I couldn't stop her. She didn't stick to the script like I told her.*

Justice Zannis's clerk interrupted his thoughts. "The judge is ready for you."

The judge was still in her black robe, sitting behind a desk, the court reporter at her right hand. Andy Kwon took the chair to the judge's left, as if they were still in the courtroom. Parker slid into the empty chair.

"Yes, what is it, Mr. Parker?"

"Your Honor, I have reason to believe there is significant new evidence tending to exculpate my client, which the prosecution has failed to provide to us."

Justice Zannis looked grave. "Please say more, Mr. Parker. That is a very serious allegation."

"Judge, we have learned that a major organized-crime figure informed the federal authorities a week ago that Tony Burke was killed by a Mafia assassin, likely a woman. That organized-crime figure, Dominic D'Amico, was himself murdered last weekend."

"Yes," Justice Zannis said, "I saw that in the news."

"And we know that the federal authorities are actively investigating to determine who killed Tony Burke, and why."

Andy Kwon blew air out through his nose. "Maybe they should attend this trial, Your Honor. Or wait for the verdict; then they'll know."

He really is becoming an overconfident dick. Parker ignored the sarcasm. "And, Judge, we have reason to believe the feds told some or all of this to the DA's office, which has not provided anything about it to the defense."

"So how did you learn of it, Mr. Parker?"

"I'd prefer not to say, Your Honor. The most I'm comfortable saying is 'from a reliable source close to the investigation.'"

"That's fine. I'm not going to press you. But I'm not sure what your claim is at this point. *Brady v. Maryland* and its progeny simply require that the defense be aware of material evidence helpful to the defense. If you already know the information, it's hard to see how the prosecution can be faulted for not telling you what you already know. Am I missing something?"

When he didn't answer, Justice Zannis gave him a break, turning to Andy Kwon. "Mr. Kwon, is there additional information of which the prosecution is aware that should be made available to the defense here?"

"Not that I know of, Judge."

"Well, I'd ask you to check with your office and be sure. I'll want something on the record to that effect."

"Of course, Your Honor."

She turned to Parker. "Well, Mr. Parker, I'm not sure what your motion is, but if it is based on some kind of *Brady* violation, I'm sorry, I don't see it. Will you have further witnesses tomorrow morning?"

Parker paused for a moment before answering in a soft voice. "No, Judge, I don't think so, but I'll know for sure by the morning."

"Okay then. If the defense rests, I expect we'll do summations and charge the jury in the morning so they can start deliberating after lunch. Please let the court know as soon as possible if you'll be calling any more witnesses, Mr. Parker. See you tomorrow."

Justice Zannis rose and left the room, followed by the court reporter.

Parker turned to Andy Kwon. "You little fucker. You know you've got this wrong. You're prosecuting an innocent woman."

Kwon was almost formal in his reply. "Mr. Parker, with all due respect, I don't see it that way, nor does my office. But maybe the jury will. We'll know soon. I'll see you tomorrow."

He popped up and walked out, leaving Parker alone in the robing room. He was in no hurry to rejoin his client in the courtroom.

CHAPTER TWENTY-ONE

The mood was dark in Parker's law-firm conference room. "Jeez, Kyra," Parker began, not hiding his irritation. "Woulda been nice for me to know all that stuff about your name. Kinda felt like I was standing there with my pants around my ankles."

She didn't look up. "I get that, now, but it didn't seem like a big deal. Until Kwon made it sound like one."

"Yeah, I gotta tell you, it made us look bad. And where was the Kyra I know?" he asked. "Especially toward the end of cross, and on my last question?"

She didn't look up. "I'm not sure. I started to get tired, I think. Was it that bad?"

Not gonna crush the poor woman, but hell yes. "No, not at all," he said. "I was just hoping for a more forceful rejection of Kwon's suggestions, and then maybe a home-run swing when I asked you at the end if you did it. But let's not waste time looking back, let's look ahead. It's gonna be important that, from here on out, you radiate the nice, kind, innocent Kyra. The jury is always watching, whether you're on the stand or not. Okay?"

"Got it. Nice. Kind. Innocent. So what's next?"

"Nothing for you tomorrow. I complained to the judge that the prosecution hadn't given us the stuff on the mob maybe hitting Tony. Got nowhere."

"What's your friend say?"

"They're working as hard as they can to see if they can prove who did it. And it doesn't feel like you're one of their suspects, that's for sure."

Kyra didn't answer, but Parker could see her eyes filling with tears. "Hey, hey," he said, "hang in there. This thing ain't over."

She dropped her head as she spoke. "I know I blew it on the stand and I'm scared. I actually had a dream last night about Rikers Island."

"Hey," Parker said, waiting for her to lift her head. "Hey. Don't do that to yourself. First, you aren't going to get convicted. Second, even if you did, I would fight to keep you out on bail before sentencing."

"But you said that would be hard. If they 'step me back,' as you said, I do go to Rikers?"

"Ah c'mon, Kyra."

When she didn't respond, he answered her question. "Yes, female defendants pending trial or sentencing are usually held there. Only men are held at the Manhattan jail next to the courthouse—and who would wanna be at a place they call 'The Tombs' anyway? And I know Rikers doesn't do well on TripAdvisor, but stop with the dreams; you aren't going there. The system works for innocent people, and it helps that your lawyer is awesome."

She wouldn't even look up. "I told you, I can't be locked up. I just can't. I will die first. I will."

Parker waited, watching Kyra, her head bowed, working to control her breathing. In a few moments the panic passed and she lifted her head, took another deep breath, and changed the subject.

"You know, the whole mob thing actually makes so much sense to me now. Tony dealt with some slimy characters. I know politics is dirty, but he did stuff for union guys and construction guys who always creeped me out. I never sat in, but what's the governor doing after hours with those characters in his apartment?"

Parker was too tired to talk about it. "Go get a good night's sleep. I gotta work on my summation. And tomorrow, you radiate kindness and innocence, clear?"

"Clear."

"Oh, and one other thing: Radiate that kindness and innocence as much as possible directly at Juror Seven. Nothin' weird, but try to make eye contact a couple times. You know who I'm talking about, right? White woman, second row, silver hair with pink streaks, big dangling earrings every day?"

"Yeah, I know which one. Kinda funky. I think she said she worked in an art gallery or something."

"Exactly. Her. Our jury consultant has been watching her and thinks she's on team Kyra. Some body-language mumbo jumbo or something. I'm gonna pitch directly to her tomorrow as well. If she loves you, we need her to stay strong for you. At this point, a hung jury may be our best shot."

"I thought you were going for all twelve."

"I am, I am, of course, but always gotta have an insurance policy. Weird-hair art lady is ours. So throw her your beam of projected innocence, okay?"

"Got it. See you in the morning."

CHAPTER TWENTY-TWO

The lights were on at Nora's end of the fourth-floor hallway. She was at her computer, with Jessica and Benny next door on theirs, all loudly offering updates. "Definitely wasn't Kyra at the Joey Cufaro wake!" Jessica shouted. "Customs and Border Patrol just hit us back; Kyra was out of the country. Greece."

"Good to know," Benny said. "I was already positive it was Gina, but good to verify. Where we need the FBI's help is developing the picture of the relationship between Gina and Conor. Need to see their entire lives and how they mesh. 'Cause it sure looks from the picture I took that they may have been doin' a whole lotta meshing. As they say: A picture's worth a thousand words."

Nora leaned in through the doorway. "Wow, I kinda thought Conor was gay." Turning to Jessica, she asked, "So what do we have so far on the two of them and the, uh, meshing, to use our colleague Mr. Dugan's term?"

"Gina lives full-time in Palm Beach Gardens. Been down in Florida full-time since her father died. Has what looks to be a pretty successful real-estate brokerage there. Repping buyers and sellers of single-family homes and condos."

Benny interrupted. "Probably selling second homes to wise guys from up here."

Jessica continued. "Uses her real name, lives alone in a townhouse condo she's owned since moving there. Financials we have so far say she's worth a lot, maybe more than would make sense if she were only a realtor, but can't be sure yet. Very little indication that she ever leaves Florida. If she's hitting the road, she's probably doing it under another name."

"Conor, on the other hand, is almost an adopted son of the Sunshine State. He's down there all the time. His Amex has him flying to Miami about once a month and renting a car. No hotel, Airbnb, nothing like that. And no indication he owns something. So he's either sleeping in his rental car or he's driving the two hours up to Palm Beach Gardens for some, uh, meshing. But weird that he doesn't fly to Palm Beach or Fort Lauderdale. So much closer."

Benny laughed. "Maybe the little mesher doesn't want people knowing where he's going. Might be time for a chat with that dude."

"Still a little early for that, don't you think?" Nora asked. "I'd like to see what the Bureau's technical whizzes can put together on his life and Gina's. We may get only one shot at him, and I want as much info in our pockets as possible."

"And we can put together some pretty cool graphics from their digital dust," Jessica said.

"Okay, young hipsters, you know tech ain't my thing. But please do enlighten this dinosaur. Digital dust?"

"That's the term for all the markers we leave in our lives, all over the place, whenever we drive or pay or call—"

Nora jumped in. "Or text or email or visit a website or post on social media or appear in someone else's post or—"

Benny held up both his hands. "Okay, okay, enough. Got it."

But Jessica was too excited to stop. "In a hyperconnected, wired world, we leave digital dust wherever we go—with every log-in, every 'like' or page visit. And we—your government—can collect that dust and sweep it into a pile that offers a pretty detailed picture of a life."

Nora picked it up. "And the good news, if you're us, or the bad news, if you're a bad guy wanting to hide your tracks, is that the Supreme Court hasn't gotten around to fully changing how the law thinks about this dust in terms of the Fourth Amendment. We need a warrant to read somebody's emails or texts or listen to their calls—and we now need a warrant to get somebody's phone location history—but we can sweep up all kinds of dust because it's still considered 'non-content'— doesn't show you what the person said—and the consumer 'voluntarily' gave it to a company someplace by using their devices or websites. So we get it without probable cause, using the subpoenas or court orders I've been pushing out. And, like I said, I got warrants to find out where Gina's and Conor's phones have traveled."

"That'll teach me to ask," Benny said, grinning. "So we collect dust and then I get to have a chat with sneaky Mr. Conor McCarthy. You let me know when I'm up to bat."

Nora was back at her computer typing out requests for stored electronic communications information when Benny leaned through the doorway, gently rapping on the frame. "Hey Ms. Smooth, got a minute?"

"Sure," she said, turning her chair.

He came in and quietly closed the door, settling in the chair facing her desk. "Okay, so what's the deal with you knowing Kyra as Lizzy?"

"What do you mean?"

"What do I mean? I didn't just fall off the truck. There's a story here and I need to hear it from you, especially if this connection means you should step away from this thing."

Nora's cheeks turned pink as she looked down and told the story to her desktop. "When I was a freshman at Fairfield, we would sometimes go to bars in New Haven 'cause it was a city and it was close. It was either that or come all the way into New York. One night, I was at a place near the Yale campus and I met a girl who was a senior there. Her name was Lizzy. We hit it off right away and talked almost the whole night. I went back quite a lot that year to meet her for lunch or dinner. Sometimes we'd study together, but mostly we'd just walk and talk."

Now she looked up at Benny, the redness fading from her face. "Let's just say I thought there was something there, a real friendship and a strong connection, but then she graduated and totally ghosted me. I really hadn't seen it coming. Texting wasn't a big thing then, but she stopped calling or returning my calls. I sent her a few emails—actually, more than a few—and they started bouncing back. Then her phone number was disconnected. I felt like some kind of stalker and finally stopped reaching out. I never heard from her again. Honestly, I was pretty hurt and embarrassed by the whole thing. Eventually, though, I decided to just forget about it and move on. I've barely thought about it since until seeing that photo, and then it all kinda came pouring back, and I'm feeling pretty embarrassed again."

She blew out an audible exhale. "So that's the story. I know: It's a lot. But I'm positive it was this same person, the one who is now Kyra Burke, on trial for murder."

"Why didn't you recognize her when we were in court?"

"I'm not sure. I felt something in the courtroom, maybe from the way she moved or walked or something, but it didn't click. I think because of all the makeup she wears. The Lizzy I knew was not fancy at all. I think that's why the mugshot in the file from the morning she was arrested, with no makeup, hit me like it did. That's the way I remember her, although a lot younger."

"So ya think you're okay to work this case? Nothin' gonna mess up your amazing prosecutorial judgment? You know I gotta ask this, right?"

Nora nodded. "I'm glad you asked and I am actually fine. The Lizzy I knew no longer exists, and I don't know or really care about Kyra Burke. All I care about is finding the truth and that justice is done."

"There she is! Ms. Smooth is back. Truth and justice is what we're all about! Excellent. Now I gotta get back to being a superhero."

Benny launched himself from the chair and bounded out of her office, almost hitting his head on her door frame as he took exaggerated leaps. Nora shook her head at the near miss.

CHAPTER TWENTY-THREE

"**M**r. Parker?"

Even though Matthew Parker knew New York's peculiar criminal procedure rules—where the defense lawyer speaks first in summation, followed by a single prosecution summation, with no rebuttal permitted—he hadn't tried enough state cases to internalize it. So it didn't register that Justice Zannis was calling his name, until it did.

"Mr. Parker?"

"Oh yes, thank you, Your Honor," he said, standing quickly. He started speaking even before he reached the podium, as if what he had to say couldn't wait. "I want to talk to you folks about four words that Mr. Kwon only bothered to say once in his opening, even though they are the bedrock of our justice system and the central obligation he bears."

Now he raised his voice to near shouting. "Beyond. A. Reasonable. Doubt." Then, dropping back to a normal tone, he said, "This isn't about 'maybe' what happened or what 'musta' happened or what 'might' have happened."

Wheeling to point at Kyra, he said, "Before the state may take that woman's liberty, they must *prove* her guilt to you. They must prove it beyond a reasonable doubt. The reason Mr. Kwon didn't spend a lot of time on those words is because they are a problem for him. Let's go through it.

"Kyra had a motive, he claimed. Did she, though? Was there a single piece of proof that Kyra knew anything about Tony's will? No. Oh, but the prenup. Well, you heard Conor McCarthy's testimony, and Kyra's. She believed he wanted to be generous with her. And without that, what's the motive, exactly? That he was a sexual predator? Well, we all know that, don't we? And we find it appalling. Why aren't we all suspects, then? It's just smoke, ladies and gentleman, not proof beyond a reasonable doubt.

"Now let's turn to the 'but she was in the lobby' bit. Does that make any sense to you? Kyra Burke is a highly intelligent woman—highly. Mr. Kwon wants you to believe she was determined to kill her husband. So what does this brilliant woman do? She walks through a lobby she knows is covered by a camera, past a doorman she has known for years, kills Tony, and then walks out the same way immediately after killing him. So is she a brilliant schemer or a total idiot?"

Parker paused to let that sink in, pretending to look at his notes before looking up again.

"Your common sense tells you it wasn't Kyra in the lobby. It sure was somebody who looked like her, wearing the kind of clothes she might wear, although I can't imagine why she would wear sunglasses at night. But you know it wasn't Kyra, because she isn't that dumb. And you know it for another reason, because you know what people are like. Kyra Burke would never give the back of her hand to Mr. Ramirez. Never. She was a person of great good fortune, but she never treated other people rudely. He told you that.

"Oh, wait, but Kyra doesn't have an alibi because her phone was off. Very suspicious, right? Except not at all, because the phone records show you that's something she does all the time. Now maybe Mr. Kwon is going to get up here and argue that she laid the groundwork for the killing by spending weeks and weeks carefully turning her phone off to prepare for the night of the murder. Again, is she a genius or a moron? Why would she deprive herself of alibi evidence? Why not just keep the phone on and leave it at her house? You don't need your phone to go kill your husband. Done.

"And why stab the needle through his sleeve if you are trying to make it look like a suicide? She's smart enough to know that would give it away. Or to imagine that a favorite dinner might be delivered, something a person committing suicide would wait for. Again, is she a diabolical criminal or a total idiot? The prosecution can't have it both ways.

"The truth is that it wasn't Kyra in the lobby that night. The evidence tells you that. But I don't actually need to prove that to you. Mr. Kwon needs to prove it *was* Kyra—Beyond. A. Reasonable. Doubt. Do you have doubts based in reason about whether she was dumb enough to march through the lobby? How can you not?

"Ladies and gentlemen," Parker continued, and then found himself choked with emotion. Maybe it was that he thought his client may have blown it with her testimony. Maybe it was that he knew her raw terror at the idea of being caged again. Maybe it was that this was his last case. But whatever it was he stopped, looking down and then up at the ceiling before coughing into his fist.

"Ladies and gentlemen," he tried again, "I don't know whether you liked my client during her testimony or not. I hope you did, but this case isn't about that. It's about the evidence and whether the prosecution has proven her guilt beyond a reasonable doubt." He had tears in his eyes now, looking directly at Juror 7, who was also crying. "They haven't. Please end this nightmare for Kyra. That's your sworn duty. Please do it. Thank you."

As he took his seat, he saw a note in front of him in Kyra's hand-writing: *So my testimony was pretty bad, eh?* He scribbled back quickly. *Radiate. #7.*

Andy Kwon was wearing his best navy blue suit, a crisp white button-down shirt, and a red-and-blue striped tie. This was his big moment. He rose in the packed courtroom, buttoned his jacket, and picked up his notebook. All the jurors watched him walk slowly to the podium, which was at the middle of the jury box. He set his notebook on the podium, took a deep breath, and silently swept his eyes across the jury. Then he began, still going thin to win.

"Ladies and gentlemen, as I told you in my opening, this is a simple case. Based on the testimony and exhibits presented in this courtroom, these are facts you know: Somebody Tony Burke knew killed him in his own study. It was somebody who could just walk into a fancy apartment building, who knew the elevator code, who knew where to find him. It was somebody he wouldn't fight, somebody who even knew about his insulin. Who was it? You don't need to guess, because you saw it with your own eyes."

Wheeling toward the defense table, he pointed at Kyra and raised his voice for the first time in the trial. "*There* is the person who was in the lobby that night. You saw the video and you heard Mr. Ramirez. Despite all the noise, there she is, the person who murdered Tony Burke."

He then walked the jury slowly through all the prosecution's evidence—crime scene, medical examiner, lobby video, doorman, finan-cial motive proof, statements from Kyra's Columbia colleagues—and ended by picking up the large map showing how close her place was to the murder scene.

He twisted to look at the map, studying it, then turned back to the jury and continued in a quiet voice. "And where was she that night? She says she wasn't in the lobby, she was less than a mile away at her place, reading. She says that what you saw must have been some look-alike, some actor playing Kyra Burke. She says a lot of things, but she can't show us where she was that night because she turned her phone off, so there is no proof where her phone really was. Let's be clear about this, because I worry there is confusion around this phone thing. There is no evidence that Kyra Burke was someplace else that night. None. The only evidence you have is what you saw with your own eyes. She was in the lobby, moments *before* her husband died and moments *after.*

"Now why would an accomplished person like Kyra Burke want to kill her husband? Well, the evidence and your common sense tell you why. She had a powerful financial motive, which you've heard a lot about, but it was even more than that. She hated him for what he had done to other women, but she hated him most of all for what he had done to her. Sometimes it's hard to make sense of why people hurt each other. Not here. He was a bad guy who had done terrible things and was going to keep on doing them, to her and to others. That doesn't make it right—in a civilized society, murder is never okay—but it explains it. Your common sense tells you that.

"You also got the chance to see her testify. In our system, a defendant doesn't need to testify, doesn't need to say anything at all. That's the way it should be. But she can. That's her right. She can get up there and tell her story. And when a defendant does, the jury is entitled to consider it—to evaluate it—just like any other evidence. So think about Kyra Burke's testimony. Did she strike you as someone who regretted the death of another human being? Did she strike you as someone who couldn't possibly form the intention to harm him?

"I would suggest to you the answers are no. In many ways, I suppose, you have to admire her candor. She showed you in this courtroom how much she hated that man. Well, maybe she had good reasons, but she must be held accountable for killing another human being, no matter the reasons."

He paused, getting ready to wrap up.

"Mr. Parker has done his best to make this case sound complicated. It isn't. If you listen to the law as Justice Zannis gives it to you and apply your common sense—your ability to assess situations and people, which is the product of your lifetime of experience—you will conclude that the evidence establishes beyond a reasonable doubt that Kyra Burke is guilty. Thank you."

It was Justice Zannis's turn. "Thank you, Mr. Kwon. Ladies and gentlemen, it is now the court's duty to instruct you on the law that will govern your deliberations." She launched into the invariably too long "jury charge," telling the jurors how they should consider different types of evidence, what "reasonable doubt" means, and the elements of the crime. When she finished, she invited counsel to sidebar to see if there were any objections or suggested corrections. There were none, so she sent the lawyers back to their tables, and then thanked the alternate jurors for their service and excused them, sending the remaining twelve out to deliberate.

Only Juror 7 glanced at Kyra as the jury walked out. The rest either looked at Andy Kwon or stared straight ahead. Parker turned and nodded to his jury consultant, who quickly rose and walked out of the spectators section. Her job was to follow the alternate jurors out to the street and see if any would speak to her about their impressions of the case.

When the jury was gone, Justice Zannis instructed the lawyers to stay nearby in case there were early notes from the jurors. Parker and Kyra went to a defense conference room adjoining the courtroom and sat in silence for about five minutes before the jury consultant returned. Two of the jurors had agreed to speak with her, but only briefly as they'd walked to the subway.

"What'd they say?" Parker asked.

The consultant hesitated, glancing at Kyra. "Lay it on us," Parker said. "She can handle it."

"They both said they weren't sure you were guilty until your testimony. I'm sorry, but they said you came across as cold and they thought you did it. Maybe you had good reason to kill him, but they thought it was you."

Parker dropped his head. "Thanks, Sheila. I appreciate you hustling after them. And thanks for all your work on this."

"My pleasure," she said. "And we still have number seven."

"Yes, we do," Parker said.

When they were alone, Kyra waited a long time to speak before saying, "So we're just going for a hung jury here, aren't we? Meaning, best case, I get to do this again."

Parker let out an exhausted breath. "Yes, I think that's the best we can hope for right now. But the best case is actually no retrial because we convince the DA to stop this bullshit."

They sat in silence as Parker picked up his phone and sent yet another text to Benny Dugan.

CHAPTER TWENTY-FOUR

Benny had silenced his phone hours ago and stopped looking at texts. He knew his buddy Matthew Parker was in agony waiting on a jury with an innocent client. He didn't blame him for blowing up his phone. But there was nothing Benny and the team could do about it, except work the case, which is what they were doing almost around the clock. So he'd muted the text conversation with Parker.

Suddenly, he was shouting from his desk chair again. "Okay, here's a weird one on Gina." Before he could go on, Nora leaned in the office door so he lowered his volume and continued: "I've been talking to my sources—both crooks and cops—tryin' to come up with a list of unsolved mob hits anywhere in the country over the last ten years, right? So I've got about a dozen, mostly in the Northeast, but a few near Vegas, Chicago, Atlanta, stuff like that. I took what you got me on Gina's historical cell location. And that's where it gets weird. On the date of every one of those hits, her cell is at her Palm Beach Gardens condo. And not just the day of. On the days around those hits, it's still at her condo. Doesn't go to the grocery store or nothin'. What are the chances that her phone, which is always boppin' around in Florida, goes no place whenever somebody gets whacked by a mystery killer?"

"And so, Mr. Holmes?" Nora asked.

Benny gave her a confused look.

"Sherlock," she added, shaking her head. "I was going for Sherlock Holmes. But the moment is ruined now, so please just tell us what you make of this."

With a quick smile, he continued. "She's traveling with a burner phone whenever she goes out on a job. Thinks she's bein' smart leavin' her phone at home, but she's now done so many jobs, it ain't smart any longer. It's a pattern of its own."

"Wait," Nora said, "what about on D'Amico and Tony Burke?"

"Phone was home in bed in Palm Beach Gardens for both of those. They're two of my dirty dozen."

"Whoa," Nora answered.

"So what next?" Jessica asked.

"We see if we can show she traveled around those dates and to those places," Benny said, "to see if Sherlock's hunch is right. Unlikely she drove to those places, so we gotta put her on a plane somewhere, or at least in an airport. Gotta assume she's got an alternate ID for travel. Once we get that, we can find her other flights."

Jessica spoke up. "No way she drives her own car to the airport. I'll check for cabs or Ubers from near her place to an airport on the days bracketing the killings. If we can put her in an airport at an approximate time, then we can narrow the flights, maybe get an ID that way or from airport cameras."

"Yup," Benny said, "and my guess is she flies outta Miami. Bigger than West Palm or Lauderdale, and she's less likely to see somebody who knows her as Gina."

"FBI has got this," Jessica said, picking up her desk phone.

Nora moved her chair closer to Benny's desk to avoid interrupting Jessica's call. "And I can give you Jessica's update on Conor's movements," she said. "He's less careful, takes his phone everywhere, so we see him on every trip to Miami picking up a rental car and driving straight from the airport to Gina's condo. He keeps the visits short, usually just a night or two—never more than three. We checked every visit and his phone never leaves the place until he drives back to make his flight. You must be right about the meshing."

"They go no place together, because they don't want nobody to know about them."

"They sure don't," Nora said. "But now we do."

"I'll get all his Florida dates from Jessica so I can see if he's ever there when she's traveling to kill people."

CHAPTER TWENTY-FIVE

The first afternoon of deliberations, the jury sent only one note, asking to stay late and have dinner. Justice Zannis looked up from the note with a smile. "An industrious and hard-working group. I'll ask my clerk to get them menus. Again, counsel, please stay nearby. I expect this jury may move quickly."

Back in the defense conference room, Parker checked his phone. Nothing. He texted Dugan a long string—*?????????????*

At eight P.M., Justice Zannis brought the jury back into the courtroom to dismiss them for the evening, instructing them to return in the morning.

"Miami Field Office has Uber pickups from Gina's Palm Beach Gardens place to Miami airport," Jessica said, "and they line up with about half of Benny's hit list. Rest may be too old for Uber, or maybe she was taking cabs back then. She uses an Uber account in a fake name that's connected to a debit card that's connected to a bank account, all in the fake name. The bad news is that she's not using that fake name for her flights. Our people already checked with the airport, where we have great relationships. No sign of that name on any reservations going back ten years. So a bit of a dry hole."

"Shit," Benny said. "Thought we might get lucky."

"But Miami airport is definitely where we focus," Jessica replied.

Nora had been standing in the doorway for this update and now returned to her desk. Ten minutes later, she was back in the door. "Hey, here's a thought. Looking at Gina's life—Palm Beach Gardens realtor Gina—I see only two loyalty-program memberships, Publix supermarkets and Starbucks."

"Yeah?" Benny said.

"So there are no supermarkets at airports, but there are always Starbucks. And coffee drinkers are creatures of habit—speaking from personal experience—so maybe the place we get lucky is her getting a coffee at the airport."

"So you think she mobile-orders from the Uber?" Benny asked. "Can't be that dumb."

"No, I'm not sure what it might be, but it's worth running down. Never know. And it can't be hard. Gotta be a retired FBI guy in regional security at Starbucks. They're everywhere."

Jessica smiled. "Retired FBI or Starbucks?"

Nora and Benny laughed and answered at the same time. "Both."

"Worth a try," Jessica said. "I'll ask my bosses."

CHAPTER TWENTY-SIX

A t nine A.M., the judge's clerk told Parker and Kwon that the judge wished them to know that all the jurors were present and deliberations had begun again. In the defense conference room, Parker and Kyra sat well apart, which was now their habit, without speaking. She read a book, he struggled with his morning Wordle, trying to guess the five-letter daily word in fewer than the six allowed attempts. He got it the third time, which lifted his mood, so he opened his text app and sent Dugan a long string of triangular turd emojis. *He'll know I'm just fuckin' with him, but we need some answers here.*

Just before lunch, Justice Zannis summoned them after receiving a second note. The jury wanted to read the testimony of the prosecution's Columbia witnesses, the ones who recounted Kyra's harsh view of her estranged husband. They also wanted the testimony of the lawyers about the prenuptial agreement and the will. She intended to send them the requested transcripts on an iPad, after first giving counsel the opportunity to see if there is any portion that shouldn't be included.

"This is a bad sign, isn't it?" Kyra said when they were back in the defense conference room.

"No," Parker answered. "There is absolutely no way to tell. Believe me. I gave up years ago trying to interpret jury notes. You don't know whether it's one juror wanting to check before acquitting or a split jury fighting over everything, or a juror who won't vote to convict without hearing something again. You just can't tell. I know it's torture, but you've got to stop yourself from reading tea leaves or whatever."

"Kinda hard," she said.

"Very," he replied, turning back to the iPad, before stopping again. "Now, if we get a chance to see them when they come back in, maybe at the end of the day, then we can get a read. Faces, body language, that kinda thing. But not until then."

He finished with the iPad. "No issues here," he said and walked out to return it to the clerk.

They heard nothing more from the jury until five thirty, when the foreperson sent a note requesting to leave at six P.M. and asking whether they would be deliberating over the weekend if they weren't finished the next day, which was Friday.

After reading the note aloud, Justice Zannis said, "I'll bring them back in here just before six. At that time, I'll explain that we will not be deliberating on Saturday or Sunday, but will resume Monday at nine, if necessary."

As they waited in the courtroom at the defense table, Parker leaned over to Kyra's ear and whispered. "Forget what I said earlier, because it wasn't entirely right. This is a sign—that they are starting to get stuck—and they can see it's gonna be a long slog. Guessing is dangerous, but the way this case has gone—and the bad mojo from the alternates—I'm still betting most of them want to convict you but somebody, or somebodies, is holding them up. I'm praying it's our gallery woman, Juror Seven."

At six P.M., the jury returned to the courtroom so Justice Zannis could deliver her normal admonitions and answer their weekend question. It was hard to read anything from their expressions. None of them looked at the prosecution or defense tables. They nodded along with the judge, then got up and left for the evening.

Back in the defense room, Parker texted a long string of middle-finger emojis to Dugan.

Jessica hung up the phone and spoke loudly enough for Nora to hear next door. "Starbucks update. Maybe something, maybe not."

Nora leaned in through the door. "Do tell."

"We can put Gina at a Miami airport Starbucks one time near a date on the hit list. Because she used points to pay for her drink. Probably didn't even think about it. So Miami is working with the airport to see if they can find her flight. The hit around then was in Chicago and there's a million of those flights, but they're working it."

"Okay," Nora said, turning back to her office.

"But wait, there's more, as they say. The South Florida regional security guy for Starbucks is, shockingly, retired FBI. Apparently, he was struck by what she ordered. Grande Frappuccino with a biscotti cookie blended into it. And she also got one pump of white mocha syrup in it."

Benny made a face. "Jesus, that ain't coffee. Sounds like fuckin' Dairy Queen."

"I don't know about coffee," Jessica said. "But I do know the security guy said that's a really unusual drink—off their 'secret' menu—and he thought he could pull a short list of every time it's been ordered at a Miami airport Starbucks going back to the beginning of Benny's list. If it's Gina's regular order, we may really get lucky."

Five hours later, Jessica and Benny came through her office door, the giant behind the FBI agent, both with arms overhead. Benny pulled his arms down so he could clear the doorway, but then raised them again.

"What?" Nora asked. "We got something from Starbucks?"

Benny started to speak, then stopped and turned to Jessica with mock seriousness. "Would you like to brief our colleague?"

"With pleasure," Jessica said with a faint British accent. In a normal voice, she continued, "We got that Biscotti Frappuccino with a single white-mocha pump ordered a few days before almost every hit, including D'Amico and Governor Burke. Every damn one except the Atlanta hit. It's her drink! We got this bitch, and her fancy-pants Starbucks secret-menu shit. We got her. Now Miami is all over the saved airport camera coverage, watching her walk with her secret drink. Only a matter of time before we put her on flights, collect the flight manifests to find the common passenger, and figure out the name she uses. We'll know fast. Bam."

CHAPTER TWENTY-SEVEN

I t was cold and raining on Friday morning. *I hate this place*, Parker thought, taking the five stairs into the criminal courts building, holding his umbrella high enough to give both him and Kyra some coverage. Inside the defense conference room, they took their normal seats on opposite sides of the room and he pulled out his phone. Nothing from Dugan. *C'mon man, I know you're workin' hard but gimme something.* He texted one red heart emoji and a question mark. Having sent positive thoughts to Benny, he started his Wordle. Six tries later, the day was ruined. *VIVID? Seriously? Who the fuck would go with a double-V word with a double-I too? Pricks.*

The jury asked for more testimony transcripts and then sent another note, this time asking whether they would be deliberating all of Thanksgiving week if they didn't reach a verdict.

Justice Zannis looked up after reading it. "I intend to send in a short answer—'Yes, except for Thanksgiving Day itself.'"

Parker was on his feet.

"Your Honor, I'd be concerned about anything from the court that unduly pressured the jury. Perhaps you could just tell them you will discuss their schedule with them early next week, if necessary?"

"I appreciate that, Mr. Parker, but I don't think being candid about their need to commit to deliberation is pressuring them. So overruled. Send the jury my response."

At the end of Friday, again around six P.M. at the foreperson's request, Justice Zannis returned them to the courtroom to repeat her "don't read the news" instruction, because they would be going home for the weekend. They didn't look good. Eleven of the jurors were stone-faced, most with arms crossed. Juror 7 was pale and red-eyed and looked like she had been crying, darting her eyes to Kyra before looking back at Justice Zannis.

Stay strong, lady, stay strong! Parker screamed inside.

When the jury was gone and they were alone, Kyra looked at him and raised both eyebrows. "Again," he answered, "it's dangerous to read too much into this stuff, but I'm starting to get a hang feeling. There's an old expression—*An ill wind blows through courthouses on Friday afternoons, bringing with it convictions.* If they didn't convict you this afternoon, I'm feelin' better. Course we got the pressure of Thanksgiving comin' up. But you saw our juror, right? She's in there fightin' for you. So let's get some rest this weekend and think good thoughts."

His mood lifted, he texted thinking-face emojis to Benny.

Jessica hung up the phone and raised her voice. "Mildred Jamison. That's our Gina. Check your email, both of you. We got her flying to and from on eleven of Benny's twelve hits."

Benny turned away from her to look at his computer screen, which now showed Mildred Jamison's driver's license photo. "Specfucking-tacular. Next move is to focus on our two—The Nose and the guv. Can we put her at the scene?"

"Exactly," Jessica said. "We got a dozen agents and analysts working that now, seeing if we can take her from the airport here to the hit. But it may be easier than it seems."

"How so?" Nora had finished reading her email and was now in the doorway.

"Just like she uses the same fake ID for all the hit travel, it looks from the airline records like she's traveling with the same burner phone while hers stays home in Palm Beach Gardens. And her mistake is that she has Google on the burner."

Nora and Jessica looked at each other and smiled.

"What?" Benny asked. "Why's that matter?"

Nora nodded to let Jessica take it. "Because Google's whole business is advertising, they work very hard to know where you and your phone are at all times, so they can give you the right headlines, the right weather, and suggest the right purchases for you. With the right *court order*, they can give *us* a moving map of the device's past travel."

Nora was so excited she had to jump in. "You know we can get stuff from historical cell-tower information, but Google's data is much more precise. They can give us a fricking movie showing the little dot moving. We can see where she goes like we were in a drone overhead that day."

"Holy shit," Benny said. "I'm almost starting to feel sorry for the bad guys. Almost."

On Monday morning, the jury asked for what amounted to the rest of the testimony in the case. That took some time because there were objections and sidebars to remove, but they got it. In the afternoon, they asked for a copy of the court's definition of "beyond a reasonable doubt." At four P.M., they followed with a note reading, "Justice Zannis, we regret that we are unable to reach a verdict."

Parker rose from behind the defense table. "Yes, Mr. Parker?" Justice Zannis asked.

"Judge, after this long of a period of deliberation, you can't give them a deadlock charge. It would be coercive, and the defense would strenuously object."

"Mr. Kwon?"

Andy Kwon rose slowly. He was tired and frustrated. "Your Honor, the People request the charge, which the Court of Appeals has said is not coercive but instead an important public service to avoid wasting taxpayer resources on a retrial."

Justice Zannis didn't hesitate. "Mr. Parker, I understand the strategy behind your objection. But Mr. Kwon is right that the Court of Appeals strongly encourages the use of a supplemental instruction to remind the jurors of the need, if possible, to reach unanimity because the case will have to be retried in any event by jurors no more qualified than they are. So your objection is overruled. But I will ensure the instruction is appropriately balanced. Please bring in the jury."

The situation was obvious once the twelve were in the box. Eleven of them seemed to lean away from Juror 7, who was sitting with a straight back and crossed arms. She now looked furious, not sad. Justice Zannis began reading, glancing up and down and urging the jury to try again to reach a verdict. She paused at the end, as if she wanted them to not miss the finish. The pause went on so long that all eyes in the courtroom went to her. Then she continued, with emphasis that was not in the written sample instruction she was reading.

"I want to emphasize that I am *not* asking *any* juror to violate his or *her* conscience, or to abandon his or *her* best judgment. Any verdict you reach *must* be the verdict of each juror, and *not* mere acquiescence to the conclusion of others."

Parker could swear she looked directly at Juror 7 while reading that part.

"So, please return to the jury room. I'm asking you to continue deliberating and resume your deliberations with an open mind."

The jury stayed until six P.M. before going home, without a note. Reporters rushed from the courtroom to get their phones from security so they could tweet new headlines: KILLER KYRA HUNG JURY? and LUV GUV CASE JAM.

Parker didn't text Benny.

CHAPTER TWENTY-EIGHT

"T his'd be some place to watch a ball game," Benny said. He, Nora, and Jessica were seated before a wall of TV screens at the FBI's New York Field Office, just across Foley Square from the Thurgood Marshall courthouse. The Staff Operations Specialist finished typing on the podium keyboard and looked up. "Okay, here we go," he said. "This is Google data from Saturday, September 14, the day before the Dominic D'Amico killing."

They sat mesmerized as the dot representing Mildred Jamison—Gina Cufaro—moved smoothly from LaGuardia airport to locations in Brooklyn before stopping for the night at an apartment building in the borough's Bay Ridge neighborhood. Sunday morning, the dot went to the Caffè Giardino on Eighteenth Avenue in Brooklyn. About an hour later, the dot returned to the airport.

"Kinda chilling, actually," Benny said. "So she whacked him at Giardino. Makes sense. Couple goombahs musta been given the job of dumping the body, and probably the gun too. And she's gone."

"She go anywhere near Conor McCarthy, that we can tell?" Nora asked.

"No," Jessica answered. "Not that we know yet. But that changes when you go back in time to the Governor Burke hit. Watch."

The specialist leaned toward the keyboard again and soon they were watching Google's version of Gina's early spring visit. As before, the dot moved from the airport—Newark this time—to various spots in Brooklyn, before stopping for the night in Manhattan, at the Lucerne Hotel at Seventy-Ninth Street and Amsterdam Avenue.

"Shit, she could almost see Burke's apartment from the Lucerne," Benny said. "Three blocks, tops."

"Yup," Jessica answered, "and she had company that night. We can't show both dots on this graphic right now, but Conor goes to the Lucerne and stays the night. Next day, he leaves for his own place, and then this happens with Gina's phone, a little before eight that next night." She gestured to the specialist, who continued the movie. The dot left the Lucerne, moving down Amsterdam to Seventy-Seventh and then east two blocks to Central Park West, where it turned north, going past the museum to Burke's building at Eighty-First. A short time later, the dot retraced the route, going down Central Park West past the museum, then right on Seventy-Seventh to Amsterdam and back up to the hotel. The next morning, the dot returned to Florida.

The room was silent when the movie finished. After several beats, Nora broke the quiet with a loud exhale. "Wow," she said, turning to Benny. "*Now* you go to bat with Conor. We need to talk to that weasel."

"Maybe just a little longer," Jessica said. "We want to see if we can bring this movie to life. NYPD did a video canvas after the murder but came up empty because there's nothing in front of the museum and they didn't know where to start. We know exactly where she started and when she walked to and from the building. We know what she looked like in the lobby . . ."

"Yeah," Nora said, "like Kyra Burke."

"Right, but we want to see if we can pick her up on video getting in and out of the Kyra getup. There are all kinds of cameras in front of doors along the route she walked. It's unlikely she left the hotel or went back in looking like the killer, so she must have whipped on the scarf and glasses—and maybe the blonde wig—as she walked. We may be able to see it. Agents are out now knocking on doors of homes and businesses all along those blocks to get a look at their cameras. And we're hitting the MTA because all the city buses have forward-looking cameras. I'm hoping we catch her costume change."

CHAPTER TWENTY-NINE

Tuesday morning was clear, but raw and windy. As he climbed the five stairs, Parker sent up a silent prayer. *PLEASE let this be over today.*

The jury was quiet until four P.M., when the foreperson signed their final note: "We the jury are unable to reach a verdict, despite our very best efforts."

"Zannis can't give a second deadlock charge," Parker said to Kyra, with a big grin. "This thing is done."

Kyra didn't share his enthusiasm. "For now," she answered glumly.

Justice Zannis took the bench and repeated to the courtroom exactly what Parker told Kyra. She couldn't push a deadlocked jury twice without being guilty of coercion. She recalled the jury to thank them for their service and send them home for Thanksgiving.

In the box, the division was again obvious. Eleven jurors kept their eyes locked on the judge, with a few adding an apologetic glance at Andy Kwon. Number 7 looked directly at Kyra, a tired but satisfied look on her face. *I saved you*, her face seemed to say. *I alone rescued you.*

When the jury was gone, Justice Zannis addressed Kwon. "Do you have any applications, Mr. Kwon?"

Kwon quickly stood and was clearly angry, speaking louder than necessary. "Yes, Your Honor. The District Attorney intends to retry this case as soon as the court gives us a date, and we ask that the defendant be detained pending retrial. She has now seen the strength of the prosecution's case and surely knows she narrowly avoided conviction. Her incentive to flee has increased immeasurably. Only with her at Rikers Island can the People of New York be sure we will have a retrial."

At the word *Rikers*, Kyra took a sharp breath and put her hand on Parker's arm. He began to stand, but Justice Zannis held up her palm to stop him. "No, Mr. Parker, no need," she said calmly. "Mr. Kwon, I believe your application to be ill founded. This defendant has had a clear view of the evidence ever since you provided the required pretrial discovery. There were few surprises at this trial, at least to my understanding. Your failure to convict surely doesn't *increase* her incentives to flee. The conditions of release will remain in effect."

Justice Zannis stopped for a moment, before adding, "With the additional condition of an electronic monitoring bracelet for Mrs. Burke."

Smart, Parker thought. *She's worried the DA will appeal on bail. Hard for them with the addition of electronic monitoring.* He decided not to fight the bracelet. He could explain it to Kyra. Parker tried to meet Kwon's eye before exiting the courtroom, but Kwon was having none of it. He gathered his files and left without a word or a nod. *Kid's gotta learn. Never let the other side see your emotions, because that equals weakness.*

Back in the defense room, he was surprised when Kyra gave him a long hug and held it, thanking him again and again. She didn't even ask about the monitoring thing, but he explained how it would work anyway. "I'll put Columbia's campus in the judge's order as a place you're permitted to go. And get me the address of the South Bronx mentoring place you talked about."

"Oh," Kyra answered, "that isn't necessary. I said I *started* it but I just got too busy to keep it going. And the city has lots of programs for kids. So Columbia is fine."

Parker paused but he was too tired to follow up. "Just go home and stay there for now. Avoid the press, avoid everybody, and don't talk to anyone you don't completely trust." Then he grabbed his phone and sent Benny a long string of kissy-face emojis before heading out to the gauntlet of media, and a few stiff drinks.

They were back in the FBI conference room and Benny was whispering to Nora as the technicians set up. "Ya know, I badmouth the Bu from time to time, but when they put their minds to something, especially if it's some tech shit, they are unfuckingbelievable."

Nora gave him a kind look and faced forward as the show began. The FBI had assembled a movie from dozens of camera clips. There was no sound, but somehow that made it more chilling to watch Gina get in the elevator on her floor at the Lucerne Hotel, her hair already covered by a blonde wig, ride to the lobby, and walk out to the street. She strolled as if enjoying an after-dinner walk on a Manhattan evening, her hands in the deep pockets of her black Prada gabardine raincoat. When she reached Seventy-Seventh Street, she paused in front of a store window, pulling a blue Hermès scarf from her pocket. Looking directly at the camera, which recorded her as if behind a two-way mirror, she faced the glass to knot the scarf under her chin, tugging gently at the wig with gloved hands to ensure the blonde hair still showed. Next, she removed Jackie O sunglasses from her pocket and put them on before continuing her stroll. Down two blocks to Central Park West, she turned and headed past the museum to Burke's building. For that section of the walk, camera coverage was less complete, but she soon appeared in the now-familiar footage passing Mr. Ramirez.

Several minutes later, she left, raising the gloved hand to acknowledge Ramirez's greeting and walking south on Central Park West. The camera coverage of the route past the museum was again limited, but a city bus camera captured her near the spot where the bronze equestrian Teddy Roosevelt once looked over Central Park. At that moment, she smoothly pulled the scarf from her head and removed the glasses, returning them to her raincoat pocket.

The movie became more complete when Gina reached Seventy-Seventh Street and its many doorways, and they watched her make her way back to the Lucerne. The next morning, a now brown-haired Gina departed the hotel. She and her dot went back to Miami and the presentation ended.

"Okay, now I'm up with Conor, right?" Benny asked.

"Yep. It's time to bring him in," Nora said. "Let's go back and game that out."

As they stood, her phone buzzed and she looked down. "So there's some good news for the American justice system," she said.

"What?" Benny asked.

"News alert from the *Times*. Kyra Burke, a person we now *know* to be innocent, didn't actually get convicted. Just close. Hung jury. But the DA has already announced his intention to retry."

Jessica leaned in with a grim smile. "Innocent *white* people getting prosecuted? Wow. Who says things don't change in this country?"

Neither Nora nor Benny could figure out the appropriate reply to that, so they walked to the elevators in silence. As they rode down, Dugan looked at his phone and smiled. Matty Parker really did have a gift for emojis.

CHAPTER THIRTY

I t was late on Tuesday evening by the time they finished briefing unit chief Carmen Garcia. "That's some nice work," she said, looking at Jessica. "You okay if I call over there and thank the Bu leadership for all of this?"

Benny spoke before Jessica could answer. "Sure, and would be nice if you made it clear that our rookie here has been driving the FBI bus."

"Uh, actually," Jessica said, "I appreciate that, Benny, I really do, but one of my instructors at Quantico told us about the 'tall-poppy syndrome,' where the tall ones get cut down first. Think the idea comes from Australia, but we have the same thing in the Bu, he said. Do the work, but don't stick your head up, especially early."

Benny shrugged. "What a fucked-up organization."

"Got it," Carmen said. "No tall poppies. But I'm still gonna call. So what's next, squad?"

Nora took that one. "Next big item is the Conor interview. We got some more stuff coming in from the tech companies on both him and Gina, but we have enough to go at him. We're thinking Monday. That'll give me a chance to get a warrant for his phone and a grand-jury subpoena to hand him if he tells us to go screw."

Carmen nodded and looked at the tired team. "Makes sense. So let me issue a direct order. It's Thanksgiving, so go home. Hug somebody, eat lots of good stuff, drink responsibly, sleep. Get away from this case for a few days. It'll make you better."

"I guess I don't work for you," Jessica answered, "but I'm gonna follow that order anyway. Flight early tomorrow to San Fran to see my family. Back Sunday."

"And you two?" Carmen asked, nodding her head at Nora and Benny on the couch.

"The great feast of Hoboken awaits," Nora answered. "And, it's good that you're seated to hear the news that Mr. Rough here is actually going to spend Thanksgiving with his family."

Carmen made a face of mock surprise.

"You two are hilarious," Benny said. "Dinner with my two boys, them and theirs. I'm bringing whiskey, wine, and presents for the granddaughter. Been a while, and that's on me, but I'm lookin' forward to it. Bunny would want me to figure out this grandfather thing, and I guess it's better late than never."

They knew who he meant. "Bunny" was Benny's nickname for his wife, Moira. He was the only person she let call her that, and he started doing it in the eighth grade at St. Cecilia, when he began his quest to convince her, as he said, "to marry way, way down." She had relented and they'd raised two sons in Brooklyn. Of course, Benny also liked to say, "She raised two sons while I was out on surveillance." And when a stroke killed her without warning and Benny was dealing with a broken heart, their boys drifted away from him.

The room was awkwardly silent as the three women weighed and then passed on follow-up questions, deciding on smiles and nods of support.

Nora broke the silence, "What about you, Carmen?"

"It's just gonna be a quiet holiday for the three of us this year. Thankful for no traveling. Okay, team," Carmen said, standing, "eat, drink, and be merry. See you Monday. Hit me on my cell if you need anything."

"Got it," Nora said as she got off the couch. "I hope you and Marguerite and Eli have a wonderful Turkey Day." Then pointing at the ceiling, she added, "You still don't see a need to brief up there?"

"Not yet," Carmen said. "We're close, but let's wait to make that call until after you've seen the whites of Conor's eyes."

"Got it. Happy Thanksgiving."

On Park Avenue in Hoboken, Sophie's paper turkey creation was still taped to the fridge, although it was drooping quite a bit. Nora quietly pulled a yogurt and a beer from the fridge and sat on a stool at the counter. She heard her mother's slippers gently slapping into the kitchen.

"Hey baby-girl, another late night for justice, huh?"

"Yeah, Ma, but I'm here for the whole long weekend."

"That's wonderful, Nora. Sophie will be over the moon." She paused, then added, "You know Nick's gonna be here tomorrow night and Friday."

"Sure, like every year," Nora said. "We each get at least two days here at Thanksgiving, no matter whose week it is."

"Yeah, course. I only bring it up because he's gonna have Vicki with him."

When Nora didn't reply, Teresa added, "So there's that."

Nora chuckled. "Ma! You're killing me. Can we talk about it tomorrow? I promise I'll feel all the feels when we're making pies. But tonight, I'm just too tired. And my bug is gonna jump on me at dawn."

"Sure, sure," Teresa said. "Tomorrow, we feel." She came around the counter and hugged her daughter, wrapping her arms around her from behind. "But you do have to feel, at some point."

"Great, Mom. Sleep tight."

"And you. Sweet dreams."

Sophie was still in her pajamas, perched on a stool at one end of the counter, headphones on, watching *Frozen* on an iPad for the thousandth time. She couldn't hear herself chewing on her toaster waffle. The rest of the counter was covered in pie-making paraphernalia—a mound of freshly peeled green apples waiting to be cut into eighths, rhubarb stalks about to be chopped, moist crust laid on wax paper, mixing bowl at the ready. Nora's mother reached for the remote control with a flour-covered hand and increased the volume on the little TV by the coffeemaker. The Macy's Thanksgiving Day Parade now shouted at them.

"Ma, she can't hear anything with those headphones on," Nora said.

"I know, I know," her mother replied, not changing the volume. "So tell me how you're feeling about this Nick-Vicki thing."

Nora shook her head. "Really, I gotta feel before I get a second cup of coffee? And can I at least joke about the name thing? We gonna call him 'Nicki' now?"

Teresa shook her head. "No jokes. We said we'd talk about it this morning. So talk."

Nora sighed. "The most important thing is that Sophie's okay with it, and she seems good. She likes Vicki and is really excited about the wedding and the flower-girl thing. But honestly, I feel weird about it. Vicki seems nice, and it's really not about me and him. I don't care if he has somebody; in fact, it's good that he has somebody. It's not jealousy, at least not in the normal sense. But I actually think I'm jealous that *he* has somebody and I don't. Ma, I worry I'm gonna be alone forever."

Teresa put down her spoon and faced Nora, grabbing her face with two hands. "Hey, hey. First, you'll never be alone. You have me and, most of all"—she nodded to Sophie—"you have that amazing little human . . ."

"I know that, Mom," Nora said, gently grasping her mother's hands and sliding them off her face, leaving white streaks. "It's not that. I just worry I'll never have a partner, like you did, like Nick will. Somebody to lie in bed with at the end of a day, somebody to scratch my back, tell me I'm full of it, make me laugh. You know what I mean. You had that."

Teresa smiled tightly. "I did, and it was the joy of my life. That's the second thing I was gonna say. When your father died, I lost a piece of myself that I'll never get back, because he was what you just said. He was my partner—in everything. And as much as I loved you kids, as much as you were the center of my life—of our life—he brought a joy that nobody else could, and I miss it every day."

They were both crying now. "I want that for you, Nora. You deserve to have that in your life, and you'll make someone else's life so full. I really think you should make time to focus on that, on trying to find that person. I hear about these apps—where Nick met Vicki, you know."

Nora cut her off. "Ma, stop. I can't get advice about dating apps from you. Please. Too creepy. But I get what you're saying."

"Good," Teresa said, returning to pie-making. They were quiet for a few moments, the kitchen filled with the sound of someone loudly lip-syncing from a Sesame Street float in front of the landmark Macy's. Then Nora spoke without looking up from the crust she was pressing into the glass pie pan.

"One of my problems, Ma, is that I'm not sure what I'm looking for."

"What does that mean?" her mother asked.

Nora took two deep breaths before answering. "When I was in high school, it was me and Nick, me and Nick, all the time. I liked him, but I never felt what I always thought I was supposed to feel, and I figured that was it. Seen too many movies, right? But when I got to Fairfield, I met a girl from another school. She was cool, smart, fun, and really pretty too. The more I got to know her, the more I started to feel the things I didn't with Nick. It was really confusing. She kissed me kinda casually once and I felt so much it actually scared me.

"I'm not sure I even realized what I was feeling until she ghosted me—stopped calling, emailing, just gone. It crushed me. I think I was falling in love with this girl. I'm not sure she felt it, but I sure did, especially as I look back at it. I've never had anything else like that, college, law school, ever. And, yeah, I had Sophie with Nick—which I'm so glad about, best thing that ever happened to me—but even the 'having'—if you get me—didn't feel good the way I thought it would. I never thought of myself as gay or bi, but I guess I am, and I still feel confused, all these years later. If I'm honest with myself, I think maybe I should be looking at women on those apps of yours."

Without warning, Teresa pulled her into a hug and then pushed her away, leaving her hands on Nora's shoulders. Shaking her gently, she said, "You know God made you perfect, right?"

"Thanks, Ma, although I'm not sure who made me besides you and Dad. And I don't think Father Frank would agree with you, and all the homilies I've heard over the years make this harder for me."

Nora sniffled loudly before continuing. "I'll figure it out. But not now. Now I got you and Sophie and this case, but when things settle down a bit, I promise I'll figure it out. I will find my person."

Teresa grimaced. "Well, times are changing and Jesus said we should love and not judge, so I think Father Frank will be just fine and I'll help him get there if he needs it. In the meantime," she began, "I've read great things about this Bumble app—"

Nora cut her off. "Ma, no," she said sharply. "I'm serious. Stop."

Immediately regretting the flash of anger, she added, "But for *you*, that might be just the thing. Finally meet that nice Italian man your parents always thought you should be with. Yeah, I should have thought of this earlier. We should start working on your profile. Piña coladas, getting caught in the rain, not into yoga. That kinda thing."

"Okay, okay," her mother laughed. "No more with the apps. I surrender."

Nora turned serious. "And, you know I couldn't do any of this—single motherhood, job, any of it—without you in my life. I'd be lost without you."

"And me you, baby-girl."

"Now can we turn the fricking parade down? If Al Roker yells at me again I'm gonna scream."

Teresa laughed and reached her floured hand for the remote.

CHAPTER THIRTY-ONE

The Monday after Thanksgiving was always hard for Nora, ending four days of being with Sophie full-time. After walking her to school, she made her way to the PATH train and then to the office in a bit of a daze. As she approached her office door, a booming Brooklyn baritone snapped her out of it. "Nice of you to grace us with your presence, Ms. Smooth. Was beginning to think I would have to solve this thing all by my lonesome."

She leaned into Benny's office with a smile. "Mr. Rough, were you the good person I know you to be this Thanksgiving?"

He gave her a full smile, a rare thing from Benny Dugan. "Indeed I was. A model father and grandfather, if I do say so myself."

"Whoa, hold that thought," Nora said, stepping into her office to put her shoulder bag on her desk. As she came back into Benny's office, she gestured to the empty desk. "Jessica not back yet?"

"She texted they bumped her last night, so she took a later red-eye. Be in this morning." Somehow still sounding cheerful, he added, "How the fuck they bump an armed federal agent? Heads *way* up asses out there."

"You *are* in your happy place, big guy," Nora said. "Tell me and don't leave anything out."

"First, let me say you were totally right," Benny began.

"Always nice to have a story open that way, but go back to the beginning. You went to Cal's place, right?"

Benny had spent Thanksgiving weekend at the home of his eldest son, Calvin, who lived with his wife and their two-year-old daughter in Seaford, a middle-class town on Long Island's South Shore, about thirty miles due east of Benny's office. Benny's younger son, Kenneth, who was still single with no kids, had planned to come down from Boston to join them. Both boys worked in the financial services industry, avoiding the law-enforcement path taken by men in their family for generations. They had been very close to their mother and she had been the glue that had held their family together, but after the stroke killed her, Cal and Ken saw very little of their workaholic father, which had been the pattern anyway.

"I got there Wednesday night," he said, "after Claire was in bed. The boys were there, and Sheila—Cal's wife—"

"I remember," Nora protested. "Go on."

"Right. So we all sat in their living room. I brought a bottle of Jameson and poured us each a glass so we could toast Bunny—this'll be the tenth Thanksgiving without her. They seemed surprised by that, but knocked on their asses by what I did next." He paused.

"What, what?" Nora pleaded.

"Exactly what you told me to do. I just told them the truth. That I had been a shitty father and shoulda been a better husband, that I was so fuckin' sorry for that and I knew I couldn't give them those years back, but that I would do everything I could to make it up to them. That I would be a real dad to them and a real granddad to Claire. That I didn't expect them to accept my words, but I hoped they would see it in my actions and judge me by those."

"Wow. What'd they say?" Nora asked.

"Nothin', for a long time. The boys just looked into the whiskey in their glasses and Sheila looked at me like she was gonna cry. Then Kenny finally said, 'Who the fuck're you? You got a *Mission: Impossible* mask on or some shit?' And he leaned in like he was gonna peel my rubber skin up from the neck. Expose the imposter. We all started laughing and before he could lean back I grabbed him and held on to him. Actually started cryin', saying how sorry I was. Then he cried and Cal cried, and Sheila, well, she was already gone. It was like fuckin' *Oprah* or something."

Nora had tears in her eyes. "Oh, Benny, I'm so happy for you. For them. For all of you."

He looked embarrassed and happy. "Now don't start with how good a person I am. Baby steps."

"Well, maybe you're a little better than you realize." She got up, walked behind his desk and leaned down to hug the big man. He reached up and returned the embrace, pressing two balled fists on her back.

"Geez, there are zero hugs at the FBI," Jessica said loudly, stepping into the room and dropping her bag. "I'm gonna be sad to leave this kind and gentle place."

Nora was now standing awkwardly next to Benny's chair, her face still streaked with tears. "Those case-related tears I should hear about?" Jessica asked.

"No," Nora answered, "Happy tears from hearing what a great Thanksgiving Mr. Rough had. So how was your trip?"

"It was great. It always is, with our crowd. I got to play cool Auntie Jess with the nieces and nephews instead of helping in the kitchen. So a perfect holiday on my end. Exhausted 'cause I can't sleep on planes, but ready to get back to work."

"Is it finally time to talk to that little prick Conor?" Benny asked.

"Yep, see if you can bring him in." Nora said.

Benny had the touch. Somehow he convinced people to "come down-town for a chat" without lawyering up. In the real world, there was no such thing as "taking you in for questioning." There was only "taking you," which required probable cause and an arrest and reading *Miranda* rights, or there was "please come talk to us without a lawyer and say things that we may hang you with." Nora always marveled at Benny's ability to create a world in which people came, voluntarily, and didn't ask for an attorney.

Benny and Jessica were in an elevator headed up to Conor's parents' place. The McCarthys lived on the top floor of a six-story Bronx apart-ment building—an "elevator building" it was called in the old days, in an effort to look down on six-floor walk-ups, of which there were plenty in New York. Conor had spent Thanksgiving weekend at his parents' and, as of noon on Monday, he hadn't left, except to buy some groceries a couple hours after his father had left for his Upper East Side doorman job. Conor's mother stayed home as a rule because her arthritis made it hard to move around. She had long ago retired from her job as a hotel maid.

The team knew where Conor was because Special Surveillance Group teams had been covering him for days. They even had an Airbnb rented just down the hall from the McCarthy's apartment with a thin fiber optic camera snaked into the hallway to give a clear video feed of the door. They knew where he was.

Dugan made it a practice not to go to the homes of mob guys. He would call them and tell them he had a subpoena or needed to ask some questions and offer them the chance to meet him around the corner. It was about letting them avoid embarrassment with the wife and kids, a deposit in the bank of goodwill that led those who later wished to change sides to reach out to Benny. But Conor wasn't some capo. He was a schmuck. With him, Benny wanted to use the potential for embarrassment as leverage.

Benny pressed the large black button beneath the door's peephole, which produced a sad metallic imitation of a doorbell. Violating his training to never stand directly in front of a closed door, he saw the light in the peephole flicker as Conor examined them and apparently decided an enormous white man in a tie and Westport Big and Tall black raincoat and a Black woman in a dark suit were no home invasion threat.

"Can I help you?" he asked after opening the door.

"Maybe," Benny answered. "We're with the United States Department of Justice." Benny and Jessica held up their badges. "We were hopin' to get a chance to have a conversation. May we come in and have a brief chat?"

Conor stiffened, reacting as Benny hoped he would. "Uh, uh, well, my mother is here and she's not well, so I don't think this would be the best venue for a discussion."

Where are you from? Benny thought. *Venue? Discussion? Jesus, man, this is the Bronx.*

Benny could see Conor thinking, so he turned up the heat, moving as if about to enter the apartment. "It'll only take a minute." That did it.

"There must be a better place," Conor said, blocking the way.

"Sure," Benny answered. "You ride with us now to my office and we'll have you done in a jiffy. No need to bother your mom."

Relief washed over Conor's face. "Good, good. Give me a minute to get my things and we'll go." He closed the door to a crack. They could hear him telling his mother he had to go to an important meeting and thanking her for a wonderful Thanksgiving. Then he was at the door, his overnight bag in hand. "I appreciate your patience."

"No problem," Benny replied. "Like I said, this should be quick. When we're through we can drop you wherever you want."

Benny kept up a New York sports monologue the entire ride to the US Attorney's office, reviewing the history of New York baseball and its many stadiums—"Over there's the site of the Polo Grounds. Actually there were four versions of that, going back to the 1800s, where the New York Giants played, until they moved out to your stompin' grounds, Jessica, and the Giants football team played there too"—then moving to more football and basketball—"Did you know the Knicks are named for the original Dutch settlers who were called Knickerbockers for the short pants they wore?" They got to One St. Andrew's before he could turn to hockey to fill the time, and they entered the fourth-floor conference room without one word having been spoken about the reason for their trip.

Nora was waiting for them in the conference room. She was the good cop, the only role available when doing an interview with Benny. Given that this was Jessica's first interview since Quantico role-playing—where professional actors did a very good job of being difficult—she had no assigned role. Nora invited Conor to a chair on one side of the rectangular table, directly across from Benny. Conor put his bag next to his chair and sat, before leaning to one side with a wince and removing his Pop Tart–sized iPhone from his tight pants pocket and setting it on the table. Jessica sat to Benny's left and Nora took the empty chair at his right elbow.

When they were seated, Benny went right at it. The amiable New York sports fan was gone.

"The fuck you doin' at Joey Cufaro's wake with your arm around Gina?"

Conor didn't seem rattled that the game's first pitch was at his head. "I don't know what you mean."

Benny slapped an eight-by-ten color picture on the table, right side up in front of Conor. Stabbing the picture with his thick pointer finger, he said, "That's you. That's Gina. That's Handsome Joey's wake. That's what I mean."

Conor paused before speaking. "Gina is an old friend of mine from the neighborhood. Her father died. I paid my respects. That's what that is."

"You two were an item?"

"We were close, but not steady boyfriend and girlfriend, if that's what you're asking."

"You still close?"

"We stay in touch."

"Like horizontal, no-clothes in touch? Like that?"

"I'm not interested in discussing my personal life with you."

"Well maybe that's where we diverge, then. 'Cause we're very interested in your personal life as it pertains to Gina, and to your professional life as it pertains to Gina."

"What's that supposed to mean?" Conor asked.

"Let's just say we have reason to think there's some overlap there. That your personal connection to Gina may have led to Gina using her professional abilities with your boss, who died as a result of her abilities."

"You're suggesting I killed Tony Burke? That's absurd."

"No, no," Benny replied. "I'm suggesting you *know* who killed Tony Burke, and I want to hear that from you."

"Well, I'm sorry to disappoint you, but I'm not interested in talking to you about Gina, or about Tony Burke's death."

There was an awkward pause. Nora broke it.

"We have a search warrant for your phone," she said, gesturing to the black iPhone on the table in front of Conor.

He grinned, still appearing confident. "Except I'm not required to unlock it for you. I remember that from the news."

Directly across the table, Dugan's face flashed red. He leaned forward abruptly, his massive chest almost on the table. "You little prick, how 'bout this? How 'bout I fuckin'—"

Conor was frozen by the burst of verbal violence. To Dugan's left, Jessica silently reached across and picked up the phone. "Hey Conor," she interrupted, lifting the phone just as he turned his head toward her. The phone clicked open at the face recognition. "Done," she said, looking at Benny, who was confused by what just happened.

Jessica stood, holding the phone. "Gotta get this to our forensic people." She turned toward the door, then paused, looking down at the phone. She turned back to face the table. "Hey, you got WhatsApp on here, Conor. That's smart, 'cause that's end-to-end encrypted so nobody can read those." She waited a beat before adding, "Except somebody who has your phone." Then she was silent, her thumb scrolling and scrolling. Ten seconds later, she said, "Whoa, do you know that this has all your messages back and forth with Gina? Looks like a heck of a story. Gotta save some time, right? Lemme get the tech guys to make a copy real quick." She opened the door and left.

Dugan wasn't tracking all this but he leaned back heavily in the chair and smiled, giving Conor his best satisfied look before adding, "Dumbass." When Jessica returned, Benny spoke again. "Okay, so let's not waste our time. Tell us about you and Gina, and start at the beginning."

And Conor did, for two hours.

When he was finished, Benny asked, "So why would she want to frame Kyra?"

"I'm not sure she did, but it's odd she's dressed like Kyra in those pictures. I also remember how weird she got once when I told her I thought if I couldn't work for Burke's son, then Kyra would be an amazing candidate and I'd love to work for her. She wouldn't speak to me for a while after that. It was bizarre. Gina always had a thing about me and Kyra, going back to Yale. Since we were kids, she's been a jealous woman."

"So you think she kills people for a living?" Benny asked.

"I can't say for sure, but she is a scary, scary person. Gina wasn't always like that, but I know for sure she would kill me if she knew we were having this conversation."

"If it came to it, you'd testify against her?" Nora asked.

"If it came to it, I'd tell the truth. I've looked the other way, sure, but I've never broken the law and I've tried to be a decent public servant. I never should have let myself get used by bad people. So, yes, I will testify if necessary, but I hope like hell it never comes to that."

CHAPTER THIRTY-TWO

The team was back in Carmen Garcia's office in the usual seats—Nora and Benny on the blue couch, Jessica in the side chair. After they finished briefing her on Conor's interview, Carmen leaned back, tented her fingers, and stared at the ceiling.

After five second of silence, Nora asked, "Something wrong?"

Carmen leaned forward, dropping her hands on the desk. "No, no. Just thinking. Trying to figure out how we're gonna navigate two problems—one mine, one yours."

Nora grinned. "Whose you wanna talk about first?"

"Yours for sure," Carmen said, returning the smile. "Much easier than mine. Yours is about how you're gonna connect Gina's hits to the mob so we can prosecute in federal court and not have to hand it off to our good friends at the DA's office or other local prosecutors. Mine is about what I tell him," she said, pointing at the ceiling. "Thoughts on yours?"

"First," Nora said, "no chance we are giving this to anybody, so we *will* find the nexus."

"Nexus?" Jessica asked. "Missed that in class at Quantico."

Carmen took it. "Nearly all murders are charged in state court because Congress only classified certain homicides as *federal* crimes. The one we use all the time in this unit is called 'murder in aid of racketeering.' That requires us to prove the defendant killed somebody either because the mob paid for the hit or because the killers did it to grow or keep their position with the mob. We call that the 'nexus' between the murder and a 'racketeering enterprise'—here, the Mafia."

"Got it, thanks," Jessica said. "So it's not enough to prove Gina murdered Burke and D'Amico and maybe ten others."

"Right," Carmen answered. "Of course, that's a helluva start, and if the jury thinks you've proved that many murders, it's not gonna take a lot to prove the nexus, but you need enough so a judge will let it get to a jury in federal court. Somebody's gotta testify that Gina is not just a killer but a mob killer, and I'm hearing you say that's not Conor."

"Right," Nora answered. "Maybe he's lying, but he says he intentionally didn't learn exactly what she did and for who, and he thought she was going to 'talk' to Burke that night."

Carmen looked at Benny. "You gotta go through your mental Rolodex of mob cooperators. Must be somebody who can testify that Gina's regular gig was killing people for Cosa Nostra. Even somebody from another family."

"Yeah," Benny answered. "Been sitting here doing exactly that. Rolodex is comin' up empty. Nobody ever gave us anything solid on this ghost killer. Just heard rumors it might be a woman. And that she—if it was a she—might be outta Joey Cufaro's world. The Nose was the first who mighta nailed it down for us, and he ate a canary. But lemme think on it."

Now Carmen looked at Nora. "So you need to decide how to make an actual federal murder case on Gina. Conor and the cool tech stuff put her in Burke's place when he died, and that, plus our travel and phone proof, buries her on being a killer. All that is great, but we can't indict without the nexus proof the statute requires.

"Yup," Nora said, "and I thought this was supposed to be the easier problem. Let us chew on it and we'll talk again. Now your problem?"

"Up there," she said, gesturing to the US Attorney's office four floors above hers. "Do I tell him that Conor locks down Kyra Burke's innocence and Gina's guilt? And that, with the digital proof and Conor, we can prove she killed Governor Burke and the DA is full of shit? And that we don't know yet whether we can charge her federally, without the nexus piece?"

She shook her head, looking down from the ceiling. "And what does he do with that information? Does he tell the DA before we're ready? Does he tell us we can't charge it because we aren't ready? And not to get too dark, but we still don't know how it got out that The Nose was cooperating. Simpson was one of the few who knew."

"Yeah," Nora responded, "I don't think we should be too dark on that last piece. Other people knew. The judge, that weird WASPy lawyer friend of the judge . . ." She paused and looked at Benny, giving him the chance to do it first. He took it.

"And, idiot that I am, I told Matthew Parker."

Carmen made a sour face.

"I know, I know," Benny said, holding both palms toward her. "It seems stupid lookin' back, but I trust him. He had your job once and he was representing an innocent person who was almost convicted. I wanted to give him a heads up that we had somethin' going that might help. It was a mistake and it was mine alone. I didn't tell the team 'til after."

"The team?" Jessica said sharply. "You didn't tell *this teammate* until this moment. Yeesh." She turned to Nora, her brow furrowed. "For that matter, neither did you. Some team."

Carmen cut it off. "Okay, okay, you all have some stuff to work out. I don't wanna get stuck in that. Look, I don't know where the leak came from, but it coulda been our man upstairs—I'm not saying he's dirty, but he's definitely a gossip who likes to make himself seem important, and even if there was no bad intent, I don't trust him with confidential information. I just don't know, and that's a heck of a thing to say about the United States Attorney.

"On top of that, if I go to him before we have our ducks in a row, there's a chance he blows the whole thing up. Of course, he's gonna be majorly pissed when I walk in two weeks from now and tell him we're ready to go to the grand jury on a bunch of murders"—pointing at Benny—"because you figured out how to connect them to the mob. Oh, and that includes Tony Burke—the one that ends our relationship with the DA."

She looked at Nora with a wry smile. "If I didn't get $7,000 more per year, plus the couch, I might start to doubt whether taking the promotion to supervisor was worth it. Okay, so go, heal your team, figure out our nexus proof, and then come back to make me happy."

Nora, Benny, and Jessica walked down the long fourth-floor hallway without speaking. As they reached the adjoining doors of their offices, Benny tilted his head toward his office. "Hey, can we have a quick team meeting?"

When they were together, he closed the door, something he almost never did. "Hey," he said, looking at Jessica, "I'm sorry. I fucked up." Then he jabbed a thumb toward Nora. "But don't be mad at her. She didn't tell you because she didn't want to make me look like shit. That wasn't about hurting you. That was about protecting me, which I'm sorry I made necessary."

"But it was still bad of me," Nora interjected. "I should've told you, Jessica, and I'm sorry. We're a team. Won't happen again."

After a long pause, Benny looked at Jessica and asked, "We good?"

"Yes, we're good," she said, then looked at Benny with an impish grin and added, "I know you're just a catty bitch from Brooklyn who lives for drama, but I can do without it."

He boomed his laugh. "Fair enough. Fair enough. And no 'I' in team or whatever."

"Okay, break it up," Nora said. "And you, Mr. Rolodex, by coffee tomorrow we need this problem solved."

"Yes, ma'am," Benny said.

The next morning, Benny was already behind his desk when Nora and Jessica arrived for work. "Mornin' Jessica and Ms. Smooth, thought you two would never get here. It's time for another team meeting!" he shouted when Nora walked into her office.

She dropped her bag and came in smiling, holding the coffee she bought on the plaza. "I was only kidding about you solving it by this morning, Mr. Rough."

He ignored that and looked over at Jessica. "You said you've kept your leadership up to date, right?"

"Yes," she said, "this is the FBI. We brief up or die. That much I know."

"And they're fired up?"

"Totally, all the way up to the ADIC," she said, using the acronym for the Assistant Director in Charge. The New York office was by far the FBI's largest and, unlike most offices—which were headed by a Special Agent in Charge—New York was led by an ADIC—pronounced, despite the irresistible jokes, as "ā-dick."

"Good," Benny said. "We're about to test that enthusiasm. See if you can get an FBI plane for us to use. For tomorrow morning. We're going to New Mexico to visit an old friend. Four of us."

CHAPTER THIRTY-THREE

The Gulfstream G600 twin-engine private jet felt like it was going straight up as it roared away from Teterboro Airport, the general aviation airfield just across the Hudson River in New Jersey. The plane could go as fast as 610 mph and as high as 51,000 feet, so it was a much quicker way to get to Albuquerque than Southwest Airlines, and without TSA security lines or baggage claim carousels. The FBI has dozens of propeller planes that it uses for surveillance, but only a handful of jets, which Congress funds primarily for transporting international criminal suspects and for moving the Director and the Attorney General safely.

Nora sat in one of the big cream-colored leather armchair seats and pressed her forehead against the enormous oval window, watching New York City quickly recede from view. She and Jessica had the four-seat front cabin all to themselves, facing forward, slipping off their shoes to prop their feet on the leather seats opposite each of them. The cockpit door was closed and Benny had also closed the door behind them, to the rear compartment where he was sitting, so they were alone in a world of leather and polished mahogany. Large wall-mounted screens showed the plane's progress superimposed on a digital image of the globe. The picture gradually zoomed in, showing landmarks, before switching to a home-screen photo of the Cleveland Browns football team, then returned to the zooming globe.

After watching the loop—and the Browns—several times, Nora looked across the aisle and gave Jessica a quizzical look.

Jessica knew exactly what Nora's question was. "One of the pilots said we bought the plane from the owner of the team and nobody has figured out how to change it."

Nora shrugged. *Suppose it's not a high priority.*

A black FBI Chevy Suburban drove onto the tarmac at Kirtland Air Force Base, which shared runways with Albuquerque International Airport. It stopped at the G600's stairs to collect the passengers before roaring out, headed into the desert. Not long after they'd left Albuquerque's far suburbs, the vehicle turned off the main road, driving up a long rise. At the crest of the rise, they could see a two-story structure sprawling out below them, down in a wide and desolate valley. This was one of the federal government's prisons reserved entirely for inmates in the Witness Security program.

Even though the jail was full of witnesses for the United States, it was still surrounded by a high double perimeter of concertina wire–topped fencing. "To keep the good guys in and the bad guys out," Benny explained. In fact, he said, the prison was a bit like a fraternity; no new inmate could join unless every current inmate approved of his joining. If an inmate was black-balled as a potential threat, he would have to try one of the other WITSEC facilities. It was a tough place to get into. Benny had been here many times working with witnesses to build mob cases, but this was his first time bringing a guest.

◆

Frenchie looked tan and fit in his prison clothes as he stepped into the room, breaking into a wide grin the moment he saw the mountain that was Benny Dugan. "The big man returns!" Frenchie almost shouted. He began to say something to Nora when a figure slipped from behind Benny's big body, freezing Frenchie with his mouth slightly open. Frenchie's eyes filled with tears, then flashed a worried look. He turned to Benny, searching the big face.

"What's wrong? What happened? Why is he here?"

Then he looked directly at his son and asked, "Why are you here?"

"He's here because we need to ask you to do something hard," Benny said.

CHAPTER THIRTY-FOUR

I t had all been Benny's idea. "I could kick myself," he said as they sat having coffee a day earlier. "We never asked the Frenchman about Gina. Why would we? But we shoulda. When I go back through his file, he *had* to know about her. We just didn't ask, and for reasons I can guess, he never volunteered. But he did stuff with Joey Cufaro's crew, and we also know how tight Frenchie and The Nose were and what a mouth D'Amico had. Dollars to doughnuts, The Nose—and probably other guys he dealt with—told him about Gina."

"And all of it would be admissible evidence," Nora said—for Jessica's benefit. "Statements by coconspirators in furtherance of a conspiracy—even statements about who's who and who does what—are not considered hearsay. When mob people gossip about mob stuff, it comes into evidence. It could be all the nexus we need."

Then Nora started shaking her head. "But I'm getting way, way ahead of myself." Turning to Benny, she asked, "So how're we gonna get Frenchie to tell us about Gina and then volunteer to testify? That seems like a steep hill."

"Very steep," Benny replied. "But I think two things will get it done. First, we explain to Frenchie that Gina is sending an innocent woman to prison for life. Underneath it all, Frenchie is both an honorable guy and sees himself as a bit of a knight. And we show him some pictures of Kyra. He'll like the idea of rescuing a pretty damsel."

Nora and Jessica both rolled their eyes.

"Hey, hey," Benny quickly added, "I'm talkin' about Frenchie, not me. It is what it is."

"Second," he continued, "we reconnect him with his son. It's the right thing to do—something I know from recent personal experience—and hopefully Frenchie will like the idea of showing his boy that he's willing to do something good, especially when it's very hard. The kid is a solid citizen, good job at a big bank. I'm guessing he'll be offended by what's happening to Kyra and will want his old man to help."

Nora chuckled. "That's totally nuts, Benny, and just might work. And it's at least as good as our alternatives, which are none right now. So what's our next step?"

Benny explained that he knew where Frenchie's son worked in lower Manhattan and he proposed to walk over to see him with Jessica, tell him it was a matter of critical national importance, and that an FBI jet was waiting to take them to New Mexico the next morning, where he could help his country convince his father to do the right thing.

It had been two hours since they left Frenchie and his boy, Albert—now a man—alone in the conference room. "What could they be talking about all this time?" Jessica asked, staring into her vending-machine coffee cup.

"Wait 'til you have kids," Benny said, "and basically ignore them for years, then try to put it back together. In a WITSEC jail. On zero notice. It might take a while. But I recommend not doing any of that. Just be a good parent from the get-go."

Jessica nodded in mock seriousness. "Got it."

After another hour, a prison official knocked quietly on their waiting-room door. "He's ready to talk to you."

When they walked into the room, Frenchie and his son were sitting together on the same side of the table, but all the chairs looked disturbed, as if father and son had slowly made their way toward each other, chair by chair.

Frenchie turned toward the team. "Okay, gonna do it, but I don't want him here for the debriefing. Better if he can say he doesn't know what I said about anyone."

"Agreed," Nora answered. "Albert can sit outside and have some lunch while we chat."

"Of course I know about her," Frenchie said when they were settled in the conference room. "She's a stone-cold killer. A lot worse than her old man—who was a vicious fucking bully in his own right, by the way—maybe because she has a chip on her shoulder because she was born a girl and can't get made. I don't know, but it really doesn't matter.

"What matters is that everyone was afraid of her and also wanted her for the toughest jobs. Gambinos even lent her out to other Families, both for money and so the others would owe them. I never met her personally, mind you—she hung out in Florida and violence was not my thing, as you know—but I heard plenty of conversations about her. None of you feds ever asked me about her and everything I know came from talking with mob guys, so it didn't occur to me to bring it up. But hell yes, I heard a lot about Gina. It doesn't surprise me one bit that she whacked the governor and then set up some cutie to take the fall, and then whacked The Nose to protect herself and the mob. Like I said, she is stone-cold."

The room was silent until Frenchie spoke again. "So, now that you convinced Albert I'm some kind of American hero, how do I avoid disappointing him?"

"Not sure," Nora said. "But I think we're going to indict her on a bunch of murders now, including the governor—and The Nose—"

"That cocksucker," Frenchie interrupted, before adding with a smile, "Please excuse my French. May he rest in peace. Go on, go on."

"—and then confront her with the pile of evidence we've got on her—most of which doesn't come from you at all—and see if she'll give it up—"

"Which she won't do," Frenchie interrupted again, "not in a million years. I know I keep saying it, but she's a stone-cold killer with bigger balls than most men. Which means?"

"Which means," Nora answered, "that if there's a trial, we'll need to call you as a witness."

When he didn't respond, she added, "For the last time ever."

Frenchie laughed at that and nodded toward Benny. "Yeah, until Brooklyn Bubba here decides he needs to find out who really killed JFK."

Benny smiled. "You fucker, you been holdin' out on the Kennedys?"

Nora jumped in before it got too far off the track. "Trial sometime early in the new year, probably. Marshals will bring you in, safe house, same drill as before. It'll be easier than it is here to see Albert."

"Yeah," Frenchie said, "about that. I appreciate what you did, connecting me and my boy. I know you did it because you're fucking manipulative sons a bitches, but no matter. I'm glad you did."

"But I gotta ask," Nora said, "what kinda threat to him is Gina once she learns you're a witness?"

Frenchie paused for a moment before answering. "Actually, as strange as it may sound, not much. You have to understand: From everything I heard, this Gina chick is as Cosa Nostra as they come. If she'd been born a dude, she'd be boss of the Gambino Family. She's old school, all about honor and rules, unlike that piece of shit The Nose. And one unbreakable rule for somebody like her is that she doesn't kill civilians, and Albert's a civilian. Now, she'd kill *me* in a New York second. Resurrect me and kill me twice if she could. She'd whack the governor if he was in bed with them and trying to screw the Family somehow. That's all business. But it doesn't make me worry more about a civilian like Albert."

"I hear ya, Frenchie," Benny said, "but I still think we offer WITSEC to your boy again. Or at least some kinda lighter protection."

"I appreciate you thinking about it," Frenchie said. "Don't want him worrying, and maybe he'll be interested in seeing me more. And speaking of seeing me more, anything you can do to cut my state time if I testify?"

"Maybe. That's the most I can honestly say," Nora answered. "You provide truthful testimony here and we'll ask the state to reduce your sentence. But you should know our relationship with the DA is not great, and this case is part of the problem between us for reasons I can't go into. So I doubt they're going to feel charitable. Course, there's always a possibility the current governor could commute your sentence, but that's way down the road. Too long an answer, but don't assume we can get it done."

"As always," Frenchie replied, "I appreciate your candor. But I've seen the rabbits you feds can pull out of hats, so I won't give up hope."

"Great," Nora said, switching topics. "Now that we're all the way out here, we can spend some time and go over the details on what you heard about Gina. From who, where, when, that kinda stuff. You okay with that?"

Frenchie nodded and the work began.

CHAPTER THIRTY-FIVE

United States Attorney Freddy Simpson seemed irritated to be meeting on the case again. "I thought I told you to handle it however you thought appropriate," he said, staring at Carmen Garcia as she finished her briefing.

Simpson and Carmen sat in oxblood leather wing chairs facing each other across the length of a coffee table, which rested on a different rug now. Nora, Benny, and Jessica were squeezed together on the couch down the long side of the rectangular table, like tennis fans watching a match between the two leaders. As tight as it was, though, Benny still managed to get comfortable, resting his left ankle atop his right knee, holster and gun visible on his sockless lower leg.

Nora was looking down, avoiding the angry glare of their boss. *New rug doesn't tie the chairs and carpet together nearly as well as Georgene's stolen rug did*, she thought.

"Yes, sir," Carmen answered, "you did, but we're about to take a significant new step with this indictment. This will be the United States Department of Justice saying the DA is prosecuting an innocent person. I didn't know whether you wanted to give the DA any kinda heads-up or anything before we launched."

Simpson's eyes swept the room, pausing almost imperceptibly on Benny's ankle. "You've already told them we think they have it wrong, as I recall."

"Yes," Carmen said, "and they were, uh, uninterested in what we had to say. But in fairness, our case against Gina Cufaro has gotten a lot stronger since then. I could imagine them agreeing to not retry Kyra Burke if they saw all our evidence, maybe even wanting to do a joint announcement with you."

That seemed to flip a switch in Simpson. "*They* might want to do a joint public announcement that *we* have brought to justice the most notorious Mafia killer of the modern era? After they indicted, tried, and intend to retry an innocent woman for that killer's work? I'll be damned if I'm going to let Henry Stern film another ad for his reelection. He's in a one-party town anyway. More likely to be an oppo ad against me someday."

Carmen wasn't following this. "Sir?" she asked.

"Forget it, forget it," Simpson said quickly. "Just thinking out loud. Go and indict it. Get a draft of the indictment and some talkers to the press office and we'll schedule my press conference."

They filed out of the United States Attorney's office in silence, although Benny couldn't resist turning his head to Georgene and mouthing "Nice rug." She beamed but said only, "Have a nice day!" as the four of them went out into the hall and down the fire stairs to four.

CHAPTER THIRTY-SIX

T he FBI's Miami Field Office in Miramar, Florida, occupied one of the few architectural gems among modern federal office buildings. Named for Special Agents Benjamin Grogan and Jerry Dove, who were killed by bank robbers during a 1986 shootout, the undulating glass sides of its two connected six-story office towers seemed to rise out of the Everglades, somehow making the secretive agency literally transparent. But Benny Dugan wasn't looking around at the architecture. Everybody was too pissed at him.

FBI ops-plan meetings are usually straightforward. The SWAT Team Leader presents the written plan to the investigative team and office leadership, with arrest tactics driven by risk. Here, given that Gina Cufaro was a contract killer, the plan called for a major SWAT presence to execute the arrest warrant at her Palm Beach Gardens residence. They would hit her front door at six A.M. without knocking—under authority granted by a federal judge—utilizing an explosive door breach, flash-bangs, a robot, and a canine. Sniper overwatch teams would cover all windows and doors.

The plan briefing was met with nods all around the large conference room until a deep Brooklyn voice from the back ruined the meeting. "Big mistake, if you'll excuse my sayin' so." The team from

New York was here as a courtesy. Responsibility for executing the arrest was Miami's, because it was their people who would be at risk.

"She's killed a lot of people," Benny continued, "but she ain't gonna hurt law enforcement, unless she doesn't realize it's us. You go in that heavy, wakin' her up and all, explosions and such, she may react like it ain't us. Then it goes sideways in a hurry. Plus, you put something in the goodwill bank if you treat wise guys like the honorable people they like to pretend they are. Flipped a lot of guys by giving them a little rope in spots like this."

The Team Leader—"TL" in FBI-speak—was professional but cold. "And so you would do what, exactly?"

"I would call her cell when we're outside, give her a chance to get dressed, get her hair and makeup right, then have her open the front door and walk out with me."

"A subject with a dozen bodies on her," the TL said. "A subject with a known facility with weapons of all types. That's your recommendation? And your consideration of officer safety is where, exactly?"

"Look," Benny said. "I know you got history. I respect and honor that history. I hate that this building is named for those two good guys. I hate that you lost two more in that child porn case in '21. I really do. And I respect your skill. You know tactics like nobody's business. No disrespect at all. But I know Cosa Nostra. I know how they think. Gina thinks she is a *uomo d'onore*—a 'man of honor'—even though she's a *donna*, a woman. The rules matter to her: No killing with explosives, no killing civilians, and no killing law enforcement, ever.

"I know you're sittin' there thinkin' we'll have a barricade situation if we call her out. We won't. We will put fewer of you guys at risk. And we gain somethin' with her that may be useful down the line: we let her walk out in front of her neighbors the way she wants to be seen."

The room was silent. "And I will walk up to that door, alone," Benny added. "If it's gonna break bad, it will break bad right in my face. I'm not askin' anybody else to take that chance."

The TL seemed to admire that last bit. "Roger that," he said. "Let me talk to our bosses. We'll let you know."

Gina's cell rang five times before a groggy voice came through Benny's speaker phone.

"What?"

"Gina Cufaro, this is Special Agent Benny Dugan with the US Attorney's office in Manhattan. Can you hear me okay?"

"Yeah, yeah," she said, coming awake. "Whataya want?"

"I'm actually outside your place right now, with just about the entire Miami FBI. We have a warrant for your arrest. They're gettin' ready to hammer down your door and drag you out. But I wanted to offer you a few minutes to get yourself together and come meet me at the front door. Do this like pros insteada like some fuckin' drug dealer gettin' pulled from a house. Whaddaya say?"

There was a long pause. "I know you, Dugan. You been around. Amiright?"

"Long time," Benny answered. "Go way back with your old man. Since you were a kid."

"Thought so." Gina was fully awake now. "No need for the army here. Gimme five, maybe ten, and I'll meet you at the door."

"And, hey," Benny added, "no fuckin' with any evidence inside."

"As if," Gina answered and hung up.

Benny looked at the TL, who was standing looking down at Benny's phone. "We good?" Benny asked.

"We're good. But we're gonna have red dots on her the moment she opens that door. She threatens you, she dies there."

Benny made a tight smile. "Appreciate the concern. But I think we're gonna be okay."

Nine minutes later, Gina's front door opened several inches, then paused as she peeked out at the massive Dugan before opening all the way. In heels, gray dress pants, a matching jacket, and a blue blouse, with her hair and makeup flawless, Gina looked ready for a day showing homes to buyers. *Why the hell do they always say they need an hour to get ready?* Benny thought.

"Hey," Benny said, "got your whole neighborhood out here gawkin'. How 'bout we step inside and I cuff you?" He gestured to the suit jacket she was wearing. "I'll do it in front and we can put that over the cuffs so nobody sees 'em."

"I appreciate that," Gina said, shrugging the jacket off.

Moments later, Benny and a well-dressed woman holding a jacket in front of her walked down the front steps and slipped into the back seat of an unmarked FBI Ford Explorer driven by a SWAT agent, with the TL in the passenger seat, and they were gone.

"Do you understand these rights as I have explained them to you?" Benny asked after giving Gina her *Miranda* warnings in the back seat.

"I do," she said, "and I'm grateful for your courtesy just now, but I'm not saying a fucking word"—it came out *woid*, her New York accent strong now. "I wanna speak to my lawyer"—*law-yah*—"Salvatore Butler."

Benny chuckled. "Sal's your guy? Shoulda figured. You know he represented The Nose, right? Don't know whether he'll have feelings around now representing the person who, uh, ended that particular engagement. But I'll call him while you're gettin' processed by the Bu."

Gina didn't react to any of this, staring straight ahead as they drove toward the West Palm Beach FBI branch office—called a Resident Agency or "RA"—where she would be fingerprinted and photographed before being taken to federal court.

"Sal, Benny Dugan here."

"Benny!" Butler boomed, as loud and theatrical on the phone as he was in court. "My old friend. You in trouble? Need quality legal representation?"

Benny laughed. "God forbid, Sal. Nah. Down here in south Florida. Just locked up Gina Cufaro on an indietment outta my office up there. Gave her *Miranda* and she said she wanted to talk to her attorney, who is you."

"What're the charges?"

"Whole lotta murders for somethin' called Cosa Nostra. Maybe you heard of it?"

"A creation of Hollywood and ambitious prosecutors, my friend. You know that. This so-called maf-eye-ah."

Benny laughed again. He always got a chuckle out of Butler's practiced denial of Cosa Nostra and his intentional mispronunciation of *Mafia*.

"Save it for the courtroom, Sal. You representing her or not?"

"Well, that will depend upon whether she and I are able to achieve a certain meeting of the minds, a certain symbiosis"—he drew out each syllable so it came out *sym-bye-oh-siss*—"a certain—"

Benny cut him off. "Got it, Sal. Just so you can relax, she's got a lotta dough. Should buy a lot of mind-meeting."

"Then we should be able to achieve that necessary symbiosis, my friend. I'm optimistic, in that event."

"Before you get too deep into your symbiosis, you should know that one of the murders she's charged with is The Nose."

Butler paused before saying, "And why should that concern me?"

"Well, you may remember that the guy was your client, before she shot him twice in the forehead and stuffed a canary in his mouth. Thought you might have some feelings around that."

"None whatsoever," Butler replied quickly. "You will recall that Mr. D'Amico at the time was engaged in a misguided attempt to save himself by making patently false statements about other alleged members of the so-called maf-eye-ah. An effort of which I had absolutely no knowledge, by the way. Reckless beyond belief. And, in any event, I am a professional and Ms. Cufaro is in need of competent representation against charges that are utterly without merit—"

Benny cut him off. "Sal, you don't know shit about the charges."

"Well, in broad strokes I do. You said she had allegedly killed a lot of people. That's absurd and again, assuming adequate symbiosis, we intend to mount a vigorous defense."

Benny chuckled again. "Whatever. Just so you know, she's being processed now at the West Palm RA and will be presented on the charges in front of the magistrate judge at noon, in case you wanna have one of your Florida associates there. Nora Carleton is the SDNY AUSA and she's down here to handle the initial appearance with one of the Florida AUSAs."

"I'll call Nora. Thanks for the heads-up."

CHAPTER THIRTY-SEVEN

T he lobby of the US Attorney's office for the Southern District of New York was dominated by an art installation suspended from the ceiling. Called *Kayaks in the Storm*, it was a collection of long, narrow, brightly colored papier-mâché boats that appeared to be crashing into each other. Every so often, a new United States Attorney would inquire about removing the gigantic baby-crib mobile, only to be told it was protected by the 1990 federal Visual Artists Rights Act and so would require the artist's consent to remove it, which was never sought because there was too much else to do without starting a war with a papier-mâché artist.

Now Frederick Simpson was noticing the kayaks for the first time as he stood at the big wood podium waiting for the crowd of reporters and camera crews to settle down. Behind him was a nine-foot-tall dark blue curtain suspended from aluminum piping that ran along the ceiling in the corner of the lobby. He had slipped through the media-backdrop curtain too soon, without waiting for the signal from his press officer, which would have come after the press aide gave the media a one-minute warning so they could settle down. But Simpson found it too awkward standing among the administrative staff cubicles behind the door covered by the curtain. He had nothing to say to the people sitting at their desks pretending to work, and he was ready anyway. So he opened the door and pushed his way through the gap in the curtain.

The press was quiet, finally, but now he had to wait as his staff put a huge poster board on the easel to his right. It featured a large and sinister-looking surveillance photo of Gina Cufaro in the center, with the names of twelve homicide victims arranged around it in a circle like the hours on a clock. Each name was written inside what appeared to be a skull-and-crossbones graphic and connected by a black line to the Gina picture at center. Governor Tony Burke's name was in the skull at the top, in the twelve o'clock position.

Simpson had spent a long time practicing with the poster in his office. The "money shot," his press aide explained, would be him standing next to the poster pointing an accusing finger at Gina's image. But he shouldn't stand so close that he blocked the view of the poster, or so far that he might be cropped out of the picture. And, given that his right side was his best side and there wasn't enough room for the easel to the left of the podium in the cramped corner of the lobby, he would have to walk past the poster, then pivot back and extend his left arm at Gina while looking up at the photographers, who would now be off to his right. And he shouldn't smile. Also, he needed to hold the pointing pose long enough to give every camera the chance to record multiple good images of him pointing. It was a lot, but the photo of him splashed across NYC media would be worth the effort.

Simpson had memorized his remarks summarizing the indictment and now delivered them from the podium as if the text was rolling behind his eyeballs. His face took on a faraway look and his voice was flat. He also hurried, as if he couldn't wait to get to what he had practiced. Finishing, he began the move, realizing, as he made the final turn to point, that he hadn't adequately considered whether extending his arm with his suit jacket buttoned would cause the garment to look awkwardly tight at the button, as if he had a big belly. So he improvised, forcing his upper body to rotate left with his pointing arm, while his head and his lower body faced right to the photographers. The suit button didn't pull, but it looked painful. He held the twisty pose for a full minute while the cameras clicked, a period of time that had never seemed long to his press aide until she watched Frederick Simpson stay frozen and contorted for sixty entire seconds.

At long last, Simpson broke the pose and returned to the podium, where he introduced the FBI ADIC, a smooth public speaker who, as the New York FBI typically did, went well beyond the language of the indictment to offer click-bait soundbites about Gina Cufaro's "reign of terror," "pandemic of murder," and "slaughter on Central Park West." Carmen Garcia was visible behind the podium, but did not speak.

The media questions were all predictable. "So Kyra Burke is innocent?" a reporter shouted.

"Yes," Simpson answered. "This indictment alleges that another person killed former governor Burke."

"Have you coordinated your investigation with the District Attorney?"

Here Simpson looked down at the podium to read exactly what he had written. "We have a cooperative relationship with the District Attorney's office and we have had conversations with that office during the course of our investigation, and I'm not going to get into the specifics of those conversations."

"Will the DA drop the charges against Kyra?"

"That's entirely their concern," Simpson said.

"You mean you think they might prosecute Kyra while you prosecute somebody else?"

"I'm not saying that. I'm just saying that questions about the DA's office should be addressed to them. They are a fine and independent group of professionals."

Carmen Garcia had already spoken to Andy Kwon. She called him to break the news shortly after Gina was in custody in Florida, and walked him through all the proof the feds had assembled. While they were on the phone, she emailed him the FBI video compilation so he could follow along as she narrated Gina's movements on the night she killed Tony Burke.

He was quiet for a long time after she finished.

"Andy, you still with me?" Carmen asked.

"Yeah, yeah, I just feel like shit, like I almost did the wrong thing, which is scary as hell."

"You didn't have all this," Carmen said, "and *we* didn't have it while you were trying the case."

"Yeah, I know, I know, but it still feels shitty. I was so *certain* we had it right, that Kyra Burke did it. I almost sent an innocent woman to prison. Damn, that's chilling as hell."

"Hey," Carmen said, "in the end you're gonna be in the right place."

"Yeah, thanks," Andy replied glumly, "I appreciate that but . . ."

He didn't finish the thought. Instead, he said, "I'll brief my bosses. I'm sure they're gonna dismiss on Kyra. I'll let you know if they need anything else."

Before calling his supervisors, Andy Kwon made a different call.

The phone was answered after the first ring. "Andy Kwon, to what do I owe the pleasure?" Andy could never tell whether Matthew Parker was being sarcastic or not.

"Hey, Matt," Andy answered. "Listen, I'm calling to update you on some developments in our case. They aren't public yet, and I haven't even told my bosses, but I felt like I owed you and your client this call."

When he hung up, Parker sent a text to Benny Dugan—without emojis. *Thank you, thank you, thank you*, it read. Then he grinned and called Kyra. *I never have to go back to fucking 100 Centre Street*, he thought, waiting for the phone to ring. *There is a God*.

Parker was wrong, as it turned out. Before Justice Zannis would grant the DA's "in furtherance of justice" motion for dismissal and release Kyra from the terms of her bail, she wanted them all back in court one last time.

Parker didn't find the five little stairs so depressing this time. Maybe it was the weather, or that the throng of media now seemed strangely muted, even sympathetic, or maybe it was nostalgia now that he was committed to retiring. But whatever it was, he felt a spring in his shiny black shoes. Kyra didn't seem to feel his sense of energy and lagged a half step behind as they made their way through security and to the courtroom. *Bit of a bad dream for her, I'm guessing.*

Andy Kwon was at the prosecution table, but didn't look at them. Justice Zannis took the bench, looking grim. She announced that she had received the DA's motion to dismiss the indictment. "But as I read section 210.35 of the Criminal Procedure Law," she said, looking down at a book, "I am required to find the existence of some compelling circumstance clearly demonstrating that conviction or prosecution of the defendant upon such indictment would constitute or result in injustice. Mr. Kwon, what is that circumstance, exactly?"

Andy Kwon stood straight. "Your Honor, newly discovered evidence has established, to the People's satisfaction, that another individual was responsible for the death of Mr. Burke and has, in fact, been charged with that crime by the federal authorities. We have reviewed that evidence and believe further prosecution of Kyra Burke would result in precisely the kind of injustice the statute contemplates."

The judge turned to the defense table. "Mr. Parker, anything to add?"

"No, Judge," Parker answered, "except that we are grateful for the way Mr. Kwon has handled this."

Now Justice Zannis shifted her gaze slightly. "Mrs. Burke, please rise. Do you have anything you wish to say?"

Kyra stood and cleared her throat. "Just that I hope we can all take this as a lesson that our criminal justice system is well designed and well intentioned, but it is run by humans with all the susceptibility to error that comes with being human. This has been very hard for me, but I choose to look forward and intend to devote the remainder of my life to serving those who lack the access to resources, the privilege, that I enjoy." Parker turned to watch as she spoke. *Wow, my client hit that out of the park.*

"Thank you, Mrs. Burke," Justice Zannis said. "I admire your maturity and good grace. On behalf of this court system, which I assure you *is* committed to justice, I am sorry for what you have been through. The conditions of your release are vacated and the indictment is dismissed with prejudice in furtherance of justice. You are free to go. The court will stand in recess."

When the judge was gone, Kyra walked over to Andy Kwon and extended her hand, which he took. "I'm very sorry," he whispered.

"You're a good prosecutor," she whispered back. "Just doubt yourself more, because we all make mistakes."

Kyra turned back to Matthew Parker, who put his arm around her shoulders and walked her through the packed courtroom and into the elevator lobby.

Out on the sidewalk on Centre Street, Kyra held an impromptu news conference to repeat for the cameras—word for word—what she had said in the courtroom, with one additional line: "And I will be back with you shortly, my fellow New Yorkers, to explain how I think I can best serve the people of this great state."

With that, she brush-kissed Parker on both cheeks and got into a waiting car. As the media members scurried off to post their stories, he was suddenly alone on the sidewalk. He decided to walk back to his office so he could grab a coffee up the street on St. Andrew's Plaza, maybe relive old glories in his mind. *It goes by so damn fast.*

CHAPTER THIRTY-EIGHT

The federal magistrate judge in Florida ordered Gina to be detained without bail, on the grounds that she was both a flight risk and a danger to the community. That meant a trip for her on the real Con Air. Few people know that the United States Marshals Service operates the largest prisoner transport network in the world. Based out of a separate government terminal at Will Rogers Airport in Oklahoma City—with hubs in Las Vegas, Puerto Rico, and the Virgin Islands—the Justice Prisoner and Alien Transportation System—called JPATS, not "Con Air," and the reference to the Nicholas Cage movie irritates the marshals—moves federal prisoners around the country on a fleet of 737 planes.

That meant Gina's flight from Miami to Stewart International Airport, about ninety minutes north of the Manhattan federal jail, connected through Oklahoma City, where she and the other passengers shuffled off the plane with ankles and wrists cuffed to a chain that wrapped around their waists and hung down between their legs. And there was no Starbucks in the JPATS terminal. After reaching her final destination at Stewart, a former Air Force base on the west side of the Hudson River, Gina was transported in a US Marshals van to the Metropolitan Correctional Center next to the US Attorney's office and housed with other female pretrial detainees in a separate unit on the eighth floor.

◆

They were in courtroom 318 of the Thurgood Marshall courthouse, waiting on Judge Whitney to start the first pretrial conference. The case had originally been assigned randomly to another judge, but Whitney had convinced the chief judge to transfer it to him on the grounds that his prior familiarity with the D'Amico case would "promote judicial efficiency." Nora smirked as she looked at the judge's empty chair. *What it promotes is your desire to have a high-profile case.*

The New York media was loving that another attractive woman was accused of murder, and this time as a prolific mob killer. One tabloid had already gone with the sexist MURDEROUS MOLL headline for Gina. The other was toggling between ANGEL OF DEATH and BEAST OF A BEAUTY.

Salvatore Butler was behind them at the defense table, huddling with Gina, who sat in her dark blue prisoner smock and pants, with her feet chained just above her slip-on prison shoes. Judge Whitney had affirmed the initial magistrate's decision to hold Gina without bail, given the charges she faced.

"It just feels so weird to be back here," Nora whispered to Benny. "Same place, same judge, same lawyer. Except she killed the guy who sat in that chair last time we were here."

Before Benny could reply, the clerk called out, "All rise!" and Nora heard the metallic rattle of Gina's chains as she stood, Butler using one hand to help her up. "Please be seated," Judge Whitney said, adding to his clerk, "Call the case."

"*United States v. Gina Cufaro,*" the clerk intoned. "Counsel, please state your appearance."

Nora stood first. "Assistant US Attorney Nora Carleton for the government, Your Honor."

And then booming from the back table, "Salvatore Cutler, Esquire, Your Honor, for Ms. Cufaro, whom I am honored"—*on-ah'd*—"to represent."

"Yes, about that, Mr. Butler," Judge Whitney said. "I'm sure you received a copy of the government's letter raising concerns about potential conflicts of interest in your representing Ms. Cufaro after having represented Mr. D'Amico, whom she is charged with killing."

"Yes, Your Honor, we saw the letter and my client is fully prepared to waive any potential issues with respect to that representation."

"Very well," Judge Whitney replied. "Let us first arraign the defendant and then we will proceed to the issue of waiver."

After leading Gina through a lengthy series of questions to preclude any later claim that her lawyer was conflicted, the judge said, "Let us now turn to the matter of a trial date. Ms. Carleton, I was very surprised to see this case designated as Wheel B, which is supposed to be for cases that will take fewer than twenty trial days. As I read the indictment, you intend to prove twelve separate homicides. I can't imagine how we can try it that quickly."

"Well, Your Honor, we thought about that pretty carefully. The case against Ms. Cufaro will come in largely through digital evidence showing her connection to the murders. And given that I assume Mr. Butler's defense will be that his client had nothing to do with any murders, we will be able to present crime-scene evidence largely by stipulation. Then the government will use some fairly straightforward cooperator testimony and the case will be done. We actually think in fewer than twenty days, Judge."

"Very well, Ms. Carleton. That still seems ambitious to the court, but we shall see. And aren't these offenses death eligible? Will we need to deal with the death penalty? Because that is an entirely different kettle of fish."

Nora had no idea what he meant by the fish reference, but answered anyway. "Judge, our office has already communicated with the Department of Justice. As you have no doubt read, the current president believes being pro-life means, among other things, being against capital punishment, so we expect to hear back quite quickly that the maximum punishment will be life in prison without parole. So none of the complications that a death-penalty case would bring."

Butler was on his feet. "Your Honor, we request a fast trial date. I agree with Ms. Carleton that we should be able to do this quickly. My client is innocent and incarcerated before trial, as you know—a detention I have not yet chosen to challenge with the Court of Appeals. Understandably, she is eager to have this over. Once I receive discovery from the government, I'll know what motions I'll be making, but we'd ask the court to set this down for February, March at the latest. We'd want it even sooner, but we recognize the complications that Christmas and New Year's present to the court's calendar."

"No objection to that, Judge," Nora called out.

"Very well," Judge Whitney said, as he always did. He looked down at a calendar on his bench, then said, "Jury selection will begin on the second Monday in February. Agreed?" Like a childhood jinx moment, both lawyers responded, "Yes, Your Honor."

Nora stood again. "And I forgot to mention that the government will be making a motion for an anonymous jury. We will do that promptly."

"Very well. The court will stand in recess. Let me take this opportunity to wish all of you a Merry Christmas, including you, Ms. Cufaro."

Did he really just wish Gina Cufaro a Merry Christmas? Nora thought. *What the hell? At least her Christmas will be behind bars.*

CHAPTER THIRTY-NINE

I t was a ridiculously small snowman, but Sophie didn't know that. They were in the tiny backyard of Nora's childhood townhouse in Hoboken and had scraped together enough of the new-fallen wet snow to make a two-foot-tall creature. It was more of a lump than three balls, decorated with a baby-carrot nose, stick arms, and raisins for eyes and a happy mouth. As they sat on the back steps admiring their work and sipping hot chocolate, Sophie was going on about how the snow would make Santa's work that night so much easier, and Nora was fully engaged.

She wasn't thinking about work, because there was nothing left to do until the New Year. She'd gotten all the discovery out to Butler, filed her motion for an anonymous jury, and notified the court and the defense that the Department of Justice, as predicted, had quickly approved them not seeking the death penalty—something they would never get from a Manhattan jury anyway. It felt good to really focus on family this Christmas.

And she was thinking about family—constantly, including on those back steps. For the first time in Sophie's life, Nick would have another woman with them at Christmas tomorrow—his fiancée, Vicki. It felt weirder still that Nick and Vicki would be taking Sophie with them to Westport, Connecticut, the week after Christmas to visit Vicki's parents. It was only a ninety-minute drive, but the thought gave Nora a dull ache in her chest. Their lives were changing, and Nora did not like change.

After she tucked Sophie in that night—"Happy thoughts, ladybug, and sleeping position, because Santa won't come until you're asleep"—Nora went downstairs to the kitchen, where her mother was at the sink, finishing some dishes from dinner. With a loud sigh, Nora slumped in a chair at the small kitchen table. Teresa turned with a gentle smile. "How's my badass prosecutor?"

Nora just looked up at her, tears filling her eyes. "Not feeling very badass right now."

"I'm making tea. Want some?" Teresa asked.

Nora nodded and her mother lifted the hot kettle, poured two cups, and set them on the table, repeatedly dipping a tea bag in one before moving it to the second cup, then wrapping it around a spoon and setting it on the table.

"Work?" Teresa asked.

"Nah. Work is fine. I just feel like I'm losing Sophie, like the traditions we built are slipping away."

"You mean like Vicki is gonna be here tomorrow?"

"That, and they're taking Sophie to Westport and I won't see her for a whole week, including New Year's. It's never been like that, and now that they're getting married it'll probably happen more and more."

Her mother tried to make her smile. "You wouldn't wanna go to Westport. Houses too far apart, no sidewalks. Can't be fun for New Year's Eve."

Nora gave her only half a grin, so Teresa took a deep breath and tried something else. "Look, having children is amazing but it's also agony, because nothing is constant except change. You can't freeze them, you can't keep everything the same. Things never stop being different."

"Yeah," Nora said, looking into her tea, "but this feels different from her learning to ride a bike or going to kindergarten. This is about strangers taking her away for the first time in her life."

"Well, first, not *strangers*," Teresa answered. "This is her father and the woman who will be her stepmother. But second, this is the kind of agonizing change I'm talking about."

"I know, I know," Nora said, without looking up.

"Hey," Teresa said, "look at me."

Nora lifted her chin to look at her mother, who continued: "Traditions will change, they just will. But you know what will never change? *You* at the center of her life. Think of how powerful a force I've been in your life, right? Even when you wanted to get me out of your head, you couldn't. You are that little girl's *mother*! Nothing threatens that, nothing can ever change that. No Vicki, no Westport, nothing can ever touch that."

Teresa leaned over and took Nora's tear-covered face in her two hands. "You really should come with me to Florida. Vero Beach is lovely and your Aunt Irene would love to see you. Could be wild fun to hang out with a bunch of late-middle-aged snowbirds. The four thirty P.M. buffets we could hit together!"

That finally made Nora laugh. "Tempting, Ma, but I've already done Florida in December this year to lock up Gina Cufaro. Carmen's been on me about coming out to stay for New Year's. I'm gonna do it. I won't be alone, don't worry."

Carmen Garcia and her wife, Marguerite, lived in the left half of a two-family house in Maplewood, New Jersey, a leafy and increasingly hip suburb about twenty miles due west of lower Manhattan. Their place was just down the street from the train station, making Carmen's commute to the city easier, and near both the fire station and the swings and duck ponds of Maplewood Memorial Park, all of which were sources of enormous joy for their three-year-old son, Eli.

It had snowed again but it wasn't too cold for a walk on the afternoon of December 31, so Nora pushed Eli in the stroller up the plowed sidewalks of Dunnell Road toward the fire station as his two moms walked behind. The station's big garage doors were closed—always a major disappointment for Eli—so they walked for a bit and then turned left into the park to watch kids sledding down the steep hill from the train station parking lot. They didn't have a sled, so they pushed on rather than torture poor Eli, crossing under the railroad tracks and into the little town center of Maplewood. They found a booth for a late lunch at the Mapleleaf Diner, a longtime town fixture.

As Eli dove into mac and cheese with French fries and chocolate milk, the three women ate omelets, drank coffee, and chatted. Nora talked of Sophie and Nana and Nick and Vicki and Westport, the words gushing out of her until she stopped short with an apology. "I'm so sorry for dominating the conversation. I don't normally do this. I think I just miss Sophie too much."

"Please," Marguerite said. "It's so nice to meet a real person from Carmen's world who does something besides talk about people getting 'whacked' or who's gonna 'flip' or whatever. Thank you for being normal."

"Hey," Carmen said in mock protest, "I talk about all that stuff and I'm normal."

Marguerite laughed. "Jury's still out, as my prosecutor wife might say."

Carmen leaned her forehead against Marguerite's. "I pledge to be more normal."

"I didn't fall in love with 'normal,'" Marguerite said, smiling. Looking at Nora, she said, "So, a lot about Nick and what's-her-name, but nothing about *your* love life so far. What's up?"

Nora acknowledged the question but avoided it with a smile, calling out "Check please!" Carmen and Marguerite laughed and let it go.

On the way home, they stopped in Memorial Park again to let Eli play on the slides and playground climbers. It was cold but he needed to burn energy before his nap. The three women huddled together on a bench as the little boy enjoyed the snow-frosted equipment, which he had all to himself. Nora noticed a white man who appeared to be about thirty standing at the edge of the play area, watching, his hands deep in the pockets of his black leather coat, his head covered by a green New York Jets knit hat. Without taking his eyes off Eli, the man slowly made his way to the bench nearest theirs and sat. Now Carmen noticed him too, and that he didn't appear to be with a child.

Still staring at the little boy, the man spoke in a loud voice. "Must be so nice to have a happy family. Treasure it. Things can change fast." Then he stood and began walking toward the exit, passing just behind their bench. Nora jumped to her feet, reaching in her pocket for her phone as she turned to face him. Without stopping, he glanced at her and said, "And that beautiful little girl of yours. Hope you keep her safe."

Nora was so startled by the comment that it took her several seconds before she got her phone open and started taking pictures of him from behind. She got a series just before he stepped into the front passenger seat of a waiting car, which roared off.

She turned to Carmen and Marguerite. "Hurry, get Eli and let's get back to your place."

Once they were in the house, Nora called Benny, who was at his son's Long Island home, to tell him about the encounter.

"Motherless fucks," he said when she was done. "Send me the pictures. Lemme see if I can ID him. I'm gonna call Maplewood and have a car sit on Carmen's tonight. Hoboken PD too, for when you get back."

"Thanks, Benny, I really appreciate it. Any reason you think we should send word to Nick? You know he's up in Connecticut with Sophie."

"Don't think so. This isn't normal Cosa Nostra stuff. Someone stupid is just trying to fuck with you, to scare you, and no sense spreading it."

"You see the pictures? I just texted them."

"Lemme put you on speaker." Benny was quiet for a moment. "Yeah, I see them. Don't recognize him. Hard to believe it's a wise guy 'cause this is shit they just don't do. They know how stupid it is to fuck with the feds. But lemme work it."

"Thanks, Benny, I really appreciate it."

"No problem. Hey, put me on speaker so Carmen can hear."

When she did, he said, "Hey boss, happy New Year, amiright? Listen, don't let this take over your life. That's what this mope wants. Gonna ask your PD to sit on your house tonight, but remember: People who want to hurt you tend not to talk to you first. This guy just wants inside your heads. Don't let him in."

"Appreciate it, Benny," Carmen said. "Let us know if you turn anything up. And happy New Year to you as well."

Hours later, after Eli was asleep upstairs, the three women had the "wild" New Year's Eve Carmen had promised, despite the distraction of a police car parked on the street in front. They sat in the tiny living room talking, then playing Settlers of Catan and drinking champagne, occasionally glancing at the muted TV playing *Dick Clark's New Year's*

Rockin' Eve, even though Mr. Clark had been dead for a long time. When Marguerite went upstairs to check on Eli, Carmen turned to Nora. "Hey, it might be the champagne making me crazy, but I'd like to be your second chair on the Gina Cufaro trial. I've been outta the trial game for a while and would love to help. You lead, I sit there and do whatever you want me to do."

"Are you serious right now?" Nora asked. "After what happened today, you want *deeper* into this?"

Carmen nodded. "Yup, now I *really* want a piece."

"You remember you second-sat my first trial when I was in General Crimes?"

"I do," Carmen said. "You didn't really need me then and probably don't need me now. Think of it as a favor to a dinosaur. Get me another trial before they put me out to pasture for good."

"Done," Nora said. "You're in. This'll be a ton of fun."

Carmen chuckled. "What has this work done to us that we're talking about the *fun* in prosecuting someone for twelve murders?"

Nora lifted her glass. "To the end of the 'Murderous Moll.'"

Carmen clinked her glass against Nora's. "I like the 'Beast of a Beauty' thing better, but here's to us putting her away, whatever she's called."

At midnight, Nora felt a twinge of loneliness and pain watching Carmen and Marguerite kiss. She hugged each of them and then excused herself to go to bed in the small guest room upstairs next to Eli's.

The next morning, Nora got up early and walked into town to surprise her hosts with bagels and coffee from the little shop they'd pointed out on their walk. She waved to the officer in the MPD car as she passed by and saw no sign of the creepy stranger in the Jets hat. As a Hoboken native, she knew bagels tended to get less dense and chewy the farther one got from New York, with the size of the bagel's hole being the tell. The best bagels had no holes. They were lumps of thick, cooked dough with a crusty surface bearing just the faintest hint of a navel. Now she stood in the Maplewood bagel store staring at bins filled with nearly Panera-sized circles she could use as eyeglasses. *Oh well*, she thought, *this is their store so they must like 'em this way.* She walked back with a mixed dozen, and a coffee for the officer parked outside.

After coffee and bagels—which were a big hit—Nora took a nearly empty train home, staring out the window and thinking of Sophie as the NJ Transit train passed through Newark, crossed the soggy Meadowlands marshes, and slowly made its way into the deserted Hoboken terminal on the Hudson River's edge. No point in going to her mother's house, which was empty, so she walked to her basement apartment. It was empty, too, and quiet, but her work laptop was there, and that would help push away the sad thoughts. There was a lot to do, so she began mapping out the order of proof for *United States v. Gina Cufaro.*

CHAPTER FORTY

The murder of former governor Burke would be the center of the government's case because it was the one murder of the twelve charged where they thought they had Gina totally nailed. The jury could actually watch her walk toward Central Park West, slip on the Kyra disguise, enter the elevator to the penthouse apartment while the victim was still alive, and then depart shortly before the body was discovered.

The problem was that the Burke killing didn't fit Gina's pattern. The other eleven—including Dominic "The Nose" D'Amico—were all shots to the head, not some clever effort to fake a suicide. Gina always managed to get close to her victims, and then shoot them, except Tony Burke. That gave Butler something to argue, but, after sketching it all out, Nora thought she had enough circumstantial evidence to overcome that.

She looked up from her computer and out the front window, where the Bloomfield Street sidewalk was visible at the top. She could see the lower legs of people walking past. Her outline made it clear: *Gina is going down*, she thought, *if the government can get a fair trial.*

For decades, the Gambino Family had specialized in corrupting jurors in trials of its members. She laid out all that history for Judge Whitney in her motion for an anonymous jury. But she knew anonymity alone would not protect the jury from corruption, because the bad guys would know what the jurors looked like and could follow them. A juror might even reach out to the mob through relatives or friends, looking for a payday. It had happened.

In the new year, Carmen started coming to Nora's office to talk case strategy, something Nora initially found very strange—given that Carmen was her boss—but as the trial drew closer, it became the new normal.

"Should we offer her any kind of plea?" Carmen asked from her side chair across the desk.

"Not sure," Nora answered. "What would that even look like? She pleads straight up and goes away for life, which makes no sense, right? Why not take a swing with a jury? Or she pleads and cooperates to try to get a 5K"—the shorthand for the provision under which a defendant could receive a sentence reduction for assisting the government—"and to get that, she's gotta tell us every bad thing she's ever done and go against the mob."

Benny's voice boomed from the doorway. "And she ain't gonna do that, for two reasons: She's all 'we never betray Cosa Nostra'—more than any of the men, for sure—and she also knows there are murders we haven't connected her to, hits she did before she got stupid with the phone and the digital dust youse are always talkin' about."

"I agree with Benny," Carmen said, "but I thought I should at least raise it. If Butler wants to approach us about a plea, let him—he knows our number."

"Agreed," Nora added. "And if we reached out to him, it would telegraph weakness. And we aren't weak, are we, Mr. Dugan?"

"No, we are not," Benny answered. "And speaking of our strength, I think I got a line on the creepster in the park from New Year's. It appears to be a shithead named Rico Faraci. He's actually Gina's half brother. Seems ol' Handsome Joey got somebody other than his lawfully wedded wife pregnant when Gina was about ten. Woman had the baby and he's been in a loose orbit around their world ever since. I say 'loose' 'cause he's half a lunatic. Too unstable for the mob, if you can believe that. Even though he's descended from royalty on his father's side, they won't make him. But he may think standing up for Gina is somehow gonna help his prospects. Don't wanna give him too much attention, but gonna keep an eye on him."

Benny rapped the door frame twice with the knuckles of his right hand. "That's my report, and I'll keep you updated if we find him."

CHAPTER FORTY-ONE

Jury selection went smoothly in courtroom 318 until the very end. Only one of the potential jurors made Nora and Carmen nervous about jury tampering: a man who said he was of Italian heritage and worked in the finance industry. Although the judge stressed that the jurors were to be anonymous and asked only for county of residence, this guy volunteered that he lived in the Belmont section of the Bronx, an area that had long been known as the Italian center of that borough. It was also Gina's childhood neighborhood. Nora had tried to get the judge to remove him for cause after he specified his neighborhood. But Butler countered that tens of thousands of New Yorkers lived in Belmont, which persuaded Judge Whitney to leave him on.

When the time came for the government to use its final peremptory strike—which allowed removal of a juror without cause—Nora was most worried about a fifty-three-year-old woman who worked in the publishing industry, lived in Manhattan, and thought the FBI was part of the Republican party. The juror also maintained, strenuously, that, despite those beliefs, she could be fair and impartial in this case. She would be on the jury unless they struck her now.

"No, leave the Bu-hater," Benny whispered. "Gotta use our last strike on that fucker from Belmont. Too many goombahs around Arthur Avenue."

"Benny," Nora answered, her voice barely audible. "We are in the *courtroom*, for God's sake. She's more dangerous for us."

Carmen agreed. "If we strike him, then the FBI-hater is definitely on the jury and she can screw us," she whispered. "Can't take that chance. Gotta get rid of her and leave Belmont guy."

"Okay, okay," Benny replied, "but I'm tellin' you, Belmont guy is gonna be a problem."

With the government's final strike, the jury was set—twelve plus alternates. Judge Whitney cleared his throat and addressed the entire courtroom. "Ladies and gentlemen, those of you who were not selected are excused from further service with the thanks of the court. Those of you who were selected will now follow the clerk into the jury room. We will begin the trial in the morning, with opening statements at ten A.M. And please bring your belongings with you now, because you will be departing from the jury room. Good evening."

When the jurors were assembled in the jury room, a Deputy US Marshal explained their new commute. Three blacked-out vans driven by the marshals would depart from the underground courthouse garage each day after court and drop the jurors at one of three meeting places—a parking lot for those commuting by car, and two different train stations for those coming by train or subway. Each morning, the process would reverse, with the marshals' vans meeting them and driving them to the courthouse. The vans would take different routes every day. The jurors were never to travel on their own between home and court. They all nodded, the gravity of their anonymity getting heavier.

Benny apologized as he dropped heavily onto the couch in Carmen's office. "Sorry to hold the team up, but I had a weird one just now from the Bureau of Prisons."

Turning to Carmen, he added, "You know I have a standing request at BOP to keep me posted on new visitors to our mob defendants at the MCC."

"Yeah?" Carmen answered. "So?"

"Fuckin' Marian Burke went to see Gina last night."

"What?" Nora almost shouted. "How could that be?"

"Dunno," Benny answered, "but I think we gotta find out."

"Yes, we do," Nora said, "like yesterday."

Marian Burke now lived in a mansion between Fifth and Madison avenues, almost directly across Central Park from her former penthouse—and the site of her former husband's death.

"I like the Upper East Side better," she explained to Nora and Benny as they sat on a leather love seat in her brightly lit drawing room—or that's what her assistant had called the room as she escorted them in. "Closer to the Met, less ethnic, fewer underemployed actors. I do miss Zabar's, though."

Nora was tempted to ask what a "drawing room" was, but instead she got right to the reason for their visit. "Mrs. Burke, did you visit Gina Cufaro at the Metropolitan Correctional Center yesterday evening?"

"Yes," Marian answered immediately. "I did visit Ms. Cufaro last night at that awful jail."

"Why?" Nora asked.

Marian lifted her chin slightly. "Because she's a human being, now reduced to a tabloid headline. I saw what the media did to poor Kyra. And I've met this girl, more than once I think, with my former husband at some of his boring political events. I remember her when she was just a young girl; she stood out, in a good way. The least I could do is show her some humanity. She is innocent until proven guilty, correct?

Aren't we people of faith supposed to be 'doing unto the least of these,' or something?"

Benny had now mostly recovered from being hunched over in a tiny metal elevator cage for the creaking ride to the mansion's fourth floor—"Why the fuck we gotta be in this rat trap?"—but the experience still lingered.

"Yeah," he said, leaning forward, thick forearms landing on his thighs, "that's mighty Christian of you, visiting the woman who offed your ex. But—and excuse my frankness in your drawing room—that seems like some bullshit to me."

"Benny—" Nora began.

"No, no, that's fine," Marian said quickly. "I appreciate your directness, and even your charming bovine reference. It was a favorite of my former husband—may he rest in peace."

Benny was not charmed. "Yeah, so, bovine excrement aside, what's the real reason?"

Marian was unfazed. "An act of charity, Mr. Dugan. As I said."

"Okay," he said, "since you appreciate directness, let me be direct. Did you kill your husband?"

"I did not," she answered.

"So that wasn't you in the lobby that night, in your Jackie O getup?"

"It was not."

"You line up Gina to kill him instead?"

"I did not."

"Then what the fuck were you doin' at the MCC?"

Marian looked down at her hands resting on the front of her dark green taffeta dress.

"This is a very complicated situation," she began, before a loud voice cut her off.

"No, no, that's quite enough," Edward Burke announced as he stepped into the room through a door directly behind his mother. He stopped behind her chair, touching her shoulders with the tips of his fingers. "There is nothing complicated about this at all. My mother has answered your questions, welcoming you into her home on very short notice and without insisting counsel be present. Now I will ask you to leave. Good day."

Benny lifted his head to look up at Edward standing stiffly behind Marian in his suit and tie. After holding the stare for several beats, he dropped his eyes to Marian. "That what you want, Mrs. Burke? What junior here said?"

Marian paused. Benny could see Edward's fingers redden slightly as he pushed down on his mother's shoulders.

"Mrs. Burke," Benny asked, "you sure you don't want to visit with us alone?" Lifting his head to Edward, he added, "Adults-only kinda thing?"

Marian exhaled audibly. "I'm sure. I will thank you to leave my home. Good day."

With that, she stood and followed Edward back through the door he had used. Nora and Benny sat in silence for several seconds before Marian's assistant stepped in from the main door to guide them to the elevator. Benny insisted on taking the stairs. Back on the street, they walked to his car, which was parked in front of a fire hydrant—protected from towing by a priceless FDNY placard in the front window.

"What do you think?" Nora asked.

"Twenty minutes of my life I'll never get back," Benny said across the top of his car. "Weird as hell, maybe bad, but I can't prove the bad. Honestly can't imagine that tight-ass doin' her own dirty work, and I never bought the idea that it coulda been her that night in the lobby, but hiring Gina? I could see it. Matty Parker told me there was this weird angle at Kyra's trial, about Marian maybe inheriting under the will if the guv croaked. But I don't know; seems like she has plenty of dough. And what's sonny-boy doin' listenin' through the wall? Somethin' stinks. Just don't know what it is, exactly. You wanna take care of briefing Carmen?"

"Yup. Can't wait to tell her about you firing shits and fucks around a Fifth Avenue drawing room."

Benny beamed as he squeezed into the driver's seat. "They never taught me how to act in drawing rooms at St. Cecilia's." He chopped the car into drive. "Let's get outta here before they decide I'm too ethnic or something."

CHAPTER FORTY-TWO

The next morning, Nora delivered the prosecution's opening statement, walking the jury through the proof that would finally end Gina's career as a professional killer, spending extra time on the centerpiece of the government's case—the murder of former governor Burke.

"Who murdered Tony Burke?" she asked in a loud voice. She turned and pointed at Gina, no longer in prison scrubs, sitting next to Butler in a dark green sweater and gray flannel skirt, her thick brown hair brushed and falling straight to her shoulders, her face carefully made up. Two female Deputy Marshals sat close behind her. "That petite, attractive woman did. And she killed eleven other human beings."

Turning back to the jury, she lowered her voice and added, "Her looks are her disguise. Being fooled by her was the last mistake many people ever made."

When she finished, the judge called on Salvatore Butler, who rose and paused at the defense table to button his double-breasted suit jacket. He was a block of a man—five foot nine and 220 pounds—and still carried himself like the pugnacious New York City high school football player he had long ago been.

As he walked toward the podium with his notebook, Butler noticed something. The small garbage can was gone. When court began just a short time ago, it sat in its normal spot—next to the clerk's desk, on the side nearest the jury box. Butler now had his back to the jury and appeared to be looking for it.

"Mr. Butler?" Judge Whitney asked.

"Yes, Judge, sorry," he said, without looking up. "If I could just have a moment."

He spotted it where Benny had hidden it, under the edge of the government's table. Glancing at Dugan with just a hint of a grin, Butler retrieved the can, returned it to its normal spot, and turned to face the jury.

"Good morning, ladies and gentleman," he began. "I have the honor of representing Gina Cufaro, yet another victim of the government's obsession with a Hollywood myth." He then launched into his "mah-fye-ah" shtick, thundering about anti-Italian bias and the injustice it produced. Then it was time for the part Benny had tried to mess with.

Butler reached into his notebook and retrieved a copy of the indictment against Gina, which was thirty pages long. Holding it aloft and at arm's length, as if it were something rotten he found behind the refrigerator, he said, "You've heard a lot about the indictment in this case. Well, here it is. You've heard the judge tell you that my client is presumed innocent, that the indictment is merely an allegation. But it's worse than that in this case."

He shook the indictment, its pages now fluttering audibly. "It looks all fancy, all professional. Right? It's brought to you by the United States, after all."

Raising his voice, he thundered, "But there's nothin' fancy about it. You know what it is? Garbage!"—*ga-bidge!* With that, he turned, raised his arm high, and angrily threw the indictment down into the little trash can. "Garbage!" he repeated.

At the government's table, Jessica jolted at the noise of the can moving from the impact. Benny leaned toward her ear and whispered, "Does it every time. Someday, I'm gonna just remove all the fuckin' cans. Let 'im bring his own."

"You know who killed Tony Burke?" Butler shouted. "His wife did it—and it's on video, which you probably already know from the news—and now that rich, powerful woman is gonna get away with it because the federal government would much rather go after the alleged mob and my innocent client."

Nora considered objecting, but decided not to look defensive. There was no need. The evidence that Gina killed Burke was powerful.

Butler devoted the rest of his opening to condemning "rats" and the evils of circumstantial evidence before finishing where he began, denouncing the witch hunt that had landed this fine Italian-American business woman in a courtroom.

As he returned to his seat, Nora whispered to Carmen, "I don't get why he's so cocky about this case."

"Me neither," Carmen whispered back. "Well, he's always cocky, but this is cockier than usual. Doesn't make sense when we have so much on her."

Behind them, Gina Cufaro was sniffling audibly, with Butler dramatically rubbing her upper back, before pulling his enormous pocket square, snapping the bright yellow hanky open and offering it to his client. Gina took it and gently dabbed each eye.

Benny, who was sitting at the end of the government's table with his chair turned so he could see what was happening behind him—"Lifelong habit of not lettin' bad guys get behind me," he explained—grinned sardonically and whispered to Jessica. "Couple Oscar nominees back there. Gina wouldn't cry if you stuck a pencil in her eye."

CHAPTER FORTY-THREE

FBI Special Agent Jessica Watson was the government's first witness. Carmen did the questioning and used Jessica's testimony to explain Gina's Palm Beach Gardens life with surveillance photos and financial records: the house, the realtor job, the money in investments and bank accounts in amounts far beyond what a realtor might have earned, the ski mask and boxes of surgical gloves found in her dresser, and her phone and its location at the time of all twelve murders—in her house.

Next, they told the story of "Mildred Jamison," her travels, and the different phone that accompanied her wherever she went.

The trial's first day ended with a merger of the two, with surveillance camera pictures of Gina checking in at airline counters as Mildred Jamison. After debate, they decided to skip the Starbucks evidence that helped them discover Mildred was Gina. "I know you love the coffee thing," Carmen had said, "but we really don't need it. We have the pictures of Gina being Mildred. Thin to win, right?" Nora really did love the Starbucks secret-menu story, but she agreed to drop it.

The second day of testimony was focused on the story of Tony Burke's death. They used crime-scene and medical-examiner witnesses to describe the murder, just as Andy Kwon had, but they had no need for the doorman, Ivan Ramirez. If Butler wanted to call Ramirez to say he thought it was Kyra that night, let him. They would argue that Gina obviously wanted him to think that, and it worked, until the video compilation.

Instead, another FBI special agent showed the jury records of Mildred Jamison's trip up from Florida and the movement of her phone to the Lucerne Hotel the night before the murder. Then they watched the video montage showing a blonde woman with the same general build as Gina/Mildred going from Mildred's hotel floor to Central Park West—pausing to put on the sunglasses and scarf—then in through Burke's lobby to the elevator, out through the lobby, back to the hotel, and up to Mildred's floor.

It was a strong collection of evidence. The one hole was that they couldn't prove for sure that the blonde woman who left the fifth floor to go kill Burke was Gina. It would have to be one heck of a coincidence for the female killer to be staying on the same floor as Gina but, still, it was a small doubt Butler might exploit. They would fill the hole later.

Next, Nora offered into evidence the airline records showing Mildred's flight back to Miami the next day and her phone returning to Gina's Palm Beach Gardens home.

Butler's voice boomed. "Objection, Your Honor, objection! There is absolutely no basis for the admission of such records. I've let all this stuff go until now, but enough! My client deserves a fair trial."

Judge Whitney glared at Nora like she had done something wrong, lifting both eyebrows.

"Judge," she said, "Mr. Butler signed a written stipulation that all these records are admissible."

Butler inexplicably doubled down. "That's a canard, Your Honor, an utter canard. I recall no such thing."

Benny leaned over to Jessica, whispering. "First, I have no idea what a 'canard' is, but this is what Sal does. He thinks his mob clients like to see him fight. This is for Gina and the Family—capital F."

Whitney was no longer glaring. He seemed somewhere between confused and amused.

Nora walked calmly to the government table and picked up a document. "Your Honor, I'm now handing the court Government Exhibit 23S, a written stipulation covering all these records, signed *yesterday* by Mr. Butler and government counsel."

Judge Whitney looked at the document, then lifted his eyes. "Mr. Butler, is this your signature?"

"It appears to be, Your Honor, but I feel as though there has been some chicanery"—it came out *chai-cain-erie*—"and I intend to get to the bottom of it. But I don't wish to belabor the court while I investigate it. I will withdraw my objection at the present time."

"Very well, Mr. Butler, the objection is withdrawn and the records are now in evidence. And this seems like a good time to break for the day. Perhaps that will afford additional time to sort out any confusion."

Butler didn't mention it again.

CHAPTER FORTY-FOUR

E arly the next morning, Carmen was waiting in Nora's office when she arrived, a Ziploc bag in her lap.

"Hey, what's up?" Nora asked, setting her shoulder bag on the desk.

Carmen lifted the plastic bag, which held a white greeting card–sized envelope. "This was in our mailbox at home last night."

"Got one too," Nora replied, pulling her own Ziploc from her bag. "Nice to see we both preserved for prints."

They had received identical greeting cards, addressed to them at home, with no stamp and no return address. Each was a get-well card with a yellow canary-like bird on the front. Inside each was a picture of their children—one of Sophie, one of Eli—taken from a distance. A large X—which might have been a target crosshair—was drawn across each child's face.

Benny exploded when he saw the cards. "That's it. Sick of this shit. It's gonna stop, now."

"What are you going to do?" Carmen asked.

Benny ignored the question and spoke to Jessica, who was at her desk. "Jessica, you submit these for forensics, see if we can get anything from them, but it ain't no mystery. It's that dickhead Faraci again."

Now he looked at Carmen. "Look, youse just try your case. Don't let them in your head. Lemme see if I can send my own message."

That morning, the trial turned to the other eleven murders, with Carmen taking the lead for the prosecution. The jury mostly heard summaries of what witnesses would say if called to the stand. As expected, Butler stipulated to factual evidence because he didn't want to prolong the live testimony, so the jury learned the circumstances of the other killings, the phone and travel records documenting Gina's/Mildred's movements to the crime scenes, and the overnight FedEx packages Mildred sent to herself on nine of the twelve killings. Nora and Carmen intended to argue those were the murder weapons. It was too big a security risk to try to get them in the cities where she would do the killings. She couldn't bring them on a plane, so she shipped them to herself and must have discarded them after the hits rather than risk a shipment back to Florida. It was easy to get more guns in Florida.

There were no packages sent in connection with Tony Burke, who was killed by injection, or the hit on The Nose, but Gina had plenty of friends in New York with guns. And there was no package sent for an Atlanta murder, but they showed Mildred moved by car for that hit. The ballistics for Atlanta also matched that of one later killing. They intended to argue Gina must have driven back and forth from Florida to Atlanta with that gun, which allowed her to ship it to the site of a later killing, before dumping it.

After all the records and stipulations, Carmen put Benny on the stand to offer expert testimony about Cosa Nostra and give the jury context for The Nose's death. The jury seemed fascinated as Benny explained the origins of Cosa Nostra, "this thing of ours," and its roots in Sicily, its organization into Families run by an administration made up of a boss, underboss, and consiglieri, who presided over capos leading crews composed of made members and associates, with money from criminal activity flowing upward at all times. He explained the requirements for getting "made"—males only, with Italian fathers—and the promises made during the induction ceremony, with a particular focus on the commitment to keep Cosa Nostra's secrets. He told them of New York's five Families, whose bosses formed a commission to referee disputes, and of the history and dominance of the Gambino Family in particular.

With Mafia 101 completed, he testified that Dominic D'Amico had been on trial for racketeering, and near the end of the government's case had passed a note to Benny seeking to cooperate, teasing information about Tony Burke's murder. He told the story of meeting with The Nose and his new lawyer—without mentioning that his old lawyer was one Salvatore Butler—and added that the information he provided concerned the identity of the actual killer. But he didn't give the details of what The Nose said that day—that it was a professional hit by somebody out of Joey Cufaro's crew and rumored to be a woman—because all of that was hearsay. D'Amico wasn't trying to help the mob by saying it, so it wasn't an admissible coconspirator statement; it was pure hearsay, and Nora told the judge they would leave it out.

While she had Benny on the stand, Carmen showed him a picture from the D'Amico crime scene—showing The Nose dead with a small bird stuffed in his mouth—and had him confirm that it was the same man who had attempted to tell them who really killed Tony Burke, and that the canary was a longtime Cosa Nostra message about the costs of "singing" to law enforcement. Carmen seemed to finish, then paused and said, "Oh, Special Agent Dugan, I forgot to ask. What color is the bird in that picture?"

Benny paused and seemed to stare at Carmen, his face a mixture of amusement and anger. "I don't know for sure," he answered. "I'm color-blind."

Carmen announced that she had no further questions.

When Butler was up beginning his cross, Nora leaned toward Carmen and whispered, "What was that about?"

Carmen smiled and whispered back. "Oh, I know he's completely color-blind. We try to find a way to ask him something about color every time he testifies. It's a thing in the unit, going back years. Matthew Parker used to do it. Surprised you didn't know."

Butler had battled Benny Dugan for decades and knew Benny would follow the court's instruction not to reveal the identity of D'Amico's lawyer.

"Benny," he began, shaking his head. "Benny, Benny, Benny."

"Sal," Benny answered, "is there a question?"

"This Dominic D'Amico you testified about, his trial was not going well for him, was it?"

"Didn't seem to be, to my eyes."

"Despite his being represented by highly competent counsel."

Benny mostly suppressed his smile. "Yes, despite his excellent lawyer. Sometimes the evidence is just overwhelming, as you know."

"He wanted to become a rat?"

"He wanted to cooperate in an effort to reduce his own sentence."

"In violation of the oath he claimed to have taken to join this alleged organization."

"Yes, in violation of the rules of Cosa Nostra, an organization that exists."

"So you say, so you say," Butler replied, clearly enjoying this. "But not demonstrating *la forza*—the strength—you have seen other defendants display, people who stand by their principles, no matter what."

"That's increasingly rare, as you know, Sal."

"But it happens, doesn't it? There are still people—of the old school—who make promises and keep them, aren't there?"

"There are," Benny answered. "Doesn't make a lot of sense to me, when the organization you made promises to is utterly amoral, but it happens, even today."

"Yes, it does," Butler replied. "Yes, it does. I have no further questions for this witness, Your Honor."

"Is there redirect?" Judge Whitney asked.

"No, Your Honor," Carmen said.

"Mr. Dugan, you are excused," the judge said.

Benny stepped down from the witness box, walked halfway along the jury box railing and turned right to slide his enormous frame behind the prosecutors' chairs, headed for his own. "Hilarious," he whispered. "Does this shit ever get old for you comedians?"

The daily lunch break was scheduled to end at two P.M. At 1:50, Benny wandered into the courtroom, knowing the marshals routinely delivered Gina to the courtroom early so they could remove her handcuffs and seat her at the defense table well before the jury returned to the box. As in every trial, they worked hard to conceal that a defendant was in custody, although the stone-faced women sitting just behind Gina were hard to disguise. Butler wasn't back from his regular lunch at Giambone's yet, so Benny scooted his rear-facing seat a little closer to the back table. Gina heard the chair scraping and looked up.

"Hey," Benny said, "I always treated you like a professional, right?"

Gina nodded slowly.

"Your nutcase bastard brother, Rico. You need to get a leash on him."

Gina squinted at Benny. She didn't know what he was talking about.

"That motherfucker's out there threatening these prosecutors, and their kids."

Now Gina made a surprised face.

"It's gotta stop," Benny said. "It ain't who you are and it's gonna start a war with us, and nobody wants that."

Gina exhaled through her nose, shaking her head slowly from side to side, and finally spoke in a low voice. "He's a stupid fuck." Looking down, she muttered, *"Scemo"—shay-mo*, "fool" in Italian. "Taken care of," she added. Benny pulled his chair back.

After three days of travel records and phones and FedEx packages, Nora and Carmen knew the jury wasn't connecting all the dots, but they would do that for them in summation. It was time for Frenchie to link Gina to the Gambino Family.

CHAPTER FORTY-FIVE

"**S**o the gang's back together again. Feels like that movie, *Groundhog Day*," Frenchie said, looking around the familiar witness room behind courtroom 318.

"You're tellin' me," Benny replied. Nodding his head in the direction of the courtroom, he added, "Everything's the same in there. Judge, Sal Butler, everything. Except Gina's sittin' in the chair of the guy she whacked. It's a beautiful story."

Frenchie laughed.

"Why aren't you more nervous?" Benny asked.

"Jeez," Frenchie said, "trying to ruin the mood, are we?"

Nora cut in. "What I think he means is, how are you doin'?"

"As I told you last night at the WITSEC place," Frenchie answered, "I'm good. Honestly, I'm not sure why, exactly. I'm about to testify against another mobster, but I don't feel like I did last time. And it's not because she's a she. I know what she's capable of. It's not that. I'm just in a better place than I was last time we were here."

Frenchie looked at Benny. "It's probably what you did with my boy. I just feel like there's a life for me now, after all this."

"There is," Nora said. "There is, and we're happy for you." She paused, then asked, "Any last-minute questions before we hit it?"

"You don't want me to try to ID her, right?"

"Well," Nora said, "you told us you don't think you've ever seen her, so there's no basis for identification. Just stick to what we went over—all the stuff you were told about Joey Cufaro's daughter. That's it. And, like we practiced, be specific as to who told you what. The judge is going to need that if Butler objects."

"Got it," Frenchie said. He looked at both of them, then added, "I know it's crazy, but I think I'm going to actually miss working with you two."

"Hey," Benny said, "don't get all soupy. Do your fuckin' job, then get on with your life."

Frenchie turned to Nora, "I'm not sure how you bear all his sentimentality."

With a grin, she said, "It's a burden," and stood to go into the courtroom. "See you in a minute."

Frenchie entered the courtroom, walked to the familiar witness stand between the jury box and the judge, raised his right hand and took the oath. When he sat, Nora saw him look toward the defense table just as she said, "Please state your name." Frenchie didn't acknowledge her—still staring at Butler or Gina—so she audibly cleared her throat and repeated the question more loudly. "Sir, please identify yourself for the jury." That did it. He gave a little shake of his head and then turned his eyes to her. *Oh no*, Nora thought, *not again. Please no.*

But Frenchie's direct examination went smoothly. As Nora had in the D'Amico trial, she led him through his life of crime, his work for D'Amico and other Gambino Family members and associates. Then she had him describe his contact with Joseph "Handsome Joey" Cufaro, Gina's father. He recalled D'Amico introducing him to the powerful Cufaro, who had a very specific request.

"He wanted me to obtain a stained-glass piece by Marc Chagall." Frenchie pronounced it correctly—*shuh-gaal.*

"Who is Marc Chagall?" Nora asked.

"He was a famous twentieth-century French artist, a modernist. Worked in all kinds of media, including a lot of stained glass. Did some famous stuff, like the *Peace Window* at the United Nations."

"How do you know so much about Chagall?"

"First, I'm an art thief," Frenchie answered, eliciting some light laughter from the jury, which was charmed by him. "Second, I was born in France and my mother always loved Chagall. Also, I had stolen some of his stuff before."

"You said Mr. Cufaro asked you to 'obtain' the stained-glass piece. What did you understand him to mean by 'obtain'?"

"Oh," Frenchie answered, "I don't think he used that actual word—obtain. He wanted me to steal it and he would pay me to do it. So he used some word like that. 'Get,' maybe. I don't remember exactly."

"What happened next?" Nora asked.

"Well, it took a lot of work, because the piece was actually in some fancy guy's apartment in Manhattan. Somehow Joey'd seen it, and wanted it. Eventually, I got in and got it for him."

"You stole it."

"Yes, yes, that's the only way I got stuff." Again the jurors smiled and chuckled.

"When was this, Mr. Joseph?"

"Ten, twelve years ago, not long before Joey died."

"And how did you get the Chagall piece to him?"

"I had forgotten before, but just remembered when I walked in here where he had me deliver that piece. I didn't understand why it was so special before now."

"Objection!" Butler shouted, having no idea what he was objecting to but deciding whatever Frenchie was remembering could not be good.

"What is the basis for your objection, Mr. Butler?" Judge Whitney asked.

"He just admitted changing his answers right there on the stand, Your Honor. He's just sayin' stuff. That ain't right."

That didn't make it any clearer, but Nora cut in. "I'll ask a question to clear this up, Judge."

"Very well," the judge answered.

She then broke the sacred rule to never ask a question in court if you don't know the answer, but she was pretty sure she now knew why Frenchie had frozen when he first looked at the defense table. They hadn't shown him a picture of Gina because he said he had never seen her. Showing him a photo after that would have opened the prosecutors up to a charge that they engaged in a suggestive identification procedure. But now, in living color, Frenchie remembered something.

"Mr. Joseph, did something in this courtroom refresh your recollection about the Chagall delivery?"

"Yes," he said, nodding vigorously.

"And what was that?"

Pointing at Gina, he said, "I remembered when I saw *her*. Joey had me deliver that beautiful piece to her and I thought she was his mistress or something, but now it makes sense. She's his daughter."

Nora took a chance with a leading question. "So you first met with him in the Bronx, but he told you to deliver the item somewhere else?"

"Yes. I talked to him about the job at his social club in the Bronx, but he didn't want the Chagall delivered there. He wanted me to bring it to some place in Florida, some place near Palm Beach, like a townhouse or condo. Not on the beach, but a few miles inland."

"And what happened?"

"I did what he wanted, because he was Joey Cufaro. I drove, because you can't roll up stained glass, and I couldn't take it on a plane or Amtrak."

"When you got to Florida, to whom did you deliver the stolen Chagall?"

"To her," he said, pointing, "his daughter."

Nora looked toward Judge Whitney. "Indicating the defendant, Your Honor."

"Yes," the judge replied, "the record will reflect that the witness has identified the defendant."

Butler started to stand several times, but didn't. He couldn't figure out whether this hurt him. Joey Cufaro *was* Gina's father, after all. And she was on trial for multiple murders, so who really cared if her dad threw her a stolen piece of glass?

Nora decided to move away from this, turning to Frenchie's accounts of his many conversations with Gambino Family members about Gina. Frenchie buried Gina in a pile of things he was told about what a valuable Family asset she was, and the power her killing brought the Gambinos, who even lent her out to other Families to use her special talents. It was strong nexus proof.

Judge Whitney called the lunch break between direct and cross.

"You gonna eat?" Benny asked Jessica.

She was sitting at her desk scrolling through photos on her computer. "Yeah. Just wanna finish looking at these."

Seconds later, she shouted, "Hah! That must be it."

"What?" Benny asked.

"The Chagall. Been going through all the photos the search team took at Gina's place in Palm Beach Gardens. I don't know anything about art, but that sure looks like stained glass."

Benny came over and looked at the picture of a poster-size piece of glass hanging in front of the window over Gina's kitchen sink, its irregular patchwork of blue pieces catching the early morning light. "Don't know art either, but I'd bet that's it. One thing's for sure: Frenchie's been there. He saw her, in her own house. Son of a bitch."

"I'm sending this to one of our art people. See if they can confirm it's a Chagall and get a copy to Nora while Frenchie is still on the stand."

CHAPTER FORTY-SIX

Butler had been to Giambone's for lunch, as was his habit. Nora had heard the rumors—that he liked to have two martinis at lunch, especially when he thought a trial was going well.

"Nora! Kid! How ya doin'?" he said loudly, walking up toward the government table as they waited for the judge and jury to return.

"I'm good, Sal, how're you?" Nora replied.

"Livin' the dream," Butler replied, as he twisted the cap off a travel-sized Listerine bottle, tilted his head, and emptied the 3.2 ounces into his mouth. He was close enough that Nora could hear him forcing the Listerine over his teeth, puffing out his cheeks as he did so. Then he pitched his head back, gargled audibly, and spit the liquid into the garbage can that had once held the indictment, dropping the empty bottle in after it.

"Keep bein' you," Butler said as he turned and walked back to the defense table.

Nora leaned forward and looked left down the table, to where Benny was in his usual seat, keeping an eye on the defendant and the spectator section. He had witnessed the Listerine show before. He leaned toward Nora. "Now you've seen it," he whispered. He smiled and added, "You need any more stips, this afternoon would be a good time to ask."

Back in his seat, Butler removed a gold-topped green bottle from his briefcase and shook Polo cologne into one palm. He set the bottle down and began rubbing his hands together, patted his cheeks, and then smeared the scent over his bald scalp before capping the bottle and returning it to his briefcase. Benny smiled and shook his head. *The mob's idea of a good lawyer is a different thing from a good lawyer.*

Butler swung wildly all afternoon, but didn't land a glove on Frenchie, who stayed feisty but dignified.

"Mr. Joseph," Butler asked near the end of his cross, "you aren't an official member of this so-called mah-fye-ah, are you?"

"No," Frenchie answered, "I was not an official member. An 'associate' is what they called it."

"And that's not because you weren't a criminal, because you were, right?"

"Yes, that's correct."

"It was because you weren't an honorable enough person, right?"

"Well—" Frenchie began.

"You weren't a person who could adhere to a code of honor, one that stretched back centuries, am I right?"

Frenchie made a confused face. "Are you right that I'm not such a person or are you right that this organization you say doesn't exist stretched back centuries?"

"I'll withdraw the question and rephrase it, if that makes it easier for you," Butler said.

"Suit yourself," Frenchie said.

"You weren't a member, is that your testimony?"

"It still is."

"Yet you expect us to believe that made men—*uomini d'onore*—men who had taken solemn and ancient oaths, entrusted the secrets of this so-called Cosa Nostra to you, a thief who couldn't get in?"

"They told me stuff about Gina Cufaro, yes."

"But you don't know who killed Governor Burke or any of the other victims named in the indictment."

"I don't."

"Because nobody ever told you my client killed a particular person."

"That's right. They just told me, a lot, that she was a very special killer for them."

Butler looked toward the bench. "Judge, I'd ask you to strike that answer as non-responsive."

Judge Whitney was tired now. "No," he said, "overruled. This is cross and you asked the question, but Mr. Joseph, please do try to answer only the question you are asked. Mr. Butler, how much more of this do you have?"

"If I could have a moment, Your Honor." Butler walked to the defense table, leaning in close and whispering to Gina, who seemed very unhappy with her lawyer.

Hope she likes Listerine—and Polo, Benny thought, watching the scene.

Butler straightened up, still standing by his client. "That'll do it, Judge."

"Very well," Judge Whitney replied. Looking at the government table, he said, "We'll go right into redirect."

Nora popped up. "Just one, Your Honor. May I approach the witness?"

"You may," the judge answered.

She handed Frenchie an eight-by-ten color photograph identified earlier as one taken during the FBI search of Gina's home. It depicted her kitchen.

"Mr. Joseph, I'd like to direct your attention to Government Exhibit-in-evidence 52F, as in Frank."

Because the photograph was already in evidence, it also appeared on the monitor screens in the jury box and around the courtroom.

"Would you take a look at that and tell me if you recognize anything about it?"

Frenchie seemed genuinely surprised and pleased, as if seeing an old friend. "Yes, yes, that's it, that's the Chagall! You see the way he uses the lead tape to join so many different blues in all those strange shapes? Amazing. And it looks great where she put it."

Nora was eager to end this before he got too relaxed. "No further questions, Your Honor."

Whitney nodded to Frenchie, "The witness is free to go."

Frenchie was not free, but he was done.

Now Judge Whitney turned to the jury. "It seems we have reached a logical stopping point for the day. I wish you a good evening, ladies and gentleman. Please remember my admonition that you should avoid any media that may concern this case. Safe travels."

When the jury was gone, the judge looked to the government table. "Ms. Carleton, how much more do you have? For the court's planning purposes only."

"I'm not sure, Judge. We are still working through some things. Can I let you know in the morning?"

"Very well," he replied, standing and turning toward the door. "The court will stand in recess."

Butler ambled up to Nora as she was packing up. "Kid," he began, the word stretched out—*key-iddd*—"so what's the big mystery about tomorrow?"

Nora answered without looking up from her packing. "No mystery, Sal. We're just still sorting out how we're going to finish up."

"That's not like you feds, wingin' shit. Can ya gimme a hint, maybe some of the possibles?"

"Can't Sal. But not winging stuff."

His tone darkened abruptly. "Hey, don't fuck with me. My client needs to know what's comin' next. She has questions and I need to answer them. Don't leave me standing here with my you-know-what in my hand."

Now Nora stopped and looked down at Butler, who was several inches shorter. "Actually, Sal, I don't know what and I don't want to know. And I have no additional information to provide you at the present time.

"See you in the morning," she added and brushed past him toward the door by the judge's bench.

Butler turned back to the defense table, where Gina sat glaring at him, and walked to his client with both hands in front, palms up, shrugging his shoulder pads. He then sat and Gina leaned toward his ear, whispering intensely. Butler whispered back, his head now red. They went back and forth, mouth to ear, mouth to ear, until a Deputy Marshal rose holding handcuffs and touched Gina on the shoulder. Time to go.

CHAPTER FORTY-SEVEN

First thing in the morning, Butler was back at the government table. "*Now* can I tell my client what's happening? She's entitled to know. She wants to know."

Before Nora could answer, Judge Whitney came through the door and swept to the bench, smiling at the jury as Butler retreated to the defense table. "Good morning, everybody. I trust you had a restful night." Dropping the smile, he turned to look at Nora. "Call your next witness."

As Nora began to stand, a slight twinge of anxiety hit her stomach. It was very unusual for federal prosecutors to call a surprise witness.

The door to the witness waiting room opened before Nora could announce the witness, but Gina didn't need the name, because stepping into courtroom 318 was the handsome man who had been her lover since high school.

"The government calls Conor McCarthy," Nora announced as he reached the witness stand.

Benny was staring at Gina the entire time. Her demeanor didn't change when Conor walked in, but some of the color drained from her face. Butler looked confused and repeatedly turned his head to Gina, then to the stranger entering the courtroom. But from Gina, nothing. *Now that's kinda impressive*, Benny thought. *Crazy cold, but impressive.*

As the clerk administered the oath, Nora walked to the podium, pausing to hand Butler a copy of the 302 Jessica wrote after their interview with Conor and a copy of his testimony at Kyra Burke's trial. Butler slid the documents to Gina, who picked them up and leaned toward his ear, whispering energetically. Several times he held up his finger to quiet her before she finally stopped. Then he stood up.

"Mr. Butler?" Judge Whitney said.

"May I approach, Your Honor?"

"Certainly," the judge said, sliding his chair to the side of the bench.

The sidebar was theoretically out of the jury's hearing, but Butler was hot and very loud—clearly hoping both the jury and his client would hear him.

"Judge, in a clear violation of law and practice, I was given this witness's 3500 material as he walked into the courtroom. I have had *no* chance, *zero*, to review that material and prepare my cross-examination. I *object* to the government's *devious* tactics and move for a *mistrial* or, in the alternative, a continuance of at *least* several days to address the extreme prejudice."

Judge Whitney had finally stopped having strong reactions to Butler. Instead he just looked at Nora. "Ms. Carleton?"

"It's true that we just now gave Mr. Butler this witness's 302, which includes a list of the times we met to prepare him to testify, as well as a copy of his brief testimony in state court. For a variety of security-related reasons, we thought that appropriate and it is exactly what 18 USC Section 3500 contemplates, although I recognize our office's normal practice is more generous. The material consists of a five-page summary of his interview, which largely tracks what he will testify to today, and his thirteen-page public testimony in state court. Mr. Butler could read it in ten minutes, but we have no objection, given the hour, if Your Honor wishes to give him a reasonable amount of time after the direct to read it and prepare for his cross-examination."

"Very well, that's what we'll do," the judge said. "Mr. Butler, your objection is noted but the court believes a brief continuance will remedy any prejudice you perceive. We will complete the direct today and your cross will begin at ten tomorrow morning. The court has unrelated matters to attend to, in any event. Now step back, please."

Back at the podium, Nora went for it right away.

"Mr. McCarthy, do you know Gina Cufaro?"

"Yes, I do."

"How?"

"We've been close since we started dating in high school."

"Your relationship has been a romantic one to this day?"

"Yes, you could say that."

"Is she in this courtroom?"

"Yes, there," he said, pointing to the defense table. Gina just stared back. *If looks could kill*, Benny thought, his eyes never leaving Gina.

"Your Honor, may the record reflect that the witness has identified the defendant?"

"It will," Judge Whitney answered.

"Mr. McCarthy," Nora continued, "did you spend a night at the Lucerne Hotel here in Manhattan the evening before Tony Burke was killed?"

"I did."

"Were you alone?"

"No, I was with Gina."

Nora nodded to Jessica, and the monitor screens came to life.

"Mr. McCarthy, I'd like you to watch what has been admitted into evidence as Government Exhibit 70."

The video compilation played, showing the journey of the blonde killer from the elevator at the Lucerne to Central Park West and back.

When he finished watching, Conor looked up. Nora paused until the jurors did the same, then asked, "Who is that in the video?"

"Gina," he answered, sounding sad.

"How do you know that?"

"Because I know her. I've known her walk, her body, almost my whole life. She's obviously wearing a wig, but that's her."

"As you look at the video, does she resemble anyone else you know?"

"Yes, Kyra Burke, Tony's wife."

Nora then paused and, almost as if beginning again, asked a new series of questions so Conor could introduce himself to the jury—his working-class Bronx upbringing and falling for Gina at the Catholic high school they both attended.

"You mentioned that your mother worked cleaning hotel rooms for over twenty years and your father was a doorman in Manhattan. What did Gina's father do?"

"Objection," Butler shouted.

"No, I'll allow it. Overruled," Judge Whitney replied.

"It wasn't clear to me, at first," Conor said. "He just seemed to spend a lot of time sitting in front of a social club just off Arthur Avenue. Lots of people would come and go, talking with him all day long. He seemed important and respected in the neighborhood."

"Did there come a time when Gina told you what he did?"

"Yes."

"What did she say?"

"Objection," Butler shouted again.

"Overruled," Judge Whitney replied. "Calls for a statement by your client, Mr. Butler."

"She said he was in the Mafia, a big guy in it."

At that, Butler let out an audible "Hah!" and leaned back in his chair, arms crossed. Judge Whitney abruptly moved his head toward the sound and appeared to be about to speak, but Butler quickly looked down and the judge turned back to the witness.

Nora ignored the noise. "Did you come to know her father better?" she asked.

"I did. I hid it from my own folks, but I got along well with Mr. Cufaro and would sit and talk with him a lot at the club. He would send me to do errands and pay me for it."

"What kind of errands?"

Butler was on his feet again, objecting. He was clearly trying to break up this testimony.

"Overruled," Judge Whitney said. He was done giving reasons.

"Just going to pick up an envelope from a guy, or deliver one, that kind of thing."

"You said you hid it from your parents. Why?"

"They didn't like Mr. Cufaro—or his world, at least—and didn't want me hanging around him. I used to tell people it was because the Irish didn't like the Italians, but it was more than that."

"And how did you explain the money you were making?"

"Told them I got a job at Macy's downtown."

"Was that true?"

"No. I was hanging out at the club."

"You told the jury what your parents thought. Did *you* like Mr. Cufaro?"

"Yes, very much. I liked Gina most of all, but I also thought he was a cool guy. He talked all the time about how much potential I had. As a kid, I think I craved that affirmation and my family didn't have any extra money, so it made a big difference when he paid me for jobs."

"Objection, relevance," Butler called out.

"Overruled."

"What did you understand him to mean by your 'potential'?"

Butler was up again. "Your Honor, I'd like to have a continuing objection to this witness's testimony."

There was no such thing in federal criminal procedure but Judge Whitney was tired of Butler, so he nodded. Thinking he had his "continuing objection," Butler sat back down and remained seated.

"He was never specific about his expectations for me," Conor said. "He didn't talk about his work, but Gina explained that only men could join his thing, and it had to be men with an Italian father. So we were both out. Still, he used to talk all the time about the great things I could do with my life to make myself useful and he really pushed me to go to a great college. He told me that the guys in suits with fancy degrees ran the world and made big money. He made me want those things."

"Did you?"

"Did I what?"

"Go to a great college?"

"Yes, definitely. I applied to a bunch of schools and got into Yale, which was my top choice."

"How could you afford Yale?"

"Mr. Cufaro was really excited about it and said he would pay. And he did."

"What did your parents think about that?"

"Nothing. I told them I was getting scholarships and could cover the rest with on-campus jobs. So they never knew."

"Did Gina go to college with you?"

"No, she stayed home and commuted to Iona, which is a Catholic college in New Rochelle, not far from their house."

"Did your relationship continue?"

"It did, although it got kinda tense for a while. Gina had this idea that I was gonna have Ivy League girls all over me or something. I would actually see her on campus following me sometimes, like to check up on me. We had a couple bad arguments over it. Finally, I decided I would just tell everyone at school I was not looking for any kind of relationship. Told my parents the same thing."

"Was that true?"

"No, of course not, because I was in one with Gina, but it was the best way, actually the only way, I could think to handle the situation. I cared a lot about Gina—still do—and she was getting really upset. It was making her dad crazy too—and he was paying my tuition. So that took care of it. She was actually really touched by me doing that. Made us closer, which was good."

"What did you major in at Yale?"

"Political science."

"What did Mr. Cufaro think of that?"

"He said he loved the idea and pushed me after graduation to get a job with a politician and start working my way up in that world."

"Did you get that kind of job?"

"Yes, with a state legislator named Tony Burke."

"What did Mr. Cufaro say about that?"

"He loved it. He used to say, 'That guy's goin' places and he's gonna take you—and us—with him.'"

"Did your parents approve?"

"Yes, very much. I used to joke it was because Burke was an Irish name, but they loved it. And I loved it. Felt like I was doing something good."

"What did Gina do after graduating from Iona?"

"Her dad set her up in Florida—Palm Beach Gardens. She got a realtor's license so she would have a legit job to point to."

"What do you mean by a legit job?"

"Well, she was going to continue doing stuff for her dad, but that's not the kind of stuff where you get a W-2. She needed something to explain her income."

"Why didn't Gina stay in New York?"

"The sexism of the mob drove her crazy. Believe it or not, it bugged her dad a little, too, that she couldn't be an official part of the Family because she was a woman. So they came up with the idea to have her move away from it but still be part of his crew."

"What did being 'part of his crew' involve?"

"I didn't know. Never really knew, and actually didn't want to know. It was one of those things you didn't ask."

"Did there come a time when Mr. Cufaro wanted something from you in connection with your work with Tony Burke?"

"Yes. After I'd been there a few years, he started asking to meet local New York politicians I knew. And he wanted to meet Tony Burke—who was a state senator by then."

"What did you say?"

"I told him I didn't feel comfortable doing that."

"What did he say?"

"He got really angry. I had seen him mad at other people before but this was the first time it was directed at me. So I actually remember it pretty clearly. He said, 'Well, this ain't about your feelings. F your feelings'—except he said the curse word. 'This is about you owing me and you doing the right thing. Capisce?'—which means *understand* in Italian."

"Did you understand?"

"I did, very clearly. I made the introductions, including to Tony, but I also made it clear that my help didn't go beyond introductions. I didn't want to know what came next, with any of them."

"Did you continue working for Tony Burke when he first ran for governor?"

"I did, although I went on the campaign payroll, so I wasn't a state employee for that part."

"What difference did that make?"

"He was able to pay me a lot of money. And he did. The campaign had a lot of cash coming in—I think from a lot of the connections I helped make—and—"

Butler stirred, apparently deciding his "continuing objection" may have expired.

"Objection to his speculation, Your Honor."

"Sustained," Judge Whitney said, turning to Conor. "Only testify to what you know."

"I know the campaign had a lot of money," Conor said, "and they paid me a ton, which I saved and invested. Then I went back to being a state employee when he was reelected."

"What did you do with the money from the campaign?"

"Like I said, I held onto it and tried to grow it. Also used some of it to help my parents so my mom could stop working on account of her arthritis. Tried to get my dad to retire, too, but he loved his work. He still works in the same building to this day."

"What was the nature of your relationship with Gina during this time?"

"Still romantic, I guess. It wasn't what you would call a normal relationship, but we loved each other and enjoyed our time together. But then her dad died, from cancer, and things got harder between us."

"What do you mean?"

Conor looked down to his folded hands in his lap and spoke more quickly—with new emotion in his voice. "After he died, she never wanted to come to New York anymore. Always wanted me to come see her in Florida. She said that I was the only man she cared about now that her father was gone. I had to come at least once a month or she would get really angry. She told me she wasn't involved with her father's crew anymore and that she was just a realtor now."

"Was that true?"

Conor looked up, his eyes filling with unshed tears. "I don't know. I always avoided knowing and never asked questions. But I did know she started making big money after her dad was gone and also started traveling, which I never understood—for a realtor to travel. I felt us growing apart, like I didn't know who she was anymore."

"At any point after Mr. Cufaro died, did you consider ending your relationship with Gina?"

"I thought about it but I couldn't. It's hard to explain. I knew I should but I also cared about her a lot. She's literally the only woman I've ever loved."

"Do you still love her?"

Conor started to answer, then stopped and looked down, drawing deep breaths through his mouth.

Benny never took his eyes off Gina, who responded to Conor's evident emotion by dropping her head heavily, as if overcome by her own feelings.

Judge Whitney pushed a box of tissues across the top of the bench and nodded to the witness. Conor turned and took a tissue from the box, wiping his eyes. When he looked up, they were wet.

"I'm sorry," he said, his voice cracking, "can you repeat the question?"

Gina now looked up, her face still a piece of stone. *You can't even fake it*, Benny thought.

"Yes," Nora said, "I was asking whether you still loved Gina Cufaro."

He sniffled again. "I don't know. I'm not sure I know what love is anymore, but our relationship hasn't been okay for quite a while."

"Were you ever afraid of her?"

"Sure, sometimes, especially after her dad was gone and she got angry a lot more often. But she could also be so kind to me. Always said she was sorry after she got mad."

"What happened to your job after Tony Burke finished his second term as governor and left office?"

"I still had a job—he wanted me as his chief of staff, for him as a private citizen—but I thought my political career was over."

"Why?"

"Well, all kinds of bad stuff came out around the time he left office about his treatment of women. Mistreatment, I should say. He denied it all to me and I believed him at first. But then people I really trust came to me with proof of his bad behavior and I knew it was completely over for him. But he was still talking about running for president, again, which was crazy."

"What did you do?"

"Nothing right away, but a couple weeks before he died I finally worked up the nerve and went to tell him he couldn't run for office anymore, that he had too much baggage—I think I said 'too many sexual skeletons in the closet'—and that he was finished as a politician. I told him I was going to sign up with another candidate. I didn't tell him at the time but my plan was to go with his son, Edward Burke, who I'd known for years and who didn't have Tony's issues."

"What did he say?"

"He got very angry and said that I was the one with the skeletons. Then he called me 'Mr. *Nostra Amico*,' and said I should 'shut the F up.'"

"What did you understand him to mean by 'Mr. *Nostra Amico*'?"

"It was a reference to the Mafia. They refer to someone who is part of a Mafia Family as a 'friend of ours'—*nostra amico* in Italian. I wasn't, but that was the reference."

"What did you take that to mean?"

"I took it as a threat, to reveal stuff about me and the people I introduced to him and other politicians. He was going to ruin me if I didn't stay with him."

"What did you do next?"

"I was down at Gina's that weekend and I told her what he said."

"What, if anything, did she say?"

"She offered to talk to him. She had met him a few times when he was in Florida for fundraisers and he knew who her father was. I said there was no way he would want to see her, especially not in New York."

"What happened next?"

"Gina was really insistent, as she can be, saying she wanted to help me keep my career going and that it was also important that her father's business remain confidential. She said she would just 'stop by' and tell the governor to apologize to me, quit politics, keep his mouth shut, and retire. She said I deserved to have a career and she could make Burke understand that. She believed he would listen to her. Eventually made me believe it too."

"So what did you do?"

"I said, 'He'll never let you in,' but she said to just give her the elevator code to his place and she asked me about his schedule. She came up the day before, stayed at the Lucerne, like you saw. I told her he was always home after six P.M. during the week. I assumed she would distract or pay off the doorman, then use the code to get upstairs, have a quick conversation, convince him, then leave. All good."

"Did she tell you she would dress up to look like Kyra Burke?"

"No, most definitely not."

"To your knowledge, did Gina know Kyra Burke?"

"She knew who she was, because Kyra and I have been friends since college—and Kyra was one of the people Gina was initially jealous about, which was crazy—but to my knowledge they never met."

"Did you speak to Gina Cufaro after her visit to Tony Burke's penthouse?"

"Yes, I think we talked on the phone that night, before she went back to Florida."

"What did she say?"

"That the conversation had gone well, although she was worried about Tony. Said he seemed really worn down by all the accusations against him. He'd told her he knew he was finished and that I had to move on—everybody had to move on from him. His time was done, he'd told her. That's what she said."

"Did there come a time when you learned he was dead?"

"Yes, I got a call from the police late that night. They were looking at it as a suicide, which was horrible but didn't surprise me, after what Gina had said."

"When did you learn the police viewed it as a homicide?"

"I don't remember, exactly; in the week after or so."

"Did you tell the police that you knew Gina had been to see him the night he died?"

"No," Conor answered, his voice beginning to crack.

"Why not?"

"I don't know. I didn't want to believe she'd done anything, so I did what I've always done—just pushed it away."

"You're aware Kyra Burke was charged by the local authorities with killing her husband that night."

"I am."

"In fact, you testified at her state trial."

"I did. They asked me questions about a prenuptial agreement Tony and Kyra had."

"Why didn't you tell them you knew who had done it?"

Conor answered rapid-fire as he began to cry, his words running into each other. "Because nobody asked and I really care about Gina and I'm also afraid of her and I didn't *know* she had done it and I still don't to be honest. I told you the truth when you asked about Gina, but the rest . . ."

Conor's voice trailed off. For a moment he dropped his head, shoulders jerking, breath audible. Then he looked up, tears running down his face, and seemed to speak to the defense table. "Tony Burke was so good to me, and Gina is like a piece of me, or me of her. I still don't want to think these things."

Judge Whitney reached over and nudged the tissue box even closer to the witness.

Nora paused and looked down at her notes.

"Anything further, Ms. Carleton?" Judge Whitney asked, turning a concerned glance toward the witness, who was now visibly crying on the stand.

Nora said, "If I could just confer with cocounsel, Judge." She walked to the government table and leaned down to Carmen. "Miss anything?" she asked.

Carmen shook her head "no," but tapped her pen to alert Nora to a Post-it note stuck to the table. In Benny's handwriting, it read, *Rico*

Faraci's body found in the Gowanus Canal. Fredo Corleone? Nora immediately understood the reference to the murder of the unreliable brother
in the movie *The Godfather.*

Whoa, she thought, *life imitating art in a really dark way.* She stood
up straight and said, "No further questions, Your Honor."

Judge Whitney explained to the jury that he was taking the afternoon off to deal with unrelated cases and sending them home. They
were off until the morning.

The team gathered back at Carmen's office to hear Benny's report on
Faraci, which wasn't much more than the Post-it note had said—NYPD
pulled his body out of the heavily polluted two-hundred-year-old canal
running from New York Harbor up into the heart of Brooklyn, cause of
death not yet determined. "Could be 'cause of the stupid shit he pulled
with you two," Benny said. "Or it could be somethin' unrelated, or could
be it all just piled up to a point that he had to go. Hard to say right now."

CHAPTER FORTY-EIGHT

Before court the next morning, the judge's clerk motioned to Nora and Butler and they approached her desk, situated just below the front of the judge's bench. "Judge Whitney would like to see counsel in the robing room, with the court reporter."

When they walked in, Whitney was already in his robe, sitting behind the big wood desk. "I've received a communication from the marshals that one of the jurors has asked to speak to the court, urgently. I intend to invite the juror in here now, and wanted counsel present and a record made. Only I will communicate with the juror, is that clear?"

The lawyers all nodded.

"Which juror?" Butler asked.

"He is currently juror number twelve." Whitney replied.

Belmont guy, Nora thought. *What the hell?*

The door opened and the juror entered, his eyes nervously sweeping the room. The judge directed him to a chair placed in front of the three set out for the lawyers, so he would see only the judge when he spoke.

Whitney spoke first. "Welcome, Juror Twelve—and I again remind everyone that we are not to know the names of our jurors. I understand you wished to speak with me. Of course, I need to have the lawyers present to do so, but please relax and tell me what's on your mind."

The juror's voice was shaking. He lifted his hands as he started to speak. Nora could see that they were shaking as well. "Judge," he began, "I need to get off this jury."

"That's a very unusual request," the judge said. "Can you tell me why?"

"Twice this week, including last night, my wife was approached by people from the neighborhood who tried to talk to her about the case. Once in the beauty salon, last night in the grocery store. People she knows, but only from seeing them in the store and whatnot. Not quite pushing her, but trying to make conversation—send a message. Twice. These people may be dangerous and they know I'm on this jury, people near me, they know who my family is, and I can't be on this jury anymore."

"And why does that make you believe you can't be on the jury any longer?" Whitney asked.

"Because I'm not going to let it get to a place where there is an ask. I'm just not. I won't put my family in that position. Because I would say no to any ask—I'd have to, 'cause I took an oath—but that would put me in a bad spot, put my family in a bad spot. And I'm not gonna do it to them."

Whitney kept pushing. "But, as you said, there have been no improper contacts to this point—"

The juror cut him off with the magic words. "Judge, I can no longer live up to my promise to be fair and impartial. I just can't, given what's happened. I'm sorry."

"Very well, then let me ask you to go with the clerk to the other room, just for a moment, while I confer with counsel."

When he was out of the room, the judge turned to the lawyers. "Well, any objection to my excusing this juror?"

Butler gave it his best shot. "Judge, it's all theory. What's really happened here? Couple conversations in a store. That's it. He's an honest person who will tell us if anything improper happens. And I'd also note that he appears frightened by the government's constant harping on organized crime and violence. My client wanted this fair-minded juror, and his departure will operate to her substantial detriment."

Nora wanted to say, "Are you serious right now?" Instead, she said, "The man is frightened. His wife has been approached, when honest people would have no reason on earth to know of his connection to this case. On top of that, he's told you—he can't be fair and impartial—and for good reasons. He can't stay."

Belmont guy was excused and Juror 13 moved to his seat. Butler's objection was noted.

Back in the courtroom Nora leaned toward Benny's ear to tell him what had happened in the robing room.

"That must be why Butler was so full of himself," Benny grumbled. "The motherless fuck figured he was gonna hang the jury. Big mistake leavin' Belmont on."

"You really want to relitigate that?" Nora asked sharply.

Carmen cut it off as the door next to the bench opened. "Hey, hey, everybody to their corners."

Benny sat up and nodded to Gina as she was brought into the courtroom and had her handcuffs removed by the federal marshals. She was dressed in a pink turtleneck sweater and black dress pants with her hair pulled back in a ponytail. Benny thought she looked exhausted and much older than when the trial began. She pursed her lips and slowly nodded back before taking her place at the defense table. Butler stood up to hold her chair and leaned over to whisper in her ear.

Then the judge and jury entered the courtroom and Conor was back on the stand.

"We'll go right into cross-examination," Judge Whitney said. "Mr. Butler?"

"Thank you, Judge." Butler got up from the table holding what looked to be a pile of pages torn off a yellow legal pad. He laid them on the podium, smoothed the stack with the palm of his hand, and began questioning—reading a series of assertions.

"You've been in love with Kyra since college."

"That's not true."

"You've always loved Kyra."

"Not true."

"In your eyes, she was a high-class woman, especially compared to your high school girlfriend from the Bronx."

"She was a fine person, but so was—so is—Gina."

"Twice a week during your senior year of college, you used to meet Kyra at—"

Butler paused, then carried the top yellow sheet to the defense table and leaned down to Gina, pointing. She whispered something and he returned to the podium.

"—the Yankee Doodle Coffee Shop at the corner of Elm and York."

Benny watched this entire exchange. *Holy shit, she wrote out a bunch of questions last night and Butler has to read them.*

"That's actually true," Conor answered. "I studied at Sterling Library and she took a class at the law school. We would meet at the Doodle for coffee after her class because it was right there. It was never romantic. Ever."

"Joey Cufaro was very good to you."

"He was."

"In fact, Joey Cufaro made you."

"Not in the Mafia sense, but I owe him my education for sure, if that's what you mean."

"That actually is Kyra in the videos, just as the DA thought."

"No."

"You and Kyra conspired to frame Gina for Burke's death."

"We did not."

"Gina has loved you nearly her entire life and you repay that by lying about her and stabbing her in the back."

Nora considered objecting to the form of that question but let it go. The entire thing was too painful.

"That's not true," Conor said. Turning his head to look directly at Gina, he added, "It's really not."

Now Butler looked up from the yellow sheets and the tone changed. It was time for his own questions.

"You a good liar, Mr. McCarthy?" he asked with a snarl.

"I don't know what you mean."

"You don't know what I mean," Butler echoed. "Let's take the romance thing. You told the people closest to you something about you that wasn't true for years and years—that you were not interested in a relationship—am I right?"

"I did."

"I know you said you did it because you had to if you were gonna keep your girlfriend, which makes no sense whatsoever, but it was still a lie and nobody made you lie, right?"

Nora was close to jumping up, but let it go; she didn't want the jury to think Conor was on the government's team.

Butler didn't let him answer anyway, instead asking a new question. "So you lied about one of the most important parts of being human, is that right?"

"I suppose it is. People throughout history have felt like they had to lie about their love lives. They all had their own reasons and I had mine."

"And the people you told, including the people who knew you best, they believed you, didn't they?"

"I think they did, yes."

"Because even those who knew you best, even the woman who carried you in her womb and brought you into this world, they couldn't tell you were lyin', correct?"

"I think you're correct. And I'm deeply sor—"

Butler cut him off, his tone sarcastic. "Yeah, I can't speak for the jury, but I'm not real interested in your expressions of regret." Then he raised his voice almost to a shout. "The point is, people can't tell when you lie, even if it's about important stuff, right?"

"I suppose that's true."

Now he simply yelled. "So why are you wastin' this jury's time with these fairy tales?"

Nora was on her feet but Judge Whitney didn't wait, his own voice just below a shout. "Mr. Butler, you will conduct yourself like a member of the bar of this court. Do not make me speak to you again about it. The objection is sustained and the jury will disregard the question."

Butler's tone came back to earth, as if the whole thing never happened. "Certainly, Your Honor. I have no further questions."

Not bad, Benny thought. *Not much more he could do with a guy who's been with his client forever.*

"Redirect, Ms. Carleton?" Judge Whitney asked.

"Briefly, Your Honor. Mr. McCarthy, did you tell the truth at Kyra Burke's trial?"

"Yes."

"Did you tell the truth in this court?"

"Yes."

"Why?"

"Because I'm under oath and I take that seriously. I lied in my personal life—for love," he added, looking at Gina, "but a court of law is different."

"Nothing further, Your Honor. The government rests."

After sending the jury to lunch early, Judge Whitney invited Sal Butler to make his Rule 29 motion for a judgment of acquittal, which a judge could only grant if, drawing all inferences in favor of the government, no reasonable jury could convict. It was a steep hill for the defense to climb, but the motion had to be made if they wanted to argue on appeal that the evidence was insufficient. Butler's heart wasn't in it but his mood was still sunny, even after the loss of Belmont guy.

"Your Honor, at this time," he said, "I'd like to make the usual motion under Rule 29."

"Very well, Mr. Butler, that motion is denied. Be prepared to begin any defense case immediately after lunch."

"I'll be ready, Judge," he said with smile. "We should finish today given how cooperative the government has been in stipulating to the testimony of various witnesses. They've been complete professionals."

"Glad to hear it," the judge said. "The court will stand in recess until two P.M."

As they packed up, Nora and Carmen exchanged looks. "Sal's still on happy pills after losing his hanging juror?" Nora whispered. "Makes no sense."

"Yup," Carmen answered. "Something else has him all giddy. Just wish we knew what it was."

The defense case began with Maybelline Rocco, the owner of the Florida realty company that employed Gina Cufaro. Rocco was of an indeterminate age between fifty and seventy-five, with long straight platinum blonde hair, drawn-on eyebrows, ruby red fingernails, and heavy makeup on her deeply tanned skin. She walked very carefully up the stairs to the witness box on four-inch red heels, her movements further limited by her sleeveless knee-length body-hugging red dress.

Gina had been one of her "stars" for the last eighteen years, she said, moving people in and out of the white-hot South Florida residential real-estate market. She was diligent, trustworthy, hardworking, and efficient, and her clients loved her.

At this point, Butler interrupted the direct examination to read to the jury from stipulations between the defense and the government. If called as witnesses, the agreements said, in substance, five former customers of Gina's would testify that she was an amazing realtor. The details were all in the stipulations, which Butler read loudly while facing the jury.

He then turned back to Maybelline Rocco. "Do you have an opinion as to Gina's reputation for honesty in your community?"

"I do," she replied, the New York accent of her youth still very fresh.

"And what is that opinion?"

"People find her honest, hardworking, and law-abiding."

"Ms. Rocco," Butler asked, pausing to increase the drama, "do you believe Gina is a professional killer?"

"That's crazy, no," she answered.

"I have no further questions, Your Honor."

"Any questions, Ms. Carleton?" Judge Whitney asked.

Nora stood quickly. "Just one, Judge, and I can ask it from here, with your permission."

When he nodded, Nora asked, "Who is Mildred Jamison?"

The witness answered quickly and honestly—as near as Nora could tell. "I don't know anybody by that name."

"Nothing further," Nora said, sitting in her chair. Carmen scribbled a note and slid it to her. *Thin to win, baby!* it read. Nora flipped the note and wrote: *I could have gone into all the financial stuff, but there's so much power in the one question.* Carmen nodded her agreement.

Next, Butler and a paralegal acted out the state-court testimony of Tony Burke's doorman, Ivan Ramirez, who thought it was Kyra Burke who passed through the lobby that night. Butler wanted to avoid live testimony because he feared Ramirez might compensate for his role in Kyra's prosecution by now nailing Gina. For her part, Nora could have insisted Ramirez testify live, but agreed to the transcript because there was always the possibility Butler would push him into saying more if he were on the stand. And she wasn't worried about what was in the transcript. *Of course he thought it was Kyra. Duh. That was the point of Gina's disguise.*

When the transcript reading was done, Judge Whitney asked, "Mr. Butler, is there further defense evidence?"

Butler paused and then answered with exaggerated solemnity. "Yes, Your Honor, there certainly is. At this time, the defense calls . . . Mildred Jamison."

Nora thought she must have misheard. She turned her head slightly to look at Carmen, who was squinting. *Musta misheard the same thing*, Nora thought. She glanced at Benny, who was facing backward, eyes fixed on the back of the courtroom, the same place all the jurors were looking.

Through the public doors came a woman who bore a resemblance to Gina, escorted by one of Butler's assistants. She walked through the swinging half doors separating the gallery from the well of the courtroom, navigated around the tables, and stepped up to the witness stand. Following the clerk's instructions, she remained standing, raised her right hand to take the oath, then sat in the chair and stated her name. "Mildred Jamison."

Feels like a bad dream, Nora thought, her face a mask.

Whatever was happening, Butler was loving the moment. "May I proceed, Your Honor?"

"You may," Judge Whitney answered.

"Ms. Jamison, where do you reside?"

"Loxahatchee, Florida."

"And can you tell the jury where that is?"

She turned to the jury box. "Palm Beach County, the far west side, long way from the ocean. Think dirt roads and alligators."

Mildred Jamison then told her story. She was a forty-one-year-old Florida native who worked at an IT consulting company in Palm Beach County. She handed Butler her driver's license, which he displayed on courtroom screens. She said she traveled quite a bit for work and preferred to fly out of Miami because it offered more flight options. She owned a cell phone, which she had brought with her, and she recited the phone's number for the jury. It was the number of the "burner phone" the prosecution said was Gina's, although the government had never found that phone.

On the courtroom monitors, Butler displayed a listing of the air travel the prosecution associated with Gina's murders.

"Did I ask you to look at your travel records before coming to court today?"

"You did."

"And what did you conclude with respect to the flights listed on Government Exhibit 29?"

"I took all those flights, to client jobs or conferences."

"Now let me show a collection of airport surveillance photos that the government has put into evidence. Would you take a look at those and tell me if you know who that is in those pictures?"

"Yes, it's me. On those trips."

Butler left the podium and walked to stand behind Gina, putting his hands on her shoulders. "Ms. Jamison, do you know this woman?"

"I do not."

"I have no further questions," Butler said and walked to his seat.

Nora's world was spinning. "We'll go right into cross-examination," Judge Whitney said.

The spinning slowed enough for Nora to ask, "May we approach, Your Honor?"

At sidebar, Nora spoke first, trying to sound only mildly irritated. "Judge, we were given absolutely no information about this witness and the government will need time to prepare."

The judge turned his head to Butler.

"That's rich," Butler began, "given the chicanery"—again *chai-cane-erie*—"with Conor McCarthy. But we have no information to provide. I have no prior statements of this witness, who has never been in trouble with the law. I don't know what it is Ms. Carleton thinks she's entitled to."

Judge Whitney turned back to Nora, who said nothing. *Maybe some advance notice that a witness is going to tell a lie so massive I can't figure out what to do about it? How 'bout that?*

"Very well," the judge said, "I see no basis for the court to act here. We'll go right into cross-examination. Please step back."

Nora was working hard not to look panicked in front of the jury. She returned to the government table to retrieve her notebook. Carmen was affecting the same nonchalance as she reached over and put a sticky note in front of Nora. *Great,* Nora thought, *an idea.* Nora palmed the note and walked slowly to the podium glancing down at her hand as she positioned her notebook. The note read: *Now we know why Sal was so happy.*

As Nora pretended to look for the correct section of her trial notebook, a strange calm washed over her, a peace that often came to her in moments of stress. In a flash, she could see what to do. She stopped searching in her book and looked up.

"Ms. Jamison?" she asked. "May I call you that?"

"Well, it's my name," the witness replied.

"So you said," Nora answered. "Do you drink coffee?"

The witness seemed confused. "I'm sorry?"

"Coffee. Do you drink it?"

"No, I like tea."

Now I got you. Nora paused and took a deep breath, just as Carmen rose from her chair at the government table and walked quickly out of the courtroom.

"Do you know what a Grande Biscotti Frappuccino is?"

"No."

"Well, it's from the Starbucks secret menu, so a lot of people don't, I guess especially tea drinkers. How about a Grande Biscotti Frappuccino with one pump of white mocha syrup in it? Ever order that at the Miami airport?"

The witness looked more confused than irritated. "As I said, I don't drink coffee, so no, I never did."

"But the woman who flew to all those places as Mildred Jamison did—are you aware of that?"

"No."

Nora turned and pointed at Gina as she asked the next question. "Are you aware that it's Gina Cufaro's favorite Starbucks drink?"

"No."

"And that she bought one every time she pretended to be you at the Miami airport?"

"I have no idea."

Turning her head to the government table, where Jessica sat at the laptop controlling the exhibits, Nora said, "Government Exhibit 37K, please."

All around the courtroom, a picture appeared of the blonde woman with the Jackie O sunglasses and Hermès scarf in Tony Burke's lobby.

"Is that you?" Nora asked.

The witness hesitated.

Oh, now I really got you, Nora thought. *They didn't tell you that you'd have to confess to a murder to help Gina, did they?*

"Ma'am," Nora said, raising her voice and hammering her words, "Is. That. You?"

The witness answered quietly. "No, I don't think so."

Nora was feeling it now, so she took her voice up another notch. "Did you walk from the Lucerne Hotel in Manhattan to Tony Burke's penthouse, murder him, and then walk back?"

"I did not," she answered.

Now Nora shifted to a concerned tone, worried for the witness. "Your name really is Mildred Jamison, right?"

"Yes."

"But you didn't do the traveling we've talked about in this court-room, did you?"

The witness's eyes darted for just a moment to Gina, but Nora caught it, and she wanted to make sure the jurors didn't miss it.

"Don't look at the defendant, ma'am, just answer the question. You lent your identity to Gina Cufaro, didn't you?"

Now the witness looked terrified, her face pale. And she was no longer trying to conceal her effort to look at Gina. She turned her head to the defense table, her eyes almost pleading to be released from whatever had brought her to this place.

At that moment, Nora decided to save her life. Most prosecutors would savor the chance to tear the witness apart with question after question she could not answer. Maybe the payoff would be some dramatic confession implicating Gina. But Nora was different from most. She didn't need it and didn't want it. She had shown the jury this was a fraud; anything more and this woman might end up sleeping with alligators.

"Judge, I'm going to withdraw that. I have no further questions for this witness."

Judge Whitney seemed confused as Nora took her seat, but he pressed on. "Is there redirect, Mr. Butler?"

Butler didn't even try to stand for the answer. "No, Judge."

"Very well, the witness is excused."

The jurors watched her retrace her steps, with the addition of a very slight shrug of her shoulders in Gina's direction as she passed through the swinging half doors.

Butler had used the moment to regroup. He rose, buttoned his suit, lifted his chin high, and announced, "That concludes the defense case, Your Honor."

Judge Whitney excused the jury and then looked at Nora. "Is there rebuttal?"

She stood and paused, looking at the door next to the judge's bench. "I think so, Judge. Ms. Garcia went to see if—"

The door opened and Carmen appeared, walking quickly to Nora's side. "If I could just have a moment, Your Honor," Nora said, leaning her head down to listen as Carmen whispered, "The Starbucks guy is still at his hotel. He's coming over now."

Nora whispered back. "You think we should ask for time to investigate this Mildred Jamison? Maybe get some agents to check out her address in Florida? Like they should have done months ago when we saw the license Gina used?"

"No," Carmen answered into her ear. "Judge'll never give us enough time, and you ended it with the coffee thing anyway. Now we close it off completely and move on. Look at Mildred for perjury down the road."

Judge Whitney cleared his throat. "I don't mean to rush you, Ms. Carleton, but . . ."

Nora stood up straight. "Yes, Your Honor, sorry, we were checking to see if a Starbucks witness we had subpoenaed was still nearby. He is, and can be here in twenty minutes. We would propose in rebuttal to present his testimony and the record of the defendant's purchases, on her Starbucks loyalty card, at the Miami airport. Should be quick once the witness gets here."

Judge Whitney looked over her head toward Butler. "Perhaps even fertile ground for a stipulation, Mr. Butler? The court will stand in recess while counsel confers."

Butler knew, or should have known, what the Starbucks records showed because he got them from the government in pretrial discovery. When the judge was gone, he agreed to a stipulation essentially putting a Grande Biscotti Frappuccino with one pump of white mocha syrup in Gina's hand at the Miami airport shortly before each Mildred Jamison flight departure.

The government rested after reading the stipulation to the jury. Whitney excused the jury for the evening, heard and denied Butler's obligatory renewal of his Rule 29 motion, and set summations for the morning.

CHAPTER FORTY-NINE

Back at his desk, Benny picked up his office phone and called his old friend Matthew Parker, Kyra's former lawyer, now retired.

"Hey bud, got your text. What's up?" Benny asked.

"Thanks for getting back to me, man. I was reading in the *Times* that Conor McCarthy testified in your case yesterday."

"Yup. Strange dude, but he really hurt her and helped us."

"That's why I reached out," Parker said. "I'd forgotten it, and also forgot to tell you when I still remembered it, but Conor knew what you told me about D'Amico cooperating. I didn't give him the name or any details, but I think I said enough that he knew somebody was cooperating."

"What? You fucking *told* people? Son of a bitch, Matty, that was for you only, me tryin' to help you."

"I know, I know," Parker answered. "And I'm sorry. Look, I didn't give him specifics, but I was having a drink—well, *some* drinks—with him and Kyra, not long after you gave me the heads-up. I was trying to give my client some hope and so I let slip that some mob guy was cooperating with the feds and had the dope on who really killed Tony Burke. I'm fuckin' sorry I said it, but I did, and I don't hold out on you, so I'm tellin' you now. Didn't think much of it until I saw from the paper just how tight he was with fucking Gina Cufaro."

Benny was quiet for a moment. "Look, I'm pissed at you for shootin' off at the mouth, but you're a stand-up guy for tellin' me. You coulda just buried it."

"Yeah," Parker replied, "we don't do that shit to each other." He laughed and added, "Much as I might want to in this particular situation."

"No, we don't," Benny said. "Okay, thanks."

He hung up the phone and stared out the window. *What the hell?*

CHAPTER FIFTY

Carmen handled the government's main summation, which focused mostly on tying together all the records connecting Gina, aka Mildred Jamison, to the charged murders. For ninety minutes, she walked the jury through each of the twelve murders, weaving all the evidence together to show that Mildred Jamison was Gina and Gina went to all twelve murders. She only briefly touched on the defense witness Mildred Jamison. "I don't know what that was about, exactly, but it had nothing to do with the truth. She wasn't the one taking those flights. It's a fair inference that Gina Cufaro made some kind of deal to use that woman's identity. Maybe Mr. Butler can explain what I'm missing."

When it came time for his summation, Butler was no longer the happy warrior. He walked to the podium and snarled the first word out of his mouth. "*Ga-bidge!*

"I told you in my opening it was all garbage and now you've seen it. I represent a woman of character, of strength, of principle. I'm honored to be her lawyer. And she didn't do what they say."

For the next two hours, Butler delivered his greatest hits: the so-called may-fye-ah and the proliferation of rats as witnesses. He went with "my client can't be that dumb."

"So which is it?" he thundered. "Is Gina a master criminal or an idiot? She's marching around the country using the same name and the same phone, killing people? Really? Didn't occur to this alleged hit woman that she oughta change up the phone, maybe try out a different alias? It's nonsense, is what it is. The government says it's sinister. Hah. I say it's evidence of innocence, that's what it is.

"But you also know it isn't her phone anyway and she didn't travel with it. The real Mildred Jamison did, a person you met. It was her phone, not Gina's. She's a different person from my client. They may look alike, which is why the government got it wrong, but they are two different people. Both innocent, by the way."

That's how he's gonna handle the Mildred crap? Nora thought as Butler continued to yell. Conor was a "little weasel" who couldn't be trusted. Frenchie was a "career criminal and a liar." He was simply repeating things other liars told him, and the jury should know it was all lies because "no actual man of honor would gossip to some thief about a stand-up person like Gina Cufaro."

It went on and on, until sweat was rolling down Butler's head onto his face and neck, darkening the collar of his light blue shirt. He finished when he seemed physically drained, quietly urging the jurors not to let the awesome power of the federal government destroy an innocent woman.

Nora's rebuttal summation was brief. "Mr. Butler spent so much time on Daniel Joseph and Conor McCarthy because you can't condemn pictures, or phone records, or videos; you can't call them names, impugn their integrity. They just sit there, quietly showing you Gina Cufaro is guilty. And one of the things they show you is that the Mildred Jamison nonsense is just that—nonsense. I can't stand here and tell you exactly what the story is with that woman named Mildred Jamison, who seems to have lent her identity to the defendant. But you know for sure that tea drinker isn't Gina, with her love of the secret Starbucks menu. Gina, with that phone, was in a blonde wig walking to and from the murder of Tony Burke."

Now she held up her hands in air quotes. "'Mildred Jamison,' if that's even her real name, told you that wasn't her in those pictures. No way. It's not clear why she loaned Gina her identity, but the deal clearly didn't involve admitting to a murder Gina Cufaro committed. It seems there is more than one person in this world using the name Mildred Jamison, but only one of them killed a dozen people."

She turned and pointed. "And that Mildred is sitting right over there. And this business about Gina being either a master criminal or an idiot? Well, you know the answer. She was a very careful criminal—traveling under an alias, shipping weapons to herself, using a disguise. But she wasn't perfect, which is why she's sitting here today. If she had a chance to do it again, she would probably handle her elec-tronics differently, but this case is about making sure she doesn't get another chance to kill."

Nora ended with an appeal to common sense. "You were chosen for this jury because you have lived lives—incredibly diverse and interesting lives, to be sure—but you have all spent years listening to people, watching situations, and asking yourselves, 'So what's really going on here?' If you use that common sense, that lifetime of experience, you will see what's going on here. Gina Cufaro killed twelve people for the mob—including Governor Burke—and she is guilty of the crimes charged. Thank you."

Judge Whitney spent the final hour of the trial day giving his legal instructions to the jury, then sent them home for the night. He would dismiss the alternate jurors once the first twelve returned in the morning to begin deliberations. They piled into their assigned vans and headed off, swerving and stopping as directed by the FBI surveillance teams, which saw no sign they were being followed.

The jury sent no notes the next day. They deliberated in the room behind courtroom 318 for most of the day, then sent a late afternoon message that they had reached a verdict. Back in the courtroom, Judge Whitney read the jury's completed verdict sheet, then handed it back to his clerk, who returned it to the jury foreperson.

"Madam foreperson," Whitney said, "has the jury reached a verdict?"

The juror rose. "We have, Your Honor."

"Ms. Cufaro, please rise," the judge said, adding to his clerk, "we will now take the verdict."

Gina stood straight, back in the green sweater she wore the first day of trial. Butler rose next to her, making the usual display of buttoning his jacket.

The clerk then spoke loudly. "As to count one, how do you find the defendant, guilty or not guilty?"

"Guilty," the foreperson answered.

Gina didn't flinch. The process was repeated for all counts, with the same answer. About midway through the list, Butler, standing beside her, lifted a hand to her shoulder. She angrily shrugged it off as the litany continued.

Gina Cufaro was guilty of everything.

"Ms. Cufaro," Judge Whitney said, "you may be seated."

Judge Whitney thanked the jurors for their service and excused them to take their final van rides.

As the jury departed, the Deputy Marshals behind Gina inched their chairs closer to her. They had seen too many defendants do crazy things after conviction. But Gina didn't move. Her facial expression hadn't changed all day.

Judge Whitney scheduled sentencing for two months later—allowing ample time for the probation department to prepare the standard pre-sentence report—but the result was foregone. Gina was going to get mandatory life without parole in a federal penitentiary. There was no other sentence permissible under the law.

The Deputy Marshals handcuffed Gina and led her from the court-room. Butler came up to shake hands with Nora and Carmen, the scent of his Giambone's lunch beverages and post-meal Listerine and Polo cologne all preceding him and lingering in a dizzying combination. "My worthy adversaries," he said. "A battle well fought."

"Thanks Sal," Carmen answered for the group. "Always fun to be with you."

With a smile, Nora added, "Let us know if Gina wants to cooperate."

Butler chortled. "Never. Old school, you just saw. Take it like a man, even if you're a woman. Dying breed in my view, which is sad."

Neither of them could think of something to say in response to that, so Butler waited an awkward beat and returned to pack his things.

Benny leaned over after he was gone. "Ladies, despite the color-blind bullshit, it was a pleasure. Meet back at Carmen's office to discuss drinks?"

They both nodded. "FBI in on this?" Jessica asked.

"Are you kidding?" Nora said, smiling broadly. "Team for life."

The team went out the judge's door in the wall of courtroom 318, cut past the robing room, and went into the hallway to the bridge back to the US Attorney's office. As they passed the door to the Marshals cellblock, which led to the separate bridge to the Metropolitan Correctional Center, the chief Deputy US Marshal knocked from behind the bulletproof glass and gestured to Benny. "Youse go ahead," Benny said to the others. "Must be somethin' on another case. Meet you at Carmen's."

"Hey Phil, what's up?" Benny asked when the cellblock door was open.

"You got a second?"

"Sure," Benny said, following him in toward the cells that lined the hall leading to the prison walk-bridge.

They stopped just before reaching the first cell, and the chief Deputy whispered, "It's Cufaro. She's asking to talk to you. Won't take no for an answer. She's been so easy for us—total professional to this point. Can you talk to her before we put her in for the night?"

Benny hesitated. "Okay, a minute. Which?"

Phil gestured toward a cell. "Nobody else in here now. We'll wait down the row. Gimme a shout when you're done."

Benny peered into the cell at Gina, who was sitting on the bench staring down at the shackles and chain connecting her ankles.

"You rang?" he asked.

She got up and came toward him, whispering through the metal mesh cage. "Yeah, thanks. I know we aren't supposed to talk without my lawyer, so I won't talk about anything. But I want to have a separate conversation, just you and me. You find the right spot."

Benny started to speak but she cut him off. "And don't get excited. I'm not looking to cooperate. Ever. I did what I did and I was raised to take my lumps. So I'm gonna take 'em. Fuck it. But there's some shit that isn't right and I want to set it right. Capisce?"

Benny nodded. "Got it. When?"

"Doesn't matter," Gina said, lifting her cuffed wrists. "I'm not going anywhere. Wanna make sure you hear from me before too long, but it's not urgent. It can wait until they send me out, but it's gotta be in a way that doesn't burn me. If I'm gonna take my lumps, I don't wanna get labeled a rat in the bargain."

"Got that," Benny said. "I'll figure out a way to do it that doesn't heat you up."

Benny turned his head and shouted, "We're all set here, Philly." Then he left the cellblock and headed up to Carmen's office, shaking his head as he climbed the stairs.

At Benny's insistence, the team celebrated at McSorley's in the East Village, the oldest Irish pub in New York, where beer had been served in frosted glass mugs—two at a time for each customer, whether you wanted two or not—since 1854. Benny loudly narrated the history as he pushed through the battered swinging wooden doors, sliding his feet on the sawdust that covered the bar's floor.

"Didn't allow women in here until 1970," he said, oblivious to the wide-eyed looks his colleagues shared behind him. "Nothin' removed from these walls since 1910," he said, sweeping his arm around the crowded single room. "Those're Harry Houdini's handcuffs on the bar rail there, and up there's the wishbones hung by boys going off to World War I. The ones still hanging are the boys' who didn't come back."

The charm was lost on the other team members, but they grinned politely, pulled chairs up to an ancient wood table, and ordered. As the waiter returned, somehow using all his fingers to hold their eight mugs in a semicircle of beer, Jessica held up her phone. "News alert. Kyra just announced she's running for New York governor." She held the phone sideways and played the video of Kyra Burke's announcement that she would be seeking the nomination that summer. In the noisy bar, it was impossible to hear what she said, but Carmen pointed her finger to the corner of the screen and paused the video. "Isn't that our boy Conor standing there? Look just at the edge of the group behind her, second row. Isn't that his head back there?"

"Yup, that's him," Nora answered. "That little climber. Looks like he already found his new horse."

Carmen was right. It *was* Conor, in the literal background. He was too controversial after his testimony at both Kyra's and Gina's trials to have a prominent role in Kyra's campaign, so he was simply a "campaign volunteer" to anyone who asked. Of course, he was the only volunteer who spent hours with the candidate at her Pomander Walk kitchen table, plotting strategy.

CHAPTER FIFTY-ONE

Not long before the gubernatorial primary, Gina was finally sentenced—after probation finally finished the report on her life—to the expected mandatory life term without possibility of parole. She would die, someday, at the federal prison built just for dangerous women, the Secure Female Facility in Hazelton, West Virginia, a place where several federal prisons were clustered together on an elevated plateau the inmates called "misery mountain."

Now Benny and Nora were headed up that mountain to see Gina. After she got to her final destination—in more than one sense—Gina began an email correspondence with Benny. The messages were vague, but their meaning clear: She was inviting him to come visit her in Hazelton. *I look forward to traveling soon*, Benny typed in reply. *Of course, I can't travel alone. My tall colleague is up to speed and she will travel with me.* Gina would know he meant Nora.

She was now fully up to speed. As soon as Gina was sentenced, Benny told Nora about his contact with the killer, although his delay in telling her was not well received.

"What the hell, Benny?" Nora said, her voice tired. "I thought we were done hiding shit from each other. You had this conversation *months* ago and *now* I hear about it?"

"Hey," Benny replied, "I'm sorry, but there was nothin' to be done with it then and I didn't want to get you in any kind of crack over somebody having contact with a represented defendant. You're a lawyer. I'm not. I figured the less you knew right then, the better for your ability to remain a lawyer."

Nora shook her head. "You gotta stop making decisions that you think protect me. Let *me* protect me."

With a smile and a shrug, she added, "But it's probably better I didn't know."

Now they were in the far northeastern corner of West Virginia, after flying into Pittsburgh and renting a car for the two-hour trip south.

"You sure she's not worried about us coming up here?" Nora asked as Benny steered around switchback curves.

"She said she ain't afraid of any of the women she's locked up with and doesn't give a shit what they think. And, as she said at the start, she ain't gonna flip anyway. Just wants to get somethin' off her chest."

Up on top of the plateau, he pulled into the visitor lot of the sprawling two-story sand-colored prison.

Gina looked different. She had cut her thick brown hair short. "One of the other inmates has a side hustle," she explained. "I had one of my people on the outside put some money in her commissary account. Now I got a lifetime of free haircuts. And I'm gonna live a long time in here."

Benny and Nora couldn't tell if she was trying to be funny. She was across a silver metal table from them, sitting in the unmovable chair where the guards had placed her. She lifted her handcuffs, which were chained to a metal ring soldered to the table. "This isn't a counsel visit so they won't let these go. Whatever."

She dropped her hands to the table, where they landed with a metallic crash. "Okay, let's not have some awkward thing here. I'm not looking to cooperate. I made my lawyer withdraw my appeal because it's a waste. Lemme just say what I wanna say and you can get the hell off misery mountain. And don't take notes. It isn't complicated."

Benny nodded and folded his arms across his chest. "Got it. So what should we know?"

Suddenly sounding more like a realtor than a killer, she answered in a calm voice. "I want you to know the truth about Conor McCarthy. That needs to be set right. I don't know what he told you about me, but I took care of him all these years, giving him money and lots of—let's call it 'comfort'—when he visited me in Florida. For years, he acted loyal to my father and like he really loved me, but now I know he was just using us. All he really cares about is power and money.

"He's right that things changed after my father died, but what changed was *Conor*. He started taking me for granted, asking for money all the time, and treating me like crap. I'm guessing he was too afraid to do that when my old man was around."

Benny leaned in, "I don't wanna hurt your feelings, Gina, and that's all sad, but didya really bring us all the way up here to tell us your love story?"

Gina laughed. "You really are a hard case, Benny. No, that's just background. What you need to know is that Conor knew *exactly* what I was, what I did for my father and later to make big money on the side. Hell, I never offered to come to New York to talk to Burke for Conor.

"Conor asked *me* to 'talk' to Burke," she said, holding fingers up in air quotes. "And one hundred percent, he knew what that would mean. It was *his* idea to make it look like he killed himself. How do you think I knew about the insulin? Are you kidding me?"

She leaned forward so she could tap the center of her chest with one chained hand.

"Now me, I came up with the idea to look like little Miss Perfect—the future governor—when I went in there. I've known for years that Conor has a thing for Kyra. There's been a weird connection since Yale, and it isn't something I imagined. He can claim I'm some crazy, jealous bitch, but something is going on there.

"Anyway, I figured if this job went sideways somehow, it'd be nice to have Kyra on the scene, maybe killing her awful husband. Of course, no way it goes sideways. It couldn't, 'cause this is what I do, right? Burke killed himself. Done. I'm out. Would look like a suicide. Nobody would even check to see if there was some tiny hole in his shirt. Nobody would even know when it happened. He'd be found the next day, stiff as a board. Gimme a break."

She paused and stared at her hands, as if trying to control herself.

"But it went bad, didn't it?" she said, looking up. "It went bad 'cause a fucking food delivery showed up and the putz doorman had to go up there, find the body *way* too early."

She looked down again, really struggling with her temper, and took two deep breaths before continuing.

"So you gotta ask yourself—how did that happen? Bad luck? A coincidence, maybe?"

Gina lifted her hands until the chain was tight, then slammed them down on the table. She was spitting the words out now, her eyes narrowed. The realtor was gone. Benny and Nora were sitting across the table from a killer.

"No fuckin' way. I killed a lot of shitheads in my day in all kinds a ways—more than you know—and I don't believe in coincidences. I think that lyin' little bastard set me up. That cocksucker Conor

McCarthy knew I would be in there doin' Burke in a way nobody would ever know. But he fixed it so the world *would* know. No way Burke ordered food. That's the shit Conor was paid to do. So he did it alright, and fixed it so there'd be video of me walking in and out of that lobby right when Burke is supposed to be killin' himself. No fucking coincidence! He set me up!"

Suddenly she was calm, gently rubbing the shiny table with the palms of her hands.

"He musta shit a brick when his sweet thing Kyra showed up on that video and got arrested instead of me. That nearly fucked him—and her—good. Then I had to do The Nose, before he ratted me out. And you know how I knew he flipped? Your boy Conor told me, even had D'Amico as the name. Don't know where he got it from, but he was right. Nose didn't even try to deny it before I did him. Then you assholes started diggin' into *that* one, and I end up with a lifetime of haircuts 'cause I was stupid, but that's another story."

Gina looked from Benny to Nora and back to Benny. Now that her story was out, she looked exhausted. "So that's what I wanted to set right. I wanted you to know your little star witness is a lyin' mother-fucker and that's on you. What you do with it is your business, but you really should do something to set Conor straight. I'd kill him if I still had the hooks, but lucky for him those days are over. Once I got life, nobody's lookin' to do me those kinds a favors."

Now she stared directly at Nora. "So I'm hopin' your obsession with the truth might matter here. Because your witness lied his ass off. I'm thinkin' maybe that shit matters to you and you'll do something about it."

Gina smiled tightly and turned to Benny. The realtor was back. "And now, we're done. Don't take it personally, but don't come back here again. I'm no rat and have nothing more to say to you. We're finished."

Before Benny or Nora could speak, Gina leaned her head back and shouted to the ceiling. "Guard!"

"Wait," Benny said, "one question: What the fuck you doin' with Marian Burke visiting you at the MCC before trial?"

Gina laughed as the guard unlocked the chain and guided her to her feet. "Not about whacking her ex, if that's what you mean. She had business with my old man, helping out her son, who was not the financial genius—or Christian family man—he pretends to be and got himself in a tight spot, both money-wise and pant-around-his-ankles-wise. A favor was done. She wanted clarity from me on how things stood. I told her we keep our promises, and those details will remain private, between her and me. Have a nice life."

They drove in silence for five minutes, the lush late-summer West Virginia hills rolling past. Nora spoke first. "You believe her?"

Benny squeezed the top of the steering wheel with both hands. "Yep, I do. Can't be certain, course, but it sure rings true."

He paused before adding, "And I know she's onto somethin' about The Nose thing. Matty Parker says he told Conor what I told him about there being a mob cooperator."

Nora slowly shook her head but Benny spoke before she could. "And I know I promised no more secrets, but that was from before."

"Before when, exactly?" Nora asked.

"Matty told me after Conor was off the stand."

"Oh Benny," Nora said.

"Didn't mean much to me then. Matty also told his client, and who knows who she told. And the judge knew and his lawyer buddy knew and our fuckin' untrustworthy US Attorney knew. Coulda been a lotta people. But now it makes me believe Gina."

"So did Conor lie to us? Did he lie on the stand?" Nora asked.

"If Gina's tellin' the truth, sure. And how would we nail him for that? With Gina as our star witness? Like she's the queen of truth-telling? Fugetaboutit."

Nora was quiet for a long time before saying, "I think that's probably right, but I feel like we can't let it go. I feel like we gotta dig into this food-delivery thing and what Gina says about getting a heads-up about The Nose. Coincidences are real, no matter what Gina says, but I feel like we can't let it go."

"So we're really gonna do what Gina wants?" Benny asked. When Nora didn't answer, he said, "Hey, if that's what you want, we start digging."

"It's about finding the truth, Benny. That's supposed to be what this job is all about. Right?"

"It is," Benny said quietly, "but in a messed-up world, it's also about makin' sure bad guys don't get away."

"We can do both," Nora said. Then she repeated it, as if trying to convince herself. "We can do both."

Benny exhaled through pursed lips. "Hope so. Really do."

CHAPTER FIFTY-TWO

Nora tiptoed down the stairs and into the kitchen, where her mother was reading at the table, nursing a cup of tea. "She's finally asleep," Nora said quietly. "She loves *The Monster at the End of This Book*, but it gets her worked up. I'd rather we stick with *Goodnight Moon*."

Teresa smiled. "That one puts me straight to sleep," she said. "At least I make it through the silly Grover book."

Nora grabbed a mug from the cupboard. "And you should know that Sophie just told me picture books are getting too babyish for her, now that she's six. Evidently her teacher reads chapter books to the class. So we're gonna start the Magic Treehouse series next week. Ma, she's growing up so fast."

"They sure do," Teresa said, shaking her head.

Nora now had her own tea and joined her mother at the little table.

"What?" Teresa asked as Nora sat.

"Whataya mean 'what'? I can sit and have tea with my mother."

Teresa beamed at her. "Sophie is asleep and you aren't doing work emails. So, again, my love, what?"

Nora took a deep breath. "Nick and Vicki are gonna move to Connecticut to be near her family. He told me her dad wants to help me get a job at some hedge fund there in Westport so we can all be close. Lotta money, yada yada."

"Huh," Teresa answered. "Whaddaya think?"

"Don't know," Nora said. "This is our home, I love my work, but I also think it would be hard on Sophie to have him there and us here. And some extra money would really be nice."

She paused and took a sip of tea before adding, "You, me, and Soph are a package, so what do *you* think?"

Teresa sighed gently. "You know I love that part from the Book of Ruth: *'Where you go I will go, and where you stay I will stay.'* So that's my answer. You and that little girl are my life and I will be happy wherever we are, together."

She put her cup down and looked at Nora. "Hey, now, don't start cryin'. Let's analyze it. Maybe you go to the US Attorney's branch office in White Plains and we live somewhere between there and Westport. That'd make it much easier for Sophie to see her father, and I'll bet we could find a place around White Plains that we could afford on your government salary—especially if we sell or rent this place."

Nora looked around the kitchen as she answered. "Maybe. But not a place like this, Ma."

"Well, what would a job with a hedge fund be like? And what even is a 'hedge fund'?"

"It's the name for a financial manager for rich people and things like pension funds. They try to make more money than you would make just passively investing in a market. I know about it from some financial fraud cases I've had, but I'm no expert."

"They pay a lot?"

"Yes. If they've been in business for a while, it's because they've made money, a boatload usually."

"They honest?"

"Some are, some aren't, kinda like people in general. They're regulated by the government, which tries to weed out the bad. I'd have to check on the one Nick is talking about. But even if they're honest, there's no way the work is as meaningful as what I do. I'm sure they'd want me in some kind of compliance role, helping them avoid doing things that might get them in trouble. So that's okay, but it's not like putting bad guys away."

"So if you went there, we could afford to live close to your work, maybe get a house, be near Nick too. And you know that area from college, right? Isn't Westport right by Fairfield?"

"It is," Nora said. "Really nice area." With a smile, she added, "Of course, it doesn't smell like coffee, but no place is perfect."

They were quiet for a moment before Nora continued. "Look, I think the work change would be the biggest hurdle for me. A former boss of mine used to say that what we do has moral content. It's doing good for a living, or at least it's supposed to be. That's why I love it so much. I love being in a place where the only important question is—what's the truth? Would be hard not to have that."

Teresa nodded and reached for Nora's hand. "Whatever you want to do is what I want. And kids are resilient as heck. Even if we have to shuttle Sophie between here and Connecticut a bit, she'll be fine."

"Thanks, Ma."

Teresa flashed her own smile, an exact copy of her daughter's. "Meantime, I'll get on Zillow and see what's what around Westport and how much these hedge-fund people would have to pay you for us to live in the style to which we've become accustomed."

"You do that," Nora said, returning the smile.

◆

The digging took months. They couldn't prove Conor tipped Gina to The Nose's attempt to cooperate, but they made progress on the dinner order. Tony Burke's dinner had indeed come through Seamless, the popular food-delivery service in Manhattan. The company found an account opened in Burke's name and billing to his American Express. But Burke didn't have a Seamless app on any of his personal devices, and an examination of his computers didn't turn up any orders.

Seamless was finally able to provide them the computer IP address from which the Wagyu coffee-rubbed strip-steak order had been placed. After weeks of work, they determined the computer bearing that IP address had been located at the time in the member library of the Yale Club of New York City, a private club in Midtown Manhattan. The last piece fell into place when they obtained location data for Conor McCarthy's cell phone on the evening Burke was killed. He was at the Yale Club.

Nora made an appointment to go see Conor at the temporary transition offices of New York's newly elected governor, Kyra Burke, who had ridden a wave of publicity and sympathy to victory in November with Conor at her side, although usually far enough away to be out of any camera shot. There was talk that she may be America's first female president. And it could be a family contest because her former stepson, Edward Burke, was another early presidential favorite.

The transition offices were high in a Midtown office tower on Sixth Avenue, across from the flagship New York Hilton. Conor greeted Nora and Benny with a practiced smile, explaining as they walked to his office that these were exciting times. He was even helping Kyra redecorate the executive mansion in Albany, although he expected they would be spending most of their time in Manhattan at her place.

"Wait," Nora said when they were inside the office, "you and Kyra are an item?"

"I'd prefer not to discuss my personal business," he said calmly, "if you don't mind."

"What happened to Edward Burke?" she asked. "I thought he was your guy."

"Have you met his mother?" Conor asked, raising his eyebrows. "There's only room for one person behind that throne.

"But enough about me," he added, "you didn't say what this was about."

Benny took that. "Yeah, Conor, here's the thing. We had a conversation with Gina about you."

As smooth as he was, Nora could still see his jaw muscles squeeze at that.

"And she had some interesting stuff to say," Benny added, before laying out what Gina had told them.

When he was finished, Conor literally batted it away, flexing his hand and swinging his arm in a backhand motion. "Oh please, the desperate lies of a convicted mass murderer. Surely you aren't taking anything she says seriously?" He ended by pushing air between his pursed lips, making a *puhhh* sound.

"Yeah, well," Benny responded, "Gina does have her baggage. But there's one thing you could help us with that doesn't come from Gina."

"What's that?" Conor asked.

"Did you order the steak dinner that was delivered the night Burke was murdered?"

He answered without hesitation. "Yes, I did."

"Why?" Nora asked.

Conor smiled tightly, holding the grin for a beat before answering. "Why? Because the governor wanted me to. That's why."

With that, he stood quickly and said, "And that completes our interview. If you'll show yourselves out, Governor Burke and I have a great deal to do for the people of New York." He stepped past them and disappeared into the warren of cubicles.

They sat in stunned silence.

"Which governor, you motherless fuck?" Benny asked the empty room, pushing himself up out of the small side chair.

"I've never known what that charming phrase means," Nora said as she stood, "but—motherless fuck."

CHAPTER FIFTY-THREE

Nora was sure this was the right place; she had followed the directions carefully. Three miles west of Interstate 684 in northern Westchester County, she had turned left into Lasdon Park and driven three-tenths of a mile to the empty parking lot. As directed, she left her car—really her mother's car—and walked into the memorial garden, past the busts of the wealthy couple who once lived on these two hundred acres, and up the handful of stairs to the formal garden. She followed the path around the central fountain, ringed by miniature boxwoods and crowned by statues of two naked boys dancing and spitting streams of water through what looked like wind instruments—flutes, maybe, or recorders.

Strange place, she thought. At last, she found her way to the wooden bench on the far side of the fountain and sat. This was the most private public park she had ever seen. And no cell service, in a county of more than one million people, bordering New York City.

Nobody else visited the garden during the long time Nora sat there and she didn't leave the bench, for fear of missing her meeting. Instead, she sat, watched the boys spit water, and checked the time on her watch every minute or so, her mind racing, as it had since she started the drive up here.

How could someone like Lizzy become someone like Kyra? Was she like that all along? Did Conor, a bad guy, change her? Or is she the bad one? Why the hell did I agree to meet here?

Suddenly, it occurred to her that maybe there was some dark reason Kyra chose this remote location. *That's crazy. She wouldn't want to hurt me. I'm meeting the governor, for God's sake. And I'm a damn federal prosecutor. I'm here for an adult conversation with someone I used to know.*

About twenty minutes past the meeting time, from her bench in the elevated garden, she saw a black Suburban pull into the parking lot by the entrance, its multiple antennas shaking as it came to a stop. Shortly, a young woman in business clothes and an earpiece climbed the stairs, swept her eyes around the garden and then motioned to someone behind her. Governor Kyra Burke appeared, followed closely by two other women in business attire with earpieces. *Okay, that's cool—all women on her protection detail.*

Nora stood, wondering whether she should stay at the bench, or move toward Kyra. As she watched, Kyra seemed to speak to the members of her security team, motioning with the palms of her hands down, as if telling them to stay. Then she walked on alone, coming around the fountain, feet crunching quietly on the path. She came all the way to Nora, smiling widely, pulling her into a hug, then kissing her on both cheeks.

"It's so great to see you," Kyra said. "All grown up and prosecuting the world. Wow."

"Well, you, you . . ." Nora started to say.

Kyra pointed to the bench. "Sit." Nora complied. It felt like an order. Kyra sat sideways, her feet on the ground, knees pointing toward Nora, who turned to copy the posture, their knees almost touching.

Nora swept her eyes around the garden. "This place . . ." she began, but Kyra cut her off again.

"Nora, dear, it meant so much to me to hear from you again, after all this time. I know you had to keep your distance during the trial . . ."

Kyra stopped herself, pulling her iPhone from her inside jacket pocket. "As you know, New York is a one-party consent state, but I still make it a practice to notify people when I'm recording a conversation." She lifted the phone and shook it slightly, side to side. "Do you mind?"

Nora felt as though the bench was shaking. *What. Is. Happening?*

Kyra went on. "It's not about you, it's about me. There are people out there who want to bring me down, who want to stop me from doing all I'm doing for vulnerable groups, who hate the idea of a strong woman actually *leading*. For the sake of the people I'm trying to help, I try to keep a record of everything."

Apparently deciding not to push Nora for consent, she said, "Anyhow, just so you know," and put the phone back in her pocket. "So how *are* you?"

"I'm fine, thank you," Nora answered.

"I heard you had a good conversation with Conor, and I'm glad things can now get back to normal. As you know, he's a good person who was trapped in awful relationships. He's in such a better place now, doing a tremendous amount of good for me, and the state."

Holy shit, she's making a record here. I drove fifty miles to this weird place so she could try to lock me down? Are you kidding me?

Nora decided to veer abruptly off Kyra's script. "So what happened to Lizzy? What happened with us back then?"

Kyra let out a little laugh. "I changed my name, silly, from one I never really liked to one I like. That's what happened. Look, I know you had feelings for me—a college crush—and I'm sorry I had to step away, but I was a senior, you were a first year at another school, and it was the right thing—for you, most of all. I thought you would be a good friend—but you wanted something more, a lot more—and that just couldn't happen. I'm sorry."

Nora didn't answer, so Kyra went on. "Look, I hope you've found the loving relationships you were looking for. In some ways, I envy you that you have a beautiful little girl, although I have to confess it would be hard being the mother of a six-year-old in my current role."

The world started rocking again. *How the hell does she know about Sophie? She* just *turned six, for God's sake. How does she know that?*

"In fact," Kyra continued, "I don't know how *you* do it, being a mom while chasing the mob. Although I'm grateful you do it. Without you, Tony's killer might still be out there. Without you, I might have been tried again for something I didn't do."

Kyra paused and reached her hand to touch Nora's. "I can never repay you for what you've done for me, for justice."

Did you practice that fucking line? "I was just doing my job," Nora replied.

"No," Kyra said, "it was so much more than that. You threw everything you had into a case, into a *cause* really."

She paused, then added, "I'm glad we had this chance to connect because I need someone like you. No, *New York* needs someone like you. After the poison of the past, I am trying to hire talented women for all important roles. How many women is too many? Well, as RBG said about the Supreme Court, 'when there are nine.' When all my key people are women, I'll be satisfied. I'd like you to be one of them. I'm going to ask my personnel chief to be in touch with you."

Kyra looked at her watch. "And I'm so grateful to you for meeting me in this place. I know it's a bit out of the way. But it's right between my meetings. I just came from Martha Stewart's place in Katonah—she's a great supporter and, of course, had her own experiences with our flawed justice system—and I'm on my way to the Northern Westchester

Women's Resource Center up in Mahopac. They do great work for victims of domestic violence."

Kyra started to stand, then stopped, dropping back down to the bench. "Oh, I should have asked. Was there something you wanted to talk about? I actually think you reached out first, although it was great to catch up."

Yeah, maybe you stop gaslighting me and tell me what happened to Lizzy, somebody I loved and who loved me back. Where did that sweet, honest person go, and how did she end up as someone named Kyra and married to Tony Burke? What happened to turn her into this twisted, ambitious politician?

Nora suddenly had the urge to run. *There are no answers here, just her taping me to set me up as a fucking stalker.* She stood abruptly. "Nope," she said, extending her hand. "Good luck with the rest of your schedule."

Kyra stood and took her hand. "And good luck to you, Nora. I hope you'll talk to my personnel chief. I need people around me who are strong enough to always tell me the truth."

Nora pulled her hand out of the shake, which had gone on long enough. She laughed and said, "No thanks, Lizzy. I'm taking my truth and going home."

Kyra squinted at her, a confused look on her face, then shrugged and turned quickly, the soles of her shoes scraping the path as she pivoted.

Nora called after Kyra, her voice almost pleading. "Wait, don't leave, please." When Kyra paused and turned, Nora said, "Turn off the tape. I don't want to make a record. I just have to know. Please."

Kyra hesitated, then pulled her iPhone from her pocket and stopped the recording. "I don't have much time," she said sharply. "What is it you *have to know?*"

"Did you know?" Nora asked.

Kyra didn't answer at first. She stepped close to Nora and began frisking her.

"My phone's in the car," Nora said. "I just have to ask."

Satisfied with her search, Kyra said, "Go ahead, ask your questions. Then we're done."

"You were always close to Conor," Nora said, her voice cold, no longer pleading.

"Oh, I like prosecutor Nora," Kyra replied with a tight smile. "No, not always. We were close in college, drifted apart when I was in law school, then reconnected and got close again. And despite what psycho Gina may think, it was not physical. And by the way, she wasn't always a psycho, or didn't seem to be. The older she got, the crazier she got."

"But you and Conor made a plan for you to be with Tony Burke," Nora said.

"Sort of," Kyra answered. "He made the intro after the divorce. Burke seemed like an interesting guy, and I kinda liked him, but it was also a good opportunity. Conor and I both saw that. What I didn't count on was that fucker still couldn't keep it in his pants, despite being married to me."

With a laugh, she added, "Can you imagine?"

"I can't," Nora answered.

"And then Tony blew everything up," Kyra continued, "or his victims did."

"And that's when you and Conor decided he had to go," Nora said.

"I knew I had to get away from him and I knew Conor had to find a way to do the same."

"And you knew what it meant to have Gina go visit him."

Kyra just smiled.

"Why are you smiling?" Nora asked.

"Because it does feel like I'm on the stand again. It's hard to remember what I knew at the time. I've been through so much. But, however it happened, that evening meant Conor and I each got free on the same night. A two-for-one special."

"So ordering the dinner was your idea. It would screw Gina after she did her thing."

"Nice try," Kyra answered. "But I'm not about credit. There's no limit to what you can accomplish if you don't care who gets the credit. Course who would guess the crazy bitch would dress up as me on her little visit."

Kyra paused before continuing. "But, honestly, as much as it sucked, the publicity was priceless. I think our nutjob former president called it 'earned media.' You can't buy what it brought me. Without that publicity, without being the victim of a grave injustice, where would I be today? Not having cucumber sandwiches with Martha Stewart, I'll tell you that. And it was a goddam public service—no matter who deserves the credit—protecting society from Tony *and* Gina. So a win-win if I ever saw one."

Kyra looked into Nora's eyes. "Look, I'm a lawyer, too, and you can't prove anything on me. Same with Conor. We done now, counselor?"

"Can I ask a personal question?" Nora asked.

"Okay, but quickly, please."

"Did you actually care about me in college?"

"I found you . . . interesting. And I was attracted to you. But, to be honest, I was looking for bigger fish in a bigger pond."

Kyra looked Nora up and down, before adding in a sarcastic tone, "And I hope this is the *closure* you needed."

With that, she wheeled and began walking away, adding over her shoulder, "And I do hope you'll consider a job with my administration."

Nora dropped heavily on the bench, her shoulders sagging as she watched Kyra pass the fountain and disappear from view. *Our governor,* she thought, *maybe future president. God, I need to get away from all this.*

EPILOGUE

The Brass Rail restaurant had been at Second and Washington Streets in Hoboken for more than a hundred years, and despite the stories about it being haunted by ghosts after a new bride died from a fall down the spiral staircase in 1904, Nora always thought of it as the special-occasion place in Hoboken. *And this is a special occasion because this is goodbye*, she thought, as she sat holding the table for four on the second floor by the windows.

Benny was the next to arrive, his bulk emerging from the swinging double doors at the top of the staircase. Nora waved and beamed at him.

"Mr. Rough," she said as he drew near, "welcome to Hoboken."

"Ms. Smooth," he responded, sliding into a chair. "Always a pleasure. Do you know this is my first time in your fair city? And did you also know that baseball—"

She cut him off. "Stop, stop, I don't want to have dinner with my father, as much as I loved him. Yes, I know the baseball history. Yes, I know Cooperstown is a fraud. Yes, I know anti-Italian bias is to blame for Hoboken not having its rightful place in history."

"Didn't know that last part," Benny said with a smile, "but okay, no baseball. How the heck are you?"

"Honestly, Benny, I'm still having trouble with Kyra and Conor getting away with it."

Benny made a sour face. "So I've given this a lot of thought. Forget Conor. He's just a pawn. The real chess game was between two dirtball kings—or queens, in this case. First he was with one, then the other. He's nothing. It was between Kyra and Gina all along. And the good news is that the one who was a mass murderer lost, even though the winner is still a piece of crap."

"What do you mean?" Nora asked.

He held up one finger. "The first moves were Kyra's, reconnecting with Conor to get to Burke and marrying him. Then, when things went south, she got Conor to send Gina in to 'talk' to Burke, which solved her awful-husband problem, and she told Conor to order the dinner, which shoulda fucked Gina to solve a second problem—freeing Conor from that relationship."

Now he added a second finger. "Of course, Gina had prepared her own move, dressing up as Kyra and fucking her right back when the dinner order blew up the 'suicide' thing, getting her arrested as Killer Kyra."

Then a third finger. "But Kyra got another move. She couldn't say she knew Gina had visited Burke that night, because that would splash back all over her, and Conor. Right? Her defense is that she's innocent because she helped arrange for a mob killer to go see her estranged husband? Not exactly a get-out-of-jail-free card. But she found a better way, with no splash, when I was stupid enough to tell Matty Parker that D'Amico was flipping. Kyra ordered Conor to tell Gina that The Nose was ratting her out. And you know Kyra did it because, remember, Gina said Conor gave her the actual name—D'Amico; Matty Parker never gave him that. It had to be Kyra. She knew Gina would whack him, which would bring the feds in to investigate The Nose's murder, nailing Gina and clearing Kyra. Sure, it was a two-cushion bank shot for Kyra, but better than confessing she was mixed up with Gina going to see Burke."

Benny dropped his hand. "Of course, Gina doesn't fully understand the game, which is why her final move was so pathetic—telling us from jail that Conor's a piece of shit. Of course he is, but, in this game, just a little piece. The big one is Kyra Burke, the queen behind him, and she won."

Nora looked deflated. "Yeah, I know you're right, but it doesn't make it any easier to accept Kyra getting away with her moves."

Benny nodded. "Sure, but I guess my question is, 'getting away with' what, exactly? I'm just telling you what's true, not what we can prove. Because, even with you as a witness to her very careful statements in the garden, what case we got against Kyra? We'd need Gina even if we were gonna give it a shot, and she ain't willing, and that's just as well, because the fact that she's an actual homicidal maniac would make her a pretty shitty witness for the United States against the Governor of New York, dontcha think?"

"I do," Nora answered quietly.

"And we got Conor ordering the dinner, but even if he admits it was Kyra's idea—and why would he do that?—it don't mean shit unless Gina gives context, and we're back to the same problem. There's a reason Carmen and our esteemed US Attorney agreed there's nothing there. 'Cause there isn't."

Nora let out an audible sigh. "I know, I know. It just feels like we never proved the truth. And we put up Conor as a witness when we now know he didn't tell the full truth."

Benny shook his head. "Which is why you sent Butler that letter telling him what we've learned about Conor, which does Gina and everybody else absolutely no good."

He exhaled loudly before continuing. "I worry you're aiming at the wrong target, with all this 'truth' stuff. Our job is to lock up bad people to protect good people—when we have the admissible evidence to prove it. Sometimes that means we gotta use other bad people to do it. Sometimes that means people we know are motherless fucks are gonna get away. But I've never really thought of our job as 'finding truth.' That's not what the system is for. Our job is to live in gray, find the ones who have drifted into black and hammer them, so all the people sleeping soundly in white can stay that way."

"I wish I saw it so clearly, Benny, I really do. And even if we can't prove it to a jury, we *know* our governor is, at the very least, a dishonest person, and she is quite likely a really bad person who conspired with Conor McCarthy to commit murder using Gina Cufaro as the weapon."

"Yeah, that's where I'm a bit jaded, I suppose. We've had bad people in high office for a long time—startin' with some presidents in my lifetime I could name—and somehow we stumble on. Remember, you're Ms. Smooth—you can't let it drag you down."

Nora sighed again. "I'll try. I really will." Then her face lit up as Carmen and Jessica emerged from the double doors and headed toward the table.

"Hey you two," Carmen said as they took chairs, "sorry we're late. The PATH train stopped under the Hudson for some unknown reason."

"And not even an incomprehensible and terrifying announcement," Jessica added with a smile, "like you get in the New York subway—you know, *garble garble smoke and death garble garble*. Just sat there in silence. What's up with that?"

"Jersey grows on you, eventually," Nora said. "And hey, you made it. I'm so glad the team could get together away from the office."

Unfolding her napkin, Carmen now slipped comfortably into her supervisor role. "Let's order, 'cause I'm starving, then I want a report from everyone."

After the waiter collected the menus, Nora began. "I wanted to get us together so I could tell you—I've decided to take a job in Westport, Connecticut, so my mom and I can be near Sophie, Nick, and his new wife, Vicki."

"Oh no," Jessica said. "Why?"

"Well, for the reason I said—to bring the family geography closer—but, honestly, for a couple other reasons, which is why I'm not going to try to transfer to the US Attorney's office in Connecticut. I'm a little burned out on this work, especially after what this team has been through. I need to step away, at least for a while. And I'd like to make some more money so my mom stops carrying us, and I want the money to put Sophie through college. I'm going to run compliance for a big hedge fund in Westport called Saugatuck Associates—named for the river there. They manage money for a lot of pension funds and, best as I can tell, are honest, and very rich, people. So that's my news."

"Damn," Jessica said, "bad news for the good guys."

Carmen cleared her throat. "And speaking of bad news for Team USA, I'm bailing on the office too."

Benny hadn't been surprised by Nora's news, but now he whipped his head to Carmen. "What? Oh, boss, no."

Carmen's eyes filled as she looked at Benny. "Yeah, 'fraid so," she said. "It's time for my little crew to move out of the rented left half of a house, and the only way that's gonna happen is if I bring home more bacon. One of our former colleagues—you know Dave Berkeley," she said to Nora and Benny, "who's now at Benedict and Karp—reached out to me. They need a lateral partner to work internal investigations, maybe some white-collar defense. And it's a financial offer I can't turn down. Well, it's an offer I *didn't* turn down."

Benny let out a loud breath. "Well, that's a relief," he said with a grin. "I thought you were gonna tell us it was gonna be Butler and Garcia, offering a full spectrum of legal services to America's finest mah-fye-ah members."

"No," Carmen laughed, "I'm going to Midtown, not to hell."

Benny turned to Jessica. "Okay, they're dead to us. Tell me about you. Staying in our country's service?"

"Yes, I am," Jessica answered. "Got at least twenty more left with the Bu." Turning to Benny, she added, "They, and you, are stuck with me. I'm counting on it."

"Good to hear," Carmen answered. "And you, Mr. Dugan?"

The three women all looked at Benny.

"First," he said, looking at Jessica, "I'm glad at least one of you is staying with these United States." Turning to Carmen and Nora, he added, "As for you two, it had to happen eventually. All the good ones leave. I've learned that, so it's just part of life, part of this job. Don't mean I like it, but it is what it is."

He tapped an enormous index finger on his own chest. "As for me, I ain't goin' no place. Honestly, I'm the happiest I've been since losing Bunny. I love being a grandfather and I'm slowly buildin' something good with my boys. One of the reasons I can't be pissed at you two for leavin' is that it's about your families. It always *has* to be about them, or we'll never be truly happy. You knuckleheads taught me that. It's the thing we can control, in a world where we can't lock up every bad guy or always see the right answer clearly."

The waiter set their drinks on the table. Benny lifted his Pilsner beer glass, a serious look on his face. "I wanna offer a toast," he began, looking from face to face. "This team is a family for me, and I hope for you too. We been 'through it,' as we say. This ain't the mob, but we'll be there for each other, always, capisce? There ain't extra good people in this world, so we gotta stick together. You need, you call. We'll have each other's backs. Agreed?"

The three women each looked around the table. "Agreed," they answered in unison as they extended their arms, bringing the four glasses together over the table.

There was an awkward silence after the toast before Carmen broke it. "So no dripping blood from our trigger fingers onto a picture of a saint, huh?"

Benny smiled. "I'm open to suggestions."

ACKNOWLEDGMENTS

This is a work of fiction. The places and the procedures are as accurate as I could make them, and many of the characters are inspired by people I have known, but they are just that—characters in a novel.

I'm grateful to Patrice—for literally everything—and to the rest of my family for their thoughtful advice, loving feedback, and pitiless proofreading. I love you all.

Friends are people you can never repay but don't need to, or so they tell me. My amazing friends brought their expert eyes to drafts and always made them better. I'm lucky to have you in my life.

I wouldn't be on this new journey if my former editor Zack Wagman hadn't nudged me to consider fiction, for which I will always be grateful.

I'm also so lucky that Kirby Kim agreed to represent me and share his and Eloy Bleifuss's insights about story, structure, and writing. I'm better because I know you.

And thanks to the people of Mysterious Press for extraordinary support. Otto Penzler and Luisa Cruz Smith are the dream team. Thank you for believing.

Finally, I'm grateful to have known and loved Kenneth McCabe, the greatest organized crime investigator this country has ever seen. This is a work of fiction, but I hope his family can feel some of Kenny in these pages.